P9-DMZ-345

Death by Chocolate Cherry Cheesecake

Death by Chocolate Cherry Cheesecake

Sarah Graves

KENSINGTON BOOKS

http://www.kensingtonbooks.com

KENSINGTON BOOKS are published by

Kensington Publishing Corp.
119 West 40th Street
New York, NY 10018

Copyright © 2018 by Sarah Graves

All rights reserved. No part of this book may be reproduced in any form or by any means without the prior written consent of the Publisher, excepting brief quotes used in reviews.

All Kensington titles, imprints, and distributed lines are available at special quantity discounts for bulk purchases for sales promotion, premiums, fund-raising, educational, or institutional use. Special book excerpts or customized printings can also be created to fit specific needs. For details, write or phone the office of the Kensington Special Sales Manager: Attn. Special Sales Department. Kensington Publishing Corp, 119 West 40th Street, New York, NY 10018. Phone: 1-800-221-2647.

Library of Congress Card Catalogue Number: 2017951327

Kensington and the K logo Reg. U.S. Pat. & TM Off.

ISBN-13: 978-1-4967-1128-1
ISBN-10: 1-4967-1128-9
First Kensington Hardcover Edition: February 2018

eISBN-13: 978-1-4967-1130-4
eISBN-10: 1-4967-1130-0
First Kensington Electronic Edition: February 2018

10 9 8 7 6 5 4 3 2 1

Printed in the United States of America

For John

One

It was a bright summer morning, the first day of July in the remote island village of Eastport, Maine—three hours from Bangor, light-years from anywhere else—with a salty breeze snapping in the banners over the seawall and the sun glittering on the bay.

Up and down Water Street in front of the old two-story brick or wooden storefront buildings, shopkeepers swept doorways, hung out colorful OPEN flags, and watered lush window boxes brimming with red geraniums while seagulls swooped above.

Not the kind of morning that makes you worry about finding a dead body, in other words.

But as I approached my own small chocolate-themed bake shop, The Chocolate Moose, a petite white-haired woman in jeans and a black T-shirt—the shirt gorgeously embroidered in gleaming jewel tones at the neckline, jeans fitting as if tailored—stepped from the Second Hand Rose, her vintage clothing emporium next door.

"Good morning, Jacobia," she trilled.

The accent's on the second syllable of my name, by the way,

and it's Jake to my friends. But the Rose's owner disdained casual nicknames as scrupulously as she avoided giving discounts.

Firmly I averted my gaze from the shimmery-gray wool shawl hung in her store's bay window. It was lovely, and would be even more so this coming winter. But it was expensive and I'd put all my disposable money into setting up the Moose six weeks earlier.

Plus some that was not strictly disposable. "Good morning, Miss Halligan. Hard at work already, I see."

She was lugging a bucketful of sudsy water with a squeegee in it, though her shop's window was already spotless as usual.

"Mmm," she replied, squeegeeing energetically. Her perfume, a light citrus fragrance, mixed pleasantly with the sweet smell of the bay. "I hope everything's all right."

She'd called me at 5 A.M.; Miss Halligan was an early riser. She'd said my own shop door was standing open and did I want to do something about it myself, or should she just call the cops?

Listening, I'd held back a sigh. The wind often blew that old door open—the lock had been wonky from the start, the door itself creaky and temperamental—and obviously it had done so again. So I'd merely asked Miss Halligan to close it as best she could, then made one more call before going back to sleep.

Now she eyed me, brandishing the dripping squeegee. "I'd have panicked if it had been my shop," she said.

And would've rushed down here at once to check on things, she meant. "But you must have all sorts of responsibilities at home with that big old house of yours and your family," she added.

"Uh-huh." I stepped into the doorway of the Chocolate Moose, a tiny storefront with two bay windows, a moose-head silhouette with elaborate wooden antlers hung from chains over the door, and a pair of small cast-iron café tables on the sidewalk out front.

At the moment, that big house of mine was being cleaned by

my housekeeper, Bella Diamond, who since she'd married my elderly father had also become my stepmother. Meanwhile my husband Wade Sorenson was on a tugboat bound for the enormous container vessel that he'd be piloting into Eastport's harbor later that day; my grown son Sam was in Boston visiting friends; and my father was loudly but uselessly agitating to be released from the hospital where he was recovering from a heart attack.

So I couldn't use family duties to excuse my not being here at the crack of dawn. Nor did I try; for one thing, I was too busy squinting at that door.

"Thanks for calling me," I replied absently instead. "Looks like Morris got the new lock set installed already."

Morris Whitcomb was Eastport's jack-of-all-trades, the man you called if you needed your porch light replaced, your sink drain unclogged, or your fishing boat's old, sputtery wiring transformed from a rat's nest of fuses and tattered electrician's tape into a neatly labeled model of twelve-volt order.

Morris had said he had a lock set he thought would work, and he'd go to Wadsworth's Hardware Store when it opened and have an extra key made for me, too.

Which he'd done; I'd picked the key up on my way here. And he'd have called me if he'd noticed anything suspicious while he was working, I knew. But I'd never seen these small scratches in the door frame before . . . had I?

The key turned easily and the door opened; the little silver bell hung over it jangled sweetly as I went in. And at first I noticed nothing amiss:

The shop's interior had exposed redbrick walls, a pressed-tin ceiling featuring two very lovely old wooden-paddled ceiling fans, and a black-and-white tiled floor. The single bakery display case, glass-fronted and white-enameled, was all we had room for, but we only sold what we'd baked ourselves so we didn't need more.

Three additional café tables crowded the opposite wall. The

cash register—now open and empty, the way we always left it—sat on a counter to one side of the display case, and behind that a door led back to the kitchen.

Which was where I hit trouble. My longtime friend and current business partner, Ellie White, had been here baking cookies until late the previous night. The air in the shop was still heavy with the luscious aroma of warm chocolate.

So the lights must've worked then. But when I flipped the switch now, the windowless kitchen remained a pitch-black cave.

"Drat." It was probably nothing more sinister than a single blown fuse; the wiring in many of these old downtown buildings was practically prehistoric. Still, I made my way a little nervously—*had* I seen those odd scratches in the front door's frame before?—through the sweet-smelling darkness to the kitchen cooler.

There with the aid of the small flashlight on my key ring I removed the trays of fresh baked goods that Ellie had placed in the cooler the previous night. During the ill-lit transfer I only tripped once over something on the floor that I didn't bother stopping to identify. Then, after switching on the front-of-the-shop lights—they all worked fine and so did the ceiling fans, strengthening my blown-kitchen-fuse theory—and readying the cash register and the electronic credit card swiper for the start of business, I began setting out our offerings for the day.

These consisted of chocolate pistachio brownies, cranberry-nut chocolate chip cookies, and the pièce de résistance, dark chocolate fudge. Arranged on old blueware plates lined with white paper doilies, the fudge looked so tempting that I nearly grabbed a piece and devoured it myself. But I'd already had a cookie—all right, two—so I went back outside to watch for Ellie instead.

Because the thing was, I didn't want to visit the dark cellar alone. I'd never been down there before; it wasn't included in the shop space we were renting. So I didn't even know for sure where the fuse box was located, and if I ran into anything that I needed quick help with, without her I'd be stuck.

But Ellie's arrival wouldn't only clear the way to my fixing that blown fuse. It would also signal the start of our biggest baking day yet. Since our opening a month earlier we'd had fabulous success with a small, varied menu: chocolate ladyfingers and fresh éclairs one day, whoopie pies and chocolate biscotti the next.

And while it was all pretty challenging—the day before, I'd had to battle a dozen cream puffs into submission while injecting them with chocolate filling—so far we'd managed not to overwhelm ourselves. Now, though, a dozen chocolate cherry cheesecakes were due to be delivered in twenty-four hours to the Eastport Coast Guard station. There they would be auctioned off and the proceeds used to pay for Eastport's Fourth of July fireworks, three days away.

Cheesecakes, I mean, that Ellie and I had promised to bake. And although Ellie was brilliant at following her grandmother's old chocolate-themed recipes, and we'd bought or borrowed every springform pan in eastern Maine so we could bake the cakes in only a few batches, the task still felt daunting.

Anxiously I peered up and down Water Street. With the holiday imminent, patriotic flags and banners draped the shops' fronts. The cotton candy and popcorn stands were set up along the fish pier. A corral made of sawhorses and lobster traps stood ready for the pony rides in the post office parking lot, and a gaggle of vendors—postcards and T-shirts, earrings and refrigerator magnets, ball caps and candles and coupons good for 15 percent off the price of a tattoo—gathered on the walkway overlooking the boat basin.

But there was still no sign of Ellie. Meanwhile, I supposed I could be fixing that fuse right now if I just locked the shop again for a few minutes. After all, one cellar is much like another; my working down there alone wasn't *guaranteed* to lead to disaster.

Finally I went back inside, where by now the smell of warm chocolate was so paralyzingly delicious, you could've used it for crowd control. Also a familiar humming sound was coming from the kitchen: the cooler's compressor.

It meant the power was back on. Hurrying out there, I snapped the light switch once more and this time was rewarded by a bright fluorescent glow from the kitchen's overhead fixtures.

But my relief at not having to root around in the cellar got squelched fast. The kitchen was spotless as always: a worktable stood at the room's center, flanked by a baker's rack and the oven on one side, baking implements ranged out on Peg-Board hooks on the other. Two stainless-steel sinks, one for dishes and the other one strictly for washing hands as per health department regulations, completed our equipment.

The walls back here weren't brick, only plaster and Sheetrock, evidence of some long-ago architectural fiddling that had merged two buildings, ours and Miss Halligan's, into one. Now the walls' hospital-white paint pushed the room's cleanliness quotient up off the charts.

Only two things marred the room's spic-and-span perfection, in fact. The first was a box of salt lying on the floor, its spout open and a few remaining white granules spilled out in a heap.

Which wasn't so terrible. I could just sweep the salt up, and ordinarily I would have done so at once. But the second odd thing in the kitchen that morning was so utterly incongruous that I had to blink several times just to be sure I was really seeing it:

A man's body leaned against the worktable with its feet on the floor and most of its middle sprawled across the table's surface. Its head was plunged down into the large, heavy pot that we used for melting chocolate. The pot stood on a warming pad whose dial, now that the power had come back on, glowed cherry red.

"Eep," I squeaked, stepping back sharply. And just that small movement, or my voice, or maybe a breeze or something, caused the body to begin sliding.

The body's shoes had been braced against a cardboard box full of cookbooks. That's what I'd bumped against earlier, moving it just enough, apparently, so that now the box and shoes slipped backward together on the shiny linoleum. The arms slid, elbows slanting down off the table, hands splayed across the stainless-steel top as if feeling around for something.

Finally the hideously chocolate-coated head rose, dragged upward by the body's weight, until at last—with the chin hooked stubbornly over its rim—the pot tipped threateningly.

"Oh no, you don't!" I snapped, shocked suddenly out of my horrified paralysis. Grabbing the man's shirt collar, I lifted him by it; not much, but it was enough so that his chin came free.

The pot settled. So did the melted chocolate in it. "Good heavens," said someone from behind me, startling me so I gasped, dropped the dead guy, and whirled to confront whoever it was.

Somehow I'd expected the cops, or maybe Miss Halligan. Or perhaps some kindly space visitor, here to whisk me away to some distant galaxy until any possible need for cheesecake baking was over.

But instead it was Ellie White, a slim strawberry blonde with violet-blue eyes and a dusting of gold freckles across her nose. For her bakery duties today she wore a bibbed white apron over a blue-and-white summer shorts set and white canvas sneakers. A red-white-and-blue ball cap perched jauntily on her head, and her earrings were small, brightly enameled American flags.

"Darn," she said, sounding vexed, eyeing the dead man. "Now we're going to have to throw out all that good chocolate."

*   *   *

My name is Jacobia Tiptree, and when I first came to Maine I had a young teenaged son named Sam, enough money if we lived carefully, and a heart so badly broken that you could have swept the shattered bits up into a dustpan and dumped them.

That was what I'd felt like doing, having at last left my husband to the mercy of his many girlfriends back in Manhattan. Driving up the East Coast with my whole past life little more than a smoldering crater in the rearview mirror, all I could think of was getting to the end of the Earth and flinging myself off.

But then I crossed a long, tide-swept causeway and found Eastport, a tiny town on a Maine island a stone's throw from the Canadian border. The town's narrow streets full of venerable old wooden houses overlooked a pristine bay dotted with lobster buoys and fishing boats, and the air smelled like beach roses.

It wasn't quite the end of the Earth, but it was close; I did not, though, find myself wanting to take a leap. Instead I bought one of the old houses, an 1823 white clapboard Federal with three redbrick chimneys, forty-eight old wooden shutters, and about a million acres of peeling wallpaper all of which needed scraping.

So I began to. Also I began raising Sam, who after a dozen years of hearing his parents threatening to kill one another was nearly as broken as I was, and I can't say I got very far with him.

Soon, though, he discovered the island's beaches, wide sandy expanses thickly studded with rotted pilings from vanished two-hundred-year-old wharves. There he found antique bottles, clay pipe stems, and beach glass, pale nuggets of sandblasted translucence which he began collecting in Mason jars.

Next thing I knew, he was helping out on a fishing boat and doing better in school. He had his problems, still, some of them very serious ones that would end up lingering into his adulthood, but all in all he managed to turn himself around.

And then I met Wade Sorenson, a local harbor pilot who guided big ships through the wild tides and ferocious currents for which Eastport's waters were famous. I wanted a new romance the way I wanted a chronic skin condition, but Wade bided his time, never hurrying or veering off-course. We were married a few years later; I guess he must have been practicing on those big ships.

So that's how I got here, and now with Sam grown and the old house at last wrangled into some semblance of order (by which I mean it was no longer actively in the process of falling down) I'd found a new passion: The Chocolate Moose.

Ellie had talked me into it, but to my surprise I loved it. Creating delicious chocolate treats and selling them to our customers had turned out to be a blast; too bad that at the moment our shop was the location of a dead—and almost certainly murdered—body.

"I just don't see how someone dies in a pot of chocolate," Ellie murmured, still staring.

"I think maybe he had help," I said gently.

Close up, she resembled a princess out of a fairy tale: hair of gold, long, thick lashes, a smile that could make grown men whip off their jackets and fling them across puddles for her.

"Ohh," she breathed comprehendingly. Then, tenting her clear-polish-tipped fingers, "I wonder . . ."

So did I. But I was trying hard not to. It wouldn't be the first time we'd wondered ourselves into a lot of trouble; one way or another, Ellie and I had a fair bit of experience at snooping into Eastport murders.

Which was one reason why I'd already decided that we wanted no part of this one. I was about to say so, too, but instead Miss Halligan stuck her head in and spied the dead guy.

"Let's all of us step outside, shall we?" I said swiftly, body-checking the elegant-looking little owner of the vintage-clothing emporium back out through the kitchen doorway again.

I might not know much—for example, who was the guy? His thick chocolate coating and could-be-anyone clothes, consisting of a gray sweatshirt, faded blue jeans, and running shoes, obscured his identity. But I knew the cops wouldn't like it one bit if we contaminated their nice, fresh crime scene.

I mean, any more than we already had. "Come on, Ellie, let's go," I said while she stood staring at the body some more.

Today's cheesecake ingredients were all stowed in her carryalls, fortunately, and she'd left those out front. "We'll call Bob Arnold and then lock the place until he gets here," I added.

Bob was Eastport's police chief. "Probably Miss Halligan's calling him right now," said Ellie, hurrying to catch up with me. "You know how she likes to be in charge."

I did know, and she was excellent at it, too. So I decided to let her do the cop calling: for one thing, we still had all those cheesecakes to bake; and for another, the presence of a dead man—even a chocolate-covered one—was beginning to feel oppressive.

"Ellie?" I said. She was looking back over her shoulder at the guy again, an odd expression on her face. "You okay?"

But of course she was; Ellie might've resembled a fairy-tale princess, but she was as tough as an old boot.

"Fine," she replied. Still, I wondered about the expression in her eyes, a flash of dislike aimed squarely at the dead body. Her look faded so fast, I could almost pretend I hadn't seen it.

Almost. "The cheesecakes," I reminded her.

She nodded slowly. "We'll have to bake them at your house."

Right, because the Coast Guard auction waited for nobody. One year it rained so hard that the winners wore hip boots and snagged their sodden prizes with boat hooks, but the sale went on.

I only hoped the cops would agree to interviewing us while we baked. If not, we'd be auctioning off store-bought Twinkies, and those wouldn't even begin to pay for the holiday fireworks.

"Come on," I said again, and Ellie followed me outside.

She knew who the dead guy was, I could tell. Knew, and didn't much mind finding him that way, either. We'd been friends for a long time, and I could have just about guaranteed it. But she would tell me when she was ready, I knew that, too.

Besides, sooner or later they'd wash the chocolate off his face and then we'd all find out, wouldn't we?

The kitchen in my big old house has antique hardwood floors, old pumpkin-pine wainscoting, an old butler's pantry, and old . . .

Well, you get the idea. The cabinets are varnished beadboard, the countertops vintage linoleum. The tall double-hung windows all face south, so potted geraniums grow there with wild enthusiasm, and across from the woodstove and the old soapstone sink there's a huge butcher-block table with a knife rack built into it.

Shortly after we found the body in our bake shop, Ellie set her carryalls down on that table and began emptying them while my housekeeper-slash-stepmother, Bella Diamond, watched skeptically, her ropy arms crossed over her flat chest.

Bella was gaunt and hawk-faced, with big grape-green eyes and high, angular cheekbones sharp enough to cut yourself on. A firm believer in the germ-killing properties of hot soap-and-water, she ran my old house with the firm, clear-eyed purpose and whip-crack organizational style of a crusading military general. When we arrived, she'd been down on her knees scrubbing the baseboards with a toothbrush.

"We'll clean up afterward," I promised, carrying a pile of round, shiny-metal springform pans in from the pantry and stacking them on the soapstone sink.

"Mmm," Bella said, unconvinced. Then, swiping back a hank of her henna-dyed hair with a work-roughened hand, she went on:

"You know, that father of yours is just about the stubbornest man alive."

I did know, actually, and even more so now that he was stuck in a hospital bed.

"This morning he called a taxi and was just climbing into it when the nurses caught him," Bella went on exasperatedly.

Ellie got the mixing bowls out; luckily, I am a fan of church fairs, and had collected a lot of them from the sale tables, where items like Crock-Pots, popcorn poppers, and George Foreman grills complete with instruction booklets were available for a dollar.

Sadly, there were no instruction booklets for handling my father. "Jacob Tiptree," Bella pronounced darkly, "is lucky I promised 'for better or worse.'"

That's my dad's name, and yes, I'm named after him. Bella grabbed a paper towel and began furiously polishing the door-knobs, to emphasize her point. But she didn't mean it; the truth was that she adored my father and it was her lingering fear over his recent cardiac event that was making her so testy now.

Well, that and us messing up her nice, clean kitchen. Time to change the subject. "Guess what, Ellie and I found a dead guy this morning."

Still polishing, Bella rolled her eyes. "Oh, I've heard all about that already. Matt Muldoon, it was, stone dead with his face in a pot of chocolate. Can't say I'm surprised."

"Really," I said, startled until I realized: Miss Halligan must've recognized him just as Ellie had, and the gossip wire in Eastport worked so fast and accurately that if you got a bee sting at one end of the island, minutes later somebody was getting a pair of tweezers and some baking soda out for you at the other.

So of course word was getting around. Ellie said nothing, busy cracking eggs into a bowl; she'd never liked Muldoon, but her dislike had turned to fury when he began complaining loudly about cleanliness issues in our shop.

Which was nonsense. We had no sanitation issues at the

Moose. On the contrary, Bella did all our cleaning for us (she insisted) and as a result you could have run your tongue over any surface in the place and it would come up tasting like rainbows.

But that hadn't stopped Muldoon. First it was insects, then animal hair; for weeks, now, the accusations had kept coming. As soon as we managed to disprove one, he'd presented us with another, threatening to shut us down by reporting it to his friends at the Maine State Health Department.

According to him, he visited them often at their offices in Augusta, yet another of his claims that I didn't believe. In fact, where the Chocolate Moose was concerned Matt Muldoon was nuttier than a chocolate-dipped pistachio; I didn't know why.

But as Bella finished with the doorknobs and started on the cabinet latches, I already had a feeling that he was going to be even more trouble to us dead than he'd been alive.

"Anyone home?" called a voice through the screen door, and Bob Arnold came in.

With his round, pink face, thinning blond hair, and rosebud lips always seemingly ready to curve into a smile, Bob didn't look like the kind of cop who could walk into a bar fight, separate the combatants, and minutes later have the aggressor placed safely in the backseat of his patrol car, thus ending the battle.

But Bob was a master of law enforcement persuasiveness, and if that didn't work, he had a head-swat maneuver that did. Now he seated himself on a stool at the butcher-block table, frowning.

"So you found him?" Muldoon, he meant, and he already knew that we had.

"Me," I said, getting the rest of the butter and cream cheese out of one of the canvas carryalls that Ellie had brought with her and arranging them on the table. "I found him."

Ellie went on cracking eggs one after another, and I figured it would be best to let her keep quiet for as long as possible. After all, her well-known dislike of the deceased wasn't exactly going to simplify our day, was it?

And it definitely needed simplifying; just for starters, my oven here at home wouldn't hold very many cheesecakes. Two, maybe; so even if all went well, we'd be baking until the wee hours.

"All going well" also being an idea that was fast fading into the sunset. "Okay, here's what happened," I said.

Bob listened with interest as I went through the morning's events: the call from Miss Halligan about the Moose's front door standing open, the new lock from Morris Whitcomb, the odd scratches in the door frame, and the kitchen lights not going on.

"But then they did," I added as I measured out sugar and used a wooden spoon to begin working it into the cream cheese.

"And that's when you found him." Bob let Bella put a slice of day-old mocha sheet cake on a plate in front of him.

It was yet another thing Matt Muldoon had complained about: that we brought home unsold things and ate them or gave them away, and this caused some dreadful contamination that he couldn't be specific about.

Most likely that was because, like the rest of the things he fussed over, it didn't exist.

"That's right," I told Bob. "I was out there in the dark at first, but I only saw him when the lights went on again. I didn't know who he was, but . . ."

Bob licked mocha buttercream off his fork. As usual, for his small-town peacekeeping duties—despite being Eastport's police chief, he took his share of patrol shifts like everyone else—he wore his blue uniform and black leather duty belt, complete with keys, handcuffs, baton, whistle, radio, and pepper spray canister.

And his weapon, of course, neatly holstered and with the safety strap fastened. "And you, Ellie," he inquired, "what do you think about Matt Muldoon getting killed in the Moose?"

Before she could reply, he added, "I ask because the state cops surely will. And it might be, you know, that you should think a bit about your answer before you give it."

Oh, for heaven's sake. Ellie was about as likely to commit murder as I was to jump off a building and fly. Still, Bob had a point: the state cops wouldn't know that about her, would they?

"Ellie," I began warningly; Bob was our friend, but that wasn't why he was here. She, though, was in no mood for prudence.

"I'm not one bit sorry about it and I don't care who knows it," she told Bob flatly. "Good riddance is my whole feeling about him."

"You can stop now," Bella told me quietly, and when I looked down, I saw that I'd been beating the ingredients in my mixing bowl so vigorously that not a bit of sugar remained un-creamed. Any more and I thought the spoon might be in danger of splintering.

And wood chips in the cheesecake really would have given Matt Muldoon something to complain about, wouldn't they? That is, if he hadn't already been as cold as a mocha chip refrigerator cookie.

"They should talk to his wife," Ellie said as she began punishing the eggs in the bowl very severely with a wire whisk.

"Sarabelle's the one behind the nonsense he's spouting," Ellie added. "And who knows what else she's been up to?"

Like me, Sarabelle Muldoon had been a city girl until she and her husband moved to Eastport a year earlier. A public-relations woman who'd specialized in luxury-goods clients, she'd run special events in Manhattan for high-end makers of luggage and jewelry.

Now, though, I didn't know what she did. "She might even have killed him herself," Ellie went on. "Maybe she wanted him to shut up as badly as we did."

Like everyone else in town, Bob Arnold was well aware of what my son Sam called Muldoon's smack-talking about the

Moose. We'd called it slander, and we'd even gone so far as to ask Bob what we could do about it.

But slander was a civil matter, lawsuits are expensive, and after years of old-house repairs, I had almost no money left from the little stash I'd brought here.

But back to the matter at hand: "How'd he die?" I asked.

"Medical examiner'll say for sure. But probably it was a stab wound." Bob looked grim as he went on:

"Just from a quick glance I took before I called up the state homicide people, I figure it was from the little hole I saw in the back of his neck. Not much blood, though. Most of the bleeding was on the inside, I'm guessing."

I squelched the clear mental picture that Bob's remarks summoned while he looked at Ellie, still beating the eggs to a froth.

"You notice anything missing from the shop? Barbecue skewer, maybe a long-tined fork, anything like that?"

"Nothing was missing," I told him firmly. "We don't use any skewers, and anyway we keep all our tools on the Peg-Boards. So I'd have noticed."

"Um," Ellie put in unhappily, "I'm afraid that's not quite true."

Bob nodded minutely, fingers tented over his coffee cup, eyes alert. He'd already known this, too, I realized suddenly. I'd been right about why he was here.

A similar thought seemed to dawn on Bella. "We shouldn't be talking about any of this," she said sharply. "You shouldn't be here telling us about it, either, so why are you?" she demanded of Bob.

With her jutting jaw full of yellow teeth and her henna-red hair snaking out in frizzy corkscrews from the hairnet she always wore, Bella didn't resemble any benevolent household goddess that I'd ever heard of.

But she'd have stepped in front of a train for me and Ellie, and now she was scared for us. Me too, because it didn't take a genius to figure out which way this particular train was heading.

Outside the kitchen windows, the midmorning sun made jewels of the purple irises and pink poppies that Ellie and I had planted the previous autumn. Nearby the sheets billowing freshly from the clothesline would come in crisp and smelling sweet.

And everything inside was in apple-pie order as well. In fact, there actually was a pie cooling on a rack in the windowsill, right this very minute.

Raspberry, I thought. Still, my heart thumped anxiously. *For no reason,* I hoped. But something about all this felt bad to me.

Really bad. Then Ellie began to speak.

"He came down to the shop late last night. Matt Muldoon did, I mean."

Bob Arnold sat with his clean, well-kept fingertips pressed together over his coffee cup, saying nothing. Bella and I stayed silent, too; this was Ellie's decision, and she was making it.

"It was exactly eleven-forty," she said. "I was just putting the walnut cookies in," she added to me, "that's how I know."

Bob looked a question at me. "The cookies take twelve minutes in our oven," I replied. "And after what happened with the éclairs, we don't trust the oven timer."

Everyone recalled our first try at making éclairs; you could smell their charred carcasses all over town.

"So you looked at a clock just then," Bob concluded correctly to Ellie; nodding, she went on.

"He came stomping in, all mad about something as usual," she said. "That frown of his, like someone was poking him with pins."

Matt Muldoon was sixtyish, with steel-gray hair that he wore slicked back like a painted-on helmet. The corners of his small, slitlike mouth were always turned down, and his beady gray eyes were always darting around meanly.

Ellie went on: "So he starts out all huffy with me, telling me

I certainly shouldn't be there baking while the shop is closed, because people ought to be able to walk right in at any time."

She gave the eggs another few whips. "So they could see what I might be up to," she said, her tone conveying what she thought about that.

"He walked right in," Bella pointed out reasonably. "Matt Muldoon did, I mean."

Ellie poured the beaten eggs from her bowl into the mixture in mine.

"No, I unlocked the door and let him in," she corrected as she measured out the vanilla extract, the dark liquid's aroma wafting up pungently.

"He kept standing out there, fuming through the window at me, waving and mouthing words, and I knew he was going to stay there until I did let him in," she said.

"So I figured I might as well get it over with," she added as I began stirring the eggs and vanilla extract into the sugar and cream cheese.

"He didn't make you nervous?" Bob asked. "There in the shop alone with him late at night, when you already knew he was angry?"

Bob spoke mildly, but his words sent a zing of fright through me. It sounded like maybe he was trying out arguments for lesser charges: self-defense, for instance.

But she didn't go for it. "No. He didn't scare me." A faint smile curved her lips: *Oh, come on.*

"Yeah, I figured as much," he said. If you wanted to scare Ellie, you needed something more than Matt Muldoon's bad temper to do it with. A bazooka, maybe.

"What happened then?" Bob asked.

I couldn't stand it. "Ellie, are you sure you want to go into it all right now?"

But Ellie merely began grating lemon peel, scraping the tiny bits into a pile on the cutting board. The sharp, tangy smell of lemon zest drifted into the room.

"It's okay," she told me. "Bob's trying to help."

Right, I knew that's what he was *trying* to do: getting the lay of the land before the state cops arrived, then maybe guiding their investigation away from her if he could.

Like I say, he was our friend. Over the years we'd introduced him to his wife and promoted their courtship, despite his shyness, and later via our snooping activities we'd hauled her off a sharp hook that a spiteful local prosecutor had been trying to impale her on, for instance.

Bob, in return, had hauled my inebriated son Sam home more times than I could count instead of transporting him to the drunk tank at the county jail, and he'd turned a semiblind eye to a lot of Sam's other youthful behavior as well.

So we had history together. Still, friendship could only go so far; what Ellie said now could create problems for her later, if it came to that.

As I suspected it would. "He'd had a few drinks, it seemed to me," Ellie said. "I could smell it on his breath."

I kept stirring. The mixture in the bowl started out gloppy and slimy, but soon it gathered itself into a thick batter.

"And maybe because of that, he was even worse than usual," she added, "telling me he intended to put us out of business, that we didn't deserve our shop, that *she* . . ."

Sarabelle, Ellie meant. ". . . wanted a bakery of her own and he'd make sure she got it, no matter what."

She looked up at all of us. "And since Eastport's too small to support *two* specialty bakeries . . ."

Oh, brother. Now I understood why he was such a pain. Never mind that Sarabelle Muldoon couldn't bake a potato if you turned on the oven and shoved it in there for her. She'd seen how cute the Chocolate Moose was and decided she wanted it for herself.

And what Sarabelle wanted, Sarabelle usually got, mostly on account of her having a voice that could etch glass, the dumb persistence of a housefly bumping against a windowpane, and no shame whatsoever.

I almost felt sorry for Matt Muldoon. But meanwhile, Ellie had so far admitted to having motive and opportunity. All the homicide investigators needed now was for her to have had the method.

"Anyway," she finished, "I let him blather on. He told me he had friends in the health department. Said they'd come and shut us down permanently if he asked them to."

"I don't believe he had friends," muttered Bella, who'd begun scrubbing the sink with Comet scouring powder even though it was already so clean you could have done surgery in it.

"Too mean," she said. "Anyway, could he really do that?"

"Doubt it," said Bob. "But he could make you miserable, which it seems to me he had already been doing fairly effectively."

Ellie looked glum. "He was the fly in our ointment, all right. Always walking in like he owned the place and looking down his nose at everything. Oh, he just made me so *mad.*"

She stopped. Then: "Anyway, he had his say and left. I was taking the cookies out of the oven by then, so I didn't see which way he turned when he got outside. And that was it."

Bob sighed. "Okay. Only look, when I went in, there was a big, thick needle-type thing in the trash, pretty much right on top of everything. Either of you know anything about it?"

Darn. I'd forgotten about the battle of the cream puffs. Ellie scraped sour cream from her small bowl into my larger one, making sure to include as much of the lemon zest as possible in the transfer.

"As a matter of fact, I do know about it," she said calmly. "It's a pastry needle. I saw it in there . . ."

. . . *Last night,* she was about to finish. I'd put it in the trash earlier in the day, with a cork stuck on it for safety's sake.

"I threw it out," I interrupted her. "I'd filled chocolate cream puffs with it and somehow I bent it."

Bent it enough so you couldn't squeeze custard out through it anymore. But not enough so that you couldn't pop the cork off and stick someone in the back of the neck with it, unfortunately.

I'd been hoping against hope that the needle wasn't what Bob meant by "sharp implement." But of course it was.

He got up. "All right, I get the picture. The state cops're on their way here. I put the needle in an evidence bag to give to them. And no doubt they'll want to talk to you both."

Yeah, no doubt. Like the day wasn't going south fast enough. And on top of everything else we still had the shop to run during this, Eastport's biggest holiday of the year.

"How long d'you think they'll keep us shut down?" I asked.

Bella had finally run out of things to clean, unless she wanted to start wiping out the insides of lightbulb sockets. And asking her to rest for a minute wouldn't have worked even a little bit; she wasn't built for it.

Now she began crushing chocolate wafers with a rolling pin, mashing them between sheets of waxed paper. From her face I could tell she was thinking of other things she'd like to be crushing.

Bob moved toward the door. "I don't know how long you'll be closed for," he said. "The rest of today for sure, maybe longer."

So as I'd feared, we'd be in my kitchen baking cheesecakes until two in the morning, at least.

"But one last thing," Bob went on. "The blood I saw on that pastry stabber. Either of you have any idea how that got there?"

Neither of us did.

"Yeah." He nodded sorrowfully. "I figured. Well, you two just sit tight, then, and when they come to talk to you—"

"If anyone but you wants to talk to them more than once," Bella snapped, unable to contain herself any longer, "both these girls will be getting lawyers. I'll be seeing to it myself, and don't you even start with me about it," she added fiercely when I opened my mouth to object.

So I didn't, and Bob didn't, either; he knew better. "That sounds about right, actually," he agreed instead, causing my heart to sink even lower than it already had.

"But I'm sure it'll all work out fine in the end," he added, the keys and the pepper spray and the pair of steel handcuffs on his duty belt all clattering together as he went out.

"I'm not sure," said Bella tightly when he was gone, slamming the rolling pin down onto the chocolate wafers. "I'm not sure even a little bit."

Me neither. And then the phone rang.

A lot.

Two

The first call was from Lester Vanacore, junior reporter for our local newspaper, the *Eastport Tides.*

The *Tides* was the easternmost newspaper in the United States, and Lester took his reporting duties seriously. "Hey, Jake, am I hearing this right? You had a murder in the Moose?"

"Lester, there was a body. But saying for sure how it got to be one is a little above my pay grade, you know?"

He sighed audibly. "Well, whose was it, can you tell me that much? I mean, sure enough so that I can quote you on it?"

I didn't want to be quoted on it. I thought the less any of us got mentioned in connection with it, the better. The Chocolate Moose didn't need that kind of publicity.

What I really wanted was for it all just to go away; but of course that wasn't going to happen anytime soon, especially with the easternmost newshound in the United States digging away at it. Fortunately, just then the phone clicked its "call waiting" signal at me, so I got rid of Lester by suggesting very strongly that he ask Bob Arnold about the murder, then picked up the next caller.

"Mom?" Sam's voice came through sounding hollow and distant, as if maybe he was calling from an orbiting space station instead of from a Boston apartment. "Mom, are you . . ."

He'd been staying with friends, enjoying a summer break from his job here at the marine supply store. "I'm here, Sam," I said. "I can hear you. What's wrong?"

If I ever need resuscitating, just play a recording of Sam's voice sounding unhappy at me and my blood pressure will skyrocket.

". . . weather . . . bus schedule . . . canceled . . ."

He'd left his car parked in Bangor and taken the bus from there. The phone fritzed in and out, his voice suddenly sounding as if it was coming from the bottom of a deep well.

"What? Say it again, Sam, I think something's wrong with the—"

Once upon a time, Ma Bell ran the phone system with ruthless, utterly monopolistic efficiency. Now any fool can start a phone company and provide the kind of high-class personal communication service once offered only by two tin cans and a length of string.

The phone fritzed back in again. "Mom, I had a bus ticket for tomorrow. Two, actually. But they're canceled on account of—"

The phone sputtered. Then it went dead.

I took the handset from my ear and looked at it, feeling as if more information might issue from it if only I squinted hard enough. But no information did; then the connection ended entirely. When I tried calling back, I got the kind of fast busy signal that can only mean one of the tin cans has fallen off the string.

I slammed the handset down, figuring that if the phone was going to be broken, I'd give it something to be broken about. Back in the kitchen, Bella was still crushing wafers.

"Your father," she said, "is a bullheaded old fool."

She had a small mountain of dark crumbs heaped on the

table. The bowl of cheesecake batter sat there, too, awaiting its final ingredient; Ellie had gone back to her house for more chocolate to use instead of the stuff Matt Muldoon had fallen face-first into.

"Right," I answered Bella distractedly. "He is."

I wasn't really listening to her, though. So far, I had a dead guy in a chocolate pot, a shop shuttered by homicide cops, a close friend under as-yet unspoken suspicion of murder, and a grown son stuck in Boston by sudden—and I very much feared they were also mythological—weather delays.

Not to mention those chocolate cherry cheesecakes, upon which the town's whole Fourth of July fireworks display depended. *At least things can't get much worse,* I told myself bleakly.

But then I spied Bella's own cell phone lying in the kitchen sink, where she'd apparently just flung it. "Wait, what?"

She whomped the rolling pin down hard onto another half-dozen wafers. "A stiff-necked, pea-brained old—"

I snatched the cell phone from the sink. Bella hadn't turned it off before she hurled it, so the text message she had received still glowed on the screen: See you soon.

It was from my dad. Moments later I had the nurse in charge of his cardiac care unit on the line.

"Listen, I'm really very sorry to trouble you," I told her, "but could you please just check and make sure that . . ."

He's still there in his hospital bed, where he belongs, I was about to finish. But before I could, a pair of sharp car-horn toots sounded from the street out in front of the house.

Familiar car-horn toots. "Never mind," I said, peering out just as an old dark blue Monte Carlo with four mismatched tires, ominously dark-tinted windows, and *Perry's Cab Service $1/mile* stenciled in white across the doors pulled away from the house.

"Old fool," spat Bella once more, recognizing the horn.

She slammed down the rolling pin. *That is a good thing,* I thought. Since if it had remained in her hand, my dad might have had to go right back to the hospital with a head injury.

"I *told* him," she spluttered, rushing out the back door and down the porch steps. "I told him and *told* him not to . . ."

Halfway up the front walk he stopped, swaying uncertainly: a skinny old man with a ruby stud in one earlobe and a stringy gray ponytail tied with a leather thong dangling down his back, wearing a hospital gown and paper slippers.

Hurrying out past Bella, I grabbed a plastic lawn chair and stuck it behind him. "Sit."

He obeyed shakily, his bony hands gripping the armrests. His feet, big and lumpy with arthritis and bunions, had already burst through the ends of the slippers. His IV needle, still taped to the inside of his elbow, oozed dark blood.

"Hi," he managed, looking overall as if even he was beginning to realize what a bad idea this whole escapade was.

"I'm calling the ambulance," said Bella, turning back toward the house.

"Wait," he quavered, raising a trembling hand.

"Hi, Dad," I whispered. I'd never seen him tremble before. I'd never seen him look anything but strong and confident and as if he would live forever.

But he didn't look that way now. "If it's all right with you, I'd much rather be here," he uttered humbly.

Please, he didn't add out loud.

I heard it, though, and Bella must have, too; an odd look crossed her homely old face and I thought she might break down, which I'd never seen her do before, either. But then:

"All right, you foolish old man," she snapped, "let's get you inside before you pass out."

Saying this, she took his left arm and I took his right one, startled by how light he was and by how heavily he leaned on me, and we all stepped haltingly together toward the porch.

Sun-dappled maple leaves shaded our path; a blue jay called from somewhere, its peculiar metallic cry echoing, and the mingled perfumes of lilacs and chamomile hung in the summer air.

A car went by behind us, and then another. "Just a little bit farther," said Bella, urging my father forward as best she could. "Come on, now, I can't do it all for both of us."

"I know, dear," he managed hoarsely. "I'm trying," he said, and then his eyes closed and his knees buckled abruptly.

Helplessly, we lowered him to the grass; a vein in his neck throbbed with a pulse, but we couldn't rouse him. Then Ellie got back, and when she saw us she pulled out her own phone.

But Bella stopped her. "If he wakes up in the hospital again, he won't survive it," she declared, and she was right.

If we wanted him to live, he needed something worthwhile that he could cling to, needed it right nearby.

And we were it: family, home.

"I want to be here," he managed, his eyes flickering open again. "You send me back to that place and I won't last a week."

Then Bob Arnold appeared, hurrying up the sidewalk toward us. His car had been among those going by on the street, and he helped get my father the rest of the way inside my big old house.

We put him on the daybed in the sunroom, where a sea breeze made the air pleasant and blooming lilacs shaded the windows. By the time Bob left again, my father's shape was twiglike under the cotton quilt.

"Dad, you're sure you want this?" *To stay here,* I meant, *and take your chances on the result.*

"I'll get your medicines, and we'll have a visiting nurse come to put another IV in. I think we can probably take care of it okay."

His bushy eyebrows knit; he didn't like the IV idea.

"Yeah, well, I'm not having any argument on that one," I

told him. "But Dad, you know it could go either way, right? I mean . . ."

He knew what I meant: He'd just had a heart attack; he hadn't recovered from it by a long shot; and he could die here. If he began to, I might not be able to do anything about it. But in reply he only fixed me with a look of such loving acceptance—*either way*—that I really had no choice.

"All right," I sighed, giving in. "Hey, it's your funeral," I added, and he smiled, appreciating the dark humor. Meanwhile, Bella would be here soon with clean pajamas, iced Perrier water, and anything else he needed.

Lucky for me. After all, Ellie and I had all that baking to do, not to mention the little matter of a murder investigation centered around our shop.

Also I was waiting to hear from Wade. He'd gone out very early on a tugboat to meet the freighter; by now he was on board the big ship, so he'd be calling to tell me so, I supposed.

I wanted to call Sam back again, too, to find out more about what was actually delaying his return from Boston. *Probably I misunderstood Sam*, I thought as I left my dad resting quietly and went out to the kitchen again. I hadn't heard about any storm being imminent, and certainly not one big enough to delay travel.

But ten minutes later I had, and you know, it's true what they say:

It never rains but it pours.

"You've got to stop them, Millie. I mean it, and you've got to *start* stopping them immediately," Bob Arnold said urgently into his phone.

It was five in the evening—eight hours, now, since I'd found Matt Muldoon's body with its head in a pot of chocolate.

"I don't *care* if Amber's a pretty name for a storm," Bob said with frustration. "It's a *hurricane*, damn it, and it's definitely on its way here. Haven't you been listening to me at all, Millie? The *result's* not going to be pretty," he emphasized.

I'd spent all day baking, getting my dad settled, and making arrangements for all the many home-care items and services that a recent heart attack victim required.

Especially one who'd gone AWOL from his hospital bed, and if you ever want a truly enjoyable conversation, try telling a lot of medical professionals that their patient will be staying home with you from now on, and if he dies, he dies.

Which was my dad's attitude. I was just the messenger, and as a result I was the one who got talked to as if I should be getting scraped off the bottom of someone's shoe. To escape, I'd finally come downtown to the Chocolate Moose; now Bob Arnold and I sat at one of the small cast-iron tables outside the shop.

Leaning back tiredly, I let Bob's voice drift off and worried instead about the bad weather that had turned out to be imminent.

According to the Weather Channel, Hurricane Amber had begun as they mostly do, off the coast of Africa. Then, after meandering this way and that across the Atlantic like a drunk staggering home after a colossal bender, the storm veered north and shrank to a tropical depression.

Which would've been fine. But then Amber had changed course again, dipping into the warm gulf stream just long enough to draw energy from tropical currents that swirled there. Lots of energy, and now she was coming here.

And she wasn't the only one. "Millie, we've got thousands of people headed to Eastport," said Bob.

For the Fourth of July holiday, our little island's population routinely swelled from its usual twelve hundred or so to about five thousand. But this year the third fell on Friday, which always boosted the number even higher on account of the long weekend.

"That, or they've already arrived. You've got to call back all those media friends of yours," he said, "to let them know."

Millie Marquardt was the new chairperson of the Fourth of July committee, and on account of her efforts, attendance at this year's festival was projected to be at least double that of any in the past.

"Maybe people will believe they ought to stay home if it's on TV," Bob went on. "Although half of 'em probably don't even know what a hurricane *is,* and if they do, then they think it's something that happens to other people."

Bob took a breath. "So you need to make sure that it *gets* on TV," he said. "And that they *do* understand. Because we are those other people now, okay? We're getting this big storm right here in Eastport in about . . ."

He paused, calculating it. According to the TV that we'd set up for my dad in the sunroom, Amber was racing north.

". . . about forty-eight hours," Bob said. "Maybe more, but also maybe less. So I want you to get on this starting immediately, you hear me, Millie? This is a public-safety emergency we've got here."

He took another breath. "Get it on the radio, online, on TV. Shout it through a megaphone if you have to, but get hold of them, and tell them either to go home if they're here, or not to come in the first place."

I closed my eyes, listening. Inside the Chocolate Moose, the state's crime technicians still combed over what little evidence they could find. But there couldn't be much; due to Bella's strict hygiene standards, in order to find any contamination-type particles in our kitchen you'd have needed an electron microscope.

Detectives from the Maine State Police homicide squad had also spoken to Muldoon's widow, Sarabelle, and afterward to Ellie and me. And it hadn't gone well; I'd kept trying to explain that we were a food shop and thus had to abide by the health department regulations, even without Muldoon's harassment.

But because the Moose's kitchen floor had failed to offer up even a stray cookie crumb, they still thought somehow we'd cleaned it up *after* the murder, and that of course made us look even more suspicious.

"Yes, I know the Fourth of July is a big day for everyone in Eastport," said Bob into the phone.

For the restaurants, the whale-watching tour boats, and all the little gift shops on Water Street, the holiday brought in half the year's sales, and losing it would be disastrous.

Although not as disastrous as having most of their customers blown into the water and drowned, of course. "Good for merchants, and good for the whole town, yes," Bob went on. "Yes, I absolutely agree. Makes fine publicity for us all, too."

The long purple shadows of late afternoon crept stealthily between the quaint downtown buildings, their redbrick facades glowing rosily on the sunny side and darkening on the other to the color of old blood. Tourists strolled the breakwater, and out on the bay a few fishing boats tootled along prettily.

"Yes, Millie," repeated Bob with heavy patience; by now I could almost hear the steam hissing out of his ears. "I do very much agree, this hurricane is inconvenient, that's for sure."

Across the street the amphitheater-style stone seats of Overlook Park edged down to a lawn, where a free movie (tonight it was *Finding Nemo*) was being shown to a crowd of youngsters.

"Yes," said Bob. "Yes, Millie, I . . ."

On the portable screen, bright tropical fish cavorted. To the east, the day's last ferry full of tourists chugged over the waves toward the Canadian island of Campobello, gleaming like a gold bar in the sun's angled rays.

"But," Bob said evenly, clearly struggling to keep his head from exploding, "we don't want all of those wonderfully lucrative holiday guests of ours to *float away*, now do we, Millicent?"

He stopped, listening with his eyes half-closed. I could hear his teeth gritting as he fought manfully to hold on to his temper. Then:

"All right," he conceded finally. "The vendors can stay one more day. Until sundown tomorrow, they'll want to be out by then, anyway, so they don't get blown into the bay. And if the storm's passed—*if* it has, mind you, and the cleanup's gone okay, too—then on the evening of the fourth we can still have the fireworks, probably."

Oh, great, the ones our cakes are supposed to finance. I'd been thinking that really, a huge storm might be just what the doctor ordered. Or in the baking department it could be. Ellie was working on the third pair of cheesecakes right now, so by tomorrow we *might* have finished baking them all. . . .

"But you start discouraging those visitors right now, Millie. I mean it," said Bob. "And get the ones who're already here turned around and headed west, back onto the mainland."

But even after the cakes were baked, we'd still have to decorate them, which first meant shaving a ton of chocolate curls off a big block of the stuff using a vegetable peeler. Later we'd add the cherry topping, pipe the frosting on, drizzle a satiny chocolate glaze over the top, sprinkle the curls over it all, and voila!

Or "viola," as Sam would've put it. Among his many other difficulties, Sam had a weird and quite severe form of dyslexia, although that wasn't the problem I was worried about him battling just at the moment.

"Now, Millie, I know you won't be able to stop 'em all," Bob said patiently.

Across Water Street, a tall woman in a long white sundress and strappy sandals glanced furtively over at me. The woman wore sparkling drop earrings, glittery charm bracelets, and a swathe of gold chains around her swanlike neck.

It was Sarabelle Muldoon, her platinum hair swirled smoothly into a loose chignon and her expression fixed in a scowl. Bob spotted her, too, and raised an eyebrow at me while still talking.

"But unless you want a lot of tourists bunking at *your* house for a week," he said, " 'cause that's how long it might take . . ."

To get the causeway back open and all those holiday visitors out of here again, he'd have said. But instead at this last awful suggestion—houseguests! for a week!—I heard Millie's alarmed squawk come from the phone, followed by frenzied babbling.

"Fine," said Bob, satisfied at having gotten the reaction he wanted at last. "That's swell, and if it turns out you need any assistance . . ."

He stopped short, having apparently just remembered that offering to help Millie with anything generally resulted in your having the whole job dumped in your lap.

". . . call Jake," he finished, and of course I didn't bop him over the head with a café table.

Just then a pair of crime scene technicians exited the Moose, rummaged in their white cargo van parked right outside, and went in again.

"We need to get back to work in there," I told Bob. "Ellie and I do, I mean."

My old kitchen was already proving inadequate to the task we'd set for ourselves, and we were driving poor Bella bonkers as well. "What's taking the technicians so long?" I asked.

Bob spread his hands. "Dunno. I doubt it'll be much longer, though." Another thought hit him. "So how'd Ellie know so fast that the dead guy was Matt Muldoon, anyway?"

I blew out a breath. The state's homicide investigators had asked that, too, noting that Muldoon's face and hair had been hidden under all the chocolate and that his clothes and physical build were too common to use for identification purposes.

But the answer was simple. "His shoes had orange reflectors in the heels," I told Bob, "and she recognized them from when he'd come in to hassle her the night before."

She'd seen them, she'd told investigators, when he turned and stomped out of the shop.

"Hmmph." Bob's rosebud lips pursed consideringly when I'd reported this to him. "Lucky."

That she'd had a good answer ready, he meant, and I had to agree. The cops hadn't arrested anyone or even been particularly pointed in their questioning, other than the part about our shop being dirt-free right down to the subatomic level.

But I thought it was only because Ellie and I weren't flight risks; for one thing, with all those cheesecakes left to bake, we obviously weren't going anywhere. Probably they believed that as a result we were both sitting ducks for any charges they might want to bring, whenever they wanted to bring them.

Murder charges, for instance. Which we weren't—sitting ducks for them, I mean; but hey, they were the hotshot investigators, so I figured I'd just let them find that one out for themselves.

As if overhearing my thought, Bob squinted narrowly at me. "You and Ellie aren't planning on doing anything on your own hook about any of this, are you? Tell me," he added seriously, "that you are not."

By "anything," of course, he meant snooping, a notion he could be forgiven for entertaining. Ellie and I had a reputation in and around Eastport for being . . . well, not nosy, exactly.

That word implies wanting to know things merely for the pleasure of knowing them. We were more results-oriented.

There was the time, for instance, when we'd found a local butcher cut into steaks and chops, wrapped up in white paper, and stuffed into his own freezer. If Ellie and I hadn't looked into the matter, the fellow's wife would've gone to prison.

Not that she hadn't been happy to have her better half literally cooling his heels. He'd been a batterer for a long time, as it turned out. But that was then and this was now.

"I mean it, Jake. You give 'em time, the state homicide cops will realize Ellie wasn't involved. Or you, either," Bob added.

I wasn't so sure. But the last thing I needed, just in case Ellie and I did decide to do a little freelance poking around, was the police chief keeping an eye on us.

"Fine," I told him as the evidence techs exited the Moose yet again. "We'll stay out of it."

And if he believed that, I had some clam flats in Arizona that I could sell him. The crime scene technician held out the new key I'd lent him.

"The place is all yours again," he said.

Bob looked unconvinced by my no-snooping promise; as I've mentioned, he knew me and Ellie well. But he had his hands full; between the influx of tourists, Maine's recent legalization of personal fireworks, and the number of beer and liquor trucks unloading at the island's restaurants in advance of the holiday, this year's Fourth of July would be hard enough to police even without hurricanes.

And even without murder. "Guess I'll just leave you to it, then," he said, hauling himself up tiredly.

To the Moose, he meant, and to the unfinished cheesecakes and my invalid father, my absent husband, and my still-silent son. My attempts at calling Sam back had gone straight to voice mail.

Now all I wanted was to go home and catch a quick nap before I took over the baking duties from Ellie, this time here at the shop. But instead, from where she loitered across the street by the film projector, the widow Muldoon shot me another dark look.

From the way she'd hung around with her masses of jewelry sparkling and flashing, I thought she must have more on her mind than the animated fish cavorting on the portable movie screen looming behind her.

And after Bob Arnold got into his patrol car and drove away, she proved me right.

I didn't like her, and I didn't trust her any farther than I could throw her. But I needed to talk with Sarabelle, if only to rule her out of having killed Matt Muldoon herself.

Or better yet, to rule her in. Because when one spouse gets murdered, the other one . . . well, you know the drill. It was why that butcher's wife had nearly landed in the cooler herself; after all, who's got better reasons than the nearest and dearest?

Right now, though, Ellie was in the crosshairs instead. So I let Sarabelle follow me into the Moose, where the usual delicious aromas blended with the sharp, penetrating scent of chemicals from the crime techs' kits. *With any luck*, I thought, *she'll incriminate the hell out of herself.*

But she sure didn't start out that way. "Ellie did it, you know. Your little friend," Sarabelle added nastily, "that everyone in town thinks can do no wrong."

She was a decade or so younger than her late husband and still strikingly lovely with deep-set brown eyes, perfect makeup, and the kind of small, evenly-distributed facial features that suggest a pleasant disposition. But in her case looks really were deceiving; Sarabelle Muldoon's disposition was about as pleasant as a piranha's.

And dear heaven, that voice, like a cross between a banshee and a rusty hinge. "Little Goody Two-shoes," she grated out. "That's what *she* is. Thinks she's so clever, too. But she's not."

Yeah, Sarabelle was a sweetheart, all right; she went on blathering acidly while I looked around the shop. Nothing in the front area had been too badly disturbed by the crime scene techs, and my first goal was to get us ready to open again in the morning.

So I started by wiping down the glass-fronted display case. Sarabelle, meanwhile, plunked herself down at one of the little café tables.

"I told him to be careful, but he came down here again last night, anyway," she declared.

Good, she was feeling chatty. "And why was that? I mean, he'd already talked to her about all the dog hair he supposedly saw," I said, spritzing the glass with Windex.

Sarabelle looked affronted, but I didn't care. She didn't seem at all grief-stricken, just angry and arrogant as usual.

And . . . curious. It was in her eyes, as if there was something she wanted to know from me, but couldn't risk mentioning.

"So why did he come back here last night?" I asked again.

"First of all, it *absolutely was* dog hair," Sarabelle said. Although from her tone it might as well have been ebola virus. "I saw it, too, right there on the floor yesterday morning."

She pointed a manicured index finger. "I tried to say so, but Ellie denied it. So my husband came down and tried telling her."

I already knew this part; Ellie had come to my house spitting mad about it afterward. She was worried, too, because if the Chocolate Moose got cited for health code violations, we could be forced to close.

And that could ruin us. Our money situation was dicey already and the hit to our reputation would be worse. Then the door would be open for Sarabelle to take over the place herself.

I ran a damp paper towel over the cash register, coming up with not a speck of anything visible, as she went on resentfully.

"Ellie could have just admitted it, of course, but no. She had to be stubborn about it."

This was also true, and I understood why. We didn't even have dogs, for heaven's sake, and Ellie had been too fed up to humor the platinum pest's annoying husband any further.

"Still," I persisted, "why did he bother last night—"

"Coming back here that one final time?" Sarabelle lifted her beautifully groomed head and blinked imperially at me.

"Maybe," she said slowly, "it was to give her one more chance at setting things right. He was," she added, "a forgiving man."

"No doubt," I replied evenly, and if she noticed the sarcasm, she didn't comment.

The chocolate delicacies I'd put into the display case hours earlier still looked delicious on their white paper doilies, but I doubted that anyone would want to eat them now. People would think they had murder cooties on them; I swept them into a paper bag.

"Or maybe he'd just had enough of her foolishness," Sarabelle added, and in reply I certainly did not stuff my Windex-dampened paper towel into her mouth.

"She wouldn't listen to him the first time, so he *had* to come back," Sarabelle went on indignantly. "Why should he let her make a fool of him?"

Muldoon hadn't needed anyone else to make a fool of him. He'd managed that very effectively all on his own, but I didn't say so. Sarabelle herself was a deeply unpleasant person, and as I say, I'd disliked her even before recent developments.

On the other hand, those recent developments had made her a new widow, hadn't they? And it was entirely possible that she hadn't caused them; plenty of people disliked Muldoon.

"Do you have anyone to help you make the arrangements?"

I tried to sound sympathetic. The Muldoons had no children or other relatives that I'd ever heard of, and if she hadn't killed him, then it must be awful to face such sudden bereavement alone.

But she only looked puzzled. "Oh, you mean for a funeral? No, he has a sister back in New Jersey, but they weren't close. My family's there, too. I visit them quite often actually, but they're not . . . not very supportive."

For a moment she'd nearly seemed human. But then: "Don't think you can get out of this by being nice to me," she snarled.

Her default mood, apparently, was evil. "That friend of yours killed my husband, she's got a terrible temper, and she's going to pay for it."

My sympathy vanished; Ellie no more had a terrible temper than I had two heads. "So when did your husband leave the house last night to come back down here to the Moose?"

I snapped the question out and she answered as if by reflex, just as I'd hoped she would.

"Late. After the TV news ended. I could see he was still very upset after his bad day, so I told him he should try to get some sleep."

The bad day being Ellie's fault, too, of course. Sarabelle glanced peevishly around the shop again, her gaze raking the floor as if she might spot something incriminating down there.

"That's when I went up to bed," she went on. "Later when I realized he hadn't come upstairs, I looked for him, but he wasn't in the house. I thought he must have gone out for a walk."

"You didn't worry when he didn't come back?" In Eastport you aren't going to get mugged for your wallet, but you can fall off a pier, get trapped by the tide, or tumble over a granite cliff's edge at any number of locations around our little island.

Sarabelle shook her head. "I sleep soundly. And this morning by the time I figured out that Matt still wasn't there, Bob Arnold was already at the door."

So far, plausible. "Okay. So all you know is that he went out shortly after eleven-thirty last night."

And sometime afterward wound up with his face in a pot of chocolate. "I wonder, how did he know that Ellie would even be here at that hour?"

It wasn't a regular thing, her staying so late. She'd wanted to clear the decks for our big project by doing today's baking for the shop, then starting the chocolate melting for the cheesecakes' batter and decoration.

Chocolate we still have to replace somehow, I recalled with a pang of anxiety. The stuff we used was the real gourmet deal, not the grocery store variety. Sarabelle shrugged impatiently.

"Maybe he didn't know," she said. "He might not have

meant to come here at all, I suppose, but then he could have seen her as he was passing by, saw the lights on, and . . ."

Her gaze swept the floor again, as if she just knew there was dirt down there somewhere and she'd find it if she searched hard enough. "But what I do know is that if she hadn't been here, he'd be alive right now."

She got up. "Ellie killed him, I'm sure of it. She lost her temper, or maybe she knew he was right about the dog hair and panicked over what he was going to do about it. And you must know that, too, so don't pretend you don't."

I knew just the opposite, in fact. But after the day I'd had, I was too tired to argue about it, and anyway it would've done no good. "Okay. Whatever. I'm sorry for your loss," I said.

But Sarabelle wasn't having any of that, either. "Sorry?" she drawled out sarcastically. "Sure you are."

She yanked the door open as if readying herself to slam it on her way out. But at the last moment she hesitated; her face lost its smooth beauty and her extraordinary dark eyes filled with something ugly and real.

Grief, maybe. Then the door did slam hard and her slim shape flitted past the window, ghostly white in the summer evening.

Good riddance, I thought as I gave the kitchen a thorough wipe, and not much later I headed home myself, setting the CLOSED sign in the window and turning the new key in the lock. Its sharp *click!* reminded me of the scratches I'd noticed on the door frame earlier, but I'd told Bob Arnold about them and alerted the state cops, too, so there was nothing else for me to do about that.

Outside, the kids from the movie had gone home and the rising moon cast a silver stripe on the flat-calm water of the bay.

Lingering tourists wrapped sweaters around themselves, and from the boat basin came the clank of the heavy chains holding the finger piers to the dock and the gush of bilge pumps working.

"Hello, Jacobia." I caught a whiff of citrus cologne just as

Miss Halligan's voice came from the shadowy doorway of her shop. "Cleaning up, were you?"

She stepped out onto the sidewalk. "I do enjoy being here in the early evening. So peaceful."

Across the bay, the land was a dark, low shape with here and there the faint glow of a car's headlights moving on it.

"Really." I'd intended to hurry away, eager to get home to my dad and to Ellie, still working there in my kitchen.

But now I paused. "So . . . by any chance, were you here late last night, not just in the evening like now?"

The jewel-toned embroidery on her T-shirt shone under the nearby streetlamp. "When Matt Muldoon died? No. Too bad, I might have noticed something useful. Or—"

A small boat moved through the moon's searchlight beam on the water, then vanished into the darkness again. The bay was a trap for the unwary mariner, but local boaters knew their way around it blindfolded, practically, and were often out after dark.

"Or I could've stopped it, maybe," Miss Halligan added. Then: "What did Sarabelle want?"

What, indeed? Random spewing of venom hardly seemed like a good-enough reason for her visit. "I don't know," I said truthfully.

A flock of kids on skateboards swooped by us. When they were gone, "I guess she could've just wanted company," I continued.

"I mean, she's got a funny way of showing it, and under the circumstances it seems pretty unlikely she'd come to me, but I get the feeling she has no one else to talk to."

Miss Halligan nodded sagely. "If she weren't such a rhymes-with-witch, though, she wouldn't have that problem, would she?"

She turned to me, her thick-lashed eyes glittering with some emotion I couldn't identify. But when she spoke again, I could:

"In fact, as far as I'm concerned," the elegant little owner of the Second Hand Rose vintage clothing emporium finished, "the widow Muldoon can go piss up a rope."

My big old house at the top of Key Street shone bluish white in the moonlight, its three redbrick chimneys thrust up against the twinkling stars and its old double-hung windows, each flanked by an antique pair of forest-green shutters, warmly aglow.

Climbing the hill toward it after leaving Miss Halligan in her shop, I tried coming up with a reason why she might dislike Sarabelle Muldoon so much. But my mind turned worriedly instead toward Wade and Sam.

The coming storm really is delaying Sam's homecoming, I told myself firmly. His latest stretch of sobriety had lasted for more than two years; I needn't be concerned about that.

Or no more than I always was. Meanwhile, Wade was as safe on the water as he was in his own bed, or so he often insisted; reminding myself of this, I paused in the summer night.

Fireflies glimmered in the shadows among the lilacs in the yard, a breeze rustled the maple leaves half-hiding the porch, and from behind me in the distance, the foghorn on Cherry Island let out a long, two-note honk.

Climbing the steps, I brushed through a clutter of June bugs bopping themselves silly against the porch light; inside, Ellie called out from the kitchen.

"Is that you, Jake? Good, I've been waiting for you. Listen, we have to—"

From the sunroom I heard Bella and my dad talking quietly together. So all was well on that front; I peered past Ellie to where she'd been piling a lot of things on the kitchen table.

Flashlights, a compass, two life jackets . . . not baking items, I realized with sudden foreboding. They were boating items.

"What's all this?" But I'd already guessed the answer.

In my opinion, dry land is the best possible anti-drowning precaution. But we lived on an island, where purchasing things in quantity could be a bit of a project.

And that went double for ecologically sustainable, gourmet-quality, fair-market-produced, and (one hoped) halfway reasonably priced—

"We're out of chocolate," Ellie said.

Three

"Ridiculous," I grumbled, backing out of the driveway with Ellie beside me in my car's passenger seat.

Looking south down the bay, the little town of Lubec seemed so near that you could practically touch it, especially at night. Getting there from Eastport, though, meant a long drive to the mainland, twenty miles due south on narrow, winding Route 1, and then another ten miles out a peninsula to its tip.

The round-trip could take a couple of hours. "*Completely . . . ,*" I emphasized.

That is, it takes hours unless you happen to have a boat, which Ellie did: a twenty-four-foot Bayliner with a big outboard engine and a snug two-berth cuddy. Her husband, George, had bought it for her birthday present the previous year, and I enjoyed having picnics on it when it was tied up at the dock.

But otherwise not so much. We pulled up into a rough gravel parking area overlooking the water. ". . . outrageous," I finished.

The dock at the end of Summer Street, on the opposite side of the island from downtown, lay at the foot of a steep metal gangway that rose and fell with the area's massive twenty-foot tides.

Right now it was low tide, so the gangway was nearly vertical; after I donned my life jacket, I descended by clenching the railings in a death grip while slowly and deliberately bracing my feet on the wooden blocks placed runglike on the metal surface.

"Careful," said Ellie, who'd already scampered down. And have I mentioned that it was a *floating* dock? And that it was dark out, and a stiff breeze had sprung up now, too, so the whole structure felt even more precariously unstable?

Not that it wasn't pretty. The night was thick with the rich, rank smell of seaweed and mud flats exposed by the low tide. The moon, bannered with fog wisps, cast silvery luminescence over the half-dozen other small vessels tied up alongside Ellie's.

In short, it was spectacular, and if only I hadn't wondered if it was my last night on Earth I'm sure I'd have appreciated it even more. I am not, in case you haven't figured this out by now, the world's bravest mariner.

But there was no backing out at this stage. As I stepped from the dock to the boat's foredeck, Ellie was already going through her departure drill:

Battery on, engine down, running lights on, and our lines cast off; finally came a hard shove that pushed the boat's bow decisively away from the dock. Then we were off in a roar of the big outboard, bound for Lubec and the chocolate maker, Marla Sykes, who was our regular supplier.

I gripped the rail as around us the water spread out like a sheet of aluminum foil. Behind us our engine's wake spewed up; cold spray smacked my face.

"She'll meet us at the boat landing," called Ellie over the engine noise.

"Great," I managed through clenched teeth. On our way down to the dock, Ellie had explained that if we wanted those cheesecakes baked and decorated the way we'd promised—that is, loaded with lusciously dark, mouthwatering chocolate inside and out—then this trip was a requirement, and driving would take way too long.

And of course I couldn't let her go alone. As soon as she got the boat, she'd begun taking every navigation and boating-safety course she could find, and practicing boat handling with the kind of energy ordinarily reserved for aspiring sea captains.

So it wasn't as if I were out here with Woody Allen or anything. But as a matter of principle I was nervous about cold seawater, and I was already beginning to regret my decision when a small open boat appeared suddenly out of the darkness ahead.

Zooming in toward us, the little watercraft's feeble running lights crossed our bow about thirty yards distant. Soon we were thudding through its wake, our bow diving and lurching violently. Then the other boat vanished into the darkness once more, while I hung on and waited for our voyage to end.

Which it did, finally. As we approached the town of Lubec, the water around us smoothed eerily, the flat swirls on its surface barely hinting at the jaggedness of the granite lurking below. Ellie let up on the throttle, easing us through a floating maze of brightly painted buoys, each marking a submerged lobster trap.

"Jake! Get forward all the way out on the bow, will you?" she called to me.

To watch for more lobster buoys, she meant, and as first mate I couldn't very well refuse. Swallowing hard, I crept forward up and around the cuddy cabin along the bow rail, until I reached the Bayliner's foredeck. There I found a low, flat seat thoughtfully equipped with a foam-filled cushion.

A *wet* foam-filled cushion, and personally I thought it should have safety straps like the ones that race car drivers belt themselves in with. Never mind, though, I got out to it and I sat. And I'll admit it was gorgeous there, tasting the sharp salt spray under a hazily moonlit sky with the dark water foaming and churning.

"One o'clock," I called out as a yellow-striped wooden buoy bobbed up ahead of us; Ellie veered to avoid it.

Ahead, the bright white dock lights at Lubec's boat landing beckoned welcomingly.

"Ten o'clock," I said as another buoy appeared; she steered starboard. Then: "Hey, who's that?" I gulped, startled.

Coming up fast, an open boat like the one we'd seen earlier rushed in at us again, then swung away. This time its wake slammed us broadside, drenching me with spray and loosening my grip on the seat I'd been clinging to.

Startled and slippery-handed, in an instant I slid helplessly toward the bow rail and through it, half-dangling over the water with my arms hooked precariously around the rail's metal uprights.

"Ugh," I gargled through a mouthful of salt water as Ellie dropped the engine into idle and scrambled out to me.

"I can't let go," I managed when she reached for me. "If I do, you'll be fishing me out with a net."

Ignoring me, she grabbed my life jacket in both hands, hauling me up like a cat dragging a kitten by the nape of its neck.

Spluttering, I slid back up onto the bow and scrambled to my feet. "Where is he?" I spat. "Where's that little—"

We were nearly to the dock. Boats tied up to mooring balls floated around us, their shadows rippling. A line creaked and an anchor chain rattled; a fish jumped with a splash. But no other sound broke the watery silence.

The little boat that had buzzed us was gone, back out into the watery dark. "Jerk," said Ellie, sprinting to the wheel once more. "Thought we were messing with his lobster traps, maybe."

"Yeah, maybe." I stepped down into the boat's small cuddy, a below-deck cabin with a low table, a pair of cushioned berths, and a small cabinet-and-sink unit.

"Dry clothes in the bin under the berth," Ellie called to me. Pulling a rough towel from a cabinet, I rubbed my wet hair.

Through the hull I could feel the engine's slow, steady vibration. When I got back on deck, we were ready to make our landing.

"Toss the bumpers over, please," said Ellie, her eyes on the pier we were pulling up to. I threw the rubbery inflated cylinders over the side to act as cushions between us and the dock pilings.

The pier was a lot closer, and coming on fast. *Too fast,* I thought anxiously, but just as I began feeling that a whole lot of smithereens were about to be spectacularly created, Ellie put the engine in neutral, swung the wheel hard toward the pier, and dropped us into reverse.

Whereupon the boat's stern swung smoothly and as if by magic, nestling itself against the dock. "There," she pronounced, satisfied.

"Right," I croaked, gazing around. Under the glaringly bright marina lights, small boats crowded the inner basin. From the bars and restaurants overlooking the harbor, music floated.

Shedding my life jacket, I stepped up onto the pier just as a tall, jeans-and-sweatshirt-clad woman with curly black hair and a ruddy complexion came striding toward us.

It was our chocolate maker, Marla Sykes. And although all we had planned was to pay her and take our purchases, making the transfer of the dark, gourmet-quality sweet stuff right there on the dock like a trio of culinary smugglers, Marla had other ideas.

"Come on." She urged us both uphill toward the music. "I've already ordered us some Irish coffees."

Ellie looked doubtful, and fatigue hit me, too; it had been a long day, and those cheesecakes weren't going to bake themselves. But then looking out across the glittering black water, I spotted a faint set of running lights moving away from the shoreline.

I couldn't tell whether it was the boat that had charged us or not. But either way I still had to survive the return voyage, didn't I?

Those dark waves, those granite ledges, and so on. "An Irish coffee," I told Marla Sykes, "sounds good."

The Salty Dog was an old-fashioned dockside tavern with a long, scarred wooden bar and a dozen ramshackle wooden tables and chairs scattered about on the unfinished pine floor. At the booth Marla had already claimed for us, the coffees were arriving.

"I've got your chocolate in my car," she said after taking a hefty swig. "We'll drive it down to the boat when you're ready to go."

My unscheduled soaking had sent a deep chill into my bones, and the thought of all we still had to do tonight was exhausting. But the Irish coffee, hot and loaded with enough whiskey to cure whatever ailed me, jump-started my energy.

"Good, huh?" Marla grinned mischievously, downing more of her own drink.

Only a year earlier she'd been a guidance counselor in a Connecticut high school, urging students to pick work they were good at and could love. Then, she'd told us, she woke up one day knowing that the advice she was giving also applied to herself.

Weeks later she'd bought a house here and started importing high-end cocoa paste from fair-trade co-ops whose workers weren't treated like slaves, and almost at once found plenty of demand for her product.

Two houses, actually; she'd bought the first one quickly, but like many newcomers to downeast Maine, she'd changed her mind once she got here and looked around a little. Now she worked here in Lubec, staying over on nights when her chocolate cooking demanded it, but the house she lived in most of the time was in Eastport.

"I hear you had some excitement today," she prompted now, so I described finding the body and what happened afterward.

Marla's eyes widened. "You mean they think maybe it was you who killed him?" she asked Ellie.

"I'm afraid so," Ellie sighed. "And his wife is all, 'Oh, my poor dead husband,' and *she's* accusing me, too."

"Huh. I'd have thought she'd be out celebrating," said Marla.

Ellie and I glanced at each other. "Really? Why?"

Marla shrugged. "From what I've heard, he was no bed of roses, is all. Or maybe . . . maybe she found out he had a girlfriend."

Ellie let out a low whistle at this as Marla went on:

"The two of them even came in here together a few times. But someone recognized her one night and said hello to her, I heard, and after that they never came in here again."

Muldoon and the girlfriend, she meant. Ellie frowned. "But how could they expect not to be—"

"Recognized?" Marla laughed. "Right, you can't do much around here without somebody knowing, can you? But she wasn't."

She ate two peanuts from the bowl of them on the table and washed them down with a swallow of coffee. "Too bad I never saw her myself, maybe I could ID her for you."

I got up. The Salty Dog might not have been fancy, but it was pleasant. I had a feeling the restroom would be clean, too, and it was. By the time I returned to our booth, I knew what I wanted to ask Marla.

"Who was it that said hello? To the girlfriend." Because if I could find that person, I'd just ask him or her who she was, easy-peasy.

Marla, however, looked regretful. "Guy named Wally Pryne. You're not going to be talking to him, though, 'cause see that monument out there?"

The Dog's windows faced the dock; through the nearest one I glimpsed a low granite pyramid near the dock ramp.

"That's the Lost Fisherman memorial and his name's there among many others," said Marla, and at her words I recalled the most recent accident: four men and their boat, the *Helen*

Marie, demolished when a fuel tank exploded. A pang of sorrow went through me as I remembered; that stone pyramid represented a lot of broken hearts.

"There was a birthday party here that night," Marla said suddenly. "The night when Muldoon and his lady friend were in here, I mean. I'd left early, but I heard about it later."

I felt Ellie's ears prick up as she pretended to drink some spiked coffee; she took her boat-captaining duties seriously.

"What was there to hear about?" she asked.

Marla set her own cup down empty. "The interesting part was when Muldoon tried to deck Wally for saying hello to the woman."

"Ha!" said Ellie. In this part of the world, throwing a punch at a local fisherman was a fine way to get decked. Still, something didn't add up:

"You've been here in Lubec all day," I said to Marla. She'd told us that she had been.

"And still you already know who got murdered, that's how fast word travels around here. Yet we've never heard about a girlfriend he supposedly had?" I finished my Irish coffee. "That doesn't make sense."

Marla spread her hands. "Hey, I'm just saying what I heard. As far as I know, they only came in here a few times, though, and then the accident happened, so . . ."

Of course. The deaths of the fishermen, all local guys with wives and kids, had occupied everyone's minds for days.

"Okay," I conceded. Unlikely as it still seemed, I guessed it was possible that amidst the local tragedy, the gossip had simply dropped off everyone's radar screens.

"But what were you saying before about the party that night?" I asked. She must've brought it up for some reason.

"Pictures," said Marla as if this must be obvious. "It was a party, so I'll bet that someone was taking pictures. Wouldn't you think?"

Doink. Of course. "Marla," I leaned in toward her, "do you think you could find people who were also at the party and see if they do have photographs? Get them e-mailed to me, even?"

If they existed, and if any of them had accidentally included Muldoon's companion, it would at least give the cops someone else to think about besides Ellie, wouldn't it? So Marla agreed to try, and on that note we got ready to go.

Five minutes later we all met again under the marina lamps and stowed the large butcher-paper-wrapped chocolate blocks (two of baking chocolate and four of the regular semisweet variety) on the Bayliner. Meanwhile, Marla's German shepherd pal, Maxie, supervised from the backseat of her owner's old Ford station wagon.

"Nice dog," I said, and Marla grinned.

"Yeah, you don't have to worry much with him riding shotgun," she said. "I don't care how ornery you are, you don't want to try crossing Maxie."

Which reminded me. "Hey, Marla, do you know any grouchy guys with small boats around here?"

She barked out a laugh. "Lots of 'em, you get crossways with 'em. Some get pretty mean over their lobster trap territory, too."

She slammed her car's trunk. "Anyway, let me know if you need more of anything. I'm staying at my house here in Lubec tonight, and I'll be here all day tomorrow, too," she called as we cast off.

Ellie gave the dock a hard shove; soon Lubec was a toy town again, twinkling across the water behind us.

Ahead the lights of Eastport shone hazily, seeming to dim and brighten without reason, although of course that had to be an optical illusion.

But then, "Go below and find the compass," Ellie said, her voice tautly urgent. Which was when I realized suddenly: the haze, dimming and brightening . . .

It was no illusion, and that wasn't the worst of it. Glancing back, what I saw rising behind us struck a colder chill in me than even my saltwater dunking earlier.

In the fading moonlight the fog bank looked as solid as concrete. It hadn't been forecast; they often weren't. But Lubec's
marina lights were already hidden behind it.

"Compass," Ellie repeated, more forcefully this time.

I half-fell through the hatchway, yanked open the equipment
bin, and scrabbled around among flares and a flare gun, batteries, first-aid kit, and signal horn, then simply hauled out everything and grabbed up the compass from the jumbled heap.

Finally after handing it up to Ellie, I replaced everything in
the bin, and while doing *that*, I spotted the wires sticking up
from the bin's bottom, leading to a small box screwed to its
back wall.

If I hadn't emptied the bin completely, I'd never have seen
the wires or the box they led to. And I was unfamiliar with boat
electronics, so I didn't think much of them at the time. Besides,
there was still the little matter of us being lost in the fog for me
to freak out about.

Which I was trying not to do, but still. "Okay, now, due west
a little, then north," Ellie said calmly. "Tide's halfway in, we'll
probably have enough water even if we do misnavigate a little."

Personally, I did not want us misnavigating by so much as a
millimeter. I wanted us smack-dab on course—and also not
crashed onto any rocks.

Ones, I mean, that at low tide were visible so you could
avoid them even in the dark, and at high tide were deep enough
so you wouldn't hit them, no matter what. Right now, though,
we were at midtide, so they were barely submerged.

Able, in other words, to rip the guts out of our motorboat
without us seeing them coming. "Um, Ellie?"

Oh, I didn't like this even a little bit. She looked relaxed and
in control at the helm; only if you knew her well would you
notice the squared set of her shoulders, the determined thrust
of her chin.

"Ellie, d'you see that can?" It was a large floating channel
marker, barely visible in the water with fog thickening around it.

Thickening fast. "Darn," uttered Ellie in reply; not what I wanted to hear. "We're not quite where I thought we were, then."

The fog thickened again. One minute it was a misty curtain, and the next a thick gray drapery fell.

"Okay," Ellie sounded resigned. "We're not that far off our course. And although we're stuck until this fog lifts, the good news is that it probably won't take long."

I liked the sound of that last part; well, except for that "probably." But then a loud *whonk!* blasted out of the murk at us.

Really loud. "Freighter," said Ellie. "On its way—"

"Into Eastport," I gulped. The huge container vessels came in and out of our harbor all the time to load stove pellets, wood pulp, machinery, and even livestock for shipping overseas.

"Ellie," I began, "we should really get on the radio or our phones—"

Whonkkkk! Louder this time. We couldn't see any lights on the big vessel yet, and I sure hoped we wouldn't. In this kind of pea soup we'd only see them moments before they slammed into us.

"And call the Coast Guard," I finished.

But she shook her head firmly at me. "And say what, that they should make that big ship stop dead in the water?"

She waved me up to the wheel. "Not gonna happen. And anyway, it's too late. We need to go where they won't be."

She took a breath. "And if the channel marker is *that* way"— she pointed toward where it had been until the fog swallowed it—"then I'm pretty sure . . . yes."

In the dim glow of our running lights, she nodded decisively. "All right. See that thing there?"

Mounted on the boat's dashboard was a cigarette-pack-sized gadget with a small screen glowing on it. The screen's radium-green cursor flashed steadily, and below that some numbers were displayed.

"That's a depth finder," Ellie explained. "The cursor is us, and those numbers are how deep the water is beneath us."

Oh, for Pete's sake. "Why weren't we using this all along?" It would've taken the steam out of my dashed-on-the-rocks worries, that was for sure.

"Because it doesn't work very well." As if to prove this, the screen went black briefly, then flickered gradually to wavering life again.

"I'm saving up to replace it," she said just as another horn blast split the night.

"It's for fishing, mostly, anyway," Ellie said when we could hear again. "I don't even use it much. I just always stay in deep-enough water by reading the charts."

She pushed the throttle and we nosed ahead cautiously in the enveloping fog. "You take the wheel, keep our compass needle aimed the way it is right now, and when the cursor here turns red, you drop us into neutral, fast." She pointed to the depth finder's screen. "We're going into the shallows and putting our anchor down there."

By "shallows" she meant the water over the very rocks that we'd avoided so far. I may have indicated my discomfort with this idea. But then: *WHOONK!* The horn's blast nearly collapsed my lungs.

"Okay," I agreed hastily, grabbing the Bayliner's wheel, which tried instantly to wrench itself from my hands; the currents here were fast and now the tide was running pretty energetically, too.

Also there was the small concern of the hydraulic steering system not being in exactly tip-top condition, another thing I knew she'd been saving to fix. But there wasn't much we could do about it now; instead Ellie scrambled out onto the bow while I stuck to navigating and also to hyperventilating, sweating, and shaking, all motivated by that enormous horn honking again.

Eventually, though, the on-screen cursor glowed red. *So all right, then,* I thought. *Throttle in neutral, check.*

"Ellie?" A breeze stirred the fog and I smelled Christmas trees suddenly, which meant either that Santa Claus was aboard that freighter or we were approaching an island big enough to have trees on it. And unless I was completely turned around direction-wise, the only island like that anywhere nearby was . . .

"Ellie?" A chain rattled. I couldn't see her through what was essentially a fat cloud squatting on us. The chain rattled heavily again; then came a splash and more silence.

"*Ellie?*" The boat swung around hard and stopped with a lurch that nearly knocked me off my feet. Then finally she appeared.

"I did it!" she exulted. "We're solidly at anchor now and that big ship will never dare to come this near to—"

"Treat's Island," I said. Had to be; nothing else in the bay had full-grown fir trees growing on it. We'd have fetched up on its rocky edge already if Ellie hadn't managed as well as she had.

"Look," she whispered. Behind us, the freighter loomed out of the fog with its bow wave foaming and its deck lights all ablaze.

The vessel's name was stenciled on her stern: *Star Verlanger.* Seeing it, I swallowed hard. "That's Wade's ship."

Of course, I realized; he was up there right now, guiding the freighter into port. Luckily, he didn't know we were here, stuck in the fog, and if I had anything to do with it, he never would.

I mean I loved him like crazy and all, but I wasn't stupid. Ellie must've read my thought. "I can keep a secret if you can," she said, watching the big vessel slide back into the murk.

"Deal. George wouldn't like this much, either."

Which was putting it mildly. Right now her husband was in Bangor working a construction job and wouldn't be home until next week. But she knew as well as I did that we'd better keep mum about tonight's little adventure for a lot longer than that.

The ship's engines thrummed a low note that faded and was gone. Then its massive wake rolled up out of the darkness at us and threw us around very unpleasantly until it passed, too.

But the anchor held. When it was all over, I leaned on the Bayliner's rail, letting my stomach settle and breathing in the cool mist.

"Ugh," said Ellie, sounding a little shaky.

"Yeah, me too." I don't usually get seasick, but just then my innards felt as if they might suddenly decide to become outtards.

"How long d'you really think this fog might hang on?" I asked. It would take Wade another couple of hours of paperwork at the marine terminal before he headed home.

"Maybe half an hour, ordinarily," she replied. "That's all it usually is. But I guess with a big storm coming in soon, it could be different. It could even be . . . I don't know . . . until morning when the sun burns it off?" she guessed unhappily.

She didn't know any more than I did, in other words; she'd educated herself thoroughly and practiced very diligently with the Bayliner, but she was no ancient mariner.

Still, there was no reason to push the panic button; after all, she'd brought along hot coffee. There was emergency food on the boat, even if it was only stale Fig Newtons. And Marla Sykes, bless her heart, had put a generous amount of milk chocolate into our bag as a gift.

So we wouldn't starve. Ellie went below, snapping on the cabin lights that made the enclosure into a small, snug cave; that is, if you didn't glance through one of the portholes. The fog was so thick, it looked solid enough to carve chunks from it.

The Bayliner rocked gently. The anchor chain clanked. Ellie set out the hot coffee, the cookies, and the milk chocolate, along with a deck of cards. "Want to play rummy?"

We could've called for help. We had our phones, the Bayliner had a radio, and the Coast Guard would've come at once with their rescue vessel out of the Eastport station.

But Ellie was the stubbornest creature on Earth at times like these; she'd cry uncle if she needed to, and not a minute before.

Besides, if we called anyone, all would be revealed.

So I just sat there eating slivers of milk chocolate while she dealt gin rummy hands and the fog billowed stubbornly outside.

And then we waited.

For a while I couldn't believe I was here. It was unlike me; I'm more of a sunny-afternoon type of boating enthusiast, drinks on the foredeck and a tube of tanning lotion and so on. But the darkness and salt smells, waves slopping against the hull, and the foghorns sounding mournfully in the distance all convinced me.

We were out here, all right, alone late at night in the damp, foggy darkness, floating and waiting.

And waiting some more.

Hours passed. Two of them, to be exact. But then, just as we were about to give up and call for assistance, the fog lifted and the rest of the trip home was uneventful.

Not much later we were clambering back up the Summer Street dock's gangway, hauling the blocks of chocolate.

"I could've killed him, you know," said Ellie.

"Muldoon? Don't say that."

Driving home through the silent streets, we passed only drawn shades and darkened windows. It was just after two in the morning.

"Why not?" Ellie leaned back in the passenger seat with her eyes closed. "I was mad enough, and everyone in town knows it."

"That doesn't mean you need to go around declaring it."

Rain spattered the windshield; an early warning of the storm yet to come, I supposed. The moon had vanished behind clouds.

"You think Wade's home yet?" Ellie asked.

"Hope not." Or that Bella was still up, either. The fog had been as wet as any downpour and explaining why we both looked like drowned wharf rats might get tricky.

But my driveway was empty and inside the house the kitchen was dim and quiet. Ellie got the coffee machine burbling and I unwrapped the chocolate chunks; there was plenty now for what we still had to do, so the trip had been worthwhile, at least.

"Okay," said Ellie determinedly when we'd changed clothes and drunk some of the hot, strong brew she'd made. "Six down, six to go."

Cakes, that is; she'd been busy with them all afternoon. Now while she assembled our baking utensils, I organized the rest of the ingredients.

"Have you thought any more about what Marla said?" Ellie asked as I got the butter from the refrigerator. "About Muldoon having a girlfriend?"

"So Marla thinks," I said skeptically, measuring sugar into a bowl. "Her whole story sounded kind of thin to me, didn't it to you? We'll see if she finds any pictures."

And we'd poke into the tale ourselves, too, although trying to confirm a rumor without actually starting one would take some delicacy. In Eastport, if you began asking whether or not a guy had a girlfriend, by evening the story around town was not only that he did have, but that the two of them had run off together and got married.

Thinking this, I greased two springform pans and tossed cocoa powder lightly around in them. Ellie gathered more of the batter ingredients and began mixing them. Then when I'd finished prepping pans, I crushed more chocolate wafers and started working melted butter into those.

"Anyway, if it's true," I said, pressing buttered crumbs into the bottom of the first pan with my fingertips.

"Then he was smart to pick the Salty Dog for his date night," Ellie finished, rubbing another lemon up and down on the grater.

"It's the one place you could go around here without everyone knowing about it," I agreed. "The younger crowd wants someplace with a pool table and music, and the lah-di-dah types want, well, someplace more lah-di-dah. Candles on the table and so on."

Which left the Salty Dog for the wharf rats and a few odd ducks like Marla. Ellie dug a large wooden spoon from the kitchen drawer and got busy with it: *beat-beat-beat.*

"So, do you want to tell her or should I?" she asked, her eyes on the mixture she was creating. Ellie meant that the cops would probably be visiting Marla soon.

Because if we wanted to take the focus off Ellie as a suspect in Muldoon's murder, we couldn't very well *not* report what we'd heard and who we'd heard it from, whether we believed it ourselves or not.

And the cops would want to confirm what we said by asking Marla about it. "I'll call her," Ellie said. "But you know, about this other thing . . ."

"What thing?" I checked my phone yet again for a message from Sam—*nope*—then pulled up the weather radar on the small screen. I still couldn't believe that a storm not due to strike Eastport for two more days was already wreaking havoc on the transportation system in Boston.

And then I knew it wasn't, since right now the radar had it spinning over North Carolina. So Sam must've been delayed for some other reason, and I disliked more and more trying to imagine what that reason might be.

Plenty of people do manage to stop drinking permanently and completely, I know. But Sam's all-time record was six hundred days.

And counting. "What thing?" I repeated.

"The boat that buzzed us out there," said Ellie. "Because I think maybe he was distracted, busy dealing with his lobster traps, and then he looked up and saw us and swerved away at the last minute."

Around us the house was silent, the moonless night outside as still as a held breath. I pressed more wafer crumbs up against the springform pan's vertical sides.

"Sure, that sounds possible," I said.

It did, too; out on the water at night the way he'd been, not expecting company, and we'd been idling along pretty quietly at that point, so maybe he didn't even hear our engine over his own.

"I could see it happening," I said. But when Ellie looked up from the batter she was mixing, I could tell from her expression that she didn't even believe it herself.

"Yeah." I sighed heavily, setting aside the first chocolate cheesecake crust and starting to build the second.

Yeah, me neither.

The next morning dawned clear and bright, as if the night's fog had never even happened.

"Thanks, and you have a great day, too!" I told the Moose's first customer of the day, handing over a white paper bag full of chocolate biscotti.

When I left the house, Ellie had been sliding the fifth set of cheesecakes into the oven. We'd done two pairs overnight, baked those biscotti, and then thrown together a few pans of everyone's favorite, Toll House cookies, so we could open the shop.

Also during the night Wade had returned, peered tiredly into the kitchen where we still labored, and gone up to bed. Now I swallowed some more of the jet-fuel-strong coffee I'd brought down here with me as the door opened again.

"*Good* morning, Jacobia!" Miss Halligan bustled in.

"And to you, too." From the counter I could see out across

Water Street, where it didn't seem as if Bob Arnold's warnings had produced their desired effect. If any more Fourth of July vendors tried cramming themselves onto the fish pier, I thought it might break off and float away.

The town was still full of tourists also; in the bad-storm-coming-soon department, the crystalline blue sky smiling down on us now just wasn't very persuasive.

"Any news?" Miss Halligan's bright gaze darted around.

"About the murder? No, nothing."

In a short black ruffled skirt and black leotard top, black leggings, and her usual neat black ballet flats on her feet, she looked as if she belonged in a chic Greenwich Village apartment, not a remote Maine island fishing village.

I thought she was about to say more, but just then Ellie came in lugging more bags of fresh baked items for our display case.

"Your dad's up," she told me. Briskly she unloaded a dozen frosted devil's food cupcakes and a chocolate-cream brioche into the display case.

"Bella got him into the shower, got some breakfast into him, and now he's back in the sunroom, bright as a new penny."

That was good news. I'd been worrying pretty steadily about him whenever I wasn't busy trying not to fall off a boat, get lost in a fog, or be run over by a cargo freighter.

Last out of Ellie's bag was a foil tray full of pinwheel cookies, rich with swirls of thick, melty semisweet chocolate and studded with walnut bits.

"Bella said now that your dad's settled for the morning, she'd watch the oven."

Because that fifth pair of cakes was in it, Ellie meant. "And Bob Arnold called, he'll be stopping by to see me," she added.

An alarm bell rang in my head. "You going to tell him the girlfriend story?"

Miss Halligan exited as a quintet of bagpipers marched down Water Street, practicing for the Fourth of July parade, which was now just forty-eight hours distant.

I mean, assuming it didn't get drowned out. "Not yet," Ellie said over the din. "For one thing, if I did, I'd probably also end up telling him all about the excitement we had last night."

Precisely. Bob was not only a genius at getting rowdy guys to chill in his squad car's backseat, but he was also a whiz at getting information out of them.

And he'd get it out of us, too, if we weren't careful. "Also I don't want to look like I'm grasping at straws by offering up some kooky theory," she said. "Better to know more for sure."

Right. "So maybe after you've eaten something more nourishing than cookies," she continued, eyeing the display case where a few more biscotti were missing than I had actually sold this morning. "And when you've made sure that Bella really has taken those cheesecakes out of the oven," she added.

Her eyes were wide and guileless. "Once those things have happened, I thought I'd stay here in the shop for a while, and you might try asking around a little," she said. She smiled sweetly at me. "About the girlfriend, that is, and about who might've been out there in a little boat last night?"

She didn't have to ask twice.

Four

An hour later I was in my car, headed over the long, curving causeway that linked Eastport to the mainland. A wide inlet spread to my left, its flat surface mirroring the azure sky; on my right the bay raced turbulently with whitecaps hurling themselves along.

At the Route 1 intersection I pulled over and dug my phone out. Ellie's ideas about what I should snoop into were fine, but first I wanted to talk to Marla again. Something about the party at the Salty Dog and the woman there with Muldoon that night just hadn't sounded right to me.

An eagle soared lazily over the pointed firs lining the road as I called and got her answering machine. Probably the chocolate maker was tending something delicious, and couldn't come to the phone. But she'd said she'd be there, so I turned south to Lubec again, this time via the land route.

The road was crowded with tourists in RVs, locals in pickup trucks, and highballing eighteen-wheelers from the tree-harvesting operations up north, their massive trailers packed to overflowing with eighty-foot tree trunks.

It almost made our fog-choked voyage of the night before seem safe; by the time I rolled into Lubec nearly an hour later, my hands felt permanently fused to the steering wheel.

On Front Street I parked in front of the once-busy fish-processing plant, a long wooden-frame structure with a lot of small, high windows stretching out onto the wharf. A hundred years ago the sardine-packing industry employed whole families of downeast Mainers; now local artisans rented workspaces in the venerable old building.

Crossing the street, I made my way among summer visitors in cargo shorts, fanny packs, and flip-flops. Gazing around, they blinked in wonder at the town's wooden storefronts now transformed into cafés and galleries, the harbor's glittering blue water, and the combination antiques fair and farmer's market being set up on the library's front lawn.

"Marla?" I called, entering the fish-packing plant. Inside, the fish-canning equipment of long ago had been replaced by a potter's wheel, a stained-glass artist's tools, two looms, some yarn-dying tubs, and a spinning wheel. A scrimshaw engraver's whalebone storage area—the great mammals sometimes beached themselves nearby—filled one whole end of the huge structure.

"Marla?" I called again. The high windows sent gold bars of sunlight slanting onto the bare floor. The place smelled like old wood, hot metal, oil paints, vegetable dye, and very faintly but perceptibly of fish.

No answer from Marla, and when I entered her linoleum-tiled, drywalled, and totally sealed-off cooking room—because it wouldn't do for dust from glass cutting and whalebone etching to fall into the chocolate kettles, would it?—no one was there.

"Hello?" Behind a door framed into the drywall, Marla's workspace had a gas stove and brass-shaded hanging lamps. The tables were granite-topped, the sinks all brushed aluminum with gooseneck faucets and spray handles. Pots and pans stood on low shelving and implements bristled from stoneware jugs. They all looked new and in good shape, and so clean even Bella would have approved.

Several thickly wrapped bundles stood on one of the tables. From the exotic return addresses, multiple stamped labels, and illegibly initialed customs stickers, I guessed they contained the raw cocoa paste that Marla imported and made into chocolate.

Also on a high shelf I recognized the kind of steel lockbox that Wade used for handguns. No surprise; in downeast Maine lots of people owned firearms. But there was still no sign of Marla.

I looked around some more, hunting for a way to leave a note, but didn't find any. An electric kettle, bigger and more heavily built than any Crock-Pot I'd ever seen, stood on a table of its own. Beside it was a ceramic jar labeled COCOA BUTTER and some smaller bottles: vanilla extract, several more I didn't recognize.

It all looked wonderfully supplied and well organized, as if she was getting ready to start a batch of something. No one was here now, though, so I decided to visit the Salty Dog; maybe she was having lunch.

In daylight the bar's rugged interior looked pale and anemic, the windows dust-filmed and the bar stools' leather seats patched with silver duct tape. I slid onto one of them and ordered a Moxie.

The tourists knew better than to come in here looking for food, apparently. The bartender, a wiry old guy with a shaving cut on his chin, slid the Moxie bottle at me.

"You gonna drink that or pour it in your boat battery?" he asked.

That's the thing about Maine's official soft drink: It's so versatile. You can clean barnacles off a boat's hull with it, I've heard, and it tastes like something a troll must've stewed up in a cauldron under a bridge, bitter with a harsh, rooty twang.

Even I'm not a complete fan of the stuff. But I slugged down a big gulp straight out of the bottle just to show the bartender that I could, and he looked impressed.

Not enough to confide in me, though. "Ain't seen her," he answered without stopping to think when I asked about Marla.

I got the feeling he'd have said the same whether she had been in or hadn't; what happens here, stays here, etc. To confirm my theory I asked about any recent birthday parties in the place, like the one Marla had mentioned.

In reply he looked at me like I was speaking ancient Greek, and when I mentioned a possible lunch menu, he waved a knobby hand at the peanut bowls still out on the tables from the night before.

Same peanuts, too, I was pretty sure. So I took my Moxie and went back outside into the bright day, to the dock where Ellie and I had tied up.

With an army of gleaming black seals cavorting in the water there now, the scene had a carefree, summer-holiday feel; even the wooden fishing boats, some so work-worn that they looked as if only their aging paint jobs held them together, bobbed jauntily at their moorings.

Strolling among men and a few women carrying tackle boxes and bait buckets, I bought a hot dog from a truck doing business in the parking lot and carried it down onto the lawn overlooking the seals' acrobatics.

That's when I saw the small wooden boat pulled up onto the beach. With only a five-horse engine on the rickety transom, the rot-riddled little vessel looked utterly unequal to any wild tides or twisty currents, and it had been dark the night before.

So I wasn't at all sure this was the boat that had behaved so rudely to us. But Marla might know whose it was; I wondered, too, if by now she'd located any snapshots of Matt Muldoon and the woman he'd supposedly been with, that night in the Salty Dog.

Most of all, though, I wanted to know why Marla thought the woman was Muldoon's girlfriend. It was a pretty big conclusion for Marla to jump to, I thought, especially since she hadn't actually been there to see anything herself.

So after I finished the hot dog, which was excellent, and rinsed it down with the Moxie, which was liquid and tasted like something ladled up out of an old tree stump, I drove out of town along the shore road toward Marla's house.

Beach roses lined the narrow, curving blacktop on both sides, filling the air with a fruity perfume that made the summer day heavenly. Driving along with the windows rolled down and the radio on, I stole quick glances at the Gulf of Maine's indigo water and the island of Grand Manan jutting distantly from it.

The road ran between rosebush-fenced meadows for a mile or so; then I spotted a sandy driveway with a massive old lilac bush blooming at the end of it. A weathered plank nailed to a post bore Marla's last name spelled out in seashells; following the rutted lane past a bank of solar panels mounted atop a granite boulder, I reached a graveled turnaround.

"Marla?" Her car was in the open garage next to the simple A-frame structure. "Hello?" I called.

But the only reply was the rush of wind on the high, grassy bluff overlooking the bay behind the house, which was small and a bit run-down. Around here salt air scoured paint off a place nearly as fast as a person could apply it.

Marla had tried renting the place to tourists, once she'd bought her Eastport location, I recalled, but tenants thought the house was too primitive, too isolated, or both.

Personally, I thought coming all the way to downeast Maine and then complaining about the primitive isolation was hilarious, but hey, I liked Moxie.

Or I was trying to, anyway. On the porch I touched the front door and it swung silently open at my touch.

"Hey, Marla, are you here?" *Maybe she's gone for a walk with that big dog of hers,* I thought, but then I noticed the mess.

Books, papers, manila envelopes with lengths of twine tied around them . . . everything was pulled out of the wooden bookcases on either side of the fireplace. Cookbooks, tax papers, cards with notes scribbled on them, checkbook registers . . .

When the door banged shut behind me, I must've jumped a foot. But it was only the wind blowing through the sliding-glass panels that looked out over the water, skittering the scattered papers like dry leaves across the slate-tiled floor.

"Marla?" I whispered. The small galley kitchen, all polished granite and stainless steel, gleamed emptily. Ditto for the bath and the two small bedrooms downstairs; in one of them I thought I caught a whiff of familiar fragrance, but no one was there, and I could see up into the A-frame's vacant loft area, too.

And then I heard it: "Oh." Just that one word from out on the deck sent me running; I found her sprawled on the wooden stairs leading down to the sloping backyard.

"Damn," Marla uttered. She was covered in blood.

"Wait." I crouched by her. "Stay there, I'll call somebody."

Which I did, my fingers finding the numbers on my phone even though I was so frightened suddenly that once I got someone on the line, just remembering my own name turned out to be a challenge.

It wasn't so much the blood that scared me. Crusted in her hair, dried in blackish runnels on her cheeks . . .

No, what *really* unnerved me was the idea that her attacker might still be around here somewhere.

Her eyelids fluttered, her bloody fingertips straining weakly toward the deck's top step. "Just relax," I said. "Help's coming."

". . . Maxie," she muttered thickly, her fingers still moving in an attempt to point at something. Then I spotted the dog lying on the grass below the deck's rail.

The unhappy animal looked wretchedly up at me from where it had fallen. *Or been thrown, some son of a bitch had . . .*

"Don't move," I ordered Marla, and hurried down the steps. Down on the grass I approached the big German shepherd cautiously.

He wasn't whining or bleeding. His teeth looked intact. All four legs moved when I touched them, and when I spoke to him, his tail thumped twice.

But he wasn't trying to get up, and I could only suppose that he knew he was in serious trouble, and should wait for the humans to help. "Okay, buddy," I said. "Good dog."

Out on the blue water beyond the bluff, a white sailboat came about, sails flapping. "Okay, boy, they'll be here soon."

"Wuff," the dog uttered patiently.

"It's going to be okay," I said, hoping he couldn't tell that I wasn't nearly as sure as I was trying to sound.

Probably he could, though. At the top of the deck stairway, Marla lay motionless. I couldn't do anything for her, either, and I knew enough not to try to move her.

But what I didn't know was how badly either of them was hurt, so it was a very long ten minutes before I heard the siren wailing up the shore road.

Moments later Bob Arnold came hustling around the side of the house with his duty weapon drawn, and I must say I've never been so pleased to see a loaded gun in my life.

But Bob was an Eastport cop, not a Lubec one. "What the heck are you doing here?" I demanded.

It wasn't the most urgent question on the docket, not by a long shot. But I must've been in shock.

"Sit," Bob said to me; Maxie's tail thumped apologetically. The poor thing probably thought it was a command.

"Anyone else here?" Bob lowered his weapon. But not all the way, and his pale blue eyes were narrowed professionally.

I waved at the deck. "Marla's up there." While I was focused on the dog, she'd somehow made it all the way to the top step.

"I think she must have surprised somebody inside," I said. "She's hurt and it's all torn apart in there."

Bob noticed the dog. "Criminy," he uttered in disgust. Then the ambulance screamed in, and after that everything went fast:

EMTs flocked to Marla, got a foam collar around her neck, and loaded her onto a stretcher. Bob called a local veterinarian, who arrived in a panel van within minutes and attended to the dog.

"We'll see," the animal doc replied tightly when I asked him about the canine's prognosis.

The Lubec cops got there, too, finally, and took a statement from me when they arrived, and then I was done. But as I walked to my car, Bob stopped me.

"What were you doing here?" His voice was businesslike; the coincidence of Muldoon's murder and my finding an assault victim so soon after the first crime hadn't eluded him.

Well, of course it hadn't; it didn't take but half a brain to wonder about it, as Bella would've said. I was thinking about it, too.

"I wanted to thank her for some extra chocolate she gave us the last time we bought from her," I said, repeating what I'd told the Lubec officers.

He looked levelly at me, clearly not believing this for an instant. "So you drove all the way down here?"

The vet started his van. I looked back at Bob. "You betcha," I said. "That's absolutely correct."

He kept looking at me, his rosebud lips pursed in a way I found nervous-making in the extreme. But in the end he just shook his head slowly.

"Okay." He thought about it some more, then decided not to say whatever it was that he'd been thinking about.

"See you back in Eastport," he said instead, and turned away.

His expression was disapproving, but not threatening; he knew as well as I did that Ellie was up the creek, probably, if nothing changed before the DA and the state cops got their ducks in a row.

The vet and his helper came around to the rear of his panel van, ready to depart. The last I saw of Maxie as they slid him in on a stretcher was his tail, still thumping bravely, and his long pink tongue flicking out to lick the veterinarian's hand.

Watching, I wished heartily that I felt the same way Maxie did, so certain that the human beings in charge had matters under control and that everything would be all right.

But I didn't.

Not even a little bit.

My husband, Wade Sorenson, is brawny and broad-shouldered, with brush-cut blond hair, a jawline that could give Mount Rushmore a run for its money, and eyes that are blue or gray depending on the weather.

Also he's smarter than your average supercomputer, and I needed his brainpower. So when I got home after finding Marla with her scalp split, her dog hurt, and her house ransacked, I told him everything.

Well, almost everything. The boat trip with Ellie, meeting Marla at the Salty Dog, her thinking that maybe Matt Muldoon had a girlfriend and sort-of promising photographs of the woman . . .

"Wait a minute," said Wade. "You and Ellie took the Bayliner out at night?"

We were sitting on the porch in some wicker chairs that Ellie and I had bought at a garage sale a week earlier. Up and down Key Street, kids on bikes pulled wheelies, stomped on bag bombs, and fired Silly String at each other.

"Well, yes," I admitted. I'd left out the part about getting stranded in the fog, and the little detail of Wade nearly running us over with his cargo freighter hadn't been mentioned, either.

"And Ellie handled it all okay, did she?" he asked.

His question triggered a vivid memory of her grabbing me by my life jacket so I wouldn't slide overboard.

"Yes. Fine." I almost praised the fast, efficient manner in which she'd gotten us out of his freighter's way, but decided not to push my luck.

"And you still believe this is all going to come down on her? I mean, you think they really suspect Ellie?"

"Bob Arnold thinks so. He'd told me while we were waiting for the ambulance that it's what the state cops are saying to him. He said they wanted to know if she might leave town, if they should grab her before she could."

Wade smiled, lifting an eyebrow. "Don't know her very well, do they?"

It was true, any idea of Ellie running away from anything was ludicrous. But then a detailed mental picture of Marla's bloodied head sprang to my mind again.

"Marla will be able to say who hit her?" Wade asked.

"Who knows? She was pretty out of it." Inside the house the phone rang and then Bella's sneakers squeaked across the freshly waxed hall floor to the screen door.

"For you. It's Bob Arnold," she said, handing me the phone, and when I was done hearing what Bob had to say, I wanted badly to pitch that telephone directly into the bay.

"Marla's hurt worse than I thought," I told Wade when I'd hung up. "They're deciding whether or not to airlift her to the hospital in Bangor, in case she's got bleeding in her brain." The dog, Bob had told me, was still being evaluated.

"Marla might need surgery," I said. "And . . ." Tears prickled my eyes, surprising me. "They don't know if she'll wake up," I stated.

Guilt hit me. If we hadn't gone over there the night before, if we hadn't gotten Marla involved . . .

"You think someone overheard you guys talking in the bar?"

I nodded, my throat suddenly tight. "Maybe. Guys came in

and guys went out." I hadn't been paying attention. "I guess someone could've overheard."

Wade nodded silently, mulling this. Then: "Anything else?"

Like I said, supercomputer. "Yeah, there's something else."

I described the little boat that had harassed us; I hadn't said anything about it before.

"We didn't think much of it at the time," I said, adding what Marla had said about guys protecting lobster traps. "But now . . ."

"I'll track it down," said Wade. "Marla's probably right, but I'll find out for sure."

He could do it, too, if anyone could; he'd spent his whole life on the waterfront and knew its characters well.

"Excellent," I said gratefully. "But I saved the worst for last. I guess those homicide cops didn't listen to Bob Arnold when he said Ellie wasn't a flight risk."

Inside, a triumphant *"ha!"* came from the sunroom where Bella and my father were playing chess. He'd taught her when they first met, and now she whipped him at it regularly. I wondered if she'd still be laughing when I told her she'd be helping me bake those last four cheesecakes that we needed for the auction.

Since otherwise I'd be doing it alone. "The cops took Ellie into custody just now. They found out she's got the boat, and they decided it makes her a flight risk."

"Ridiculous," Wade pronounced, which was my thought also. But it was already done; Wade and I went inside, where I grabbed a sweater and my purse.

"Probably they let her lock up the Moose before they took her, but I still need to check," I said, glancing around a little wildly. "She'll need a criminal defense lawyer. I don't even know where they're taking her, and—"

From the sunroom I heard my dad grousing that Bella should quit treating him like an invalid, damn it. So he was feeling better, at least; I, on the other hand, felt terrible, and just as

I thought things couldn't possibly get any worse, the phone rang once more.

"Jake?" It was Lester Vanacore, calling again from the *Tides*. "Good, I've got Millie Marquardt for you right here."

He'd surely known that I would avoid speaking with Millie if I knew it was her calling. I already had plenty to do getting together those last four cheesecakes, and I didn't need any more of the Fourth of July committee chairperson's last-minute, can't-do-without-it "favors" forced upon me at this point.

But she had Lester wrapped around her little finger, just like she did any other media professional she'd ever met. I don't know how, but Millie was a genius at getting publicity for Eastport—and now she was talking a mile a minute.

"Jacobia, oh, I'm so glad to find you at home. It's about those wonderful cakes, dear, that you and dear Ellie are being so fabulously kind about donating to the Fourth of July auction?"

"What about them, Millie?" I asked, hearing my voice weaken.

Suddenly I felt as if I might need to lie down. Because it had just now hit me forcefully that it's one thing to create elaborate chocolate baked delicacies with a partner who knows how. But it's something else again to be fumbling along solo, dropping eggs and spattering cake batter. Unless . . . the gleam of a plan appeared to me as Millie's voice came through the phone.

". . . so can you make extras? Cheesecakes, that is. Because we've got the bidders, people are lined up for the—"

In the Coast Guard auction, you placed your bid in advance by buying tickets; whoever bought the most tickets won the item.

"How many more cheesecakes are we talking about here, Millie? And why?"

Because so what if an energetic bidding war drove up the

cake prices? The point was to finance the fireworks, and everybody knew the auction was really just a fun way of donating to the cause.

"Oh, another dozen or so," said Millie carelessly, as if this (a dozen!) was not at all a big deal.

"Because," she explained, "they thought with the extra cakes they'd get even more bidders, and with the extra money they'd add some frills onto the show. You know, make it something special."

Oh, well, if *that* was the only reason; listening, I relaxed a little. Eastport's fireworks were already pretty spectacular, much bigger and more eye-poppingly, eardrum-hammeringly elaborate than might be expected from such a tiny island town.

"Millie," I began, relieved at being able to turn down this difficult request so easily. But she wasn't listening.

"And then on the evening of the fireworks," she went on, "we thought we'd take the kids from the special-education program out on a barge so they can watch the show from the water."

Uh-oh. I'd chaperoned a similar activity one year with a few of Sam's school friends, and it was magical.

"It costs a fair amount," Millie went on, "on account of the boat hire, the insurance, the refreshments, and so on. But we could . . ."

"*Do it if we had more cash,*" I thought she was about to finish, steeling myself to resist.

". . . give the kids some really wonderful Fourth of July memories, ones they'll never forget" was what she actually said, sounding as if she meant it.

Gosh, but she was good at this, mostly because she did; mean it, that is. "Okay, Millie," I gave in, my resolve collapsing.

Bob's dire warnings about a storm hadn't made much of an impression on her, it seemed, but that wasn't my problem.

"You can start selling tickets for twelve more cakes," I told her.

And I could start baking them, I realized in near despair when I'd hung up. Even with Bella's help it would be an enormous chore, on top of which there was Ellie's imminent jailbird status to deal with.

I absolutely had to find out what the real story was with Sam, too, before I had a nervous breakdown over it. And there was Marla's dog to worry about; I'd thought I could leave Maxie's fate to the veterinarian, but the trusting look in the creature's eyes when I'd found him had begun haunting me, and I doubted it would stop.

But before I dealt with any of those things, I had to take care of a Moose.

The door was open, the lights were on, and the paddle fans turned slowly beneath the high, pressed-tin ceiling, wafting the delicious aroma of fresh baked goods around the Chocolate Moose.

A pile of money stood by the cash register, along with some scribbled notes saying what people had taken from the display case and what they'd left in payment in Ellie's absence.

And that in a nutshell was Eastport, where the honor system still actually worked. But Ellie wasn't there, and without her the whole place felt empty and pointless. I tried finding out where she was and what, exactly, was in the process of happening to her, but the lady on the phone at the county courthouse said it might be hours before she had anything official to tell me.

Discouraged, I went back to my shopkeeping, tidying the display case, sweeping the floor, and putting coffee on. The way I felt, I should've been getting it through an IV like my dad's, and then Miss Halligan came in.

"My, aren't you the local hero?" she observed, buying a dozen pinwheel cookies and the chocolate brioche.

I thought she looked pale and her eyes seemed a little puffy. But that brioche would revive her if anything could.

"Those cheesecakes of yours have become quite the cause around town, you know."

"What do you mean?" I poured coffee and swallowed some, and felt my brain cells pop open like balloons suddenly inflating.

News of another dozen cakes had gotten around already, of course. That gossip wire, again, and it was a well-known Millie Marquardt trick that when you'd said you'd do something for her, she immediately told everyone else about it so it would be harder for you to back out.

"Good thing you've got a reliable supply of chocolate," said Miss Halligan.

Which I thought was a little odd. After all, why would she be thinking about that? But it wasn't the truly important thing about what she'd just said.

Because I was the one who should've been thinking about it. Stunned, I just stood there staring at her; she was wearing slim black jeans, a loose white blouse, and a red leather belt. As usual her fragrance was a lemony citrus blend, dry as champagne, and she'd lavender-rinsed her hair so its spiky-short fringes resembled flower petals.

She was in her late sixties, I thought, or maybe older, but she had enough energy for two thirty-year-olds, some of which I wished I could borrow since oh, boy, did I ever need it.

I found my voice. "Ch-chocolate."

We had enough for four more cakes. Not sixteen, not by a long shot. But that's what I'd promised.

Miss Halligan smiled. "Well, of course, dear. That's the secret ingredient, right? Rich, delicious . . ."

As I rushed past her, her look turned to puzzlement. "Where are you going?"

But I wasn't listening, busy cleaning out the cash register and snapping off the fans, the coffeemaker, and the lights over the display case. Shooing her out the door, I shut it and turned the key, hearing the new lock's tumblers click solidly into place.

Chocolate. A dozen more cheesecakes, and not enough . . .

And no Marla to supply it, either, even if there was time for another trip to Lubec. Nor could you obtain it in any of the local supermarkets; we'd tried, but nothing even came near to the smooth richness of what Marla made from the cocoa paste and the other ingredients that she imported.

But then it occurred to me suddenly that there might actually be some of what we needed right here on the island. Marla did have a house here in Eastport, after all.

Not only that, but for all I knew, she could've already started asking around about the party snapshots she'd mentioned, the ones that might show Muldoon and his supposed lady friend in the Salty Dog together.

Someone could even have e-mailed them to her by now. So a few minutes after leaving the Moose, I was at the far northern tip of our little island, where Water Street ends and the view across the bay to New Brunswick, Canada, begins.

On the racing waves, sailboats scudded and motorboats zipped, trailing foamy wakes. I pulled over in front of Marla's place, an Arts and Crafts bungalow with shingled side dormers, a screened front porch, and the traditional vintage stained-glass panel set into the dining-room window.

In the yard shaggy pink peonies in mulched beds flanked the front steps. Inside the porch I found a key under the doormat; in the front hall the phone machine blinked steadily. That and the untouched mail in the box strengthened my notion that just as she had predicted, Marla hadn't been here today.

Although, I thought as I moved cautiously through the parlor and dining room—Delft-tiled hearth, a dog bed with a Nylabone in it, an oaken mantel over a bricked-up fireplace with a Mission-style clock ticking hollowly on it—maybe someone else had been.

Creak . . . I froze at the sound, halfway into a bright, clean kitchen straight out of a 1950s-era *Ladies' Home Journal.* The table and counters were topped with Formica, the chairs had been upholstered in an eye-popping shade of turquoise Naugahyde, and the vintage Frigidaire was robin's-egg blue.

I half-expected one of those old TV situation-comedy moms—June Cleaver, maybe—to waltz in. But the other half of me still thought *murderer*, especially when that odd creaking sound came from somewhere behind me again.

Swiftly I identified the kitchen door leading to the backyard as my escape route, and tiptoed toward it. Past the dog's water bowl and a bin full of kibble was another door, low and narrow, that I guessed might hide a pantry.

Then it hit me: *A pantry, where food, maybe even chocolate, can be stored?* It's what I had come for; so on my way past it I grabbed the little door's china doorknob and twisted it hard.

Only it didn't turn. I tried again, whereupon it did what the doorknobs in all old houses do when you try to force them: it fell off in my hand.

Creeaak! The weird, faintly threatening sound was nearer than I'd thought; too late now to nip out the back door without being seen by whoever was already nearly upon me.

Getting seen, though, wasn't my worst worry; glancing around, I spotted a cast-iron skillet and snatched it up.

Maybe that sound was the cops here to check out the assault victim's house, in which case my emergency chocolate requirement would explain what I was doing in it, I hoped.

On the other hand, possibly it was whoever had hit Marla and hurt her dog, and maybe even killed Matt Muldoon. In which case I planned to bonk first and ask questions later.

Or just bonk. Nervously I backed up against the wall and raised my weapon. Soft footsteps approached, and the kitchen door opened. Sucking in a breath, I lunged forward, and . . .

"Oh!" Ellie caught a glimpse of the cast-iron skillet coming down and jumped aside just in time.

I jumped too, my heart hammering as the skillet fell from my hand. "Ellie, what in the world are you doing here? I thought . . ."

"I came to find chocolate for the dozen more cheesecakes that *someone* agreed to bake by tomorrow night," she replied tartly.

She sank into a chair. "Since apparently being questioned by homicide detectives isn't annoyance enough."

They'd taken her to the police station in Eastport, she told me, her words coming out in a rush. They'd sat her down in one of the interview rooms there, and if Bob Arnold hadn't finally managed to convince them that she wasn't about to take off to Canada in the Bayliner, they would have—

She stopped. "But enough about that. This big new cheesecake order that I just heard about . . . Jake, what were you thinking?"

I sighed heavily, feeling my heart rate return to normal. "Millie talked me into it. I tried to say no, but you know she can talk the birds right out of the sky when she wants to."

"Yes, I do know that," said Ellie in exasperation, "but . . . oh, never mind. I guess it's a done deal now, isn't it?"

She shook her head resignedly. "I found out about it when I stopped in to the IGA on my way back to the Moose. And my gosh, Jake, you'd have thought we'd cured cancer, the way everyone in there told me all about how wonderful we are."

As I mentioned, news travels fast, which brought her around again to what Marla Sykes had said.

"Meanwhile, I still don't get why no one else knew about this girlfriend that Matt Muldoon is supposed to have had," said Ellie.

"Well, I guess if they wanted to keep it a secret, maybe they were just very careful," I proposed. "Or . . ."

The other possible explanation for the story was just hanging there in front of us like ripe fruit, so finally I picked it: "Or because Marla made her up, maybe?" I ventured.

As for a reason why Marla would want to do that, maybe she was the girlfriend herself, I theorized, and thought she was getting ahead of the story by suggesting Muldoon's love interest was someone else.

But that didn't really fly. Why not just keep her mouth shut and hope the information never came out at all, then deal with the problem if and when she needed to?

It was among the many questions to which I had no answers. "Let's just look around for what we need here," said Ellie at last, "and worry about the rest later."

So we did, rummaging through cupboards, the refrigerator, and even the chest freezer cleverly tucked into a closet under the front stairs. But when we were finished, we had discovered not even an M&M, and although the little door in the kitchen did open onto a pantry (naturally the knob worked just fine when I didn't need it to), the shallow space inside was empty.

Strangely, we also found nothing to suggest that Marla was running her chocolate business out of the house, and there'd been no such evidence at her Lubec cottage, either.

"All the paperwork there was personal stuff," I told Ellie. "Phone bills, check registers, receipts . . . nothing work-related."

"Maybe she keeps her business records down at the fish plant workspace," Ellie suggested as we climbed to the bungalow's second floor.

"Mmm, maybe." I'd seen no desk, computer, or paperwork in the old canning factory, either. "Could be, I suppose."

But what we still really needed to find now was a stash of chocolate: blocks of it, dark and luscious, rich with cocoa fat and suitable for gourmet cake baking and decorating. Surely it was here somewhere, or so I desperately hoped.

We made our way down an upstairs hall with four rooms opening from it. In the first a set of free weights lay on a floor mat flanking an exercise bicycle. A video screen, CD caddy, and player stood on a shelf, the screen angled so the bike's rider could see it. The CD in the player was a French-language learning course.

Ellie's discouraged-sounding voice came from one of the other rooms. "Okay, maybe there really is no chocolate here, and we're out of luck. Because if it's not down in the kitchen or the pantry, then I don't exactly see where else it would . . . Hey."

Hurrying toward her, I passed the bathroom, retro-decorated like the kitchen with silver-swan-printed wallpaper, pink floral curtains, and pink chenille throw rugs, and found Ellie in a tiny alcove at the end of the hall.

"I opened this linen closet door," she said, gesturing at it, "and look what's inside!"

Not linens, definitely. Instead it was a cleverly designed tiny office unit: the desk folded down out of it. Built-in shelves at the back held ledgers, folders, stamps, and envelopes. A shaded lightbulb hung on a cord from the ceiling, and on the desk, se- cured by Velcro strips so you could tuck it back up again when the door closed, stood a laptop computer.

A *password-protected* laptop computer, as it turned out, but my first guess—*MarlaSykes1*—took care of that little problem. And because the machine was Windows-operated like my own at home, I knew how to bring its files up onto the screen.

And there, after a few swift *clickety-clicks* on the keyboard, they were: recipes, household bills, her taxes for the previous year, a folder labeled MAXIE that probably held his veterinary information. . . .

She kept records for the Lubec house in Lubec, apparently, and the Eastport-related ones here. It wasn't the way I would have done it, but hey, whatever worked.

Unfortunately, no folder labeled CHOCOLATE STORAGE LOCA- TION appeared on the screen. An icon of a trash can did show up, but when I clicked on it, there was nothing in it. And I still saw no chocolate-business records or anything resembling them.

"Huh." I frowned at the screen. The trash on my own laptop at home was spilling over, as usual. But not on this one.

"Ellie," I began, "when's the last time that you—"

"Emptied my computer trash?" She saw it, too. "Don't remember."

Saying this, she made impatient typing motions at me; moments later I'd restored the contents of the files Marla Sykes had discarded. (Whenever I do finally get around to emptying my laptop's wastebasket, I always immediately and urgently need something irreplaceable from it, so I knew how to retrieve items.)

"So they just let you go?" I asked while I arranged the dozen or so restored icons on the screen.

The detectives who had been questioning Ellie, I meant, and she nodded in reply.

"Bob stuck up for me. That's what turned the trick. But you know, me not having an alibi still makes me look awfully good to them."

"Well, that . . . and you hating him," I agreed, opening and closing the files on the screen one after another.

"And the body and the weapon both being found in our shop," I added.

The files on Marla's laptop computer were mostly the standard stuff: There was a complaint note to the exercise bike's maker about the handlebars, which were too flimsy. She had written a summer job recommendation for a Lubec high-school student whom she'd once employed. But also:

Photographs. A dozen thumbnail miniatures were in a folder labeled MM; I clicked on the first one to enlarge it and then on all the rest, so they overlapped on the laptop's screen.

"How come the detectives brought you in at all?" I asked. "I mean if they weren't ready to charge you with anything? . . ."

Ellie gazed over my shoulder as my voice trailed off. Neither of us could quite believe what we were seeing, but there it was.

"Hoped I'd say something dumb," she replied absently, still staring. "Or that I'd confess, I imagine. But I didn't. Do either of those things, I mean."

She pointed at the third photograph. "That's the best one of them, isn't it? The clearest."

"Yup." Of course she hadn't said anything dumb. Because she wasn't: dumb *or* guilty.

But I was starting to think that Bella had the right idea. "I think you should talk to an attorney before you say anything more at all," I told Ellie firmly.

She shook her head. "Lawyers cost money. And since I *was* home alone, and *don't* have anyone to vouch for me, the only way to *prove* I'm innocent is to find out who really did it. Right?"

It wasn't the way an attorney would see it, but she was right about one thing: no lawyer could guarantee that she'd be found *not guilty* if it ever came to a trial.

So being the star attraction at one would be risky in the extreme, and she had her mind made up, anyway. "That was taken in the Salty Dog," she said, pointing at the screen again.

I nodded; all the photographs had obviously been taken there, and on the night Marla had mentioned, too. Around the pickled eggs jar on the bar crowded the laughing faces of a dozen partygoers, under a homemade banner: HAPPY BIRTHDAY!

"So she must've got right on it after we talked last night," Ellie theorized. "Found someone who was there at the party and they sent her these? But then how did they get in the computer's trash can?"

I clicked more keys, opening Marla's e-mail account. We'd only asked for the pictures the night before, so this was fast results. And sure enough, she hadn't received any e-mail with photos attached, not in the past few months.

So *how* she'd gotten these was my big question now. We looked at the party shots again; in them, Muldoon's face showed clearly. His thin, downturned lips, narrowed eyes, and sour expression said that the hilarity all around him was . . .

Annoying? Not up to his high standards, apparently. But

that attitude was par for the course for Muldoon, and anyway, it was the petite, elegant-looking woman beside him that neither of us could stop staring at.

That fashionably snipped white hair, those kohl-rimmed eyes, and the little black T-shirt with the jewel-toned embroidery at the neckline were all utterly recognizable. Muldoon's companion that night at the Salty Dog had been our own Miss Halligan, owner of the Second Hand Rose.

Ellie looked up at me. "I don't get it."

"Me neither. It's like Marla had these photos all along."

"And wanted us to think those two were a romantic pair. But why?"

"I can't imagine," I said. "Not only that, if these pictures weren't e-mailed to Marla . . ."

I scrolled back through more of the chocolate maker's e-mail history. They hadn't been. Not ever.

". . . then there's only a few other ways for them to get onto her computer like this," I said.

"She could've downloaded them from an online site, or been given them on a thumb drive or CD, or . . ."

". . . Marla could've taken them herself," said Ellie.

A door slammed hard downstairs.

Five

I'd known that my friend Ellie White was quick-witted, but I'd had no idea she was so remarkably fleet-footed, too. Instantly she nudged me aside, closed up the laptop, and shut the computer desk so that from the outside it was nothing but a linen closet again.

Then she hustled me down the hall and through the door to the back stairs, putting a finger to her lips. "Shh."

No kidding, I thought as we huddled on the stairway landing. Below us we could hear someone moving stealthily around, first in the kitchen and then returning toward the front of the house.

Beckoning me along, Ellie started down the stairs. I followed, with my heart pulsing crazily in my throat, thinking that if only I'd known how exciting the baking business would be, I'd have taken up some more sensible activity.

Sword swallowing maybe, or milking poisonous snakes for their venom. At the foot of the stairs Ellie waved silently at me again. And since the footsteps had already finished climbing the front staircase and were slowly but surely making their way to where we were now, I decided to obey her again, too. But:

Had I closed that second-floor stairwell door firmly behind me? I wondered suddenly. Or did it now stand wide open like a neon sign: THIS WAY TO YOUR NEXT VICTIMS?

The footsteps started down toward us. Ellie slipped out into the kitchen with me right behind her, and some faint sound we made must've alerted someone because there was a pause, and then the footsteps *thumped* down hurriedly at us.

The back door was over on the other side of the kitchen and so was the dining-room entrance. We had no time to get to either of them. I hauled desperately on the pantry door and it opened.

I shoved Ellie inside and crowded in there with her, pulling the door shut once more until the latch clicked, then leaning back hard against the shelves to make more room for us both.

Whereupon the shelves behind us *moved:* smoothly, soundlessly, pivoting away to reveal old stone steps. Slipping past the shelves, we hustled down as fast as we could into a cellar that seemed much older than the rest of the house.

Feeling around, Ellie found a lightbulb string and pulled it. A bare bulb glared on.

Large granite boulders formed the old stone foundation, and the beams overhead showed the adze marks from where they'd been hand-shaped decades ago.

"Look," Ellie whispered, pointing to where an archway in the old foundation wall had been filled in with brick.

"Where'd that lead to?" I wondered aloud. Clearly it had been an exit at one time, but to where?

"You know," Ellie said thoughtfully as she gazed at it, "this whole island was a huge smuggler's nest, once upon a time."

Of course it was; first when the British were still levying taxes on trade, and the locals evaded the levies in their small boats, by dark of night. Prohibition in the 1920s made rich men out of Eastport mariners, too, whiskey being the contraband then.

And that stone archway, back when it was open, would've led straight out toward the water, where I happened to know there was a beach below the very cliff this house was built on.

Imagining booze casks from Canada and the West Indies being hauled up and stacked here, I jumped at another sound from above.

Ellie hissed at me from behind the furnace. "The light!" she whispered urgently, pointing at the bulb dangling in the stairway, still swaying a little.

Swaying and *shining;* weird shadows wavered unnervingly on the cellar's old stone walls, but that wasn't the worst part.

The worst part was that glowing lightbulb itself, its lit status shouting our presence here as if through a giant megaphone. While Ellie stared big-eyed from behind the furnace, the door at the top of the steps we'd just rushed down rattled angrily.

The stuck doorknob, again, but this time it was working in our favor. The light must be leaking under the door; I peered around for something to use as a weapon.

Because if that had been Bob Arnold stomping around up there, he'd be ordering us to come out by now. Instead: ominous silence.

A brick will do, I thought, *or maybe a stone fallen from one of the cellar walls.*

But there were no fallen stones down here. Unlike my cellar at home, here the elderly masonry was patched and whitewashed, and the floor, level and equipped with a drain, was coated with paint and sealer.

Even the brick in the smuggler's archway was in good shape. No tools anywhere, either. "Jake!"

It was Ellie again, this time from the cellar's far corner. She was peeking out of a smaller room, one I hadn't noticed; hurriedly I joined her in there and flashed my penlight around.

The cubicle had a low ceiling, one small window, and steel shelves lining three of the walls.

"Listen," Ellie whispered. "Is anyone coming?"

I didn't hear anything. The light from the main cellar room cast a triangle on the floor in here, reflecting up dimly to the wrapped parcels on the shelving.

Still no sound from upstairs. I crept back out to the foot of the steps and peered up.

"He's still up there. Or she is." Two shadow shapes stood side by side on the pantry door's other side, visible in the crack of daylight between the door's bottom edge and the floor.

Shoes, I thought. *Shoes with feet in them. Waiting.*

We waited, too, barely daring to breathe while one wildly impossible plan after another—break out through a cellar window (too small), cut a hole up through the floor (see *no tools*, above)—flitted uselessly through my head.

And then . . . puzzled, I squinted, hardly daring to believe it. The shoe shapes moved away from the door; then footsteps crossed over my head.

I held my breath, sure it must be a trick. But the front door opened and closed, and then someone scuffed away down the front walk, out to the street. A car started up with a low rumble, and . . .

"Gone?" Ellie whispered from the little room, where she still huddled.

"I don't know. Maybe." There was one way to find out. "Okay," I said, "stay here. Whatever happens, don't make a sound."

I put my foot on the bottom step. "If I run into trouble, you stay until the coast is clear. Don't come up until I tell you."

Yeah, sure, like that was a possibility. If anything happened to me, she'd be throttling someone with her bare hands.

But I didn't have time to argue about it; the door at the top of the stairs waited silently for me. Besides:

"Well," I amended, "if someone's actively dragging me out, do please try to see if you can get a look at whoever it is."

I took another step up. "Or if, you know, you can do anything to *stop* them from . . ."

"Oh, get on with it," said Ellie impatiently. "If I have to, I'll just hit them over the head with one of these."

She emerged from the room with her arms wrapped around some of the bundles from the steel shelves. Each bundle was the size of a shoe box. They *were* shoe boxes, I saw now, each thickly wrapped with plastic.

But whatever was in them would have to wait, I decided, as from above, that damned little door smirked at me. And if there's an expression in the world that I don't like even a little bit . . .

"Fine," I snapped, taking the rest of the steps in a fast upward rush. It was probably foolhardy, but I preferred to think of it as determined. Then:

"Gah!" First I tripped, my knee slamming the stone step; then the door stuck again. But finally it opened and I charged through.

The kitchen shimmered vacantly. So did the parlor, the dining room, the front hall . . .

No one. On the stairs a few dust motes gleamed redly in the light from the landing's stained-glass window panels.

"Hello?" I whispered. Nobody answered.

Ellie appeared beside me, causing my heart to lurch nearly to a stop for the second time that afternoon.

"Let's get out of here," I said. "I've had enough. If only we had chocolate, I'd be glad just to stand in our nice, peaceful shop and bake cheesecakes until they're coming out of my—"

"Oh, but we do." Ellie smiled. "Have chocolate, I mean."

She held out one of the shoe boxes she'd brought with her from the cellar. She'd already opened it, tearing away the plastic wrap it had been bundled in; now when she lifted its cardboard lid, a gorgeous aroma floated from it.

Chocolate. "Ellie! How did you—"

"Know what it was?" She finished my question for me. "I didn't, I just hoped."

She pulled out a chunk of dark semisweet, its tantalizing fragrance unmistakable. All the bundles were neatly labeled in Marla's distinctive back-slanted handwriting.

"This'll do it," she said. "We've got plenty of chocolate now."

"And if someone sees us carrying it out?" I asked, glancing around nervously.

Before we found all this dark, rich loot, just coming in and taking it had sounded reasonable. But now that we might actually end up having to explain ourselves, I didn't feel quite so blithe.

"We've bought from her often. She knows we're good for it, and she'd have sold it to us herself if she could and she knew that we needed it," Ellie replied confidently.

Which wouldn't stop a breaking-and-entering charge if it came to that, or make our presence here look any less suspicious. But when I said as much, Ellie had an answer for that, too:

"Everyone knows we're doing those extra cheesecakes by now. We have the perfect excuse. It's in the town's best interests that we've come in here and gotten this stuff . . . right?"

"Right," I conceded. Still, I was fairly sure whoever'd been in here with us hadn't had *our* best interests in mind; overall, this whole stunt was not only illegal, it was reckless.

Together with some very confusing information, though, it had gotten us what we needed. So Ellie and I hauled our booty out Marla's front door and stowed it in my car.

"What do we do about the pictures of Miss Halligan and Matt Muldoon?" Ellie asked as we drove toward my house together.

Upon reaching my car, we'd decided to get going while the going was still good, and pick hers up later.

"I don't know," I said. "Before we found them, I thought

him having a secret girlfriend would take the suspicion off you. Or at least dilute it."

We turned up Washington Street past the massive old granite-block post office building, draped with red-white-and-blue bunting from its windows and with flags flanking its wide front doors.

"But now I'm not so sure about that," I said.

In the post office's parking lot the holiday activities had already begun; a sign invited passersby to TRY YOUR LUCK! at a ring toss, a GUESS YOUR WEIGHT! booth, and a shooting gallery.

"Because now what's bugging me is how those pictures of Miss Halligan got onto Marla's computer at all, not to mention why."

Ellie nodded. "It seems like Marla must've had them all along. That she took them, even. So why say otherwise?"

We passed the white-clapboarded Center Baptist Church, now transformed into the Eastport Arts Center. The sign outside read PATRIOTIC CONCERT! MUSIC OF THE FRENCH REVOLUTION.

"And since I'm the one with the murder motive," Ellie went on, "and Muldoon was found in our shop, not Miss Halligan's, I don't think those snapshots will *un*incriminate me at all."

Right, and on top of that we didn't *have* the pictures, did we? We'd been chased out of there before I could get them out of Marla's computer trash and e-mail them to myself.

"The main thing, though," Ellie mused aloud, "is why'd Marla lie about them? I mean, if she had them all along?"

Yet another good question. We turned onto Key Street and then into my driveway, between a bed of orange daylilies and a pair of ancient lilac bushes, their gnarled branches covered in blooms.

I switched the car off. "Beats me. And not only that, but if we did have them and we showed them to anyone, then we'd have to explain in detail how we got them, wouldn't we?"

I'd told Wade most of it, but she hadn't told George any of it, and I wasn't eager to let Bob Arnold in on it, either.

Not unless I had to. "Oh, I'm so confused," said Ellie as we got out of the car and crossed the lawn.

Me too. As we approached the porch, Bella came out, gripping a dust cloth, looking as if she'd like to strangle someone with it.

"Uh-oh," said Ellie, which was when I realized my dad's old pickup truck wasn't in the driveway where it belonged.

"Your father," Bella stated, waving at the vacant space where the truck should be, "has gone out for a ride."

By himself. Driving the vehicle. "I tried medicating him," she said. "That calming pill that the doctor prescribed."

I knew the kind of pill she referred to; I'd been given one myself once in advance of major dental work and wound up telling the dentist to go ahead and pull the rest of them because what the heck, I was already in the chair.

That was not at all the attitude I wanted my father having while he drove an antique pickup truck around Eastport. "When did he leave?"

Bella followed us in. "A few minutes ago. He shouldn't be driving, even without those pills, I was about to call . . ."

Yeah, Bob Arnold. I was tempted to call him, myself. But that wouldn't end well for my dad, as driving under the influence was a crime Bob never took lightly.

"I'll go look for him," I said. He couldn't have gotten far. His idea of speed had been formed long ago in Manhattan, where two green lights in a row were thought of as zipping right along.

"Leave your car in case I have to go get him from somewhere," said Bella. Since Ellie's vehicle was still parked out near Marla's, I set off on foot, leaving them both in the kitchen busily unwrapping the chocolate.

Up and down Key Street flags rippled bravely from flagpoles and banners fluttered from the tops of picket fences. Kids yelled, racketing downhill on bikes and skateboards; the Fourth of July was family reunion day in Eastport, and now there were more cousins, aunts and uncles, and grandparents in town than you could shake a stick at.

Which I guessed accounted for all the freshly laundered sets of bedsheets billowing on wash lines and the unfamiliar late-model cars parked everywhere. Among these my dad's truck would stand out without much trouble, on account of it being a 1949 Dodge with a busted tailgate and mismatched tires.

But the vehicle wasn't downtown where tourists and locals thronged the waterfront in the July sunshine. There was still no big rush for the causeway, I saw, despite the ongoing storm predictions; gale-warning flags already fluttered atop the Coast Guard station but no one was paying attention.

My dad was here somewhere, though, I was sure of it; he loved this sort of thing. Among the pennywhistles tootling "Yankee Doodle" and the buskers with their guitar cases lying open on the sidewalk I peered around for him, the music and the smell of cotton candy filling my head.

Ladies in short sets, flip-flops, and visor hats passed, and men with dripping ice-cream cones in their hands hustled toward waiting kids. Down the street outside the Chocolate Moose, a few prospective customers stood, looking disappointed.

Then I spotted Miss Halligan in her own shop's doorway, alternately waving at me and pointing urgently at something across the street.

"Dad!" Hurrying toward him, I spied his pickup pulled up onto the sidewalk. He'd installed flashers, a new suspension, and seat belts when he bought the thing; now the flashers blinked steadily.

I sat by him. "Hey, what happened? Did you get restless?"

He smiled ruefully, and I noticed he'd taken the trouble to cap his IV tubing, not just leave it hanging open unhygienically.

"Yeah, it was dumb," he said, turning back toward the waves glittering beyond the breakwater. A small red tugboat was bouncing around out there, jaunty and bright.

"But I wanted to do something, you know?" he said. "Just . . . *something*. So I did. But I got tired," he finished sadly.

The tugboat's whistle sounded a decisive *toot!* as my father got to his feet a little unsteadily. He'd pulled on some navy track pants and a clean gray T-shirt; so except for the silver ring on one big toe, the venerable old braided leather sandals on his knobby feet, and the stringy gray ponytail tied in a leather thong, he looked just like everyone else.

Oh, and the ruby stud earring in his earlobe, too; he was the absolute gold-standard definition of old-school cool, and I loved him terribly.

"Hey, Dad? Do you want to go home now? Bella's worried about you."

A town squad car rolled toward the pickup truck my dad had left parked there illegally; the cop in the car—not Bob Arnold—looked purposefully at me and made a brisk gesture to move it.

My dad saw this. "All right," he said cooperatively.

I'd have thought it was on account of the tranquilizer Bella had given him if he hadn't been rolling a familiar-looking pill between his fingers, over and over like a worry bead.

"I am," he confided when he saw me noticing it, "already very tranquil. I didn't need this pill."

So he'd spit it out instead and hidden it. Repressing a smile, I replied, "I see. Maybe Bella should've taken it."

His faded blue eyes twinkled at me, but he didn't comment. "I hear we're getting a storm around here soon," he said as we got into the truck.

I drove; he didn't argue and I wished he had. It would've been more like him. On impulse I turned left on Battery Street, past the blackened bones of old wharves jutting up from the rocky mud of the inlet.

"Good," he said, meaning the detour. Rounding the curve, we drove slowly through the small beachside enclave of tiny wooden cottages called Bingville, then climbed to Bucknam's Head, with its panoramic view across the water south to Lubec.

Seeing it all reminded me of Marla once more, and of her big dog Maxie, who I hoped wasn't in even worse shape than his owner.

And speaking of not knowing what shape someone was in: "You heard from Sam yet?" my dad asked out of the blue.

"No. I wish I knew what's happened to him." I let the clutch out and the truck eased forward. "I'm very worried," I admitted.

To emphasize this I gestured as we rounded another curve, then wrapped my fingers around the steering wheel again hastily. It was a good old truck, but it handled about the way you'd expect from a '49 Dodge.

"He'll turn up." My dad gazed out at the water with a far-away look in his eyes, like maybe he was seeing it for the last time.

I didn't want to think about what that meant. "Right, I hope so," I said instead. "But in what kind of shape?"

Most of Sam's biggest troubles had happened before my dad and I reconciled, after a long estrangement extended on his part by fear of being rejected and on my part by the belief that he had murdered my mother.

The incorrect belief, I mean, which is a whole other story that I'll get into some other time. But the short version is that she was lovely, and he'd adored her; the ruby stud he wore now was the one he had given her all those years ago.

Leonora, her name was. I was three when she died, and now I didn't want to lose him, too. "Beautiful out here," I said.

Well, except for a mild milkiness in the sky and a glimmery

softness on the water to the south where the bay, cozily hemmed in by peninsulas and islands, met up with the Atlantic Ocean.

My dad nodded. "Beautiful. Maybe so." But as we rounded the next curve he peered back over his shoulder again, at the water and sky to the south.

"You know, I'm an old man." A wind gust came out of nowhere, rocking the truck as if it were a toy. "And when the barometer's just right, I've got sciatica."

The round, rubberized lid of someone's trash can tumbled bouncingly down the road, the can rolling along behind.

"Which I've got now," he added. He craned his neck to peer up at the sky through the pickup's windshield, and what he saw there made his weathered brow furrow.

"When we get back to the house, you might want to go around lowering a few storm windows," he said.

By the time we got back to Key Street, a sense of emergency had already begun spreading. Up and down the block cars pulled out hurriedly, heading for the IGA and returning full of bread, milk, and enough Allen's Coffee Flavored Brandy to float a barge, I was willing to bet.

People with company for the Fourth were especially loathe to run out of that latter substance, I imagined; also the lawn chairs got dragged in and the trash bins stowed, and all those flags flapping everywhere were getting hauled down, one right after the other.

Climbing the porch steps, I noted that Bella had carried in the potted geraniums and tied a plastic bag around the mailbox so it wouldn't get wet and rusty inside.

Inside, Bella had thought of the storm windows, too, and lowering them seemed to have used up some nervous energy; at least, when I handed my Dad over to her in the kitchen, she kept her cool.

She was so glad to see him, she'd have swallowed any amount

of exasperation, I thought as I surveyed the rest of the bustling kitchen activities.

Of which there were precisely none.

Ellie sat and read an old issue of the *Tides,* taking her usual intense interest in the local obituaries. ("Like novels," she always said, "so full of facts you hadn't known about people.")

But right now our kitchen was as dead as the departed folks. "Ellie?" I spread my hands. "What about the cheesecakes?"

The stove was stone cold. No chocolate was melting. "Because I thought that's why we went to all that trouble to get . . ."

She put the *Tides* down and slid off her chair, looking as serene as if all those cakes we'd promised were already in the Moose's cooler, which they most definitely were not.

"We have a shop," she said, "with a kitchen in it. All our tools. And an oven big enough to bake four of them at once, *while* we do business. You know, retail sales? The money-earning kind?"

She stopped to take a breath. Clearly, she'd been thinking about this. "And I know you're going to start talking about Matt Muldoon, and how at least one of us still ought to be . . ."

Bingo. You bake, I'll snoop. That had been the plan I'd been about to lay out for her. Because we both knew that although the state cops hadn't descended on us yet, it was only a matter of time.

That is, unless somebody else confessed: not a hope I was hanging my hat on at the moment.

"I know," Ellie said calmly at my expression. "I'm not in the clear. Far from it."

I could hear Bella fussing over my dad in the sunroom, and it seemed that he accepted it better than he had before, as if his escapade had satisfied something in him.

Not for long, though, I suspected. If I had to boil down the meaning of the look in his eyes, I'd say, *"Gangway!"* But whether it meant out of this house or out of this life, I didn't know.

Ellie was still talking. "Think about it, though. We don't need to snoop. Not right now. What we need to do is *think.*"

She cocked her head at me. "For instance, d'you suppose that whoever killed him had never been in the Moose before?"

Huh, she has a point. I stood there thinking about it while green-leafed forsythia branches with a few shriveled yellow blooms still attached to them tapped the kitchen windows insistently.

"Okay," I gave in finally. "Maybe less running around is a good idea. And you're right, we do have to bake sometime."

But she was way ahead of me there, too, already stowing our chocolate bundles into a drawstring tote bag.

The bag had a big brown moose happily devouring a chocolate cupcake printed on it; we'd had them made when we first opened.

"Muldoon said these bags were unsanitary, remember?"

I gave the kitchen a final glance to make sure we weren't leaving a mess. Bella had scrubbed, polished, and waxed it until the pumpkin-pine floor glowed and all the cut-glass knobs on the antique tongue-and-groove cabinet doors glittered like jewels.

"And of course I didn't pull one of the bags over his head and yank the drawstrings when he said it," I recalled, plucking a stray crumb from the table. "Although maybe I should have."

Wade was back down at the marine terminal today, and wouldn't return home for hours. Meanwhile my cell still hadn't rung, and in the telephone alcove no messages blinked on the machine.

Which meant that Sam still hadn't called, and I still didn't know what to make of it, but I knew one thing: when that son of mine did finally get home, I was going to—

"Come on," Ellie interrupted, swinging the bags of chocolate. "Let's go do this thing."

So we did. I left Bella my car again, since she thought stick shift was an invention of the devil. Marching determinedly down Key Street we dodged flying Frisbees, Super Soakers, dogs wearing flag bandannas, and a skateboarder zooming and swooping as graceful as a swan between groups of tourists.

It seemed now that the essential storm supplies were laid in—and especially the Allen's brandy, official tranquilizer of Maine summer-visitor-havers since time immemorial—the holiday was in full swing again. *"Weather be damned"* was the slogan for the day, at least until it drove everyone indoors; see brandy, above.

"Who do you suppose it was?" Ellie wondered aloud.

"In Marla's house? Well, not Miss Halligan, I know that much. Those ballet flats she wears wouldn't *thump.*"

And not Marla, of course; I spared a hopeful thought for her and her dog. Meanwhile the sky's eerie milkiness had thickened; also—and this seemed particularly ominous—seagulls were flocking by the hundreds atop the Coast Guard building and on the wharf.

But none of it fazed the holiday revelers—not yet. "All right, now," said Ellie, unlocking the front door of the Chocolate Moose and swinging it open with a flourish. "Let's get to work."

Outside the shop the Fourth of July was in high gear on Water Street, too, with a fiddle-and-dulcimer duo slinging tunes on the library lawn, jugglers tossing candlepins to each other, and food vendors enough to stuff the whole island with fried dough and onion rings.

All of which meant our cake deadline was fast approaching. So I snapped the lights on and set up the cash register as Ellie organized our worktable, and soon we were in the thick of it:

Sugar, cream cheese, eggs, vanilla . . . perched there on a tall kitchen stool with a wooden spoon in my hand, I felt my breathing slow and my heart rate drop steadily from the panicked gallop it had been stuck at.

Everything will work out, I told myself as Ellie stirred a lump of butter the size of a pigeon's egg (that's what it said in her great-grandma's old recipe, scratched out in fountain-pen ink) into the chocolate she was melting.

Sam is fine, I told myself.

My dad will surely regain his independence completely, not just that frantic grab he exhibited today.

Also I'll find some good way to tell Wade about the lost-in-the-fog portion of our Bayliner voyage, ideally without making his head explode.

And we'll finish these cheesecakes.

"Here," Ellie said gently when I'd finished with the batter, pushing a pile of chocolate wafers, sheets of wax paper, and a rolling pin at me. "Crush 'em."

The wafers crunched satisfyingly between layers of the waxed paper as I pressed the rolling pin down. And I knew it wasn't true, but it seemed to me then that as long as I just stayed right here in this kitchen—and Ellie did, too—nothing could hurt us.

And as long as we kept feeding people chocolate delicacies, no one would want to. But in order to be fed, people had to visit the shop, and sure enough as soon as we'd opened the Moose's front door, people did:

First came a crew of tourists wanting dream bars: coconut, vanilla cream, dark chocolate, and walnuts, so delicious that even Bella said that you could float right up to heaven on one of them.

Then a bunch of local kids clamored in demanding biscotti, which I supposed must have reminded them of teething biscuits. *Chocolate* teething biscuits, favored by infants of all ages.

Finally, just when Ellie and I had gotten our pair of cheesecake crusts built up, Miss Halligan came in.

And considering the photos we'd just found of her buddying up to our recent murder victim, I suppose I should've thought more in advance about what I was going to say to her.

But I hadn't. "Hi, Miss Halligan," I managed. "What can I do for you?"

Brushing my chocolate-crumbed hands on my apron, I leaned on the front counter by the cash register, hoping this looked casual and not as if my heart was suddenly thudding in my chest again.

"Just wondering if there've been any developments," she said.

For her afternoon in the Rose she'd changed into a pink Hello Kitty T-shirt and skinny jeans, and her eye makeup was elaborate as usual: thick, dark eyeliner, lash-building black mascara, and pearl-blue eye shadow.

On another woman in her sixties—or possibly even beyond; it was hard to tell—the outfit might've looked too youthful. But on her it was perfect. Spying the items in the display case, she enthused, "My, don't those look good!"

Saying this, she gestured at them, sending a whiff of her lemony cologne floating at me, and my mouth went suddenly dry.

"Y-yes," I managed. Somehow I just didn't feel like making small talk with her; maybe it was that suddenly I couldn't look at her at all without thinking about Marla Sykes's dog, Maxie.

Because that perfume Miss Halligan was wearing was the one I'd smelled faintly in Marla's house; there was no question about it.

"I'll take two dream bars and half-a-dozen biscotti," she said, pointing. Another whiff of perfume assailed me as I handed over the bag of baked goods.

"Nothing new," I replied to her earlier question about new developments in the murder investigation.

Not honestly, but I had to say something. Her eyes, gleaming from between curled lashes, were watching me carefully.

She turned to go. Then, as if this had just occurred to her at the last minute:

"Jacobia, that gray cashmere shawl I've seen you admiring, the one in the window?"

Of her shop, she meant, and "admiring" wasn't really the word. "Coveting" was more like it. Her glance at me was calculating.

"I wonder, might you accept it from me as a gift?"

I blinked in surprise.

"You and Ellie have been such good shop neighbors," she went on. "I'd like you to have a token of my appreciation, and maybe Ellie would like to come over and pick something out as well?"

Ellie was still back in the kitchen. Speechless, I could only nod. Finally: "That's . . . that's very kind of you. I'll talk to her about it, and we'll be sure to . . ."

I looked down, trying to think of something else to say, and saw her feet below the jeans hems: no cute ballet flats this time. Instead she wore stylish ankle boots in wine leather, with a small brass buckle over the instep and low wooden heels.

The kind of heels that would thud on a wooden floor . . .

My voice deserted me. Had Miss Halligan been there earlier today in Marla's Eastport house? Had she known *we* were there, too, and was she actually now trying to bribe me with an article of used clothing? And if so, bribe me about precisely what?

Popping out of the kitchen, Ellie rescued me. "Jake, we need to pour this batter before . . ."

Suddenly the Moose, with its so sweetly secure feeling just moments earlier, felt way too private and hidden away from the lively street outside.

As if, now that one very bad thing had happened in it, more things might.

Six

The rest of our afternoon was a blur of crushed chocolate wafers, buttered pans floured generously with cocoa powder, and the arm-aching labor of beating enough sugared cream cheese to sink a battleship into a chicken coop's worth of eggs.

But by late afternoon we had four cakes in the oven and four more with their crusts made and their remaining ingredients all set out and measured for the next batch.

"Miss Halligan was in both of Marla's houses today," I said. "The one in Eastport, *and* the one in Lubec."

I'd been thinking about it for several hours, and now I was sure; no one else in town wore that sharp, recognizable lemon cologne, so champagne dry and spicy that it resembled aftershave lotion.

Ellie pushed back a stray blond curl with the side of her arm. "Seems likely, doesn't it? The perfume, the boots . . ."

She was carving curled ribbons of dark chocolate from a big chunk of the stuff, for the cakes' tops.

"But they're not *proof* of anything, are they? So I don't know what we should do about it," she went on. "And we can't very well ask her about it, can we? Since for one thing, we don't want her knowing that *we* know."

"Correct." I checked the oven temperature again. Too hot and the cake tops would scorch, too cool and the batter wouldn't bake. "We need to keep our mouths shut until we know something for certain," I added. "Insinuations won't do the trick."

Outside, the late afternoon shimmered, the slanted light of oncoming evening once again making the island across the bay into a low, gold bar. But overhead the sky's thin, milky look of earlier had thickened to clotted cream, with towering clouds on the horizon to the south.

"We could go home and take naps," I suggested. We had about two hours before the next cakes hit the oven.

Ellie put the tray of chocolate curls she'd been making into the cooler. "Or we could go find out what Miss Halligan was really up to," she said. "Because," she added before I could reply, "the more I think about it, the surer I am that whatever she was doing at Marla's today, it wasn't about those snapshots of her at all."

Which was true: As we'd thought earlier, Miss Halligan must have known at the time that somebody was taking her picture. The camera had been right in her face at that party at the Salty Dog.

So why go to such lengths trying to get hold of the snapshots now? And why hurt Marla in the process?

Not to mention her dog, I thought yet again. Somehow this seemed like the worst part to me.

"You're right," I said. "The pictures don't clear you, and they don't hurt Miss Halligan, either."

So all this searching of houses and clobbering of people . . . it was about something else, but what?

Frowning, Ellie opened the cooler again, surveying the dark chocolate curls she'd placed there.

"Oh, maybe just a few more of these," she said, and began unwrapping another of the chocolate blocks we'd scored in Marla's cellar.

And unwrapping it and unwrapping it. "Ellie, how much plastic wrap is on that thing, anyway?"

Yards and yards of the stuff, it looked like. "You can't even see through it, it's so thick on there," I said.

At last she finished, and stared at the result. "What?" I said. "Is something wrong with the chocolate?"

Because if it turned out to be no good, we were screwed, you should excuse the expression, and so were the little kids who'd been promised a fireworks show, viewed from a real, out-on-the-water boat! At night! On the Fourth of July!

It sounded like so much fun, even I wanted to go. "Ellie? Is it spoiled? Moldy? *Infested* somehow?"

"No," she said mildly, a bemused expression spreading on her face. "The chocolate's fine." She looked up. "Lock the door, please. And pull the shades."

I must've looked perplexed. Our door shade existed; I'd never pulled it, though, and ditto for the front windows. But Ellie only nodded emphatically at me again, so I did as she asked.

She carried the bundle back out into the kitchen and set it on the worktable. "I think I might know now what someone was looking for at Marla's place in Lubec."

With the shades down, the front of the shop had a comfy, low-lit atmosphere, but in the kitchen the fluorescent over-heads made it as bright as an operating room.

So there was no mistaking what I saw when Ellie finished the unwrapping. "No," I managed. "Tell me that's not . . ."

But it was. ". . . money," I finished. A big, thick wad of hundred-dollar bills. Was it ten thousand dollars? Or even more?

Ellie let out a breath. "Jake, have you noticed that anytime we get an answer to something . . ."

Such as the question of what someone had really been looking for at Marla's, for instance. Ellie went on:

"Whenever we get answers, somehow they always come equipped with a lot more . . ."

Right, questions. Like where the heck did all that money come from?

My cell phone trilled; I fumbled in my bag and found it.

"Ellie, get a paring knife and cut the rest of those bundles open," I said, hoping it was Sam calling. It wasn't, though:

"Jake? Bob Arnold here."

Disappointment washed through me, along with a pang of fear. It was so unlike Sam to go radio silent this way. And what could Bob want now?

"Jake?" Bob repeated. The cheesecakes were still in the oven, now giving off an aroma so sweet that it practically seized me by the nose and floated me back out to the kitchen.

Also I was curious to learn just how much money Ellie was unwrapping. But:

"I'm here, Bob," I said. Because I don't care how friendly you are with a police officer, when you've just found ten grand in a package you stole while breaking and entering, you're polite.

Well, not technically the breaking part, but you know what I mean, especially when you found the money in an assault victim's house *and* your best friend is a prime suspect in a recent murder.

You talk to that cop, that is what I'm saying. Nicely. "What's up, Bob?"

Hey, maybe he'd report a confession. Ellie brought me a fresh coffee fixed just the way I like it, meanwhile waving another ten grand in my face. I grabbed at it, but she danced away from me; fatigue and nerves were making us both a little giddy, I guessed.

"Listen, it's about Marla's dog," Bob said, and I got *not* giddy, quick.

"I thought you'd want to know," he went on. "Dog's pretty stiff and sore, but he's fine. Bruises, but nothing broken."

"Really? That's great news," I said as Ellie unwrapped yet another fat bundle of money.

"Thing is, though, the dog needs a place to stay. Vet doesn't have boarding space and he's all full up at the clinic."

Uh-oh. Now I knew why Bob was calling me. He went on: "So I figured I'd bring the dog over to your house, maybe."

"Absolutely not," I said at once, and at my tone Ellie looked over at me inquiringly. *Don't worry about it,* I waved at her.

Bob went on without seeming to have heard me. "I know the dog would be safe with you, Jake, so could you help me out?"

I couldn't take the dog. Bella had enough to worry about, Sam wasn't here to help, and Wade didn't want a dog.

When I opened my mouth, though, what I heard coming out of it was, "Okay, bring him over."

Because I still couldn't forget how the dog had looked at me: *Help.* And my heart had already answered.

So I'm a dog person, so sue me. Hanging up, I explained and then spied a familiar look in Ellie's eyes, although she hardly giggled at all.

"Jake, you're such a softy," she teased.

"Oh, hush up," I said crossly, raising the window shades and the one in the front door once more. Thinking *Leash, collar, dog dish, water bowl . . .*

I'd compiled quite a list—*biscuits, chew toys*—by the time Bob pulled up out front, then went around to assist the big German shepherd in easing itself stiffly down from the front seat.

No leash. The dog didn't need one, calm and self-possessed despite the festival noise, people, music, and the occasional *pop!-pop!-pop!* of firecrackers exploding.

"Maxie," I said from the doorway, and he looked up at me, his brandy-colored eyes alert and watchful. He paced alongside Bob up onto the sidewalk.

"Maxie," I said again, kneeling by him. When I let my face

rest in his thick, soft fur, he leaned trustingly against me, and so of course I was doomed.

"Oh," I sighed helplessly; the dog was warm and clean and smelled faintly of Betadine from the vet's office. "Good dog."

Bob looked relieved. "Vet says to give him these." He handed over a pill packet. "For pain. Says to call, any problems."

I didn't think the vet wanted to hear my problems, the number of which had just increased exponentially. Meanwhile the dog, although he was behaving very stoically now, looked as if he could use one of those pain pills.

Around the eyes, especially. That same expression I'd seen earlier was in them: *Help*. So Ellie went home and got my car; after loading him into it . . .

. . . and synchronizing our watches because the cakes needed another hour of baking, and then an hour of just sitting there in the turned-off oven. . . .

Ellie and I headed up Washington Street toward my house, threading our way between costumed Uncle Sam figures, kids waving squirt guns, Pokémon Go players, and babies patriotically wrapped in red-white-and-blue blankets to keep them warm against the breeze now freshening from the south.

"Do you suppose they could pack any more people into this town?" she went on. "They're *everywhere.*"

We rolled into my driveway, where Ellie let the dog out of the backseat. "If that storm really hits, it'll be a mess," I agreed, but then my whole attention turned toward the animal again.

Or rather where he'd been. "Maxie?" I peered around anxiously for his large black-and-tan shape. "*Maxie?*"

"Here he is." Bella stood on the porch with her arms folded across her chest. From the foot of the steps the big dog eyed her, then sat, his look inquisitive.

"Now, Bella," I began placatingly as she fixed me in her huge grape-green eyes.

"I guess I'll be taking care of it," she said flatly.

I climbed the porch steps. "No, not at all, I'm going to be.

Well. Except this evening," I elaborated, "we do have the rest of those cakes to bake, and maybe some tomorrow. But after that—"

"I heard," she interrupted. "Another dozen." Her tone was exactly like biting into a grapefruit. Then:

"Your father is fine. Sam hasn't called. Wade ate and left again."

I absorbed the information humbly. "Thank you. Really, Bella, I do very much appreciate all your assistance."

"You're welcome," she replied, not softening a bit. But she was still looking at the dog, and although I couldn't read her expression when she nodded at him, in response he got up and padded toward her. Then, climbing the porch steps very stiffly but purposefully, he followed her inside.

"You lie down here," I heard her telling him in the kitchen. "And you stay here, too, there's a sick man in the other room and I don't want any of your dog hair getting all over him, you hear?"

Or dog drool, or dog dander, or any other doggy by-products whatsoever. If she could have, she'd have dipped the poor creature in Lysol before she brought him into the house.

"Let's go back and get its things from Marla's place," said Ellie, still tactfully not mentioning what a complete pushover I'd just been in agreeing to take the animal at all.

"Its own bed and dog dishes and food, and so on," she said. They'd been in Marla's kitchen, I recalled now.

"Oh, but I'd thought I would—" I had meant to buy them. But then it hit me, how brilliantly sneaky and determined Ellie was.

"Yes," I turned to her appreciatively, "and that'll give us a really great reason to go back to . . ."

She nodded briskly at me. "You got it," she said.

So I ran inside and gave Maxie one of the pain pills, which he took willingly, even eagerly, as if he understood what it was.

And then we went.

*　*　*

"What we need is the one thing that makes sense of all the rest of it," said Ellie.

It was late afternoon as we once more approached Marla's place at the end of Water Street.

"The problem is that we know a lot of facts. But not how they fit together," she went on, "or what they mean."

Long shadows crossed the green lawn as we pulled into the driveway. Ellie had retrieved her car; I wasn't sure when.

"We *think* Marla took those snapshots. We *think* Miss Halligan was in Marla's house," I said.

"But we don't know for sure, and we especially don't know how that money got into her cellar, or why," Ellie agreed.

I checked the rearview mirror. No one was pulling in behind us, but I still couldn't shake the feeling of being watched.

The house looked deserted, just as before. "So do we care if someone sees our car here?" I wondered aloud as we got out.

"No." Ellie slammed the passenger-side door. "Why should we sneak around?" She strode toward the house.

"We need the dog's things, so we're going to get them. I don't see who'd have a problem with that," she declared.

I did. But: "That's my story," Ellie said, plucking Marla's spare house key from under the doormat. "And I'm sticking to it."

She stepped inside; I followed hesitantly. The house had been bright in the morning sunshine, but now in the afternoon the rooms were dim and shadowy.

Ellie snapped lamps on. The spare, simple lines of Marla's handsome Arts and Crafts furnishings, the vintage rugs and leather upholstery, and the dark polished wooden floors were all even more attractive by lamplight.

"Nice," Ellie commented, following my gaze.

"Schoolteachers were paid well in Connecticut where Marla's from, I guess."

In the fireplace hearth a ceramic-glazed woodstove had been

installed; on the mantel above, the elegantly framed photograph of Yosemite was by Ansel Adams.

And the table lamp in the front hallway was real Tiffany, if I wasn't mistaken, which I wasn't. Back in the city long ago, I'd had that kind of money, too.

Ellie tapped her wristwatch. "Tick-tock, those cheesecakes aren't going to hop out of the oven by themselves."

Or the next ones hop in. Meanwhile, we weren't *really* just here for the dog's things, were we? I hurried behind Ellie to the cellar steps and down them, into the dark.

"Where's the light string?" I fumbled in my bag for my tiny flashlight, couldn't find it. From below I could hear Ellie moving around.

The light went on. Brightness flooded the cellar. Then: "Oh no."

Ellie's voice came from inside the small corner room. I hurried to join her. "Ellie, what's . . . Oh."

Inside, the steel shelves on the walls still gleamed dully and the air remained cool and still; it was why Marla had chosen it for chocolate storage in the first place, I assumed.

But now—I stared at the shelves. *Empty.*

Nothing on the gorgeously sealed and painted concrete floor, shining glossily under the fluorescent overhead lights. Nothing on the shelves, either; not anymore. *Gone . . .*

I took the cellar stairs two at a time, and the flight to the second floor the same way, racing along the upstairs hall to what we'd earlier identified as Marla's office space, cleverly hidden behind a closet door.

Pulling the door open again, I saw what I'd feared I would: Someone had been here *after* we left and had taken the laptop along with the rest of the chocolate bundles in the cellar.

And the money bundles, if there'd been any. "Now what?" Ellie asked disconsolately, appearing behind me.

We returned to the kitchen, where Maxie's food and water

bowls stood on a rubber mat by the sink. His food was in a plastic bin on the counter.

A huge sigh escaped me. "I don't know. We go on as before, I guess." We sat at the vintage Formica-topped table, on the neatly re-covered matching chairs with their bright upholstery buttons and shiny metal trim.

Money, I thought again. *All this interior design represented a lot of—*

"Wild out there," Ellie observed in discouraged tones as she gazed out the kitchen window.

"Yeah." Leaves fluttered from the copper beech tree by the back door as the wind tore at it in gusts. Down on the Coast Guard tower, just visible between the breakwater and the port authority buildings, the storm flags played crack-the-whip.

We took all the dog equipment, but left everything else just as it was. We turned the lights out and locked the door. I'd have called Bob Arnold about the ransacking, but what would I say?

Outside, the wind smelled sweet, with a touch of the tropics riding on it. *Sam,* I thought yet again as I got back into the car.

My cell phone lay stubbornly silent at the bottom of my bag, my son still not communicating. *Or maybe he's not able to communicate,* my mind added slyly, but this thought sent a bolt of fright through me and I shoved it aside.

Ellie knew, though. Like I say, we'd been friends for a long time. "He's fine," she said quietly.

"Yeah." We backed out onto Water Street. It was time to go back to the Moose, but first I drove out to where the street ended in a gravel turnaround overlooking the bay.

The tide was running hard, all the foamy white turbulence on flamboyant display. "Or I hope he is, anyway," I said.

Across the waves the narrow white beach at the end of Deer Island looked deserted, not one car in the distant parking lot of the normally crowded Canadian tourist destination.

Which made sense. The only way off Deer Island was a ferry, so people were going while it was still possible.

"All right," said Ellie, straightening. "We need a plan."

Personally, I thought a fine plan might be to forget all our difficulties, get out of town, and just live on credit cards for a month or so, preferably somewhere that did not have a hurricane or an auction in the forecast.

Palm Springs, maybe. Or Guatemala. Either way, drinks with little umbrellas in them would be—

"Don't you even think about it," said Ellie, whose ability to read my mind can be annoying.

Ignoring her, I negotiated a traffic tangle at the end of the breakwater, where a Coast Guard trailer was trying to back down onto the launch ramp. The crowds milling between Rosie's Hot Dog Stand and the ice-cream parlor made it difficult, though, for the Coasties and for me.

"Nicely done," she said when I'd gotten through it all and turned into the last remaining parking place outside the Moose.

But the rest of her mind was still on what we should do next.

"Flashlights, batteries, candles, radio . . . ," she recited as we went in.

I followed her to the kitchen where she checked the oven temperature and compared her wristwatch with our wall clock.

". . . propane cylinders, Sterno, stove wood," I added to the litany.

Out here on the island we'd been through enough emergencies—storms, mostly, but once a truck hit a transmission tower and we were out of power for a week—to know the drill.

Finally, "Once we get through this list, we'll be ready for any weather," I said. "But as for—"

"Mmm," agreed Ellie. "The other matter." Murder, she meant, and would've gone on. But instead a sharp knock came at the shop door.

"The money's a real problem, and so's Marla lying about those photographs," I said, crossing to answer.

"Because it's bad enough the weird way Muldoon died, but all those other things just make it so much more *confusing*."

I yanked open the door, feeling frustrated and overwhelmed suddenly by the other list I'd been contemplating all day: a sick parent, a son gone AWOL, a visiting dog, a looming storm, and the prospect of my dearest friend being charged with murder.

Oh, and more unbaked cheesecakes than you could shake a stick at. "What?" I exhaled exasperatedly.

Miss Halligan stood there, looking pained. "Jacobia, I'm so sorry to have to tell you this, but Bob Arnold called me just now. Is your cell phone not working, dear?"

"*What?*" I repeated, snagging the phone from my bag and opening it: battery dead. "Will you please just tell me?"

A thousand bad scenarios ran through my mind in the instant before Miss Halligan replied.

"It's your husband. There's been an accident," she said.

Wade drove a big old green Ford F-150 pickup truck whose fenders were held on with Bondo and duct tape. The truck's bed, once floored with heavy-duty metal, was a sheet of plywood, and the hood latch had been replaced by a bent wire coat hanger.

But under that hood was a vintage V-8 with enough horsepower for a locomotive, and on the wheels were an oversized set of tires with so much traction that you could give yourself whiplash just by stomping hard on the brake pedal.

Now in the gathering evening I stood with Police Chief Bob Arnold by the side of County Road, watching the Bay City Mobil wrecker hoist the truck's front end out of the ditch.

Wade was in the ambulance that had pulled over on the other side of the pavement, being checked out; I could see a swatch of bright blood on the side of his face.

When the wrecker got the truck lifted, the place where the missing front wheel ought to be gaped vacantly. Bob Arnold's pink forehead tightened when he saw it.

"Has Wade had that vehicle serviced lately, you know of?"

I shook my head, chills of lingering fright shivering through me despite the warm summer evening. "No. Nothing recently."

It would've been a decent explanation, that maybe they'd had a wheel off and hadn't put it back on correctly. But Wade did his own vehicle maintenance; besides, with him working so much lately, the truck had mostly sat undriven in the port authority parking lot, nowhere else.

Now as the wrecker hauled the vehicle away, Wade climbed down out of the ambulance and strode toward me, grinning.

"Hey, hey." He held his arms out, wrapped them around me. I'd told myself that I was not going to cry, and I didn't.

Sort of. "I'm fine," he said. "Bumped my head a little on the side window when the truck rolled."

I pulled away from him. "'Rolled'? You mean it actually turned over?"

I'd thought he'd just gone into the ditch, maybe while trying to avoid a deer. *He could've lost a wheel then*, I had told myself.

"Yeah, well." He was trying to sound comforting, but I could tell that he wasn't happy, either.

"No bones broken, no concussion." He gave me a reassuring squeeze. "Even my mental status is okay. I mean," he amended, "I did tell those EMTs that the president is Donald Duck, but . . ."

"Oh, you." Leaning against him, I laughed. He was okay, and considering how bad this might've been, I couldn't ask for more.

The F-150 went by, its front end hanging from the tow hook. Wade frowned after it. "Funny thing, though."

Bob Arnold finished recording the incident in his notebook, then came up to us, not looking particularly satisfied with what he was thinking, either.

"So you're telling me the wheel came off, no warning? You're just driving down the road and *wham*?"

Wade nodded, then put his fingers wincingly to the bloody

spot on his temple. "Yep. Weird too. I had those wheels off a few weeks ago, changing the brake pads."

He'd had the truck up on blocks out in our driveway, I now recalled; I'd spent the time cringing at every sound, listening in dread in case a block slipped and the vehicle fell on him.

Which it hadn't, of course, but now this: "And I tightened those things myself with a power wrench," Wade said.

Bob frowned. He knew that Wade, who'd been doing his own car repairs for even longer than he'd been piloting big boats into our harbor, was as likely to leave nuts or bolts untightened as he was to leave lines unsecured.

In other words, not very. In the fading light passing cars' curious occupants peered at us as they went by.

Bob tucked his notebook away. "How about I go on over to the Mobil station, have the guys there put 'er on the lift?"

Wade put his fingertips gingerly to his temple again. A lump was rising there, already purple near the split part of the skin.

"Great. I'd like to see . . . Hey." Catching sight of something, he scrambled down into the muddy ditch where the truck had dug in.

"Got it." He plucked something from the ditch, then reached out and hauled the truck's detached wheel out of the weeds where it had buried itself. Clambering up, he shoved the wheel along.

"This is interesting." He let the wheel down onto the gravel and held his hand out to show the small metal object in it.

"Oh, holy heck." Bob prodded the object with a fingertip as if uncertain what he was seeing. But even in the gathering dusk the thing's identity was clear to all of us: it was the shank of a big automotive bolt with a roundheaded nut still screwed onto the end of it.

"Cut right off," Bob mused aloud, noting the bolt end's smoothness.

"Sure was," Wade said. "Looks like somebody slid a hacksaw in there behind the nut and just cut it clean through."

Bob grunted agreement, squinting. "That possible? Someone could've got at it? "

Wade nodded. "It was parked in an out-of-the-way spot."

The truck was more duct tape, Bondo, and baling wire than it was factory original, but Wade could be driving a wooden wagon with a mule out in front of it and he still wouldn't want anyone slamming their car door into the thing.

"I guess somebody must be annoyed with me about something," he said thoughtfully, not looking at me.

But he might just as well have been. "I guess," said Bob.

Not looking right at me, either. But he gave me some side eye when he said it, as if he thought someone might've been sending me a message. Or wanted me distracted from an interest I was pursuing.

Like maybe Muldoon's murder.

"Man, when the wheel came off, I thought I was history," Wade commented.

The idea sent fury rushing through me. "Come on," I told him, putting my arm through his. "Bob, you're done with him for now, right?"

Nodding assent, Eastport's police chief waved me over. "Hey, the state cops called me. They're still hot on Ellie as number one on their hit parade. Of suspects, that is."

I let out a breath. "So how come they haven't just arrested her already, if they're so sure they can make a case against her?"

Bob shrugged. "Holiday. Storm coming. And for now, I've got 'em convinced she's not a flight risk. But I'm telling you, Jake, once the weekend's over, they'll come down on her."

Yeah, right. Boom *goes the dynamite,* I thought sourly.

"So she'd better be prepared. Also," said Bob, "Millie Marquardt's lined up a lot of media people—TV news and so on—to cover the festival. If they get wind of the murder . . . Well, you might want to avoid them."

"Thanks, Bob," I told him, and then Wade and I picked our way along the shoulder until we got to my car.

"I'll drive," he said, glancing at the deep, muddy groove his truck's axle end had dug when it hit the ditch.

Which had happened because somebody had deliberately made the wheel fall off. Sliding into the car, I felt heat spreading through my chest until I could barely breathe. Suddenly I was so angry. And frightened.

"Okay," I began as Wade pulled out. Because he was in this now, whatever "this" was. I'd put him in it.

Not meaning to, but I had, and that meant he needed to know all about it, no matter how mad he got when I told him.

"Let's go out to the park," I said. Shackford Head State Park was right here on the island: trees, trails, spectacular vistas from the high overlooks. It was where we always went to talk.

Wade looked surprised, but he turned obediently onto Deep Cove Road. The narrow blacktop curved sharply around and along a steep, high bluff, with far views of the water now darkening at day's end.

"Look, I know you're busy," I began. He'd want to get right to work on that truck of his, for one thing, as soon as Bob finished taking photographs and writing up his report.

"But there was a little more to the boat trip Ellie and I took than I told you," I added.

Wade kept his eyes on the road as it dipped abruptly and then turned sharply again, climbing the long hill above Deep Cove and the boats bobbing at their moorings in it. Finally he turned onto a rutted track meandering between cattail-studded marshlands and grassy fields.

In the park's boulder-ringed turnaround he pulled the car to a stop and shut the key off.

We got out and walked together toward the trailhead. "Wade, do you think that wheel might've fallen off by accident? That is, could you have not tightened it? Or was it defective or something?"

He shook his head firmly. "No. I don't know why it happened, but there's some funny business with it, I'm pretty sure."

"It's an old truck, Wade. You're really confident that bolt couldn't have just sheared off?"

"Yeah," he replied flatly. "I'm sure." Then: "But it sounds to me like you think you know something about it."

Damn, if he'd been doubtful, I might've just let it go. But he wasn't, and his certainty was good enough for me.

Ahead of us a low wooden bridge led over a watercress-clotted creek. On it I paused, readying myself to confide in him. Oh, he wasn't going to like this at all.

But I had no choice; the best I could do, I thought, was to ease him into it by letting him know the least bad things first.

"So," I began, trying to sound matter-of-fact. "I guess the first thing I should tell you is that we've got a new dog."

Fifteen minutes later we'd hiked up the side of the mountain, the trail winding and rising steadily among old-growth evergreens and ancient sumac thickets to a massive granite outcropping.

I'd been talking all the while: the little boat that menaced me and Ellie, the Salty Dog and Marla, finally our return.

All about our return. "Okay," said Wade, who'd been listening intently, "so you and Ellie left Lubec ahead of the fog, but it caught up with you."

"Right." From the weathered wooden bench at the top of the bluff, you could see all the way down the bay and smell the cold, briny salt water in it.

"In the dark we missed the channel marker," I recalled, then went on to explain how Ellie had navigated us out of the shipping lane, using the boat's depth finder to avoid . . .

"Rocks," I finished. Up here the wind felt as solid as a punch, and on the southwest horizon the massive clouds loomed like raised hammers.

It wasn't quite dark. Wade gazed out at the watery horizon. "Okay, first of all . . ."

Turning, he kissed me. "That's for not drowning. And for coming to pick me up just now." He kissed me again. "And for not getting run over by a ship," he said, whereupon the light dawned:

He'd already known that his huge vessel had nearly sent me to "Davy Jones's locker room," as my son Sam used to call it.

And he'd figured out the rest of it. Of course we must've been caught in the fog; why else would we in that big ship's way?

He let his arm drop around my shoulders. "Jake, when I am out there on the water, there's three things I always know: where I am, what time it is, and what the tide's doing."

I digested this. "Also," he went on, "it's not like the old days when guys hung out on ships' masts, squinting through a long spyglass. We've got high tech now, you know?"

"Oh." I felt the air hissing out of my big confession scene. "And by high tech you mean what, exactly?"

He gave me a consoling squeeze. "FLIR. Stands for 'forward-looking-infrared.' It means," he added as if I didn't already know, "that harbor pilots can see in the dark."

"Oh, for Pete's sake." Here I'd been beating myself up over not telling him and he'd known all along. "Then why didn't you—"

"Get someone out there for you?" he finished for me. To save us, he meant, or at least make sure we got in okay by ourselves.

We started back downhill between granite outcroppings covered in gray-green lichens. Spruce trees and white pines grew thickly down to where a sharp drop fell off to the waves below; luckily, we knew our way on the trail between the trees, even in the dusk.

"Well, first of all," Wade said, "I'd have to find someone

crazy enough to go out in the fog after you, wouldn't I? Or call the Coast Guard on you."

Good point. Wrapped in a zinger, but still. From the high, bare bluffs we descended to the smell of the sun-warmed evergreens, which still filled the air, and gray light slanted between the trees.

"Truth is, you looked okay where you were." Wade put a hand out to me as I picked my way over the loose stones; as steep as this trail's uphill portion had been, its downhill was even hairier.

"I knew the fog was clearing, too. It had already lifted in Cutler and Jonesport."

Two of the nearby weather stations, he meant, that his ship would've been getting reports from. "So I just asked our comm guy to let me know when you got in to shore," he added.

Above us a bald eagle in a nest the size of a Volkswagen spied down, cocking its big white head first one way and then the other.

"I know it probably felt pretty dramatic," said Wade. "But what you two did out there last night was not a whole lot more than the equivalent of pulling off the road in bad weather until visibility improves. Not fun, but people do it and survive."

I hadn't thought of it that way.

"Well, except for the nearly-getting-run-over part," he said. "Also it's just possible that the Coast Guard might have had an eye on you. Because . . . did either of you happen to notice a little black box in the emergency gear bin?"

I stared at him. "You're kidding."

He shook his head. "Nope. It's a GPS tracker, relays your signal from a satellite."

We crossed back over the small wooden bridge. From the park's gravel parking area the shoreline to the east had darkened to a black cutout against the indigo sky.

"George put it in the Bayliner," Wade said. "Boat leaves the dock, it can be located. He could track it on a computer or on his phone, and when he bought it, he said he was going to set it to automatically ping the Coasties, too. Although," Wade added, "I don't know for sure that George ever did that part."

"So that's what the wires were," I said. "From the dashboard through to the box in the gear bin."

Wade nodded, watching me digest George's . . . well, I imagine you'd call it a safety measure. But I couldn't say I approved.

"Look, he wanted her to feel free on that boat of hers, you know? Not like she was being supervised," Wade said.

I put my hand on the car door. "But she was being supervised. Spied on, even. Her *privacy* invaded."

I heard my voice rising; Wade put his hands up in a gesture of *you've got this wrong*. "He wasn't going to spy, I guarantee it."

I must've looked skeptical. "I helped him put the device in," Wade said. "I'll bet he hasn't checked it since. For one thing, I'm not sure he knows how. He was pretty flummoxed by the instruction booklet, as I recall."

His hands dropped to his sides. "It's for emergencies only, Jake. Looked at if she goes missing, but not for keeping routine tabs on her. Her privacy is not going to be invaded."

I got in and slammed the car door against the rising wind. Wade settled in the passenger seat.

"Truth is, he put it in there and then Ellie took all those boating-safety courses, navigation and boat handling, and so on," he said. "And went out and practiced like a demon."

He was right. That whole first summer, Ellie'd been on the water more than she was on land.

"So George got more comfortable, and I think he sort of lost interest in the tracker," Wade said. "We were going to go look at it again together, but we never did."

He rolled his window down; a fresh salt breeze drifted in. "That was good thinking, by the way, using that depth finder."

"And if we hadn't?" I turned the car around and headed

back toward town. "What would you have done then, if we'd still been in the shipping lane, smack-dab in front of you?"

He shook his head slowly. "Nothing I could do. It was too late. Changing course on a freighter . . . it would be like trying to turn this whole island on a dime."

A deer leapt from a thicket. I slammed on the brakes, the car stopped suddenly, and the deer vanished obliviously into a bunch of saplings on the other side of the road.

I unwrapped my fingers from the wheel. Across the darkening bay in Lubec, tiny, twinkling lights were coming on in the houses and shops.

"But never mind that," Wade went on, and I can't tell you how glad I was that he was taking such a reasonable "no harm, no foul" view of what had happened with the freighter.

"What I want to know is," he said, "are you going to tell Ellie about the tracker or not? Because I've been thinking," he rubbed a hand over his brush-cut hair, "and what I think is . . ."

If I did intend to tell her, he'd have to speak with George about it, he meant; it would be only fair to warn the poor guy that the secret was out, on account of Wade telling me about it when he must have at least implied that he wouldn't.

Meanwhile, until now, he hadn't; told me, that is. That was a fact that didn't escape me, either. But under the circumstances I figured I'd let that little omission go by.

On Key Street the kids ran, shouting and waving sparklers. From the porches wafted the sickly sweet smell of citronella candles. In the still, heavy air before the storm that was coming, barbecues spat fat flares, the flames lighting backyards crowded with kids and grandparents, lawn chairs and picnic tables.

"What *I* think . . . ," I began, turning into our driveway. No barbecue grill here, and there weren't any lights on in the house, either. The sight of the dark windows filled me with sudden worry.

"I think if you don't tell George what happened to us out on the water in the fog and so on, I won't tell Ellie about the GPS tracker he put on her boat," I said.

Not that I didn't still have misgivings—big ones. In fact, the whole idea was repulsive to me. But if Ellie and the Bayliner got in trouble, I wanted to be able to rush out and find her like *right the hell now,* didn't I?

Sure I did. And George hadn't been thinking of snooping on her for any bad reason, I was certain; he was a lovely guy and he adored her, but he was not—how shall I say this?—the most imaginative fellow on the planet.

He'd just wanted her to be safe, and he hadn't told her about it because . . .

Well, for that one I had no ready answer, and I still didn't like this at all. But Wade had to keep his trap shut about our watery adventure or George would be reading my friend Ellie the riot act about it until hell froze over.

So I was stuck. "Okay," Wade agreed easily as we got out of the car. "It's a deal, I won't tell George." Then:

"Ellie dropped that heavy anchor all on her own, though, did she? Scrambled right out onto the bow and handled it okay?"

"She certainly did. Hauled it up again, too." We walked toward the house together, his arm around my waist, through the shadows under the maple trees.

"It was a little nerve-wracking sometimes," I admitted. "But I never felt like things were out of control."

That was pushing it; in the moment of first seeing that huge freighter coming out of the fog at us, things had seemed . . . well, "unregulated" was putting it mildly.

"Ellie took care of it all," I said, "and she knew just how to tell me what to do about everything."

"Really?" On the porch he captured me in a surprise embrace. "You think she could teach me that trick? Telling you what to do about everything?"

"Ha." Flattening my hands against his broad chest, I made as if to shove him away but didn't; for pure delight Wade's embrace is right up there with a mouthful of good chocolate.

"Anyway," he said, "it still sounds to me like she handled it all just fine. It's the little boat that buzzed you that I'd like to know a lot more about."

Me, too. Besides not liking the feeling of keeping secrets from him, it was a lot of the reason why I'd told him the whole story, actually. The little boat hadn't seemed like a big deal then, but now . . .

I looked past him through the screen door.

"Not," he added with caution, "that you two ever need to pull a stunt like that *again.*"

Inside the house early evening and the lowering storm clouds cast a bluish gloom into the silence. No music or voices. No blare of a TV from anywhere.

No nothing. I pushed past Wade and rushed inside.

Seven

"Bella?" I peered into the pantry, the laundry room, and the phone alcove, then down the cellar steps and up the hall stairs. "Dad? Is anyone here?"

The private apartment I'd had remodeled for them was on the third floor, once the servants' quarters back in the 1830s when it took plenty of help to run a big house like this one.

Still did, actually. I started up the stairs, then paused at the sound of Wade's voice. "Jake."

Crooking a finger at me, he spoke quietly from the other end of the hall, his burly shape shadowy in the faint gleam from the fanlight over the big old front door.

I tiptoed toward him, and he steered me gently to the doorway of the sunroom, where the lights were turned low and a small fire burned cozily on the tiled hearth.

There together on the daybed, each with an arm curved comfortably around the other's shoulders, lay Bella and my dad, sound asleep with the quilt pulled up over them. And at the foot, positioned so his big body wasn't crowding anyone, lay Maxie the dog.

The dog's head lifted alertly. My dad's hand still rested on it, his gnarled fingers nesting in the animal's thick tan fur.

"Wuff," uttered Maxie, settling again. My dad didn't stir, nor did Bella. The firelight flickered warmly over all three of them.

"This is the dog I was telling you about," I murmured.

Wade took in the scene: dog, Dad, Bella. "I get it. Sure, I guess I can live with that for a while."

He turned thoughtfully to me. "So listen, I guess I'm going upstairs to take a shower."

Real life hit me again with the realization that I probably wasn't exactly daisy fresh, myself. "I could use one, too."

He shrugged. "In that case there's really no sense wasting water, is there?"

On separate showers, he meant. So we didn't.

Afterward we lay together in the big bed in our room, under the light-as-a-cloud blue cotton blanket that Ellie had crocheted and given to us for our fifth wedding anniversary.

"I'd better go see how she's doing," I said drowsily.

The next pair of cheesecakes was in the oven by now and while they baked she was probably mixing up a batch of cookie batter; after all, we still had to open the shop tomorrow. So we'd need just as many delicious chocolate baked items as on any other day, and probably even more.

"I'm going to try getting hold of Sam again, too," I said. But when I tried raising him on my cell phone, there was still no answer.

Wade swung out of bed and pulled on a pair of boxer shorts: blue, with little yellow bathtub duckies on them. I swear there are parts of my life that if I could just sell tickets to them, I would be a kazillionaire. However:

"No luck?" Wade asked, indicating my phone. He hauled a navy sweatshirt on, then stepped into a fresh pair of jeans.

I shook my head and began dressing as well—miles to go, et cetera. "No. And I'm really starting to get concerned."

Outside, the wind rattled the gutters; peering past the drawn shade, I glimpsed the leaves in the treetops thrashing about.

"Young guys in their twenties don't always stay in touch with their moms," Wade observed.

"Right. But Sam does. Or he always has before, anyway." It was possible, I supposed, that he was on his way here right now.

He could've had a cell phone malfunction, for example, and instead of trying to find some twentieth-century vintage relic of a pay phone, he'd figured he'd just tell me about it when he got home.

Unfortunately, though, that's not what the mother of a recovering drug-and-alcohol abuser tends to assume. At one point Sam was little more than a walking chemistry set.

I mean, when he *could* walk. Sitting there on the edge of the bed, I recalled very clearly the time the Bangor cops called me to say he'd been arrested and was in jail, and it was the best news I'd had all week.

Because he wasn't dead.

I put the phone away while Wade tied his sneakers. "What're you going to do?" I asked.

He thought for a moment before replying. Then, "This thing about the cheesecakes. Does Ellie really need you there right now? At the shop?"

"Um," I began doubtfully. Strictly speaking, she probably didn't. But before I could say so:

"Because I was thinking about that guy you said rushed you. Took a run at you in his little boat the other night."

I finished dressing: sneakers, dungarees, long-sleeved tee. The wind shook the windows harder; I pulled a cotton sweater on.

"Thinking what about him?" I took a look at myself in the mirror over the dresser: long, narrow face, dark eyes, short brown hair. I could comb it into a neat cap, but it tangled to a rat's nest again as soon as I stopped combing.

I wasn't going to scare small children is about the best I can say about my appearance; it had been a long couple of days. Wade came up behind me and kissed my neck.

"About whether the guy really came at you on purpose and if so, whether he's hooked into any of this other stuff you and Ellie have been dealing with," he replied.

Into Muldoon's murder, and the attack on Marla, the photos of Miss Halligan, the money in the cellar, and . . .

And his own truck, which somebody had sabotaged because of me, I was fairly certain now. To distract me by hurting Wade.

I turned from the mirror. "Yes, if you want to know the truth, I do think it was on purpose. I just can't prove it."

In my mind's eye I saw the little boat again, charging out of the darkness at us. Our running lights had been on; he couldn't have missed seeing us. The only way he'd missed slamming into us was to swerve away at the last instant.

"He *must* have seen us," I said, "or we'd have collided. No doubt in my mind at all, actually. I just didn't want to sound too paranoid about it."

Wade looked convinced. "Okay, then, listen to me a minute. I think I know who the guy is. Small open boat, little outboard hung on the transom? He bombs around in it at all hours, keeps it about as tidy as your average trash pit."

I recalled the decrepit small vessel that had been tied up at the Lubec dock, and the junk that was in it. "Could be the one. You know him?"

We started downstairs toward the tantalizing smell of fresh coffee and the sound of the small TV that Bella had set up in the sunroom.

"I know *of* him. You know, nod when I see him, and so on. We aren't pals or anything."

At the foot of the stairs Wade bent to greet Maxie, who'd gotten up. The German shepherd was even more imposing-looking now than he had been when I first met him: thick, wolflike pelt, huge dark paws the size of softballs, and those amazing eyes, whiskey-colored and so intelligent that they practically looked human.

"Hey, buddy." Wade crouched by the dog, who tipped his head queryingly. "How's life in dog world?"

Maxie let out an expressive sigh and put his chin on Wade's knee.

"That good, huh?" Wade smoothed the fur between the dog's ears. "Well, don't worry. You just stay here with us and we'll take care of you until your own human gets better, okay?"

The canine's ears pricked up as if he understood, and we all walked together out into the kitchen, where Bella was putting the finishing touches on a plate of sandwiches.

"Take one," she urged me, so I did, plus one of the pickles that she'd made from some of the tiny cucumbers just now showing up on the vines in the garden.

"You eat?" I asked Wade around a mouthful. I was famished, I realized, and Ellie probably was also. He nodded, sipping coffee as Bella poured lemonade and handed me a glassful.

"Yup," Wade replied, heading for the utility closet in the back hall.

"You girls," Bella began, "need to take care of yourselves if you're going to . . ."

She let the words trail off. In the dim glow of the kitchen night-light, her rawboned face was pinched with fatigue and worry.

"How is he?" I asked, because of course she was worried about my dad. I finished the second glass of lemonade, refused a third.

In the hall Wade rooted through the utility closet. Bella looked grim. "Fine," she said. "The dog helps."

Her face crumpled, ugly with tears. "But he thinks he's dying, and if he is, he insists that he wants to do it here. That he won't go back to the hospital no matter what. So now if he does get sicker again, I don't know how I'm going to manage."

She broke down, sobbing without sound. I put my arms around her thin body, all sinew and long, ropy muscles.

"Bella. Don't worry about that now, okay?" Since my father met Bella and married her, he'd gotten a new lease on life. But he was an old man, much older than my late mother, and in the end it was up to him how long that life lasted, it seemed to me.

How long, and how he would relinquish it. I took Bella by the shoulders and held her away from me.

"Because he's fine now, right?" I said. She nodded tearfully. "So let's just go with that for the moment, okay?"

She dug in her apron pocket for a tissue, which she extracted and blew hard into. "All right. I guess I'll have to."

The dog nudged her hip worriedly. "And you," she scolded him, "you're lying down on the job already. You go watch him."

His eyes narrowed comprehendingly and at this her expression softened. "Go on, now," she said again kindly, and he trotted off, his big black toenails clicking dutifully into the sunroom.

"Your dad's already in love with the beast," she said as the dog leapt back up onto the daybed with a soft, recognizable *thump.* Then came my dad's creaky old voice greeting the animal.

"It'll be a sad day," Bella added worriedly, "when it has to go back." To its owner, she meant: Marla Sykes, now lying in a hospital bed.

"Like I said," I told Bella, "let's do tonight, and we'll see what new challenges come up tomorrow, shall we?"

Wade returned from the hall closet, carrying a zippered tote. Standing in the kitchen doorway with it slung over his shoulder, wearing a battered ball cap with the words *Guptill's Excavating* lettered on it in red script, he could've easily been just another one of the local good old boys, headed out for an evening fishing trip.

But he wasn't. At my look he grinned tigerishly at me and gestured for me to come along.

"Not only do I know him," he said as we went out and the

door closed behind us, shutting off the light from inside, "but if I'm not mistaken, I also know where the guy lives."

It was full dark outside, with the wind blowing steadily and a line of clouds streaming over the thin, uncertain-looking moon.

"Where are we going?" Wade drove this time and I carried the snack that Bella had put together for Ellie: sandwiches and so on.

"Told you," he said. "I know where he lives and I want a word with this fellow."

Uh-oh. He looked more determined than angry. But on Wade, determined was plenty. He was the kindest, fairest man I'd ever met, but he was an Eastport kid at heart: born here, grew up here, got his values here.

And he still had them. The values, I mean. So you didn't mess with his wife.

You just didn't.

"His name's Lenny Crenshaw, lives out on the old Toll Bridge Road," said Wade.

We cruised past the IGA, where the floats for the Fourth of July parade were already lined up. In the dancing light of campfires and barbecues set up around the parking lot, the float teams were having a hot dog roast despite the windy conditions.

"And he'd have been out in that tiny boat on the water because why, again?"

We'd stopped at the Chocolate Moose. Ellie was there, baking steadily and, to my surprise, cheerfully, especially when she saw the sandwiches I'd brought for her.

"I talked to George, and he's fine," she'd told me through a mouthful, "and to Lee at her summer camp, and *she's* fine."

She'd looked up at me. "So that means I'm fine. Go on and do what we need done."

With a guilty pang over what I *wasn't* telling her, I'd given her a grateful hug, glanced around at the well-organized kitchen (chocolate curls here, batter bowl there, wafer crumbs in a crisp, tasty mountain over *there*), then hurried back to the car and Wade.

Now the Bay City gas station and the big new Baptist church on the corner receded in our rearview mirror as we rounded the long Route 190 curve out of Eastport.

"Let me make sure I've got this straight," I said. "The GPS tracker George put in Ellie's boat . . . it works. It's operating, I mean. It's just not being monitored."

Because if it wasn't working, it made no practical difference whether I told her about it or not. But no such luck.

"Yep. That's my understanding, anyway," Wade said. "Have you talked any more to this Miss Halligan person yet?"

I shook my head. "I'm not sure what to say to her. Like I told you, I think it was her creeping around in Marla's house when Ellie and I were there. But I have no idea why."

"Maybe she was looking for the money you found in Marla's cellar?" Wade suggested as another deer followed the first one.

"Yeah, maybe. It's all," I said, exhaling, "just too mixed-up for me at this point." I glanced in the rearview mirror again.

He nodded agreement as we passed the airport and the town garage. The rearview remained empty.

"Nobody behind us," he observed mildly.

"Good." I felt myself relax a little. On top of everything I still couldn't shake the watched feeling I'd been having; right now I felt safe, but the truth was that a man was dead and a woman lay injured, maybe even fatally.

And even though I didn't know why, somebody did. We rounded the sharp turn at Carryingplace Cove where the clam flats, fully exposed at low tide, gleamed under the cloud-veiled moon.

Another sigh escaped me. "The thing is, if we tell the state cops or even just Bob Arnold about the cash, they might decide it's all about that. That someone killed Muldoon over something to do with the money, and hurt Marla because she knew about it."

Which wouldn't clear Ellie, especially since *we* now had some of the cash ourselves. Maybe she hadn't had any connection to it before, but she did at this point.

"The money's in the freezer at the Moose," I answered Wade's unspoken question. "We didn't know where else to put it."

He nodded as we waited for several carloads of people with out-of-state plates headed to Eastport, their headlights blurry in the gathering mist. The forecast, apparently, was still either not being noticed or just not being believed.

Then we turned left onto Toll Bridge Road in the thickening darkness. "Wild out here," Wade observed, and he was right.

At this end of the island wind lashed the low salt marshes, bending the cattails sharply sideways and sending spray up onto our windshield. Ahead on both sides of the road, small houses and sheds hunkered down under swaying evergreens.

"Tide comes up high enough, this'll all be awash," Wade said. "You heard anything more about getting the visitors out of town?"

I told him about what Bob had said, and how oblivious Millie had seemed. "She said she'd get people out safely before the real weather hits, but I haven't seen any action on it."

Wade slowed between a meticulously well-cared-for double-wide mobile home on one side of the road and a factory-built ranch with a pressure-treated deck, a two-car garage, and a wheelchair ramp on the other. Both yards were thickly studded with small American flags, each lit by its own small solar-powered lamp, as if legions of garden gnomes were also celebrating the Fourth of July.

"Here we are." Wade turned in at the next driveway under a

canopy of spruce boughs, the wind whipping their tops together high above us with a sound like loud, tuneless whistling.

Or screaming. Gleams of light showed ahead, leading us toward a rough clearing that held a snowmobile with a blue tarp torn half off its ravaged seat; an all-terrain vehicle so mudspattered, I couldn't tell what color it was; and an ancient Honda sedan whose lidless gas filler pipe was stuffed with an old rag.

The Honda's right rear window had been replaced with a sheet of transparent plastic. The rear axle was up on concrete blocks.

None of this seemed auspicious. Still: "I'm coming in, too."

Wade looked doubtful. "Let me just—"

"Talk to the guy, I know." I got out of the car. At the far end of the clearing sat a small teardrop trailer. Light struggled from it through a smeary window; the music had less trouble getting out, maybe because it was loud enough to smash concrete.

"But you want one thing and I want another," I said. "Let's work on it together, okay?"

Suddenly a large dog shot out of the brush at the back of the property; coming at us, the animal resembled a buzz saw on four long, fast-moving legs.

"Darn," I said, wishing I hadn't left my cell phone in the car's charger. At first I thought maybe the dog didn't like Creedence, which was what was blasting out of the trailer at bloodcurdling volume, but when it got close and I noticed the look on its face, I figured it was probably hungry.

Or possibly it just thought we'd be tasty. Either way, Wade and I stopped short and the dog did, too. "Grrr," it said.

The trailer door flew open. "Fang!"

Of course the dog's name would be Fang. The creature slunk to his owner, then cringed sharply away from the leather leash the guy swung.

Luckily, he missed. Oh, I liked this guy a whole bunch already. "Don't you hit that dog!" I yelled, the words bursting out of me as I stomped toward the trailer.

"Jake." Wade hurried up behind me. "Jake, hold on."

But I was already at the porch steps—more of those stacked concrete blocks, actually—before he caught me.

"You hit that dog," I yelled, shaking Wade's hand off my shoulder, "and I'll break every damned bone in your stupid—"

"Didn' hit 'im." The guy peered owlishly at me. "Ain't even my dog," he said. "Damn thing won't leave, so I gotta feed 'im. Eats like a horse."

The guy was about thirty, with curly black hair and a two-day beard spreading patchily over his jaw like some dark fungus.

"Hey," he said, looking past me at Wade.

"Hey." Wade returned the greeting. "How're you doing tonight?"

"Fine." Roscoe kicked an imaginary pebble with the rotted-out toe of his leather boot. "What'cha want?"

From inside, someone insisted loudly that he had been born on the bayou. I wished heartily that he would go back there as Wade stepped briskly past me, took the leash out of Roscoe's hands, and gave the dog a pat.

"Hi, Fang. Good boy."

Whereupon Fang, far from eating Wade's arm off all the way to the shoulder, whined and sat.

"Dog ain't bad," said Roscoe. He was wearing a long-sleeved cotton waffle-cloth shirt and gray sweatpants.

"Got a big mouth, is all." He glanced back into the trailer, whose interior was all sepia-toned like an old photograph; after a moment and a whiff I realized it must be from cigarette smoke.

Lots of it. "You wanna go in?" Roscoe invited halfheartedly.

By then I'd have rather gone just about anywhere else. But Wade spoke up again: "Yeah, Roscoe. We'll come in for a minute."

The atmosphere inside was a pungent mixture of bacon

grease, old dog blanket, and the kind of ashtray that has about a quarter inch of tarry black gunk built up in it.

"Siddown," Roscoe invited, lowering the music's volume.

So my ears didn't start to bleed, after all. Tiny and low-ceilinged, the trailer had a small sink, a hot plate, and some cushioned benches to sit on; that is, if you didn't fear skin infections.

But what the hell, I was up to date on my shots, so I searched for a space amidst the clutter: lots of old socks, a harmonica, a cardboard box filled with a bunch of the bright-hued plastic-netting bait bags that the lobster fishermen used. . . .

Roscoe saw me examining them and a shy grin twisted his face. "I like the colors," he confessed.

The dog jumped up beside me and settled into the fleece-lined side of an oilcloth foul-weather slicker.

"They're very pretty," I said. "Do you collect them?"

"Nope." He'd been doing something at the sink; now he thrust a jelly glass full of something purple at me.

Grape soda, I realized when I sniffed it. "My favorite," he said with a crooked grin.

"Roscoe makes those bags, don't you, Roscoe?" Wade lifted his own glass in a *to-your-health* gesture. "Gets paid for 'em."

"Yup. Fifty cents each." (*"Fitty,"* he pronounced it.) On the diminutive dinette table lay a roll of orange netting, a sturdy pair of scissors, and a heavy-duty stapler.

"I go clamming, too," Roscoe added proudly. "Pays my way. That an' my disability money. I ain't," he declared with a lift of his shaggy head, "no moocher."

"No," I said softly through the lump in my throat. Roscoe was obviously doing his best in hard circumstances, and my heart went out to him suddenly. "No, I can see that you are not."

Wade spoke again. "So listen, Roscoe, you're not in trouble, okay? That's not why we're here."

Roscoe looked frightened at the mere mention of trouble, his not-quite-right eyes rolling wildly toward the door.

"I mean it," Wade said earnestly. "Honest, Roscoe, we're not here for anything bad."

Roscoe glanced doubtfully up at him from beneath thick, dark eyebrows that met in the middle. "Pinky swear?"

Wade offered a crooked pinky; Roscoe hooked it with his own. "Okay, then," he said, satisfied, and Wade went on:

"So remember when it was so foggy last night? Were you out in it?"

So much had happened in the past twenty-four hours, it felt like a week. If I thought about it, I'd realize how tired I was. So I didn't. Wade turned to me while Roscoe hesitated. "See, Roscoe's kind of a water rat. He doesn't care when or what kind of weather, he just likes being in his boat. Don't you, buddy?"

Roscoe nodded, purple soda staining his ravaged grin. "I was! I was out on the OCEAN BLUE!" he yelled exultantly.

But then his grin vanished and he peered suspiciously at us again. "Why?" he demanded.

I was glad Wade had come, not because I was frightened of Roscoe or of Fang, either—I wasn't now, not even a little bit— but because I'd never have gotten anywhere with him.

Wade went on: "Hey, Roscoe, by any chance did somebody pay you to try to scare someone? I mean if they did, it's okay."

Shaking his head stubbornly, Roscoe frowned. "No. No. No."

Wade leaned back, his body language conciliatory all at once, and I instinctively did the same. Roscoe was getting agitated, rocking and thumping his knees with his fists.

"Or," Wade ventured gently, "you got paid to be a lookout? Like, a guy might've wanted privacy out there, maybe?"

What Ellie had said about our island being a smuggler's haven popped into my mind. Roscoe looked stubborn; nevertheless, Wade persisted.

"Only maybe when someone did come, you went one better than you'd been told and tried chasing the intruder off?"

Roscoe's lower lip thrust out mutinously. "I was just doing a good job, is all. Ain't no crime. Didn't hurt nobody. I always," he declared, "do a good job."

I shot Wade a grateful look. But he wasn't finished.

"No. It's not a crime. Not," he amended as Roscoe glanced skeptically at him, "anything you need to worry about."

Roscoe shrugged, picking resentfully at a ragged cuticle. "So?"

"It was me, Roscoe," I spoke up. "The one you swerved at and nearly hit out there. What were you doing, trying to swamp us?"

He couldn't have; his boat was too small and the Bayliner was too big. But in the darkness he might've misjudged that, or maybe he really was just trying to scare us.

"Anyway," I went on, spreading my hands, "I'm not mad at you. I get that you need to make a living, someone offered you a job so you took it, that's all. No crime there. No harm, no foul, right?"

Roscoe nodded, then realized what he'd agreed with and looked unhappy. Outside the little trailer, the wind howled and whined in the trees.

"All I want to know is why," I finished. "Like, was it about me specifically? Do I have to watch out for somebody now?"

Because Roscoe really seemed like a decent kid. Physically older than his mental and emotional age, clearly, but not a jerk.

Well, except for the leather leash. He saw me looking at it. "I never hit Fang with it. He just thinks I will."

This time I believed him. Fang's original owner had probably put the cringe into the dog, not Roscoe.

"Anyway," Roscoe said, looking at his boots just as something banged hard against the outside of the trailer.

A blown-down branch, probably. Wade stood by the open door, looking out into the windy darkness as Roscoe went on:

"I don't know who it was," he said, "just that I was supposed to chase off anybody who got too close to—"

The window behind him exploded inward.

*   *   *

"Go, go, go!" Wade grabbed my shoulder in one big hand and Roscoe's in the other, then hustled us out. I missed my footing on the concrete block steps and came down the wrong way on my ankle.

"Damn." I let Wade drag me along, not really knowing which way we were going and not able to care through the bolts of hot anguish shooting up my leg.

"Ow. Ow. Ow," Roscoe repeated pitifully, hunched over and stumbling, and, of course, my cell was still back there in the car's charger.

Wade hauled Roscoe up from where he'd fallen. "Come on, bud, you've got to . . . Damn."

"What?" I found my little penlight at last, but its tiny beam wasn't much help as we scrambled between tree trunks and wiggled through brush, vines, and brambles.

"He's bleeding," Wade said. "Come on, Roscoe, I'll help you. You can make it, it's only a little farther."

But I had no idea if either of those latter things was true, and from the look on Wade's face when I cast the penlight's beam over it briefly, he didn't, either.

"Ow," Roscoe whispered, which I thought wasn't a good sign. When I turned the beam toward him, I saw that I was right.

"Oh." The word felt punched out of me. Roscoe's whole shirt front was sodden with dark blood, his right arm streaming with it.

But he was upright again; so far, anyway. Wade waved us to a halt and stood listening. No sound came from behind us. Then:

Wham! A load of what had to be buckshot slammed the tree trunk a few feet to my left, splinters flying in the same instant as the explosion of the gunfire hammered my eardrums.

Wade slung Roscoe's good arm over his own shoulder and

ran; I caught up with them and got under Roscoe's other arm, hoisting him.

"Where . . ." Roscoe gasped. "Where's . . ." Fang burst out of the brush at us, running full-tilt through a small, bare clearing that suddenly looked familiar.

Or what little I could see of it did, anyway. "Hey," I said. "I've been here before, I think."

I squinted around, my eyes finally adjusting to the darkness enough to make out more than general shapes.

"Ellie and I were here picking blackberries," I said, "not too long ago."

Because if you want to know what heaven is really like, try a blackberry-and-chocolate baked custard with real whipped cream and a candied violet on top.

I did not, however, want to *visit* heaven anytime soon, so I peered around at my surroundings very intently.

"That way," I said at last. Straight ahead stood an old gray concrete pillar, all that was left of a once-complete building of some kind.

"The old Exxon station," Wade commented. "It's from when the federal government had a base out here, right after the war when the Seabees were going to build a power project."

World War II, he meant, and it hardly seemed pertinent, except of course for the fact that gas stations were usually built near roads.

"I think we go that way," I said, pointing.

Nothing more came from behind us, which meant either that whoever had shot at us thought he had hit us and was going away, or he didn't think so, and was hunting us still.

"Run," Wade said. "I mean it, Jake, you've got to get out to the road if you can and get help for Roscoe."

Then a sound did come. *Click-kachunk!* It was the unmistakable sound of a shell being racked into a shotgun's firing chamber.

"*Run!*" Wade dragged Roscoe behind the battered old concrete pillar; meanwhile, Fang took off into the trees again. I followed, figuring the dog might know a shorter way to the road than I did.

Or any way to it, actually; now that I was alone, the woods seemed thicker and more confusing. Struggling along with my ankle shooting darts up my leg, I felt a target prickling on my back.

My breath came in harsh gasps. But the fear was worse: Was someone watching? Was our attacker still behind me, just waiting for a clear shot?

I didn't know, and all I could do was stagger forward while overhead the wind flung the branches wildly about. The bruised evergreens filled the air with their sharp perfume and pinecones dropped around me like small bombs.

And all the while I kept thinking I'd hear that shotgun fire again. Or I wouldn't, because I'd already be dead.

"Oof." My ankle gave up and then it went out from under me entirely, dropping me. Fang appeared, nosing me anxiously as I lay there in the weeds, cursing through gritted teeth.

Exhaustion nearly swamped me. But if I gave up, whoever had that shotgun would win. And I'm no hero, but by that point I was so mad, I'd have grabbed that damned gun and threaded our attacker onto its barrel the long way, if I could have.

The image cheered me. I summoned up similar ones—worse ones, even. And to my surprise they helped.

All right, then, damn it; if you can't walk, crawl. So I did, on hands and knees over the forest floor prickly with sharp stuff and sticky with pinesap.

Fang paced alongside me. Until: *Pop! Pop. Pop-pop!*

I froze; the dog too. It wasn't the shotgun. The new sound was something else, a little handgun or a small rifle, perhaps.

Then came the fast thump-and-rustle of someone running

hard very nearby, followed by the roar of a car starting up, peeling out with a shriek of tires, and speeding away.

Finally I heard sirens approaching.

"That's all he said? That somebody told him to keep people out of that area?"

I leaned back tiredly in my chair. The siren had been Bob Arnold, summoned to the scene where we'd been getting shot at by a passerby who'd heard the gunfire and called it in.

Now Bob sat across from me at the butcher-block table in my big old kitchen, his hands clasped around a coffee cup.

"Yup," Wade answered Bob's question. Wade had a beer in front of him; I wanted one, but a single sip of alcohol would've knocked me out.

"And you know," Wade said, squinting as he searched for the right words, "Roscoe is kind of a . . . well . . . He's not exactly . . ."

Bob brushed a strand of pale hair back up over his forehead, looking disgusted at all that had happened in the past few hours.

"Yeah, I know Roscoe. He's decent enough."

At the moment Roscoe was at the hospital thirty miles from here in Calais, the nearest market town to our north.

Bob had taken him there. "His only worry, other than getting shot in the shoulder and not quite bleeding out from it, was for the dog," the police chief said now of the challenged young man.

"He'll have worries later, though," Bella put in from where she stood by the sink.

She was right. That trailer of Roscoe's was primitive but you could bet he paid rent on it, and the medicines he'd need after getting shot wouldn't be coming out of a Cracker Jack box, either.

Also he wouldn't be able to work. Bella went to check on my

dad while I made a mental note to try getting a fund-raiser going for Roscoe. A spaghetti supper, maybe, and the Moose could cater dessert; I knew Ellie would want to be a part of it.

If she wasn't in jail. The Fourth of July cake auction was just forty-eight hours away, which was scary enough. But after that the state cops would descend upon us, most likely with an arrest warrant if we didn't come up with some way to avoid it. The thought sent a thrill of anxiety through me as Bella returned from the sunroom.

"How is the girl, Marla?" she wanted to know.

Hearing the name, the German shepherd padded in and went around the table greeting everyone, his tail wagging hopefully.

Bob Arnold smacked the heel of his hand to his head. "Right. I meant to tell you about Marla. She's awake."

"Good," said Bella, but the conflict on her face was clear. Because when Marla recovered, she'd want her dog back, wouldn't she?

And that would be bad; to my dad, Maxie had been a blessing. He'd taken on the dog's regular walk schedule and was now even talking about going all the way around the block with the animal.

Fang, meanwhile, was hanging out in Bob's squad car for the present. "But Marla's not exactly alert," Bob added, and Bella relaxed a little. "I went in to see her after I left Roscoe in the ER."

Unfortunately, none of us could describe the car that sped off from the shooting scene. Right now a couple of Bob's more junior officers were taping off Roscoe's trailer with yellow crime scene tape and looking with their flashlights for spent shotgun shells.

"I was on my way up to visit her when your thing happened, in fact," Bob went on. "But she's not fit to be questioned yet. Heck, she doesn't even know her name."

He got up. Of course, I'd told him about the money that

Ellie and I had found in Marla's basement. I'd had no choice; people were getting hurt over this, suddenly.

Now, after telling me very firmly not to poke into any of this anymore, he went back to his policing duties in Eastport, while Wade went upstairs to take another shower and Bella returned to my dad's side again.

Not much later I took a shower also, alone this time, the hot water stinging in the cuts and scrapes I'd gotten out at Roscoe's. Then, after applying more coffee and clean clothes, I put on an elastic ankle wrap pulled as tightly as I could stand it.

The pain was manageable . . . if you're the type who likes deep, penetrating misery. But what the heck, I figured a little exercise might help loosen the injury.

Also I was wide awake, my brain percolating with the kind of alertness you can only get by having a shotgun fired at you. So I scribbled a note, then slipped out of the house and hobbled on down to the Chocolate Moose. Ellie, who regularly slept only about five hours out of each twenty-four, had managed a couple of cat-naps in my absence. But now she was back in our bakery's kitchen working on the dratted cheesecakes.

The wind had dropped off abruptly again, the late-night hush like a held breath. Downhill on Key Street between the houses with their porch lights still on and their front steps flickering with citronella candles, kids up long past their bedtimes scampered in the yards.

A cherry bomb went off somewhere nearby and I jumped before realizing that it wasn't another shotgun. On Water Street a band playing Cajun dance music rollicked at the end of the fish pier, under strings of multicolored Christmas lights.

"Zydeco," said Ellie, setting coffee in front of me as soon as I got inside the Moose. "It's called zydeco music."

The smell of baking cheesecakes, mingled with the heady aroma of melting chocolate, was so powerful that it was like a drug; I sagged in the little cast-iron café chair.

"Great," I said. "Have they got a catchy tune about spilling your guts to the cops, by any chance?"

On her way back to the kitchen, where she was shaving more chocolate—you have to stop every so often and put the chocolate in the refrigerator or it melts all over your hands— she paused.

"Everything?" She turned to me.

"Yeah. Pretty much. Most of it." I described to her the many delights of my early evening.

"I'm sorry, Ellie, but after all that, I had to tell Bob about all the money we found. And our boat trip, too. And I know George isn't going to be pleased."

In reply, she agreed that anytime shotguns started firing in a person's vicinity, all bets were off. I summarized what Roscoe had said—that someone had paid him to establish a privacy zone out there, and that's why he'd menaced us.

"And I'm pretty sure somebody tampered with Wade's truck," I finished.

I plucked a chocolate-covered pretzel, one of the half-dozen kinds of treats that Ellie had made while waiting for cheese-cakes to bake, from the display case.

"And that's all the news so far," I finished, following her to the kitchen with my snack.

The whole trick, when you are making chocolate pretzels, is dipping them twice. "More mayhem, but no more answers than we had before," I said.

"Roscoe's not saying who paid him?" She checked the clock and drew two more completed cakes from the oven.

"The shooting started before Wade got the chance to ask him," I replied. "And afterward Roscoe was in no shape for answering questions."

The cake pans' shiny sides gleamed in the kitchen's overhead fluorescent lights; then the cakes' beautiful smooth tops emerged into view, lightly browned and without any cracks.

"Lovely," she said, and set the pair of gorgeous objects on a shelf away from the oven, where they could cool further. Then:

"All right, I guess I can face George. Like you said, he won't be happy. Even though," she added, "he'd have done the same thing, under the circumstances."

I took another bite of pretzel, considering whether or not to give Ellie some extra ammo for the upcoming talk with her husband. After all, Wade's half of our bargain—that I wouldn't tell Ellie about George's tracking device, if Wade didn't tell George what Ellie and I had done—was already broken.

But Wade hadn't broken it, had he? So I didn't see how my obligation to keep my promise to him had changed.

Plus George wasn't home yet and wouldn't be for another few days; meanwhile, here in Eastport, Ellie already had plenty to worry about.

So I decided I'd just go on keeping my mouth shut for now, and told her about Marla waking up in the hospital instead. But heavens, didn't I still feel just terrible about it.

"Great," Ellie said about Marla's recovery. "I'm glad she's better, for her sake and for ours."

She began rolling crumbs for the final cheesecake crusts. She was still doing only two at a time since, as she said, the oven's interior got too humid if she baked more.

"Because not to be too hard-hearted about it," she continued, "but without Marla we've got a supply problem, don't we?"

I hadn't even thought about that. "Not much we can do now except cross our fingers, though, is there?" I answered. "But what I didn't tell Bob was about the photographs," I went on. "He'd have wanted to see them, and we don't have them, and I think that would look even more like we're just trying to muddy the waters."

Ellie nodded emphatically. "It's like all the rest of it, we need actual facts that we can prove, not just bits and pieces that don't even fit together in any way we can explain."

"Right," I agreed, hearing my own voice tremble slightly, and still thinking about the secret I was keeping from Ellie. I felt lower than swamp muck about it, as Bella would have put it. Why, Ellie had delivered her baby on my kitchen floor, for heaven's sake.

Not deliberately—I'll tell you the whole story some other time—but still. And we'd been through a lot of other things together, too.

For example, one time when he'd driven up here to torment me, Ellie congratulated my ex-husband on how flexible he must be to be able to get his head so far up there, and to my astonishment it actually shut him up for a minute.

That was the day my friend Ellie became my personal hero, and nothing since had changed my opinion.

"Don't worry, Jake," she said now, misunderstanding my look. "It's all going to be okay," she pronounced, her voice full of the sort of buoyant confidence I'd always loved in her. Saying this, she finished patting the chocolate-crumb crust into the second freshly greased and cocoa-dusted pan, then poured in the batter. Sliding both filled pans into the oven, she looked at the clock and set the timer on her wristwatch.

Finally she snapped off the shop lights and fans.

"Okay, we can leave them for a while," she said, and by then I couldn't take it anymore.

"Listen, Ellie." Wade would just have to understand that I couldn't keep secrets from her, I just couldn't.

"There's something I haven't told you," I said.

She wasn't listening, though, turning to me instead with a troubled expression of her own.

"Jake. There's something I need to tell you," she said.

And then she did tell. And oh, boy, was it ever a doozy.

I couldn't believe it. "What do you mean, your fingerprints are going to be found on the murder weapon?"

I stopped on the sidewalk outside the Moose. "Ellie, how could your fingerprints possibly be in the blood that was on that pastry needle?"

Because that's what she'd just said. From the parking lot down the street, a string of firecrackers went off in a *rat-a-tat* burst.

Ellie looked miserable. "I should have told you right away, I know. But I was so shocked, I couldn't, and then there just didn't ever seem to be a right time to say it."

We started walking. "Okay, I get it. But never mind that now, what you need to tell me is how it happened."

She shook her head, her pale curls gleaming in the light from the neon OPEN sign in the ice-cream shop's window.

"I can't. It's so outlandish that I'm afraid even *you* won't believe me."

Inside the shop a long line of late-night ice-cream wanters stretched out the door; so much for Millie's promise to get the tourists off the island while the getting was still good.

"What? Ellie, of course I'll believe you."

Tired as we were, neither of us wanted to go home, so we started uphill past the breakwater and the Coast Guard station. Food carts lined the pier on both sides, forming a sort of makeshift carnival midway: blooming onions, sausage rolls, and that ever-popular, only-in-Eastport special delicacy, smoked salmon on a stick.

"Ellie, please," I said. "There's nothing you could tell me that I wouldn't swear was true, simply because *you'd* said it."

Her eyes brimmed with tears. "Yeah, you say that now."

I'd never seen her like this before. We strode on uphill past sprawling Queen Anne houses perched magnificently at the backs of wide green lawns. In its heyday Eastport had been a rich man's town: lumber tycoons, shipping barons, sardine-canning magnates.

"All right," she gave in at last with a huge sigh. "But if you *don't* believe me, I forgive you in advance."

"Deal," I told her as four teenaged boys rattled by on their skateboards in a clatter of wheels against sidewalk. It hit me again that no one seemed worried about any bad weather.

But that thought faded fast as Ellie began speaking. "First of all, I didn't kill him, of course."

That she thought she had to mention this at all sent a chill through me. I opened my mouth to say so.

"No, no," she interrupted. We passed the ferry landing and then the Chowder House restaurant, built out onto a wharf strung with bright paper lanterns. Cars filled the parking lot and music drifted from the deck area stretching over the water.

"I have to say that first, because . . . well, I already told you about Muldoon hassling me," she said. "That night, him coming into the shop, arguing and accusing. And you know, he just made me so *mad.*"

I did know. I said nothing as she went on: "But then he left, finally, just the way I said he did."

Her quick, anxious step slowed slightly as she got into her story, and even in the gloom between streetlights, I could sense her relief, that she was telling it at last.

"Then on the way out I spied that pastry needle in the trash, where you'd tossed it, and I thought I'd ask George to straighten it in his workshop. Because they're expensive, those needles."

Right, and the Moose was still on a tight budget. She'd have done it herself, but George was particular about his tools.

"So I laid it on the counter by the cash register, meaning to pick it up when I left, but then when I went out, I was still so mad at Matt Muldoon that I forgot about it."

"You locked the door?" Behind one of the houses we passed, a backyard bonfire sent orange flames leaping, lighting a family party now sliding into sozzled cheerfulness, by the sound of it.

"Yes, I rattled it, just to be sure," she said.

I was starting to have an idea where all this must be going.

We reached Hillside Cemetery and stopped at the gated entrance; the gate stood open, as it had for years, and the path ahead led between old marble stones slanting this way and that into the darkness beyond.

"But on my way home I remembered again," said Ellie. "So I went back to the shop. To get the needle, you see. And that time I had to fiddle with the door practically forever before I could get in."

Because the old, stubbornly uncooperative lock had still been in it, I realized. Her pale face was earnest in the thin, yellow gleam of the last streetlight before the cemetery's gloom.

"When I walked in, the pastry needle was on the floor. I thought I'd brushed it off the counter by accident. I didn't even see it at first. I just went out to the kitchen. I did switch the lights on out there to double-check that I'd turned off the oven."

She always turned off the oven. She always double-checked, too. "Okay," I said. "Then what?"

But I already knew with bleak certainty what must be coming.

She let out a shaky sigh.

"I had turned the oven off, of course. Then on the way out again I saw it there on the floor, glimpsed it from the corner of my eye, because you know how the streetlight shines in and . . ."

She stopped, gathering herself. "So I picked it up, not even thinking about how it got there. But it was all sticky and yucky-feeling, and that made me change my mind about keeping it."

A grimace creased her face. "So I dropped it back into the kitchen trash bin, and then I did leave."

She sucked in a breath. "When I got home and saw my hands, there was some red stuff on them. But even then it never occurred to me that it might be . . . I mean, why would I think that?"

Why, indeed. We started back toward the Moose in silence. By now in the backyards the bonfires were dying down and the voices of the cheerful, beer-buzzed people had quieted considerably; only a few overtired kids fussed in the shadows.

"So you didn't see him. Muldoon's body, I mean." The wind was rising again, gusting in puffs, but not gentle ones, more like sly shoves. A raindrop smacked my face, and then another.

"Jake, it's not that I didn't see him. He wasn't there. He just wasn't. I couldn't have missed him." She sighed deeply. "You don't believe it, do you? Why would you? I can barely believe it myself. He must've been dead, but—"

We passed the small white-clapboarded *Eastport Tides* building overlooking the boat basin. Down there no holiday atmosphere prevailed; instead men and women were on the fishing boats stowing away gear and making sure their lines were secure.

They at least understood that a storm was coming. "I believe you, Ellie. Honestly, I do."

Down the bay lightning flashed sullenly like bombs going off on the horizon. "The problem," I went on, "is that the needle was still there in the shop for you to find, but . . ."

She nodded emphatically. Ahead of us the Chocolate Moose sign over our shop's doorway swung in the breeze.

". . . somehow Muldoon wasn't."

Eight

Back inside the Moose, Ellie rushed to the oven to check that the temperature in it hadn't deviated by even half a degree.

But I went directly to the kitchen worktable, where I'd found Muldoon dead, leaning against it with his arms outstretched and his head jammed down into the chocolate warmer.

The cops had examined everything in here already. But they hadn't known what the place was like normally, of course; whether or not there were any scratches in the fresh floor wax that Bella had applied only a day earlier, for instance.

"What are you doing?" Ellie peered through the oven's window to check on the health and welfare of the pair of cakes baking in there. I crouched behind her to peer anglewise at the floor in the bright fluorescent light.

"Well, we can be sure of one thing. If he was already dead, then he didn't walk anywhere, did he?" I asked.

That pastry needle hadn't gotten onto the floor by itself, either. Someone had placed it there, ready for someone else to put her hands on it.

And deposit her fingerprints. Or so I now believed: "So

someone must've dragged or carried him," I said, squinting at the floor's gleaming waxed surface.

And sure enough, a pair of faint scrapes marred Bella's fresh wax job. The drag marks, because that's what they were, obviously, led from the worktable across the floor to the cellar trapdoor.

"Oh, for heaven's sake," I said. "Of course."

Wind rattled the shop windows as I hauled up the trapdoor by its canvas handle; because we were a commercial establishment, the handle was tucked under a piece of loosened linoleum so as not to be a tripping hazard.

I peered down. The fuse box hung on the wall at the foot of the stairs, just where the light from up here ended. But before that, on the top wooden cellar step, a dark stain had spread.

Ellie stared past me at it. "They didn't know this was here, did they? This trapdoor, the cops didn't see it because when it's shut, it's darned near invisible."

"Yep." Her husband George had refloored the whole shop for us before we opened, and the linoleum tile's perfectly matched edges fitted so smoothly together that you could easily miss them.

"So somebody stabs him *there.*" I pointed to where the heel marks on the floor began.

"It must've happened while I was on my way home." Ellie's face smoothed in thought. "And then I came back here."

She looked up at me. "But they couldn't have known I would. So why hide him?"

Because based on the timing, that's what must have happened. The bloody needle said he was dead by the time Ellie got back.

"Maybe whoever did it was still here. Saw you coming, through the front shop window. Saw you standing there, trying to get that door open."

The light dawned on her face. "And dragged him, fast. Got

him down through the cellar trapdoor and hustled down there with him, pulled the door back down on top of them both." She shivered. "What an awful few minutes it must have been, waiting down there with his body. Waiting for me to leave again."

A faint rustling sound came from next door, over on Miss Halligan's side of the wall, which divided our two shops; back here the wall was only framing and Sheetrock.

That reminded me: "Ellie, did you smell anything?" I pointed at the wall with Miss Halligan on the other side of it. It seemed the vintage-clothing seller never went home.

"That lemon cologne she wears, did you smell it when you came in here that night?" I pressed.

Not that I could imagine the elegant little shopkeeper skewering Muldoon, dragging him to the trapdoor, then hauling him back up and dragging him to the table and propping him against it.

And it turned out I probably wouldn't have to, because Ellie shook her head. "Nope. Not a whiff. And I think I would have."

As she spoke, Ellie took from the rack two of the cakes she'd baked earlier and covered them lightly with plastic wrap, then set them in the cooler; the proper aftercare of these elaborate baked delicacies is almost as important as the baking process itself.

"So," she said, sighing, contemplating the ingredients for the last pair of cakes to be baked tonight, "grab him, drag him, get him out of my sight fast. That must've been what they did."

"And hunkered down under that trapdoor with his dead body until you left again," I added, shivering. It was the creepy part, but it wasn't the cleverest part.

Wind-driven rain slammed the windows, then stopped as suddenly as it had begun. We were getting the early part of the storm intermittently, it seemed.

Later there'd be more. "Somebody tossed that needle onto

the floor," I said, "hoping someone else would pick it up. Someone like you or me, probably."

"And get fingerprints on it," Ellie agreed, taking a pitcher that I hadn't seen before from the cooler. "What a dirty trick."

From the pitcher she poured what I saw must be iced coffee into two tall glasses, dosing each liberally with cream and an ice cube. Then from a bakery bag she'd also produced from the cooler, she removed two muffins.

"Ellie, when in the world did you have time?"

She managed a smile. "This afternoon between naps, when you were out doing all that running around."

She'd made doughnut muffins, was what she'd done. I recognized *chocolate* doughnut muffins with plenty of chopped maraschino cherries mixed into them, and cherry juice in the chocolate frosting: *Zowie!*

I finished the first one, then bit into a second. To wash it down, I had a swallow of Ellie's own patented thousand-mile-an-hour juice, otherwise known as iced coffee.

She made it—I winced at the first sip, then eagerly took another—*strong*, and boy, did I ever need it. I felt, you should excuse the expression considering what had happened here recently, dead on my feet. "Um, Ellie?"

Through the doorway to the front of the shop, I could see rain splattering the window again, harder this time.

"Ellie, why are you powering us up like rocket ships, when we have only two more cheesecakes left to bake tonight?"

The muffins made me feel even guiltier about that damned GPS tracker. But now I decided that telling her about it could wait until morning; she wouldn't be using the boat tonight, and we both had enough upsetting things to think about.

"So you believe me?" she asked. She was ignoring my question about the coffee, which when Ellie does that means the answer needs parceling out gradually so I won't have a heart attack about it.

Which reminded me, I needed to get home so I could check on my dad. "Oh, of course, I believe you," I said. "I told you I did."

I finished my second muffin. "Why, I'll believe half-a-dozen unbelievable things before breakfast, if you're telling them."

A last gulp of coffee; then we shut the lights out and went outside. "Come on, though, why *have* you powered us up this way?"

Water Street was deserted, the musicians gone home. Bits of windblown trash moved on the wet pavement; Styrofoam cups and wadded napkins bounced and whirled. I fell into step beside her.

"Two things," she replied as we strode energetically toward my house. "Three, counting the dog."

She wouldn't say more, though, marching us past Wadsworth's Hardware Store, a flower shop called Petal Pushers, and the locked-up, tied-down tent city by the fish pier, still full of summer-holiday vendors occupying the parking lot with their trucks and trailers.

"Let's just enjoy the peace and quiet for a little while," she entreated, and I had to agree that we deserved it. So I didn't press her.

A couple of the pier-side pickup trucks looked ready to start hauling trailers, but no one was around and there was certainly no urgent action being taken. I wondered aloud about it, and Ellie shrugged.

"Lot of 'em are from around here," she said. "Probably they figure they're not far from home and they'll get there one way or another, never mind the weather."

They were on the wrong side of the causeway for that kind of optimism, though, as were the rest of the visitors to Eastport who hadn't yet skedaddled.

The night air felt heavy and loaded with silent menace. "I hope they're right," Ellie went on uneasily, seeming to feel it, too.

I glanced back over my shoulder, but saw nothing amiss in

the little waterfront business district. Still, I couldn't shake the sensation.

"What I hope is that whoever shot at me earlier isn't around here, somewhere, right now," I said, glancing back again.

"Unlikely." Ellie squared her shoulders defiantly. "For one thing, shooting you with me right here alongside you would spoil their plan, wouldn't it?"

Of framing her, she meant, and I thought she was probably right. Besides, the vehicle that had sped away from Roscoe's had been some kind of muscle car, to judge at least by the sound of the engine, and I hadn't heard any of those down here tonight.

Still, the thought hustled us along under a night sky racing with clouds, past the Waco Diner, with a few pickups still parked out in front of it, and the Happy Crab sports bar, with a few more.

Across the bay on Campobello an emergency vehicle raced along the shore road, its cherry beacon flaring at us through the dark. The wind whipped up even more as we hurried along the wet, gloomy street toward my house.

Inside, the hall lamp shed a golden glow and the night-light was on in the kitchen, where I found Maxie asleep. The big dog didn't lift his head when I came in, just nuzzled his long snout into his bed. But when I spoke to him, he followed me obediently out into the dark yard and back.

Only when I returned did I spy the note on the kitchen table, in Bella's jagged scrawl. From it I gleaned that my dad was still fine, and Wade was out for a few hours with his buddies. (There was a Major League Baseball game on TV tonight and Wade was the only one of his friends not rooting for the Red Sox, so it promised to be an exciting evening.)

Also Sam had called.

Suddenly I was wide awake. "What?" I blurted; Maxie glanced up at me. In the night-light's dim glow I squinted hard at the sheet of notepaper, as if it could somehow be made to give up more information.

But it didn't. Impatiently I scanned the kitchen: no blinking light on the phone machine, no saved messages on it, either . . .

And no hint from Bella's note as to what Sam had *said*. In the kitchen doorway Ellie appeared, listening calmly to my rant.

Why had he called *here*? Why not call my *cell phone*? What was he so *worried about* that he didn't want to *talk* to me about it?

Then she summed up the situation for me. "So we know Sam's alive, and he's able to call home, and he did."

I stopped short, feeling my blood pressure drop. "Oh. You're right, I hadn't thought of it that way."

I'd been on the point of going upstairs to the third floor to ask Bella about the call, even if it meant waking her.

"He'll call again, probably just misdialed the number, speed-dialed the house instead of my cell," I babbled, relieved at this new, much better interpretation of what had happened.

"Come on," said Ellie, dangling my car keys in front of me, and I was so befuddled by the number of things I'd seen and done in the past few hours that I followed her dumbly to my car without protest.

There'd been another note, too, from Wade. He'd left it on top of the refrigerator where no one else would look for it.

Be careful, it said, beside a heart with an arrow drawn through it.

And that was Wade, who wouldn't tell me what to do. Or what not to do, more to the point right now, any more than I'd tell him.

But I got the point: be careful. *Oh, you betcha,* I thought. *But whether that will be enough is another story,* I thought as I backed the car out.

"You haven't told me yet," I said to Ellie. "Where we're going, I mean."

There was no sense obsessing over Sam; as Ellie had pointed out, he was alive and that was good enough, for now. We pulled out onto Key Street just as the massive bell on the old Maine Seaman's Church tolled eleven, its low bongs vibrating heavily through the night.

Ellie didn't reply, just pointed. On Route 190, heading out of town at her direction, we encountered little traffic, except for the families of deer browsing by the road.

I forced back a yawn; my brain was still buzzed from the jet fuel disguised as coffee and from knowing that Sam had called, but my body was already begging for another jolt of the stuff.

As if she were reading my thoughts, she passed a thermos cup to me; the fragrance alone was enough to snap my eyes wide open again. "We're going to Calais," she said.

Which was not precisely an answer to my question, either. At eleven o'clock at night almost everything there would be closed, just as it was here. Everything, except . . .

The thermos coffee tasted of plastic, but it did the trick. Belted in beside me in the passenger seat, Ellie smiled as sudden enlightenment must've dawned on my face.

"That's right. The hospital is open because it always is," she said. "And even if she's not fully recovered yet, I think if we play our cards right, we can get in to see Marla."

She straightened in her seat. "And I want to," she declared. "Right now, before anyone else talks to her."

Which sounded right, actually. If we could find out who'd clobbered her, where the cash she'd had was from, and maybe even what was up with the photos of Miss Halligan on her computer . . .

Well, it was a lot to ask for, especially from an injured woman. But we needed it; I stepped on the gas.

Minutes later we crossed the long, curving causeway to the mainland, with the water on both sides spreading darkly and the sky low and threatening. At the Route 1 intersection we turned north toward Calais, the empty road winding narrowly between brackish inlets and towering spruces, gnarled orchards and old, abandoned-looking farms.

"I still don't see how we can get into a hospital patient's room at this hour," I said after a little while.

Ellie stared straight ahead, her back straight and her jaw set determinedly. "I've got a plan for that" was all she would say.

Well, all righty, then, I thought, but I trusted her. It was a key element of our success: we could depend on one another.

Which brought me around to that tracking device on her boat again. But I didn't want to tell her now: we were tired; George wasn't even here so she couldn't talk with him about it; and besides, we were on a mission.

I'd tell her, I decided, before she went out on the Bayliner again. That way she could disconnect the thing if she wanted.

"When we get there, just leave everything to me," she said. And since following her lead had very often in the past led to a positive outcome, despite my misgivings I didn't argue.

"Okay," I said instead, zooming uphill past the veterinary clinic on one side and the farm supply store on the other. After that came miles of widely separated barns, pastures, and wood-lots. An owl swooped down into my headlights and out again as I ducked reflexively, relieved that we hadn't hit it and hoping hard that we didn't encounter a moose. But then:

From the darkness behind me a pair of headlights material-ized in my rearview mirror.

"Meanwhile," said Ellie, screwing the cup back onto the thermos bottle, "I've been thinking about that trapdoor in the shop. I mean, about who knows it's there and who doesn't."

It was so obvious, I'd have hit the heel of my hand to my forehead if my fingers weren't just then extremely busy tight-ening around the steering wheel.

"Because the thing is, it's true, you can't tell it's there unless you look really hard."

The headlights in the rearview were catching up fast.

"So whoever stuffed Muldoon down there," Ellie continued, "already knew about it, I think."

Really fast. She looked over questioningly at me as the glare from the headlights lit our passenger compartment. "Jake?"

I reached for my phone, then decided against it and gripped the wheel with both hands as the headlights behind us blazed in the rearview mirror.

"Damn," I said, stomping the accelerator.

The dark road stretched vacantly ahead. Soon we'd reach the bridge stretching high over the cove at Red Beach, where a single bump from the side could send us flying over the guardrail.

I thrust the phone at Ellie. The nearest cop was miles from here, but I figured she might as well be ready. Meanwhile, I held on to that steering wheel like our lives depended upon it.

"Key in 911, but don't press 'call' yet," I told her. The S-curve ahead would be challenging, but not undoable.

"And tighten up that seat belt of yours," I added, pressing the gas down harder.

Because maybe whoever was riding our bumper really would try knocking us over the rail, sending us into the cold salt water below. But first . . .

First he'd have to catch us.

Careening downhill through the sharp curves and switchbacks before the bridge, I swiftly rehearsed everything I'd ever known about very fast driving.

Which was nothing. "Uh, Jake?" Ellie said tentatively again, her eyes huge in the glow of the dashboard lights.

Pulling away, I'd caught our pursuer by surprise, leaving him behind in a sudden burst of speed that startled even me.

The sensation was . . . interesting. Ellie craned around over the seat back. "Jake, he's catching up."

"Not for long." I slammed the gas pedal the rest of the way to the floor and we leapt forward like something shot out of a cannon. Unfortunately, though, while the car's engine supplied plenty of speed, the rest of the vehicle wasn't sure what to do with it all.

The slightest attempt at steering, for instance, produced a distinct floating sensation. It felt as if, at the slightest further encouragement, the car might achieve liftoff.

"You sure you don't want me to get help?" Her index finger poised over the cell phone's CALL button.

The road straightened. I thought very briefly that I might have a handle on all this. But then without warning a raccoon led a bunch of tiny baby raccoons out onto the roadway.

"No," I breathed. "No, no . . ."

Picked out in our headlights' glow, the small furry forms toddled adorably behind their mother. *I am not going to hit them*, I insisted to myself. *I am* not.

But there was no avoiding it. If I swerved, I'd lose control of the car. Nightmarishly, we hurtled toward the tiny animals and their mom.

Then, at the very last possible instant, she stopped suddenly. Turned lumberingly. Trundled bumblingly back to the road's gravel shoulder and on down into the ditch, with the little ones all hustling after her.

I zipped past the last one with mere inches to spare, just as our follower roared horrifyingly up behind us again, with a roar of the big engine in the muscle car he was driving.

A familiar roar. But I had no time to think about it; I was too busy steering and reviewing my past life, now passing before me like a film clip on fast-forward.

Ahead stretched the bridge. "Here we go."

I'd have glanced down at the speedometer, but I didn't dare take my eyes off the road. We crested the last hill, caught air at the top of it, and started down the other side with those damned headlights, big round ones like angry eyes, still on our tail.

"Faster," Ellie whispered. The fact that she wasn't shrieking it was vastly to her credit. "You've got to . . ."

I couldn't have agreed more; whoever this guy was—I assumed it was a guy, anyway—he'd never even heard the word "qualms."

But I had plenty. The car wasn't airborne, but it was gearing up for takeoff again as we shot around the last curve before the bridge. One last little downslope and we'd be on the wide, high-over-the-water span, and have I mentioned the concrete abutments at either end?

One of them being the one we were speeding toward now. Not that I liked playing daredevil this way, but we had no choice; if I slowed down, the guy behind us would rear-end us and I'd lose control.

And at this speed I couldn't pull over, either; one slip of the tires off the pavement's edge down onto the gravel shoulder and we'd be scrap metal.

The abutment *flew* toward us. Our attacker roared up fast and pulled alongside, engine howling. Then, just as I'd feared that he would, he swung sideways and slammed us the first time, jolting us hard toward the concrete pillar.

The steering wheel lurched as if trying to shake my hands off. I held on, the straight-ahead forwardness of our momentum now the only thing keeping us on the road. Beside me, Ellie let out a squeak.

Bang. He hit us again, harder and with an extra little weave-and-a-bobble swerve at the end of it this time. Our rear tires slid sideways and I fought the deadly urge to steer; instead, just as if we were slipping on ice, I eased off the gas gently and let the car's rear end carry us out to the end of our skid.

Only then did I steer into it, blessing the winter-driving lessons I'd learned in Maine. The car straightened, its weight and speed carrying us forward again; when it did, I slammed on the gas once more.

It was all I could do not to roll down the window and flip our attacker the bird as we roared away from him. But keeping us on the road was still occupying my whole attention, and, be-sides, I wouldn't do a rude thing like that.

Sure I wouldn't. "He's still back there," said Ellie as we sped through the village of Robbinston without flipping over or hit-ting a ditch. Only a few lights were still on in the houses as we zoomed out of the small seaside hamlet.

Next came another long, straight stretch of road. "Uh-huh," I said as I accelerated into it.

I was feeling pretty good, actually. Mostly from the massive amounts of adrenaline fizzing in my bloodstream, but still.

"Let's lose him," I said, eyeing the edge of the road for the driveway I knew would be there.

Praying he didn't know it, too. Almost . . . almost . . . *now*.

Cutting the headlights, I slowed down as suddenly as I could without losing control, then turned hard right onto a narrow dirt track that opened up suddenly between big trees.

There was a firing range back here. I'd visited it with Wade many times; he enjoyed target shooting on his days off. Huge tree trunks flew past us in the dark.

At last when I figured we'd gone far enough, we rolled to a stop; I held my breath, but saw no lights in the rearview mirror, even after waiting for several minutes.

So no one had followed us in. We'd turned before he crested the last hill, apparently, so he hadn't seen us do it.

"Whew," said Ellie, leaning back in relief.

"Uh-huh." I buzzed down the car windows and the sweet scent of pines floated in, mixed with the smell of seawater; the bay's northern reach was only a few hundred yards distant.

"He'll figure out what we did, though, if he hasn't already. He'll be back looking for us," I said.

And sure enough, in a few minutes more a pair of headlights appeared out on the paved road, moving slowly.

The headlights paused. A flashlight beam strobed the edge of the pavement; looking for our tire tracks, I supposed. But the way in had been dry and hard-packed; and in the darkness, if you didn't know the opening was here, it would be easy to miss the turnoff even if you were looking right at it.

The flashlight beam went away; I let out my breath. Then the headlights did, too, whereupon I swung the car around, put our own headlights back on, and pulled out onto the empty pavement, and minutes later we reached the town of Calais with no more trouble. The hospital was a one-story yellow-brick building with a big sliding-glass front entrance. I parked in the visitors' lot, empty except for one car, way at the back; not the car that had menaced us, I saw as we cruised slowly past it to make sure.

"You think whoever chased us just now was the same person who shot at you and Wade?"

We crossed the dark parking lot toward the hospital's glass front doors, my twisted ankle flaring with each step.

"Who else would it be?" That same person had fiddled with Wade's truck somehow, too; I couldn't prove it, but I was sure of it.

"First it was a boat that was after us, then a car . . . What's next, killer drones?" Ellie asked, trying for a light tone.

But she couldn't quite manage it, and neither could I. "Don't know," I said, "but if I tell you to run like hell at any time in the near future, just do it and ask questions later, okay?"

The glass doors slid soundlessly open as we approached. At this hour no one was at the information desk. The silent lobby smelled like carpet-cleaning solution and fresh floor wax.

Feeling like trespassers, we practically tiptoed toward a sign that read PATIENT AREA. The sign also said NO ADMITTANCE WITHOUT AUTHORIZATION, but I figured that was a little detail we'd deal with later.

"Can I help you?" a young woman in a hospital scrub uniform asked, looking up from the nurses' desk at the far end of the ward we'd just entered without authorization.

I let Ellie do the talking as I looked around: overhead fluorescent lights turned down low, heavy-duty industrial carpet, pale grass-cloth-covered walls. All up and down the corridor, doors to the darkened patient rooms stood half-open, and here and there a heart monitor beeped quietly.

I turned back to where Ellie and the nurse were nodding to one another. Somehow, despite the late hour, Ellie had gotten us past the visiting-hour restrictions.

"That way," the nurse said, pointing, "about halfway down. It's the one with the light on."

When we got there, I peeked in and saw that Ellie had been right about coming here. Maybe Marla Sykes had still been groggy from the beating she'd taken when Bob Arnold saw her earlier.

But she was awake now, with the bedside light on just as the nurse had said. Awake . . . and terrified, until she saw who we were.

"Jake, Ellie," she whispered, lifting a hand with an IV taped to it, then letting it fall. "Thank goodness you're here."

She looked like hell, half her hair shaved and iodine stains on her stitched scalp. A black eye, more stitches in her lip, and a big scrape down the back of her right arm completed the unhappy picture.

"Wow, Marla," I said inadequately. "How are you?" Of course, I felt stupid the minute I'd said it, but she laughed.

I mean, as well as she could. "Oh, just ducky. I mean, I hurt all over, but the whole not-being-dead thing is a big consolation. So there's, you know, that." Her tone turned anxious: "Is Maxie okay?"

I sat in a bedside chair; Ellie pulled up another one. "Yeah. He's fine. He's keeping my dad company."

I figured I'd loosen her up with a little chitchat before asking her why the hell she'd been lying to us, and what was going on. But Ellie had other ideas.

"Right, this is all great," she interrupted. "I mean I'm glad you're okay, and I'm really very sorry about all this." Her gesture took in the room, the IV bag with clear liquid dripping from it, and Marla's many injuries. "But we don't have much time," Ellie added. "I told the nurse out there that we're your cousins, that we drove up here from New York when we heard you were hurt."

I must've looked taken aback at this; Ellie made a face at me.

"Well," she said, "I had to tell her something, didn't I? But when I said it, I saw her face change. Like she didn't believe me, but she didn't know why."

"Damn," I said as I realized what must've happened; downeast Maine's a small world.

"Right." Ellie nodded. "She doesn't quite remember it yet, but she lives around here, you know? And any minute she's going to figure out she sold me a geranium at the school fair last May, and when she does . . ."

Just then the nurse in question came in with some pills in a plastic cup. I got up and moved toward the window; Ellie made a show of busily rooting through her bag for something.

The nurse glanced at each of us, but didn't say anything. I looked out the window again at the deserted parking lot.

Only it wasn't deserted anymore. A car was just now pulling in, swinging into one of the angled parking spaces out front.

The car's big chrome grill, round-as-a-marble signal lights, and double-barrel headlamps were the same ones that had menaced us on the way here.

The nurse went out again. Marla saw my expression. "What?" she demanded anxiously.

I crossed the room in what felt like a single bound. "Where's a good place to hide in this place, do you suppose?"

Taking her cue from me, Ellie found Marla's hospital robe and grabbed the wheeled IV pole.

"Sit," she ordered, positioning the wheelchair, and Marla obeyed.

The nurse was out in the hall, writing something on Marla's clipboard. Glimpsing us all coming out of the room together, she looked alarmed, as if she might decide to hit the emergency button on the wall a few feet away.

Before she could, though, I grabbed her, hustled back into the room and over to the window.

"See that car? Whoever's in it is about to come in here to finish what they started on our . . . our cousin." I waved at Marla. "To kill her, understand? Now where can we hide her?"

Like most nurses in my experience, this one was no fool. She made no argument, only gestured for us to follow her.

I glanced back across the room one more time; in the parking lot the big dark muscle car's inside lights were still on, but the passenger compartment was empty.

So was the parking lot itself. Which meant that whoever had been in the car was now probably crossing the hospital lobby at a sprint.

Toward us. "Go, go, go," I urged, catching up with the three women hurrying ahead of me: one rolling, the others hustling along on either side of Marla Sykes's wheelchair.

"He's going to come in here. And you're going to tell him," I instructed the nurse as she opened a hallway door marked LINENS and pushed the wheelchair through it, "that Marla Sykes has been discharged."

"But you guys . . ." The nurse knew we weren't who we said we were and now she wanted an explanation, however brief.

Ellie stuck her head back out of the linen closet. "Look at my face. That's right, you do remember me. The school fair."

The nurse nodded in recognition as the door at the far end of the corridor began opening. "Yeah, I *thought* you looked—"

"Hey, you two, can we talk about this later?" I implored. "Because we really don't have much time here."

Ellie ignored me. "I think our daughters even went to the

same preschool," she added. "And listen, I know this all seems crazy, but we're not. Honest."

The corridor's entry door finished opening. A cleaning person came through, pushing a metal cart bearing a mop and bucket. The nurse met Ellie's gaze and I saw her come to a decision.

"Okay," she whispered hastily just as the door at the end of the corridor began opening again.

I didn't see who came through it this time. The nurse closed the linen closet door on us instead.

"Darn," I said into the bleach-smelling darkness. Bella would have loved it in here. "I wish I'd told her to find out who that is, if she can."

"Never mind." Marla's voice was quiet and sad. "I can tell you. I know who it is."

I pulled the penlight from my purse, flicked it on. Marla's face looked haunted, her eyes hollow and sad; whatever she'd been up to, it hadn't worked out well for her.

To put it mildly. "I know," she repeated. Her voice strengthening with sudden resolve "I'm going to tell you, too. Both of you, right now. Only . . ."

Her shoulders slumped under the thin hospital bathrobe. All bashed up and battered, she gazed from Ellie to me and back with a look of such naked appeal that I almost felt sorry for her.

Almost. Because she'd lied to us, hadn't she? Not just once, but many times. And by then I'd figured out at least a portion of why: Marla's part of it all, anyway.

"Only you have to promise not to hate me afterward," she said.

Nine

"Hey," said Ellie from the back of the hospital linen closet. "Hey, there's a—"

"Hold that thought." I pressed the closet's door handle lever down slowly. The door opened outward; I put my eye to the crack, then backed away and gestured for Marla to look, too.

Down the corridor a tall man wearing glasses, a dark sweatshirt, and jeans stood at the nurses' desk, not liking what he was hearing. Marla leaned forward in the wheelchair and peered out.

". . . but I was told she was still . . ." The man's raised voice carried down the quiet hall.

Marla cringed back. "He must have called here, and they told him I was still a patient," she whispered urgently as footsteps stomped toward us.

"Sir!" From behind him the nurse's voice rose in protest. "Sir, you can't just . . ."

One after another, doors opened and slammed shut again as he inspected every room on the corridor. And here we were, meanwhile, trapped among the clean towels and washcloths.

"You *guys*," Ellie repeated insistently, "right here! Look!"

Angry footsteps thumped nearer as the nurse upped the ante: "Sir! I'm calling security!"

I had a feeling that our guy out there wouldn't care, though, and I wasn't interested in hanging around to find out for sure. So while Ellie shoved mountains of laundered sheets and pillow-cases aside, I pushed Marla in her wheelchair to the back of the closet.

But when we got there . . . "Darn," she breathed.

The closet, I saw, served both the small hospital's patient-care wards. So there was a door at the front, and another from the back; that way, either ward could access it.

Which meant we could get out of here, or we could if the door at the closet's rear would just open, which it was refusing to do.

The footsteps stopped outside the closet. Then came a man's deep voice: "Sir, I'm with security and I have to ask you to . . ."

"Hurry," whispered Marla as a thud shook the wall nearby: the security guard slamming the guy against it, I thought, or vice versa. Ellie rattled the door lever to our escape route once more, then let go of it and turned to me in defeat.

Whereupon the knob rattled *again*, all by itself, and the door swung open to reveal another nurse standing there, her head turned away to talk to someone behind her.

"Keeping these linens locked up," she was saying, "is such a pain in the . . . Oh!"

She jumped back as we hustled unceremoniously out past her; no one yelled *"gangway!"* but no one had to. Down the corridor, through the lobby, and out the sliding-glass front doors we ran, pushing Marla and not looking back.

"Ouch," Marla said as we bundled her from the chair to my car's backseat; I hoped one of the pills she'd gotten was for pain, because we didn't have time to be gentle.

Then glancing back, I saw a shadow cross the hospital lobby.

"Get in," I snapped to Ellie. "Buckle up."

Moments later we'd started the car and rolled downhill out of the parking lot, then around the corner onto the street, which was where I snapped the headlights on and floored that sucker.

"Talk to us," I told Marla when we'd gotten back out onto the highway. Raindrops sparkled in the headlights and splattered on the windshield.

"About the photographs and the money we found," I went on, my own voice sounding not particularly friendly.

But I wasn't feeling very friendly, either. In the rearview no headlights appeared . . . yet.

"And about who attacked you, too. Everything, Marla. Or we can just drive straight to the police station in Eastport and wait for Bob Arnold to show up."

Marla's eyes met mine. In the dim passenger compartment her sewn scalp looked awful.

"Okay," she said defeatedly, and then lights did appear in the rearview.

The car was a mile or so behind us, but coming fast. Luckily, the Robbinston volunteer fire station was around the next curve; I pulled in behind the big sand pile there and cut our own lights.

A few instants later the other car flew by. "No way he could have seen us, right?" Marla worried aloud.

"Not unless he's got night-vision equipment," I replied, and the rest of the trip home was uneventful except for the deteriorating weather.

But that was bad enough, wind and rain shoving us around on the dark road so that I clung to the steering wheel. When at last we reached Eastport and pulled in at my driveway, I let out an exhausted sigh that came all the way up from my toenails.

And from my twisted ankle, which still felt like hell. "Okay," said Ellie when we'd gotten Marla inside. "Where do we put her?"

We hadn't been able to fit the wheelchair in the car, so we'd left it behind. "I can *walk*," Marla insisted, and I'll give her this much: she took two or three more steps before she collapsed.

So we helped her in and set her up in the sunroom on the chaise lounge across from my father's daybed, where her dog, Maxie, brightening at the sight of her, plopped protectively down onto the floor beside her.

Back in the kitchen with coffee and pieces of Bella's fresh raspberry pie in front of us, Ellie and I stared in amazement at each other.

"Well, that was interesting," Ellie said finally.

With her henna-red hair wrapped in a towel and her skinny arms sticking out of an old pink chenille bathrobe, Bella padded around, pushing various forms of nourishment at us.

"Wasn't it, though?" I replied evenly. No sounds came from outside, no vehicles went by in the street, and there was no sense in alarming my devoted housekeeper-slash-stepmother, either. Not yet, anyway.

But there was still a chance that our attacker had recognized me or Wade when we were out at Roscoe's. If he had, he might just put two and two together and figure out where Marla had gotten to now, without having to follow us here.

Wade appeared in the kitchen doorway. "How's it going?" he asked, smiling.

But it was the smile on the face of the tiger. Also he was holding a small pistol, which by the smell of the gun oil that floated from it he'd recently finished cleaning.

Wade collected firearms, hunted with them, and repaired them, and goodness, wasn't I ever pleased by his interest in them now.

"Oh, we're doing just great," I said. "How about here?" I looked at the gun. "Prepared for any eventuality, I see."

He tucked the weapon into his waistband. "All quiet. I'm just being a good Boy Scout."

He patted the weapon. But Wade wouldn't be bodyguarding us with it; he had his own obligations, what with the weather deteriorating the way it was.

"It turned out the dog Roscoe was taking care of needed surgery," he added. "Bob noticed it limping. Some of the buckshot from earlier must have winged him in the butt."

At the mention of buckshot Bella glanced anxiously at him. "Don't worry," he told her, "the dog just had a little accident, that's all. Bob took it out to the vet, it's fine, now."

Much more of that and Wade's nose would start growing, but she accepted it. "I told Bob to let the vet know to go ahead and do it," he went on to me, "and that you and I would take care of the payment."

Oh, of course we would. I strode over and wrapped my arms around him and pressed my face into his broad shoulder, inhaling the twin perfumes of fresh salt air and pine tar soap.

"I don't suppose Sam called again?" I asked. I'd already learned from Bella that he'd left no message on his earlier call, just hung up when no one answered.

Which was odd right there. Wade shook his head. "Nope, still nothing more from Sam. I'm pretty sure Roscoe knows who was after us out at his place, though. Same one who hired him, I'll bet."

And chased us up Route 1 and through the hospital, too, I felt certain. Swiftly I summarized this for Wade, who frowned.

"So somebody's getting worried," he echoed my opinion. "You and Ellie are getting a little too close to something, and someone wants to discourage you."

Right, but close to what? "But Roscoe's still too scared to say who hired him, and Bob hasn't had much time to try getting it out of him, either," Wade went on.

Bella put sandwiches, a handful of cookies, and some fruit into a paper bag, her big grape-green eyes fixed on her task.

"I tried talking to Marla," said Ellie. She seems okay—alert and aware and so on—but she's in a lot of pain and she's really scared."

Ellie had rinsed her hands and face at the sink and pulled her hair into an elastic band; she looked as fresh as a daisy. "So I couldn't get much out of her," she finished.

By contrast I felt like ditch muck, despite the shower I'd had earlier; the only one here who needed a bath as badly as I did was Maxie, and he, at least, was supposed to smell like a dog.

Ellie went on, "So we'll need to talk to her more about what happened, but—"

She held her wristwatch out demonstratively; at the sight of it a jolt of anxiety hit me. "The cheesecakes! What time were they supposed to come out of the oven?"

"Right now." Ellie grabbed up her satchel, her sweater, and the lunch bag Bella had packed, and made hurriedly for the door.

"I'll deal with them," she went on, letting herself out onto the porch, "and you . . ."

Yeah, I knew: me everything else.

"Ellie," Wade called after her, "be careful, do you hear? Keep your eyes open and your phone handy, and lock the shop door."

He spoke quietly, but his tone was unmistakable. She smiled at us both while the wind, now back in full force after its brief break, whipped her ponytail around.

"Right," she promised, and vanished into the rainy night.

Which left the information-gathering portion of the program to me. And while I fully understood that Marla Sykes was probably exhausted and in pain, there were worse things.

Being dead, for instance. Because someone obviously wanted her silenced, and I needed to know who and why. So I turned to my housekeeper-slash-stepmother, as I so often did.

"Bella, could you please put some of that lovely raspberry

pie onto a small plate for me, warm it up just a little bit, and put some vanilla ice cream with it?"

Bella's lip thrust out skeptically at first, but then she caught on: "Ohh," she breathed in delighted comprehension.

Because of course she'd overheard Ellie's comment about needing to get more info out of Marla. And Marla was a chocolate maker with highly developed taste buds, wasn't she?

Which Bella knew. But chocolate wasn't the only treat around here; Bella's fruit pie was nothing short of spectacular, and the fat red raspberries on the vines out in our garden were extremely tasty right at the moment.

Tasty enough to loosen a person's tongue whether they wanted to or not, in fact. Bella smiled conspiratorially.

"Just give me a minute," she said.

Five minutes later in the sunroom I held a loaded dessert plate in one hand and pulled a wicker chair up to the side of Marla's chaise lounge with the other.

"Here." I touched the edge of the pie-laden spoon to her lip and she opened her mouth reflexively.

"Mmm." She savored the tiny bite; then she opened her eyes. Fear leapt into them as she remembered, and she tried to get up.

"Uh-uh." I guided her down again. "Have a little more."

She subsided obediently; that pain pill, I supposed. "Now," I went on, "I need to know a few things."

Her lips clamped tight stubbornly. "Look," I said, "we're trying to help you."

Right, by kidnapping her from the hospital a few hours after a serious head injury. *Way to go,* I thought. *The cops are going to love that one when they find out about it.*

Trespassing, witness tampering . . . Oh, I was going to be real popular. But I'd had no choice, and anyway, here we were.

"Marla." I fed her another bite of pie. "Correct me if I'm

wrong, but are you by any chance involved in some kind of illegal scheme?"

Because right now it was the only thing that made sense: packages of hidden money, somebody in a boat at night who didn't want to be seen or interrupted, a rash of violence . . . and murder, of course.

"Marla?"

No answer. Apparently, now that she was relatively safe, she'd rethought her earlier promise to tell all.

But I still had another ace up my sleeve. "Bella?"

She hurried to the doorway. "Bella," I said, "melt some of the stuff from the butler's pantry, will you, please?"

After we'd returned from Lubec the other night, I'd put a little stash of the semisweet chocolate away. Not much, just enough for a taste now and then.

That was why, a few minutes later in the kitchen, I was able to prepare a special truth-serum concoction.

Then I returned to the sunroom. "Marla," I repeated. The bruised, battered woman opened her eyes. "Eat this."

I spooned a bite of my newly invented secret formula into her mouth: raspberry pie, vanilla ice cream, and . . . *chocolate*! Just a drizzle, since this was, after all, the good stuff, so it didn't take much.

She chewed . . . frowned . . . and stopped. Her eyes opened wider. "Wow."

"Good, huh?" I gave her a little more, then set the plate and spoon aside. "Glad you liked it. You can have the rest of it after you tell me what the hell is going on."

I got up. "Because so far I've been shot at, car chased, stalked, and nearly drowned. And on top of that, Ellie's suspected of murder, and when the holiday weekend's over I have little doubt that she's going to be arrested."

I dropped my voice to a whisper. "And you know what? I've got a feeling it's all *your* fault, no one else's, and so will Bob

Arnold. Who, by the way, already knows about all the money we found hidden at your place, and pretty soon the state cops will know about it, too."

I leaned down, angling my head at the dark windows. "Also, in case you've forgotten, that guy who chased us tonight is still out there, whoever he is."

Marla had sat motionless throughout all this; but now at the mention of our stalker from the hospital she shuddered visibly, a tear leaking down her bruised cheek.

"So speak up the way you said you would," I told her. "While you still can. Because time is passing, and so are our chances to fix all this, whatever it is. That's my advice, at any rate."

Marla looked at me, at the dark windows streaming with rain, and at the big German shepherd still stationed loyally beside her. Then she reached for the plate of pie and ate it, and drank up the grape juice and ginger ale I'd brought along with it.

Finally she began, her voice weak but steady: "So this guy came to me this past spring and asked me if he could use some of my rented space in the old mill building."

The place I'd visited, where she actually made the chocolate, she meant. Wade came to the door and saw us, eased in and silently built the fire back up in the little fireplace, and left again.

"What for?" I asked. "Why did he want the space? And did you know the guy?"

Marla shook her head wincingly as the fresh logs stacked in the fireplace blazed up.

"He said he wanted to store a few things," she replied, "and I didn't know him. I still don't even know his name, or where he stays."

A gust rattled the windows as she went on. "I'd seen him in Lubec a few times, in the Salty Dog and so on, but only since . . . oh, a few months ago, maybe."

I thought about this. Before they'd put him in the ambulance after the shooting incident at his trailer, Roscoe had told Wade and me one thing: the guy who had hired him as a sort of seagoing security guard had first broached the idea to him this past spring.

A few months ago, in other words, around the same time that Marla's stranger had approached her about renting mill space.

"Then what happened?" I asked. "How'd you end up with all the money we found at your place?"

Marla tried to laugh, but she nearly wept instead. "That's what he was storing, it turned out," she said when she could do it without sobbing.

"And some of it was what he paid me," she added. "But the thing was, he said I couldn't spend it or even put it in the bank. Instead I had to get all of it into my business receipts somehow, then pay myself out of that."

She looked up at me. "You know, phony up some fake orders to account for the income, then give most of it back to him by making it look as if I was paying a bill he'd sent me."

"So you were money laundering, in other words?"

Suddenly I understood how a schoolteacher with no other clear source of income had been able to buy two houses, fix them up, rent a workspace, *and* stock up on all the equipment and ingredients she'd needed to start her chocolate-making business.

She nodded. "Right. Money laundering. I guess that is what it was. Not that I thought of it that way."

Sure you didn't, I thought skeptically. But never mind: "So what went wrong?"

She was tiring, but she managed to lift her head again. "I don't know. Until yesterday I had no idea anything had. I don't know the guy who chased us last night. Never saw him before."

Summoning strength, she sat up straight. "I never saw who

DEATH BY CHOCOLATE CHERRY CHEESECAKE

attacked me and Maxie, either. It might've been him, but I don't know any more than I just told you about what's going on."

Then with a deep, shuddery breath she leaned back and closed her eyes. In the darkened windows the firelight's glow reflected onto her face: pale, exhausted.

"Okay, Marla," I relented. "Just one more thing. How was *he* getting all this money? Where was it coming from? Did you ever get any information about that?"

But when I looked at her again, she was sound asleep.

Gray light crept into the sunroom, around five in the morning. I opened my eyes. The fire was out, and its ashy remains a cold heap on the tiled hearth. The slate floor was cold, too, under my back.

I sat up. Maxie lay stretched out on the daybed; Marla snored softly, still on the chaise lounge, with a blanket draped over her. From the kitchen the mingled smells of bacon and brewing coffee drifted in like a blessing; I climbed to my feet.

Wade was out there eating breakfast. "Guys're having to move boats, I said I'd come help," he explained after washing down his last bite of egg with a final swallow of coffee.

"This thing hits"—he waved at the view from the kitchen windows, rain-splashed and sodden gray—"and they could lose the whole fishing fleet."

He got up. "Hey, ask Ellie if she hears from George, let him know I went down and checked the Bayliner, okay? Tightened up the lines and so on."

He hauled on his boots. "But she should also let him know we could use his help here," he added from the back hallway, "if he can get away."

I agreed that I would tell her, and then as I was pouring my own coffee, a sound from the street caught my attention. It was a car going by, and then another.

And another. Meanwhile, Wade hadn't said anything about

our narrow escape of the night before. The getting-into-trouble part of it was what mostly I expected comment on, not the getting out.

On the other hand, what he'd be doing this morning was pretty dangerous, too, so maybe he just didn't want to hear any warnings, himself: sauce for the gander, et cetera.

Anyway, by the time he had the rest of his storm gear on, a steady parade of vehicles was passing on their way out of town.

"About time," Wade said of the fleeing visitors as he zipped up his rubber raincoat. "Like I said, if this thing *does* hit . . ."

"You mean it might not?" The first swallow of coffee had only reminded my brain cells that they existed at all.

The second one, though, had started to wake them up. Wade crossed his fingers in reply.

"S'posed to just-possibly-maybe jog east out to sea, they're saying now. At the moment, it's giving Massachusetts a hell of a pounding."

He saw my face, crossed swiftly to me, and wrapped a rubber-raincoat-swathed arm tightly around me.

"I didn't mean Sam's out in it. He's a smart guy, you know? You didn't raise any dumb kids, Jake, Sam'll know enough to stay put till it's over."

Sure he would. I just wished I could be certain of it.

"What's happened to Roscoe?" I asked as Wade opened the door to go. "That beat-up little trailer of his won't be any match for this mess, even without all the bullet holes."

The wind nearly tore Wade's hat off. "Yeah, Bob Arnold put him in the drunk tank last night. Not locked in, you understand, he just gave the poor guy a bed for the time being."

Another few cars went by. Through the streaming rain I could see that they were packed full of families, pets, and luggage, the unhappy-looking drivers gripping steering wheels, peering ahead into the murk.

"He's happy as a clam in there for now, and Fang's with him, too," Wade called back through the rain. "Dog bounced right back as soon as it didn't have a butt full of buckshot," he added as he climbed into his pickup truck.

So the veterinary surgery wasn't major, I gathered, and the damage to the truck from the accident couldn't have been too bad, either, if it was already driveable again.

But Sam was still incommunicado, and my dad had seemed so tired and tentative on our excursion together that I thought his recovery must be faltering, if not failing entirely.

And then there's Ellie, I thought as I went upstairs for a shower at last. If we hadn't figured out who'd killed Matt Muldoon by the time the Fourth of July holiday ended, she was toast.

Which was why, half an hour later with clean clothes on the outside of me and a big piece of Bella's pie and a whole lot more of her industrial-strength coffee on the inside, I was hurrying back downtown to the Moose.

A few hours of sleep had done wonders for me. But the weather had already started being unkind to Eastport; on Water Street I pulled into a parking space, noting that our shop's moose-head sign no longer hung from its sturdy chains over the front door.

"Blown down," Ellie confirmed when I got inside, the little bell ringing over my head. As usual the shop smelled like heaven, if heaven is built mostly out of butter and confectioner's sugar thinned with a little vanilla.

"I baked," Ellie explained, "a few cookies."

By which she meant two dozen chocolate chip, a couple of pans of oddballs (nuts, coconut, raisins, and Rice Krispies mixed with melted chocolate) and a few trays of needhams, chocolate-dipped potato confections that are a traditional Maine treat.

She'd caught a few hours' sleep, too, she assured me, and never mind that it was twelve minutes at a time while the cookies baked. Swiftly I summarized what Marla had told me after I'd tortured her by feeding her ice cream and raspberry pie topped with chocolate.

"Nice work," said Ellie. "But you're not the only one who's come up with new facts. And I've been thinking about them, too."

She stood by our dish sink, scrubbing out mixing bowls. I started arranging a dozen of each cookie variety on doily-covered plates. Customers would be arriving here soon; in my experience bad weather makes people need *more* chocolate, not less.

That is, they would if the huge storm cranking up its romping-and-stomping act outside now didn't end up blowing us all away. "And what I think," said Ellie, "is that Miss Halligan sleeps here at night."

I put down the needham I'd been about to bite into; potato being a vegetable and vegetables being okay to eat even this early in the morning, right?

"I beg your pardon?" I said. I'd been wondering why Ellie was speaking so softly.

She nodded, her curly blond head angled toward the thin sheet of drywall between the Moose and the Second Hand Rose.

"She's over there right now," said Ellie, rinsing the final mixing bowl—a thick white pottery one that she'd inherited from her great-grandmother, along with all our recipes—and leaning it in the dish rack.

"Quiet as a mouse, but once in a while I still hear her moving around." Ellie dried her hands on a clean dishcloth. Under her baking apron she was wearing stonewashed jeans and a purple T-shirt, which her daughter had tie-dyed at camp the previous summer.

The sight of it reminded me: "How's Lee? Have you heard from her?"

"She's fine." Ellie made worry-tamping-down motions with her hands. "She called. They're not even going to get rain."

The camp that Ellie's daughter attended with her young cousin was way over in Maine's western hills, a completely different part of the state, weather-wise.

"Seriously, though, Jake." Ellie grabbed a water glass off the shelf and pressed the open end of it tightly to the drywall partition.

Making a face at the corny spy-vs.-spy tactic, I nevertheless put my ear to the glass that Ellie held and heard . . .

Voices. Music. "She's got a little TV over there," I said.

Ellie pressed a finger to her lips. "And she's watching the Weather Channel," I finished in a whisper.

"Or she was when she went to sleep," Ellie agreed softly. "I haven't heard anything else in quite a while."

I stepped back. "Ellie, you know that if she was over there when Muldoon got killed, she might've heard something, right?"

"Yes, but she hasn't said she was. Which she would have, don't you think? Besides, what I want to know is *why* is she here? Because she has a house of her own, you know."

Right, so why sleep in her shop? And now that I thought about it, why *did* Miss Halligan dislike Sarabelle Muldoon so much, anyway?

The speed and intensity of recent events had pushed that latter query right out of my mind, but now I realized it shouldn't have. Miss Halligan had been in those pictures, after all, and Marla must have had a reason first to take them, and then to keep them on her computer.

And to suggest their existence to us that night in the Salty Dog, too; as I looked back, it seemed to me that she'd been eager to mention them. I'd have to ask her that when I got back home.

"But what's any of it got to do with Marla getting beat up, or Roscoe and his boat, or the guy chasing us last night?" Ellie wondered aloud.

"No idea. I suppose we could try to find out, though," I said slowly, and in reply Ellie's smile looked as if it should be on a cat's face and have canary feathers stuck to it.

"Uh-huh." She glanced around the kitchen purposefully. "We do have all the cheesecakes left to decorate, but we can't do it yet."

Because the last two weren't cool enough, and you have to do them at the proper temperature. Otherwise, the top is too hot to take the cherry glaze correctly, the chocolate shavings wilt, and the ganache melts down the side of the cake.

None of which we could afford to have happen. "So I think we're free for a couple of hours," my friend added, "until it's time to open the shop."

"And?" I ventured cautiously as she snapped out the lights and turned off the ceiling fans.

Outside, we sprinted through the rain to my car; by now it was full daylight, but the sky was low and lead-colored with clouds looking as heavy as boulders rolling across it.

In the car I turned on the defroster fan, the heat, and the headlights. "And if she's here at the Rose," said Ellie, "then she's not at her house."

The streetlamps still on in the gloom showed the wind damage overnight; more blown-down store signs, open trash barrels rolling, a long ragged swathe of black roofing paper torn from somewhere, tumbling along.

"So I want to go there and have a look around if we can," Ellie pronounced, frowning at the mess all around. "Because first of all, there's got to be a reason why she sleeps in her shop instead of in her own bed."

Her comment reminded me that with Sam on his way home— or at least I hoped he was—and Marla now apparently my house-guest for I didn't know how long, beds in our house were getting scarce.

After all, when you haul someone out of the hospital where they're recovering, you're responsible for them, aren't you? So

I'd been wondering, if even one more person showed up, where would I put everybody? Perhaps Miss Halligan had the same problem.

"Maybe because someone else is there?" I said. And now that I had said it, I was so sure it was true that I just nodded silently when we reached Miss Halligan's house and found a car parked in her driveway.

Which one it was, though, did come as a surprise, although by that time maybe it shouldn't have: the dark-colored sedan had a very distinctive front grill and big double-barreled round headlights.

It was the car that had chased us the night before.

Ten

Miss Halligan's house was a sweet little bungalow on Prince Street. With its low roof and gingerbread-trimmed gables nestled under an ancient pair of copper beech trees, it wore its green lawn gathered to it like a skirt, white-trimmed at the mossy hem by a neat wooden picket fence.

No light showed from inside. "Are you sure you want to do this?" I asked Ellie.

The dark car hunkered alongside the house. Looking at it gave me the creeps, as if the headlights might snap on by themselves or the engine fire to life of its own volition.

But Ellie was resolute. "She had to have heard or even seen something if she was there when Muldoon got killed, and I think she was. I think she's been there every night for quite a while, and that's why she's always there so early every morning."

She frowned at the car again. "Yet she hasn't said a word. Also those pictures of her have something to do with it, I'm sure of it. Why else would Marla be keeping them, and trying to get us to pay attention to them?"

"That lemon cologne of Miss Halligan's isn't drifting around by itself, either," I agreed, remembering the whiffs of it that we'd been encountering in places where it shouldn't be.

The storm was sending squall lines over us as its outer bands began swirling in; now as the one we'd just had pulled away, the sky brightened abruptly.

Well, not *that* much brighter, but it made me like sitting here out in the open a lot less. The house glowered silently at us. "So you don't think it's all about the money?"

Ellie shook her head stubbornly. "That money's been there all along, I'll bet. What changed was that right after Muldoon died, we talked to Marla about him, and the next thing we knew, *whammo.*"

But how would anyone know *that we had?* I wondered. "Ellie, when we were with her in the Salty Dog the other night, did you notice anyone who might've been listening to us?"

Ellie stared at the house. Nothing moved, but that didn't mean there wasn't someone inside watching us.

"Eavesdropping? No, I didn't. Doesn't mean it didn't happen, though." She sat up straight, gathering herself. "I'm going in."

Yikes! That sure hadn't been in my game plan, or at least not after I saw the muscle car. Peeking in the windows had been about as far as I'd meant to go, but Ellie was away and across the lawn before I could stop her.

By the time I'd caught up, she'd reached the screened-in side porch, which ran along the short asphalt driveway. Overhead, sneaky breezes shivered the beech leaves, releasing showers of droplets. The screened-in porch extended around to the rear of the house, where it overlooked a weedy, stream-cut ravine.

"*Ellie!*" I whispered, but she wasn't listening and I couldn't very well let her go alone, could I? The porch door opened without a sound. Inside, an ashtray overflowed onto a low table.

Miss Halligan didn't smoke. A calico cat slid in through a flap door to twine around our ankles.

"What are we even looking for?" I whispered nervously as Ellie tried opening the door to the kitchen.

The door swung wide. The kitchen was a complete mess: dishes, opened cans and packages, another loaded ashtray. The whole place smelled of burned grease, cigarette smoke, and rather strongly of the lemon cologne its owner wore, even though she wasn't here.

"I don't know." Ellie tiptoed across the kitchen toward a glass-beaded curtain in the arched doorway to the room beyond; a parlor, it looked like.

A lamp was on in there. It hadn't been on a moment ago. I grabbed Ellie and yanked her back, just as a shadow appeared on the other side of the beaded curtain.

"Shh." We ducked down quickly below the level of the kitchen counters, then moved backward as best we could toward a door that led . . . Well, I didn't know where it led, but at the moment anywhere was better than here.

We could have gone back out the porch door. But Ellie wasn't having any of that.

"She must have a desk here," Ellie whispered, "or even just a file box. There's no room for business records at the Rose."

I didn't understand how the records of a tiny secondhand clothing store in remotest downeast Maine could have anything to do with murder.

Not that I had to understand it, or anyway not right now. What I had to do now was hide; Ellie, too, because the shape on the far side of the curtain was now pushing through it into the kitchen.

The beads rattled dryly as I found a doorknob behind me and turned it. "Go," I whispered to Ellie, nudging her backward, then slipped through the door after her.

I got it closed again, just as the kitchen light snapped on; I thought we'd made it without a hitch until I felt something soft moving by my ankles and realized the cat had come with us.

"Prutt," the cat said, sounding pleased, and now of course the guy out there was calling the cat.

"Oh, for Pete's sake." My lips moved, but I didn't dare make a sound. The guy was standing just outside the door.

The cat's name was Kitty, apparently. "Come on, damn it. You flea-bitten sack of . . ."

The cat head-butted me. It wore a thin collar, with something metal dangling from its . . . *Oh, dear heaven, it's a bell.* Luckily, it was stuck in the collar at the moment, so it wasn't ringing.

Yet. Hastily I captured the feline, snagged the tiny silver bell between my frantic, grasping fingers, then swiftly slipped the whole collar over the animal's head.

Kibble clattered into a bowl; hearing it, the cat struggled in my grip, but didn't yowl. Instead he went straight to the biting portion of the program, sinking his sharp teeth into the tender skin between my thumb and forefinger.

"Mmphh," I said. Based on the sound of it, the guy out there was making himself some coffee. A trickle of warm wetness slithered across my palm as the cat let go. *The more it bleeds, the better,* I supposed, but, boy, that hurt.

We were in a little office with pine-paneled walls and a small wooden desk, plus some filing cabinets. A brass lamp stood on the desk, which had a green blotter on it, and a straight wooden chair whose seat was padded in green plaid was pulled up to it.

The guy in the kitchen belched loudly as smoke from a pan of something frying seeped under the office door. He hadn't left the kitchen at all, so we couldn't let the cat, now pacing and looking terrifyingly ready to yell in feline protest, out there to where the cat food was.

Ellie tried one of the windows that opened onto the porch. It slid up easily, the feline leapt through it, and the cat door in the kitchen flapped; we heard kibble being crunched.

"Phew." Ellie mimed her relief; in reply, I mimed vamoosing out that very same window, pronto.

But she had other plans. Angling her head at the file folders stacked atop the cabinet, she made a move toward them. She never was one to run away prematurely; the opposite, actually.

"Ellie," I whispered urgently. Because that guy wouldn't be busy eating breakfast forever, would he?

Ignoring me, Ellie plopped down onto the cozy little room's green braided rug, placing a manila folder open on her lap. Calmly she began turning pages from it. And I had to admit, the room's air of cleanliness and order suggested strongly that homeboy out there didn't visit very often.

So Ellie's calm attitude began to seem more sensible to me; if we stayed reasonably quiet, I supposed we could hunker down in here until the guy left the house and then—

Well, then two things happened: first, the cat's rubber flap door slapped shut as the animal exited the kitchen, back out to the porch.

Next, with what looked like a breakfast sausage in his jaws, the creature jumped *into* the office again, through the window we had unthinkingly left open when we'd let him out.

Then the guy must've noticed that the sausage was gone, because he roared out onto the porch, too, just in time to see the cat's tail vanishing.

Or I assume that's what must have happened, since next the guy's face appeared at the window, and the series of expressions on it when he saw us—surprise, confusion, and an urgent desire to murder us both with his bare hands were the main ones, it looked like—would have been hilarious if I hadn't been so distracted.

Fleeing for one's life, as it turns out, doesn't concentrate the mind very well at all. The guy was way too big to get through the window; as he stomped back into the house and began rattling the office doorknob—Ellie had thought to lock it, for which I resolved to be forever grateful if only I lived long enough—the only thing I could think of was to cram myself into the filing cabinet.

But since the cat was already in there, gnawing contentedly on his smoky link, I doubted I would fit.

"Psst!" It was Ellie, already halfway out the window. "Jake, what're you waiting for?"

She had a file folder under her arm. Meanwhile, on the other side of the office door, the guy yanked out kitchen drawers, loudly scattering silverware and utensils in search of—

"Ha!" he barked triumphantly, and then something jingled. *A key ring . . .*

Oh, damn it all to hell, anyway. I hurled myself at the window as the guy tried keys, one after another, snarling and cursing. The window opening was just barely bigger than my own posterior—that pie of Bella's really was very delicious, and so were all the many other wonderful things she cooked—but I was extremely motivated, and I'd made it almost halfway out when my pant leg snagged on something.

Swatting my flailing arms away, Ellie reached in and grabbed my belt, and hauled hard on it; a ripping sound came from behind me and then I tumbled out, hitting the porch deck with a thud.

A double thud, actually: one for the heel of each hand, which was where I landed, sending sharp pain shooting up both arms. By comparison my ankle, still twinging, was suddenly a nonissue.

But whatever I might've broken, it was nothing compared to what that guy in there had in store for me, and from the sound of it he was coming through the door behind me this very instant.

So I hotfooted it off the porch, down the asphalt driveway, and across the wet street right behind Ellie, and scrambled into the car. And through some miracle of good timing, by the time we zoomed away, the guy still hadn't appeared out in front of the house.

"I don't think he saw us," said Ellie optimistically when she could speak again; it was a very narrow escape.

"What're you talking about? When he stuck his head in that window, he looked straight at us," I said.

The visit wasn't a complete failure. I was pretty sure we now knew why Miss Halligan was sleeping in her shop. Some young guy—Her son, maybe? I mean, who else but a relative would just move in on an older lady like that?—had taken over her place.

He was even using her lemon cologne as an aftershave, it seemed; the light, dry fragrance, suitable for a man or woman now that I thought of it, had been coming off him in waves through the open office window just a minute ago.

On the other hand, he apparently wanted to kill us and now he knew who we were. I said as much, but Ellie was unimpressed.

"He wore glasses." She clutched the folder she'd taken.

"What?" Out on the bay a Coast Guard boat had a scallop dragger in tow, the larger vessel bulling its way through surging waves to haul the crippled boat to safety.

"He wore thick glasses," Ellie repeated patiently as we pulled to the curb in front of the shop.

Right, I'd glimpsed them on him last night at the hospital, and they'd been on the kitchen table just now in Miss Halligan's kitchen.

Not on him, and if he hadn't seen us well enough to recognize us, I could at least go home without worrying about leading him there.

Across the street a crew of men battled to wrestle down the vendors' tents and bundle them up while gusts scattered the tent poles and ripped at the large, unwieldy canvas sections, turning them into sails.

Inside the Chocolate Moose the smell of salt air mixed with

the usual lovely chocolate aromas. The powerful wind gusts were coming in around the door and windows.

But there was nothing we could do about that, so while Ellie prepped for cake decorating, I pulled on a fresh apron and got the shop opened for business. I turned on the lights and the fans, readied the cash register and the credit card reader.

"What about her?" I angled my head toward next door and Miss Halligan. "Should we ask her about him?"

Ellie slotted a Celtic harp CD into the player—her choice, don't blame me—and music so sweet it should've come with a shot of insulin poured from the speakers.

"No. Not yet. And we did learn a few things," she added as I started the coffeemaker and set sample cookies out on a plate.

She laid the manila file folder she'd been examining on the counter by the cookie plate and opened it. Inside, printouts of a dozen newspaper articles from all over New England bore headlines having to do with an arrest after a major crime wave.

I peered over her shoulder. A string of car break-ins, some burglaries, a rash of thefts, and a few brazen daylight robberies were detailed in the clippings. There were at least a couple of linked crimes from each of the northeastern states, starting as far south as Connecticut.

I looked up. "These are about him." Several clips included mug shots of the guy we'd just seen, and who'd chased us the night before; Miss Halligan's creepy tenant had a serious rap sheet, it seemed.

His name, the clippings all agreed, was Clark Carmody. Ellie poured coffee, dosed mine with sugar and cream.

"Read all the way down to the bottom of that one," she said, pointing.

So I did, discovering that . . . "Holy smokes!"

In the kitchen the oven timer let out a piercing *brrringg!* I followed Ellie out to where a dozen fresh cheesecakes, now all

cool enough for us to work on, sat awaiting their final trim-
mings.

"Okay, now," Ellie recited to herself, "first the swirls and
then the curls."

Melted and shaved in that order for the cake tops, in other
words. The piped-on chocolate ganache would come last. While
she shaved more curls off a block of semisweet with the vegetable
peeler, the rich, intoxicating aroma of melting chocolate wafted
from the top pan of the double boiler.

We were not, of course, using the electric melting pot that
Matt Muldoon had been found in—and, anyway, the police had
taken it to the crime lab so we couldn't.

I got out the ganache ingredients: more chocolate and some
heavy cream. It was still too early to actually make the stuff;
like the cakes themselves, it needed to be the right temperature.

So I started chopping the chocolate with a big butcher knife,
holding the blade lightly about midspine between my fingertips
and rocking the wooden handle in a pumping motion so the
blade's sharp edge moved rhythmically up and down.

Outside, squalls blew and subsided as the first real effects of
the storm began thundering in. People scooted past our front
window, gust shoved from behind and holding on to their hats.

But in here, at least, we were busy and content. I knew we
were in trouble and Ellie did, too; for one thing, the state crime
lab in Augusta would be open again right after the holiday ended,
and checking for fingerprints on that murder weapon/pastry needle was surely right up there on their to-do list.

Still, Ellie worked serenely. "The part about him committing
all those robberies and burglaries was interesting," she said, ref-
erencing the clippings about Clark Carmody's past crimes.
"Right?"

I weighed chocolate shreds on our kitchen scale: nine ounces,
which meant I'd need a cup of cream; the frosting made in
batches, not all at once. "You think he's up to his old tricks?"

Ellie shook her head; she'd popped a hairnet onto it before we began. I had, too, and it itched miserably, but I didn't hate it as much as I'd have hated finding a hair in the ganache.

Or worse, having someone else find one. "No," she replied, "there was way too much money in Marla's cellar for him to have gotten it all from that kind of crime, wouldn't you say?"

She was right. Thinking back, I recalled that the bills had all been hundreds; to amass that much cash around here, he'd have had to rob everyone in downeast Maine, and some of them twice.

Ellie finished drizzling thin lines of melted chocolate over the butter-colored, lightly browned tops of four cheesecakes. Next came the cherries, a ruby-red slather of fruity deliciousness, with plenty of whole cherries glistening in the mixture.

"But whatever he's been doing, he's sure getting paid really well," she went on as she worked.

I'd have to try again at getting more info out of Marla, I decided. She'd insisted she didn't know about the source of the money, but I wasn't convinced.

Just then, "Hello?" Miss Halligan tapped on the glass of our shop's front door, which I'd left locked on account of possible roving murderers, et cetera.

I hurried to let her in, dusting my chocolate-streaked hands on my apron and hastily pulling off my hairnet, which I have on good authority—namely a mirror—makes me look as if I am all prepped and ready to undergo my very own autopsy.

Miss Halligan, by contrast, looked as usual as if she'd just stepped from a fashion magazine: short spiky hair, big dark eyes, trim figure. She was wearing a tunic with elaborate smocking on the bodice, black leggings with leather sandals, and a medallion with an amethyst in it, hanging on a silver chain.

"Good morning," I greeted her. I figured I probably shouldn't ask who her roommate was. After all, she didn't know we'd as good as broken into her house a little while ago, and it was probably just as well to keep it that way for now.

"What can we do for you this not-fine summer morning?" I went on, waving at the display case overflowing with goodies, thanks to Ellie's industry. "Biscotti again? Or a pinwheel cookie for a late breakfast?"

She mustered a smile. "No, I . . . I heard sounds over here so I thought I'd check, is all." Glancing around nervously, she added, "Were you here all night?"

Translation: Did we know that she had been? Or that's how I took it, anyway. "Oh . . . no," I replied, diligently brushing a nonexistent crumb from the counter. "We both got a solid eight hours in our very own beds."

Wade's wasn't the only nose that ought to be growing this morning, and I couldn't have been very convincing. Despite the few hours of sleep I'd managed, I was still so tired that my face must have looked as if an army had marched over it.

But Miss Halligan didn't seem to notice. "Oh, that's good," she said lightly, not quite able to hide her relief.

Why does it make so much difference to her, I wondered, *that we not know she's been . . .*

Well, bullied out of her own home was my guess, and despite her sharp getup and as-usual-perfect grooming, the chic little vintage-clothing maven looked so woebegone that I nearly asked her about the guy, despite my resolution not to.

But I didn't get the chance, because just then Ellie came out of the kitchen and she wasn't as cautious as I was about upsetting applecarts. In fact, you could say doing it was her specialty.

"Miss Halligan! Just who I wanted to talk to." Ellie set her coffee cup on the counter with a sharp, meaningful little click.

Our shop neighbor blinked nervously as Ellie went on: "Because I was wondering about the other night when Matt Muldoon died."

Miss Halligan took a step back. Most days she looked like

the greeter in an art gallery, or a big-city specialty-bookshop owner, maybe: smart, sophisticated, and cultured in the extreme.

But at the moment she just looked scared. "Ye-s-s," she began doubtfully, but Ellie talked right over her.

"And what I was wondering was, did you hear that thing ring?" She waved at the shop door's bell hanging over it.

You couldn't silence the bell—not without a stepladder. If someone came in, it rang.

"I know you're here late most nights," Ellie went on, "and of course I'm sure the cops have probably asked you about it, but—"

"No!" Miss Halligan blurted. "I went home early that evening. I didn't feel well. In fact, I think I left even before you did."

Her powdered forehead furrowed. "I didn't hear it before I went, though, either. I wonder," she ventured, "if possibly your shop door had blown open already, so it couldn't ring?"

"Interesting idea," I remarked dryly, since she'd have seen it standing open if it had been. Miss Halligan didn't miss much.

But she took my comment for agreement, or pretended to. Drawing in a nervous breath, she let out a whinnying laugh that wasn't like her at all.

"And can you imagine that, me going home before you?" she added, trying to make a joke of it.

"Why, yes, it is unusual," Ellie agreed, going along with the charade. But moments later when Miss Halligan had departed, Ellie turned to me.

"She's lying. She was here, I saw the lights on, and I heard her over there, too. I'll bet she was in her shop all night, just like last night."

"So why doesn't she just say so? Unless . . . unless maybe that bell wasn't all she heard, and she doesn't want to say *that*."

Or unless she'd killed Muldoon herself. It seemed awfully

unlikely; for one thing, I couldn't envision the tiny shopkeeper hauling his body across the kitchen and down into the cellar to hide it from Ellie, then hauling the deadweight back up again and propping it against the chocolate warmer, blocking its feet against a heavy box to help keep it there.

But half the town disliked Muldoon for one reason or another, so why shouldn't she despise him, too? And people found strength when they really had to; I, for instance, had escaped my bad past life all those years ago.

"She could be protecting someone," said Ellie.

She had finished chocolate-striping the cake tops and laying down the cherry glaze. Now it was time for the second-last step of the decorating operation, the chocolate shavings.

I'd made four piles of them, heaping them up on a sheet of baker's parchment. I plucked a long curl of the shaved chocolate from one of the heaps, watched it bounce Slinky-like between my fingertips for a moment, then popped it into my mouth.

A burst of dark sweetness began on my tongue and spread rapidly all the way to my brainstem, firing off one burst of pure chocolate happiness after another.

"Mmm," I said inadequately, because I grew up on Hershey's, I still adore the stuff, and I'll never apologize for it. But the chocolate that Marla Sykes made was something else again, satiny smooth and so intense, it was like a shot of . . .

Narcotics! Thinking this, I stood stock-still with that lovely dark chocolate curl still melting on my tongue, feeling as if it had just blown open about a million brain cells.

What could you smuggle out that would bring in lots of money? Drugs were the obvious answer. But I wasn't sure where you'd be sending them from here; from what I knew, the reverse—money out, drugs in—was the way it generally worked.

Meanwhile, Ellie sprinkled chocolate curls evenly over the first cake, then mounded them at the top's center. (The trick was to do it before the chocolate melted to your hands, but not so fast that the curls got distributed unevenly.)

"Or," she said, angling her head at the wall between us and the Rose, "she might be afraid of someone."

I nodded as more chocolate curls sifted from her fingertips. "Or . . . ," I began.

But then I heard my own voice trail off; I really was tired, and it was all just so confusing, and in the next moment the shop door's little bell rang behind me—I hadn't locked it yet after Miss Halligan's exit—and Ellie's expression changed.

"Ohh," she breathed happily.

Turning, I had a moment to be glad I wasn't holding one of those cheesecakes. If I had been, I'd have dropped it; as it was, I kept on trying to speak and couldn't.

Instead I just stood there as a handsome young guy with dark hair, a lantern jaw, big long-lashed hazel eyes, and a wide grin lunged forward and wrapped his arms around me, sweeping me up into an embrace that lifted me off my feet.

"Sam," I whispered. "Oh, Sam, I'm so glad to *see* you."

Which may have been an understatement, and it's possible that I sniffled a little, too. But I did *not* cry, I absolutely did *not*.

Finally my son put me down, as from behind him a young woman with straight black hair, dark brown eyes, and a mouth like a pink flower stepped shyly forward, and suddenly I knew the whole story.

Drawing her close with an arm around her shoulder, Sam spoke: "Mom, Ellie, this is Mika. We were married yesterday."

Her smile was like sunshine. She held out her hand. "How do you do?" Her voice was music. "I'm very glad to meet you at last. Sam has told me so much about you."

Something clinked faintly to the floor, but I was still too stunned to pay any attention. "Likewise," I managed. "Not the part about telling me a lot about you, of course, but—"

Her merry laugh interrupted me. "Oh, my. Yes, we do have a lot to catch up on, don't we?"

Ellie, who'd been watching the girl closely, now went to the cooler in the front of the shop and brought back a bottled water, which Mika accepted gratefully while Sam looked proud.

"What?" I said. They all seemed to be understanding something important and wonderful that I was still not getting. Then after a quick, assessing glance around the kitchen, Mika spoke up again.

"Mrs. Tiptree—" she began.

"Jake," I interrupted her. "It's Jake to my friends."

She stopped. "Jake. I do so much wish you could've been there for our wedding."

Yeah, me too, I thought, beginning to feel indignant. *I mean how* could *he—*

"We hope to make it up to you in about six months, though," she went on, "when we present you with your first grandchild."

Ten minutes later Sam and Mika were gone, headed up to the house.

I'd locked the door yet again; goodness, this worrying about murderers was exhausting, and now I ate another pinwheel cookie. If I kept on, we wouldn't have anything to sell. But I didn't care—not enough to stop, anyway.

"Get these things away from me, please."

I waved at the plateful sitting in front of me on the shop's little cast-iron café table. By now it was nearly 10 A.M., with a few customers already sitting in their cars outside, waiting for us.

Sam and Mika had said they wanted to clean up and unpack, and get something to eat. Ellie thought I should go, too.

But I just couldn't. For one thing, I wasn't sure how I felt and I didn't want to see the happy couple until I was certain that I could behave well in front of them.

Which right now meant not bursting into tears: How *could*

he, my mind kept repeating. *She's a lovely girl, obviously, but how could he spring her on me like this?*

Also I was too young to be a grandmother; when I'd had Sam, I was practically an infant myself, but I hadn't thought he would carry on the tradition.

Besides, Ellie and I were involved in a murder case, not to mention enough chocolate cherry cheesecakes to sink a barge.

"If I were *sure* the guy from Miss Halligan's didn't see us," I said, "I might leave you here alone to finish the decorating. Or if George were here."

Ellie's husband was still working in Bangor, where the storm was not expected to be so bad.

"He says that it's triple time," she'd said to explain why he hadn't come home, "if they stay on the job and work right through the holiday."

Triple his usual pay rate, which for George, with a family to support, was no small thing. I turned the OPEN sign in the front door, unlocking it yet again but officially this time, and in response three rain-jacketed local women got out of their cars and hurried in through the raindrops.

Jane Drummond, a cheerful, freckled person who ruled Eastport's Laundromat with an iron hand, wanted a dozen needhams.

"Because my daughter is coming. Bringing my grandson for the fourth," she confided, and the other two murmured appropriately.

"I hope they'll be able to have the fireworks," Jane added with a worried glance at the ghastliness outside.

The radar, Sam had reported before leaving the shop, had the storm still aimed right at us, despite Wade's suggestion that it might be trending east and out to sea.

"Oh, I'm sure the fireworks will go on as scheduled," said Pearl Fellowes calmly, and asked for a dozen pinwheel cookies.

"And one of the pastries, please, dear," she added, brushing back salt-and-pepper curls. "My kids aren't coming this year," she added. "I'm not convinced, but they say we're going to get rained out."

She took the white paper bakery bag I handed her; I took the money and rang up the sale.

"So I think I'll just eat these myself in front of the TV," she finished wickedly, and went out.

Finally Anne Talmadge, a regal-looking woman with white hair in a braided coronet and high, round cheeks as pink as the inside of a seashell, stepped up to the counter.

"Good morning. I'm here to collect two dozen cheesecakes."

Nervously I called for Ellie, who was in the kitchen, and she came out wiping her hands on a dish towel.

"Oh," said Miss Talmadge when Ellie had explained that not all the cakes were complete, but that they all would be delivered by us late tonight for the auction tomorrow.

Not, in other words, right this minute. But now it seemed the plan had been changed.

"They're concerned that if the storm should blow in, they'll be too busy. Rescuing distressed mariners and all," Miss Talmadge explained.

Which actually made sense. But it also meant trouble for us.

"So they've moved the auction up to this evening," said Miss Talmadge, and looked at us expectantly; after all, what difference could a few hours make?

"They've alerted the TV stations' crews to come early," she added, "so they can still do their stories about the auction and the cheesecakes and . . ." She stopped, tapping her forehead with her index finger. "Oh! And I almost forgot, they want four more. Of the cheesecakes, that is. Demand just keeps growing, and they don't want to disappoint anyone, of course."

"I see. Well," said Ellie, and I was glad that she'd taken the conversational lead, since if I had, I'd have been gnashing and foaming. "Well, we'll just have to take care of it, then."

What? I blinked. Four more cheesecakes, mixing time and time in the oven for each pair, not to mention the glazing, decorating, and frosting that had to go on afterward . . . it was impossible.

Only not to Ellie, apparently. "Don't worry, Miss Talmadge," she said. "We'll deliver the cakes in time, you can count on it. Just tell them everything's under control."

Which I thought was a serious overstatement. Even if it all went perfectly, getting those cakes to the auction site by tonight would be a squeaker, and I said so when Miss Talmadge had gone.

Ellie frowned. "We have no choice. Or I don't, anyway." She turned to me. "Jake, those cheesecakes are going to tell every caterer and wedding venue in the state that we mean business."

I just stared. Not that Ellie was wrong; what we were doing was impressive. But it hadn't even occurred to me that she'd been thinking about it like that.

"I know," said Ellie, "when we started this, we only talked about having a store. Local customers, cookies and pastries, busy in the summer. But if George didn't have to be away so much, life would be a lot easier, you know? And not just for me."

Of course, I realized. She wanted to make more money, and why wouldn't she? George wasn't the only one with a family to support, after all; she was half of their team. She looked at me in appeal.

"Jake, nobody can do that kind of hard, physical work forever. And especially not as much as George does, day in and day out. And we've still got Lee to put through college, somehow."

We stood there in silence a moment, contemplating the amount of money that project would take: mountains of the stuff.

"I get it," I said finally. "A dessert catering service, why not? And with the publicity the Coast Guard auction brings . . ."

She nodded emphatically, her eyes shining with enthusiasm

even though she, too, was exhausted. "Exactly. We could have steady work all summer, big jobs, maybe even into autumn and winter."

She stopped, biting her lip. "Or I could. If you didn't want to."

"Oh, please," I replied. "Of course, I want to. There's just one thing, though."

I loved the Moose and I loved being here, doing the baking and tending to the customers. A sweet little bakery in a quaint island town . . . what could be better?

But a catering business on top of all that was something else again. Weddings, anniversary parties, family reunions . . . I wanted to bake the equivalent of a dozen cheesecakes each week the way I wanted diphtheria.

"How about if I do the cake-baking part," Ellie proposed into my silence, "and you take care of the—"

"Yes!" I agreed hastily. "You can bake. All you want, and I will help you. Anything you need, Ellie. But not right now."

Ellie looked stubborn and I could see her getting ready to resist my next idea, which was that she should catch a nap.

"I can stay here for a few hours," I insisted.

But she was shaking her head, one gold curl wispily escaped from her repositioned hairnet bobbing determinedly.

"No time," she declared firmly. "I'll need to start the next two cakes right now if we're going to meet our new deadline."

And there was no arguing with her; in fact, she insisted that I get out of there myself for a little while, a suggestion that at first I resisted as strongly as she had.

But she had an ulterior motive. "Listen," she said, pressing another needham into my hands, "about Sam's new wife."

Fortunately, I'd already bit in, so the chocolate and potato molecules were already diluting the fear chemicals that the mere mention of "Sam's new wife" triggered the release of.

Or any kind of wife. I'd been telling myself that his alive-and-well status (not to mention the whole clean-and-sober part, for which I was on my knees giving heartfelt thanks, emotionally) made up for almost any other possible complications.

"And yes, we will hash over that whole new-marriage thing, I promise," said Ellie. "I know you're upset."

We always did talk things over; it was another of the secrets to our long friendship. But now that thought pinged a guilty memory; that GPS tracking device that her husband George had incorporated into her boat's electronics.

I still hadn't told her about it; meanwhile, Sam's new situation kept going around in my head like something spinning in one of Jane Drummond's washing machines:

Sam is here; he is fine; he is . . . married? *And to a young woman I'd never even* met?

"But for right now, did you see the way she looked around at this kitchen?" Ellie went on.

I had, actually. Her glance had gone swiftly from the sinks, to the ovens, to the stainless-steel worktable. And then . . . she'd relaxed a little.

"Like she knew just what she was looking at," I agreed. "Like she had experience with it, even."

As if it had made her feel at home. Ellie nodded, meanwhile rummaging for something in her apron pocket.

"Also she dropped this."

"What . . . Oh." I peered at what Ellie held: a silver charm bracelet. It was what I'd heard clink as it fell, I now realized, and what was on it was illuminating in the extreme.

"Look at these charms," said Ellie of the silvery miniatures: a little spoon, a tiny measuring cup, a flour sifter cunningly complete with an eensy silver crank handle, and a screen.

"Ohh," I breathed. They were, well . . . charming, actually. "But what's that other thing?" I asked of the tiny object Ellie bent and plucked from the floor now.

She held it up between thumb and finger. "Look, a rhinestone. Not out of the bracelet, though. From something Miss Halligan was wearing, probably."

Those T-shirts that the Rose's proprietor often wore did shed bits of glittery stuff occasionally. Ellie dropped the gleaming rhinestone into her apron pocket; her daughter would love it.

Still holding the silver charm bracelet, I touched the tiny measuring cup dangling from it hesitantly with an index finger. "So, do you think Mika's really a baker of some kind?"

Ellie looked hopeful. "We'll find out, I guess. But if she is, then she probably knows her way around an oven like ours. Also she's nervous, eager to fit in, wants to make a good impression, and to try to help, maybe. Right?"

I started getting the picture. "So if we're correct about this, then once she's rested up from her trip, we could ask her."

Ellie nodded enthusiastically. "Or even sooner. Much better than sitting around the house trying to make small talk, yes?"

"Oh, certainly." I tried imagining Bella, freshly confronted with Sam's sudden marriage, playing hostess to his new wife and trying to take care of my dad and Maxie at the same time.

"Good heavens," I said, picturing it. Bella could be slightly difficult if you didn't know her well. Like dynamite could be explosive. "I'd better get up there right away."

Saying this, I grabbed my bag with the bracelet in it, plus my car keys and rain gear, hauling on the latter as well as I could while rushing along fairly urgently. When I glanced in the mirror behind the counter, my oilcloth rain hat was on backward.

But the hell with it; at least it was on my head, which the way I felt I regarded as a major accomplishment.

"Okay. Assuming she's on board with all this," I told Ellie, "I'll have Mika down here in . . ."

I grabbed the remaining chocolate brioche from the display case on my way by. I could smooth over just about any trouble with Bella, I had discovered, by applying enough chocolate brioche.

". . . half an hour?" I finished.

Ellie looked pleased. "Yes, she could be really helpful to me if she does know how to do things in a kitchen. Meanwhile, you could take a nap, yourself."

We'll negotiate that part later, I thought. I was relieved to have a plan, at least, for dealing with some of the knotty problems we were confronting. Not the one about my son getting married without telling me, of course; there wasn't enough brioche in the world to smooth over that little misstep.

I yanked the shop door open, and then three things happened fast: first the little silver bell over the door jingled merrily as usual. Next I got a faceful of thick, chilly drizzle; it tasted of sea salt.

And finally a man in a clear plastic raincoat and rubber shoe covers ran into me, knocking me backward halfway into the shop again as he tried entering it himself.

"Oh, I'm so sorry!" he apologized.

"No problem," I managed, but then I saw who our visitor must be, with his briefcase and his plastic clipboard and an official State of Maine name tag pinned to the pocket of his sport jacket.

And the white compact car outside had an official state plate on it, too. "Hi," he said as I turned to peer closer at him.

He was a health inspector; his name tag said so. "I'm here to follow up on a complaint," he said as he looked around.

That raised my hackles. Even dead, Muldoon was screwing us up. I couldn't imagine a health inspector working during a storm on a holiday weekend, but it was the only explanation I could think of; Muldoon must've gotten one last harassing complaint in before his murder, I thought as Ellie's warning glance shooed me out.

She was right to get rid of me. She was much better equipped, temperamentally and in every other way, to deal with Professor Bleach-Bottle, here.

So I hustled past him, telling myself firmly that I *wasn't* against normal inspections and that I *surely was* for proper food sanitation, for the Chocolate Moose and everywhere else.

But I didn't like being hassled, and especially not by dead guys, and also I was not taking any damned naps, no matter that I'd told Ellie I would. . . . *Oh, I am in a fine mood, all right, and I deserve to be, too,* I told myself irritably.

And the weather didn't help. By now it was late morning, which on a normal July 3 would be a red-white-and-blue carnival scene in Eastport, Maine. But Water Street was so empty you could have rolled a bowling ball down it and not hit anyone, and the gray, heaving water of the bay couldn't have looked more unfriendly if there'd been shark fins sticking up out of it.

Then, as if all that weren't enough, on Key Street I parked the car in my driveway and dashed through the pouring rain to the house, and met Bob Arnold just coming out.

He'd been looking for me, he said.

Eleven

Bob and I met back downtown, where he hustled me into one of the last empty booths at the Waco Diner. The rest of the place consisted of a long counter with a dozen stools plus an adjacent dining room, both areas now full of impatient customers.

"I don't get it," I said when the harried waitress had taken our orders and brought coffee. "I thought most of the tourists had left town. What're all these people doing in here?"

In the next booth two small kids battled stubbornly over a French fry. "That is not," their mother recited tiredly, "the only French fry. There are more. You don't have to fight over the . . ."

"The smart ones are gone. But the damn weather forecast," Bob groused, "is talking now about how maybe it'll be a near miss."

He waved an arm at the packed eatery. "And 'maybe' doesn't help me. All 'maybe' does is create this. *Some* left, but *lots* didn't. Can you imagine if we were having the storm right now?"

As if in agreement with him, the lights flickered. Just once, but it was enough to make his point.

"Okay," I said, "so what do you need me to do?"

Like I didn't have enough. Back at my house, by now Bella was probably so upset she was cleaning between the floorboards with Q-tips and swabbing out the refrigerator with bleach.

But if Eastport did lose power, I couldn't imagine how we would feed and shelter all these people.

"Start calling everybody you know," Bob said, "ask them to call everyone *they* know, and . . ."

Our burgers and fries arrived; I hadn't thought I wanted the food, but once I got started on it, I ate like a starving person.

". . . tell them all, if they've got any spare rooms," Bob said, preparatory to taking a bite, "that we might need them."

Which wasn't likely—the available spare-rooms part, that is. People's own relatives were in town for the holiday, so even some attics and sheds in the backyards were being occupied.

He waved around hopelessly, then took another big bite of his burger and chewed. We ate in worried silence for a while until he changed the subject.

Or more likely, he finally got around to what he had really wanted to talk about all along. "How's Ellie?"

He wiped his hands and nodded for the check. I drank more Coke, figuring that if I could pound enough sugar and caffeine down, I had a chance of staying awake.

"Seems like I should be asking you," I said. Behind me the kids gave up fighting over their food and tumbled from the booth.

"Any word from the detectives? Maybe some early lab results?" I asked.

Yes, I was, in fact, quite nakedly fishing for even the tiniest scrap of info. Bob knew it, too; he wasn't stupid, which made keeping my own cards close to my vest unusually difficult.

Luckily, he was preoccupied by the public-safety situation he was facing . . . or so he wanted me to think.

"What? Oh. No." He got up. "Health guy from Augusta stopped by my office wanting directions to the Moose. Here in town for the fourth, he said. Kill two birds, and all. But nothing new on the crime front, otherwise."

I considered what to say next. I did not want our police chief to know that we had been snooping more on our own. And I certainly wasn't telling him about Miss Halligan's houseguest: He'd most likely been the shooter at Roscoe's trailer; he'd tried running us off the road the night before. And that Ellie's fingerprints would soon be found on the murder weapon.

Because all those things were facts, but we still didn't know the reasons behind any of them. Also, even if we did know what they meant, they weren't proof of anything.

And that was still what we needed to keep homicide detectives from arresting Ellie first and asking more questions later.

What happened next made me think Bob didn't much want to hear about any of it, either. He had something else on his mind.

"Seems that Marla Sykes checked herself out of the hospital," he said casually. He put some cash down. "Friends picked her up, hustled her away from the place, and she hasn't been heard from since."

"Really," I murmured, blessing Ellie's closemouthed nurse acquaintance while trying to sound surprised.

"The whole situation needs a good, hard looking-at," he added as we shouldered back out into the wind-driven rain. "Too bad I'm so busy with this other stuff."

The Fourth of July tourists, he meant: getting them out of town, or keeping them safe here. Either way, he had his hands full.

I glanced at him, wanting to be sure I understood, and found his bright blue gaze already fixed intently on me.

And that's when I realized: He already knew we were snooping more. Not the details, maybe, but he understood that getting Ellie off the hook meant putting somebody else on it.

The somebody who'd *really killed* Matt Muldoon. But on account of the storm, and because state cops weren't eager for advice from small-town police chiefs, Bob couldn't help us much.

That didn't mean he was going to stop us, though, I gathered. "Don't screw up," he called as he crossed to his squad car, parked across Water Street in front of the hardware store.

I'd followed him down here in my own vehicle. As I approached it, he said something more:

"Your pal Roscoe's in the lockup, still. Fang's with him, doing just fine," Bob added to my unasked question. "But he's talking about hitting the road. Nothing left of his trailer, so he might just leave any minute. That's what he says, anyway."

He gestured toward the lower level of the old bank building, where the holding cells were located.

"You might want to visit him," Bob said. "Say good-bye, before he leaves town."

Delivering this large hint, Bob smiled pleasantly at me, rain plastering his thinning yellow hair to his pink forehead. "Might be he's feeling lonesome. And lonesomeness can make a guy chatty, my experience. I mean more than he was before."

Under the sign swinging wildly in the wind over the hardware store's entrance, Bob got into his squad car.

Probably that sign will be the next to go, I thought.

"Don't forget trying to line up some vacant guest rooms," Bob called from the squad car's rolled-down window.

"I'll try," I called back as customers hurried from the store to their vehicles, carrying materials and tools to snug down, box in, or shore up anything that might still blow away.

Driving home, I wondered what in the world I'd just promised.

After all, rooms meant beds, linens, food, conversation, plus all the many other items that unexpected guests might need: Shampoo! Toenail clippers!

That was what I'd ... well, not guaranteed, actually. Not quite. But Bob had just done me a solid, as Sam would say, by not pressing me on the Marla Sykes business up at the hospital; two, if you counted the little tip about Roscoe.

And I could hardly fail to repay him; meanwhile, I had other reasons for wanting everyone in my family all sitting together in one place as well. So even though it was not yet the weekend, I decided to kill about eleventy-seven birds with a single stone by reviving an old family tradition: the Sunday lunch.

Bella fussed miserably while getting out the good china. She also dug venerable crystal and silver from the butler's pantry and napkins from the linen closet, grousing about it all the while.

A meal in the dining room with everyone at the table was her favorite thing, usually. But she didn't like it now, and even the chocolate brioche I brought her hadn't helped.

"Some people," she fumed, "have the sense to go lie down when they're tired."

Me, she meant. In the kitchen Maxie looked up interestedly, wondering if he'd just heard a command, then let his big tan head back down onto his crossed paws with a low "wuff."

Which reminded me: "Where's Marla?" The happy couple wasn't anywhere around, either.

"And where's Dad?" He wasn't in the sunroom, where I'd gotten used to seeing him. "He's not out driving his truck again, is he?"

Bella floofed the tablecloth out over the dining-room table, smoothed it with a bony hand, then plunked candlesticks onto it.

"Your father's upstairs. Shaving and dressing. Wouldn't take help." Her sour face said what she thought about this.

She angled her head at the ceiling. "Sam's upstairs, too. And his"—she hesitated minutely—"wife."

"Now, Bella," I replied. "I'm sure they'll be down soon. And it's great that Dad feels well enough to shave and dress."

Thinking, *Good, they're all out of the way.* Not, in other words, wandering around downtown where they might catch sight of what I meant to do; for one thing, I hadn't forgotten about Roscoe.

"So," I said, turning back to Bella, "rare roast beef with garlic mashed potatoes, new peas, and some of those dinner rolls you make, the delicious ones. You know the ones I mean?"

Well, of course, she did, and she liked my remembering them, usually. Just not right this minute.

"And once you've got the lunch going, please try to get some rooms lined up right away," I went on.

Bob Arnold needed enough sleeping space for a battalion. When I got everyone together at the dining-room table later, I planned on pressing them all into service in this matter.

"Call everybody we know," I said, then caught Bella dragging the back of her bony wrist over her eyes.

I peered closely at her. "Bella, what's . . . Are you crying?"

Pressing a wadded-up tissue to her eyes, she nodded brokenly. "Only while you were out this morning, Millie Marquardt stopped by here, and *she* said . . ."

I put my arm around Bella's skinny frame and she allowed me to, which right there showed how much distress she was in.

"*She* said Ellie's a-goin' to jail! For *murder,* she said, as soon as those police get here again and manage to get their way."

Oh, drat Millie Marquardt, anyway, for scaring our dear Bella and for reminding me of my own worst fear as well.

"Now, now. Ellie's not going to jail." I pulled a fresh tissue from Bella's apron pocket and handed it to her. "Especially if you do what I ask of you, and help me," I said. "Now blow."

Bella obeyed honkingly, which made Maxie raise his big head again. "What else," she asked, "can I do?"

A sick husband, a house full of people, and a storm that at the moment seemed bent on tearing the shingles off the roof. . . . She was a brave little body, and I loved her.

"First of all, when you see Mika again," I began, triggering another frown. "No, we need her," I insisted. "Tell her that if Sam drives her down to the Moose, Ellie would be glad for some help there."

Bella's face softened, but the doubt in her eyes remained. "You mean to say we're just going to let some strange girl get her hooks into him?" she demanded.

"Whether or not she's strange is unknown," I said firmly. "But the 'hooks' part is already a done deal, so let's make the best of it and try to help Sam out while we're at it, too, okay?"

Whether or not Mika took my suggestion about the Moose was up to her, I decided, leaving Bella to get on with things. She was happiest when captaining her own ship.

Although none of us would be truly happy until Ellie was out of trouble. And what was going on right now would surely end very *un*happily for everyone, if I didn't hurry up and do something about it. The question was: what?

Luckily, I was beginning to have an answer. But before I acted, I wanted to sort things out quietly in my head. So I drove through the slashing rain down to the breakwater again, to think in silence. But after only a few minutes of sitting there, I saw Sam pulling into one of the parking spots in front of the Moose.

Climbing out, he ducked through the downpour around to the passenger side, holding an umbrella, which he used to shield Mika, and taking her arm protectively in his own. He accompanied her inside, and by the time he came out again, I was at the shop, too.

"Get in," I said, and finally, now that I had him alone, I let loose on him: How could you? When did you? *Why* did you?

Sam stared straight ahead until I'd finished. Then: "You and Ellie were right about Mika. She says she's an amateur baker, but she's too modest. She's won competitions, even."

I drove up Water Street through the rain. "It's not mine, by the way," he added. "The baby. I mean, not biologically, anyway."

"But she said . . . How did you . . . *Why*, then?" I demanded.

He stared out at the churning bay. "We were friends. I hadn't seen her in a while. But we reconnected in Boston not long after I got there, right after the guy dumped her."

He'd been in Boston for a month. When he got back, he'd meant to take back his job at the marine supply store. "As soon as he found out about her being pregnant, he was history," Sam said.

"I see." I could imagine the rest of it. For all his problems and challenges, Sam was a good fellow; I just hoped his kindness hadn't put him into something life-ruining.

He leaned back in the car seat. "Her parents dumped her, too, when they heard about the baby. They are very . . . um . . . traditional."

On the water the wind blew foamy wave tops to smithereens; I drove uphill past the Coast Guard station.

"So you got married so she'd have . . ."

He nodded hard, biting his lower lip. "Somebody. Not that she couldn't do it by herself," he added earnestly. "She's extremely capable, makes plenty of money. She's a nurse. The baking is just a hobby."

Well, that was promising, at least. "But she's still nervous about the baby," he went on. "Anyone would be."

I thought back to when I'd learned I was having Sam: oh, "nervous" wasn't even the word for it.

"And, anyway, she shouldn't have to do it alone," he finished stubbornly. "Neither should the kid."

He turned to me, possibly remembering life without his own father. (And with him, too, perhaps, but that was another story.)

"Mom, she's generous, and funny, and she's really smart," he added in appeal.

All good qualities. But he hadn't yet said he loved her, had he? No, actually, he hadn't, and I was afraid to ask. He'd always been a sucker for the grand gesture, I knew that much about him. Like his mom.

"I didn't call because we were in the process of getting married, and I knew you'd try talking me out of it."

So he'd waited until it was done, then showed up here: *fait accompli.*

"Okay," I said, with a sigh, "I understand. Just let me know if—"

"If I can do anything to help," I'd have said, but I didn't get to. Suddenly his arms were around me, his curly hair soft on my cheek, and his beard scratching my neck as he hugged me.

"Thanks, Ma," he replied, and I realized how hard this must have been for him. Then I noticed where we'd gotten to: all the way out to Marla Sykes's house at the end of Water Street.

I pulled into her driveway and parked. "Sam, open the glove compartment, will you, please?"

He looked puzzledly at me, but did as I asked and came up with the small, soft leather pouch I'd stuck in there when I left the house.

He loosened the pouch's drawstring. "Mom, there's a gun in here!"

A loaded .22 pistol, to be precise. "Oh, good, because that's where I put one."

Living with Wade has benefits besides the obvious ones.

He'd taught me to shoot, to handle a weapon safely, and how to make the right choice about whether I needed to carry it or not.

Today I'd decided I did; I mean heck, there was a killer running around loose. "'Don't leave home without it, right?'" I joked, but Sam wasn't amused.

"What do you need this for?" Sam didn't know anything about the murder, of course, and I didn't have time to enlighten him.

Rain slapped the windshield, unfazed by the flapping wipers. I had no business being here, but it occurred to me that right now Marla was back at my house.

Which meant she wasn't here. Sam was, though.

"Stay in the car," I told him, "and keep your eyes peeled. If anyone else shows up, you come and get me, and do it fast."

Because sitting there on the breakwater before I ran into Sam, I'd been thinking about Roscoe and what I should say when I visited him in the holding cell. But creeping into my mind also had been another question: *Could a house with so much illicit cash hidden in it hold other secrets, too?*

And now was my chance to find out.

Hustling across Marla's yard was like running through a wind tunnel with spa jets in it. On the porch steps I fumbled the key from its familiar place under the mat and went in.

Moments later Sam came in, too, to my annoyance. Some lookout he'd turned out to be. "Hey, I needed you to keep watch."

"Windshield's fogged. Can't see out." He followed me down the front hall. The house felt cold and damp as the inside of a tomb.

"Okay." I tucked the pistol into my pocket. "Go look out the front-porch window, then, and if you see anyone coming, let me know."

Sam sloped off cooperatively, leaving me to ask myself: *If I were the kind of deep, dark secret that could get Ellie out of a murder charge, where would I be?*

Which was how I found myself in the cellar again. A bare bulb dangling over the steps cast my shadow ahead of me as I descended; once I was down there, I shivered in the damp and peered around.

Rusty old tools looked like murder weapons. The open end of the slat-walled coal bin, long unused, gaped like a dark mouth.

Swallowing hard, I crossed to where the old chimney sported an ash-cleanout hatch. Ellie and I had gotten chased out before we could snoop around here; now I scanned the wall, looking for loose bricks or other signs of possible hidey-holes. And then I saw it:

Black grit speckled the floor beneath the chimney's clean-out hatch. *Fresh* grit, as if someone had opened it lately. But the fireplace upstairs was closed up, so why clean that hatch at all?

I lifted the door. Inside was a pile of old fireplace debris so charcoal black that it seemed to be sucking light *into* itself in-stead of reflecting any.

"Ma?" Sam's voice came urgently from the top of the cellar steps. "Sorry to rush you, but I think we'd better scram."

On the pile lay a large unsealed manila envelope, ash-smeared but otherwise intact. Newish-looking, even, as if someone had just put it there recently.

Sam came to the stairwell door. "Come on, we've got to go."

Just because I had a weapon, that didn't mean I wanted a confrontation, and Sam being here with me made me want one even less. So I grabbed the envelope, stuck it up under my shirt, tucked the shirt in tightly, and took the stairs in a couple of big leaps, letting Sam haul me upward by my arm for the last few steps.

Through the kitchen, out the back door, and across the sodden grass we galloped, hurling ourselves into the car, backing out the driveway in a spew of gravel and rain.

"Was somebody actually in the house? Did you see who it was?" I slowed as we drove back downtown.

Sam shook his head. "Not inside. Big black car, went by real slow, then turned around and went by again the other way. Didn't seem right to me, was all. I got a bad feeling about it."

That's my boy, I thought with a burst of pride. "You see who was driving?" Although I was pretty sure I already knew.

"Nuh-uh. Tinted windshield." He turned. "Ma, what've you and Ellie got yourselves into?"

So of course I had to explain everything, and when I was done, he quite naturally wanted to know why we didn't just dump all we'd found out so far into Bob Arnold's lap and let him deal with the state police?

So I explained that, too: "Because it's going to sound like we're just trying to shift blame. Nothing that we could say gives anyone else a better motive than Ellie's, or puts them more on the spot than she was when Muldoon got killed."

He nodded slowly. "So as it stands now, *something* must link *some* of what you know to the murder in your shop. And if you knew what those particular somethings were . . ."

"Right. Some of it's pertinent, some's probably not, and we don't know which is which." I took a breath. "And I'm not sure she realizes it yet, but if Ellie goes to jail over this, even if she's cleared eventually, it could wreck her life."

And her family's, too. For one thing, there's no bail on murder charges in Maine, so the accused can sit in custody for a long time—long enough for George to have to give up his Bangor job and stay here to care for their daughter, for instance.

"Then there'll be attorney costs, travel and lodging expenses for visiting her. And if I know George, he'll be there every minute that's allowed, so he won't be working. And who knows what else?"

And that didn't even begin to cover the dreadful possibility of her being convicted. Sam nodded. "Okay. So where do we go now?"

I shot him a sideways smile—*That's my boy, for sure*—and he grinned at me in reply. But then he glanced back and frowned.

"Hey! Somebody's following us, it looks like."

I kept my eyes on the road as a rainsquall struck suddenly. "The big dark car again?"

Sam nodded. We rounded the sharp curve toward Custom Street. "Yeah, it's him, all right. Turn in here."

He pointed to a sandy track leading down to the water. "Just do it," he said.

Sam's youthful stage as a beach bum was coming in handy. I jerked the steering wheel, bumping us downhill over a steep, sandy slope studded with tide-scoured stones.

At the bottom a weathered wooden shed sagged with age. When the tide was high, you could pull a little boat into it. But right now the tide was low; hurriedly I drove in under rickety-looking rafters.

Sam hopped out of the car and peered out between the shed's slats. Gusts threatened to reduce the old structure to matchsticks as I waited nervously; finally he got back into the car.

"The guy's gone by. Didn't see us, I'm pretty sure. Man, it's getting wild out there."

I backed out of the shed again, impressed by how unflappable my son was proving to be. "Now what?" he wanted to know.

The envelope I'd taken from Marla's cellar was still in my shirt. But Roscoe was still in the town lockup, too, and maybe not for long. *"Any minute,"* Bob Arnold had said.

Bob must've had a reason to think the young man Wade and I had visited—and been shot at with, let's not forget that part—

might be feeling more talkative than he had earlier. A reason for thinking it, I mean, *and* a reason for telling me about it.

So instead of pulling out the envelope, I gunned the car back up onto the road, and minutes later we were outside the East-port lockup.

"Ma," Sam said. "Listen, I'm sorry about everything."

"Sam, I wish you had told me about it first, that's all."

Or even asked me or Wade for advice, I added silently, not wanting to push it. "But I'm going to assume you know what you're doing," I said.

What I actually assumed was that there was nothing I could do about it, so I might as well make the best of it.

"And for what it's worth, from what little I've seen of her, Mika does seem to be a very nice girl," I went on.

"Oh, she is," Sam burst out, "and isn't she pretty? Talented too. She's a violinist, on top of everything. That's why she's been in Boston, to take lessons."

The words tumbled from him in a rush until they ran out. But all I really heard was the way his voice softened when he spoke of her, which was how I knew two things:

He was in love, all right: truly, deeply. And it wasn't my business to try to meddle in that, was it? *My boy . . .*

But the truth was, he wasn't a boy any longer; and if I wanted a relationship with him at all, I would have to accept that.

He broke the silence, changing the subject. "So what are we doing here, again?"

At the lockup, he meant. I hesitated, not ready to end our talk; the other thing I hadn't said to him, of course, was that he could marry a sword swallower from the circus and I'd still count it as a win as long as he wasn't drinking again.

He looked good, actually; his high cheekbones sun-burnished and his eyes bright. Now he caught me assessing him.

"I'm fine, Ma," he said. "Really." He peered up at the old redbrick bank building. "C'mon, let's go in."

So we did, finding Roscoe in the clean, well-lit, and decently furnished cubicle used for housing local miscreants who couldn't be transported at once to the county jail in Machias, thirty miles to our south.

"Hi," Roscoe said, getting up to greet us. Fang stayed on the rug, asleep. Some of the fur on his rear had been shaved, and he had a few small wounds where the buckshot had been plucked out by the vet. But otherwise he seemed fine.

On the wall-mounted TV, an episode of *Family Feud* played; I wondered how long it had been since Roscoe, who'd cleaned himself up nicely at the room's little sink, had enjoyed cable television.

"Howdy," he greeted Sam, sticking his scrubbed-pink hand out when I introduced them. "Nice to meet you."

The place wasn't locked. Roscoe could've walked right out. But Bob Arnold always said that when you treat people well, they'll behave well in return, mostly. In the case of the lockup this had turned out to be true; there'd never been an escape.

"Listen, Roscoe," I said. "I know you're scared of somebody, okay? And I don't blame you. I'm scared, too. But I want to help."

The wind howled between the buildings outside; Fang lifted his head and moaned, and Roscoe blinked with fright.

"This place is okay," he whispered. "Besides, I ain't got no other one to go to. But I gotta leave, because, you know, what if he finds me down here?"

His fear is realistic, I thought. "Roscoe, how about if I took you to my house? My family's there, and Wade. You could stay with us until the storm ends, anyway. Would you feel safer there?"

Roscoe brightened. "Fang, d'you hear that? We can go to this nice lady's house!"

"But you will," Sam put in sternly, "tell her whatever she needs to know?" He caught on fast, that kid of mine.

Roscoe nodded, his eyes huge. "Oh yes, I surely will. Why, if you're going to make it so I don't have to be scared of that guy no more, I'll answer whatever you ask," he declared firmly, and then he did tell.

Oh, did he ever.

Twelve

Ten minutes later, in my wind-battered driveway, I sprinted from the car to the house. A metal trash can rolled, clattering up the street, and then a lawn chair, toppling end-over-end.

I flung myself inside, with Sam and Roscoe and the dog Fang scrambling in right behind. "Bella?"

She came in a hurry with a pan of garden peas in her hands, while I stood there in the back hall, shaking the rain off myself.

"Where's Marla?" I looked around. The slicker I'd lent Marla the night before wasn't on its hook.

Bella frowned. "I don't know where she is. Not upstairs. I was up there with a dust mop a minute ago and I didn't see her."

Outside, the storm was cranking up for the main show, wind shrieking in the chimneys and thumping the roof, lifting shingles and rattling them down again with a sharp *snappity-snap-snap*.

"You know, though," Bella mused, "I did think I heard a car slowing down on the street out front, not too long ago."

A true storm veteran, she'd gotten out batteries, candles, and propane cylinders for the camp stove, and arranged them on the kitchen mantel. All the dinner materials, except for the beef roast, were out already, too, so they'd be handy when she wanted them.

And Sam was already in the sunroom with my dad, introducing Roscoe and telling him to make himself comfortable. "Get him some dry clothes, Sam," I called, "and some for yourself, too."

Marla could be just about anywhere by now, especially if she'd been picked up by someone in a car. That meant I desperately needed information of some kind, right this very minute.

So instead of going out on a rain-drenched wild-goose chase, I pulled the envelope from under my shirt, yanked the papers from it, and spread them on the kitchen table.

And stared. "Damn," I uttered. They were bank deposit receipt slips, a hundred or more all with the same account name, Sykes Chocolate Creations. Also in the envelope: a checkbook, its ledger showing both the deposits and the withdrawals that followed.

The deposits were in varying dollar amounts. To unsuspecting eyes, they'd have looked as if they represented payments from her customers for the chocolate they had purchased.

Just as she'd said. But for each deposit three withdrawals of equal amounts had been made right afterward.

And that wasn't what she'd described at all. Marla had said she was being paid a small percentage of what she deposited.

But this money, a hundred thousand or more dollars in total, was being divided into equal thirds. And after what Roscoe had told me . . .

Marla wasn't a victim, as Ellie and I had believed. Instead she was . . . Oh, what a fool I'd been.

"What?" said Bella, looking alarmed at my expression as I headed for the door again.

"No time," I told her. "Tell Sam I said for him to stay here with you and Dad and watch out for everything, okay?"

Rain hat, slicker, umbrella, keys . . . The gun was still in my pocket. "Tell him I'll be back."

The storm outside now was just flat-out ridiculous, wind and rain in torrents shoving me around as I crossed to the car. Down Key Street, rushing rivers overflowed in the gutters and boiled in the storm drains. When Bob Arnold's squad car raced by me in the other direction, with lights flashing and its siren wailing, I knew conditions were bad.

For someone else, that is. But it also meant that if things got dicey for me, Bob was already busy. And that, considering the unhappy thoughts I was thinking, didn't comfort me at all.

"Ellie?" On rain-swept Water Street I shoved open the shop door and flung myself into the Chocolate Moose. The smell of warm chocolate enveloped me in sweetness, but it wasn't enough to banish my bitter fear.

Because once Roscoe had felt safe enough to talk, he'd said that the person who'd hired him for lookout duty out on the water hadn't been a guy at all. It had been a woman: Marla Sykes.

And the deposit receipts told me why. I didn't know yet why Matt Muldoon had needed to get murdered over it all, but . . .

"Ellie!" The lights were on, the ceiling fans turning, two cheesecakes cooling, and the oven timer ticking steadily, showing a minute left to go on some chocolate macaroons that she and Mika must have been baking together.

I yanked them out; to hell with the extra minute. "Ellie, are you here somewhere?"

But of course she wasn't, and neither was Mika. I ran next door to the Second Hand Rose, where an old Joni Mitchell album was on the CD player and a small battery-run water fountain trickled prettily on the massive old mahogany cash register counter.

"Hello?" Racks of vintage cashmere sweaters, suede coats, and leather jackets crammed the shop's tiny front space, along with silk scarves and pillbox hats, lace shawls and fancy blouses.

I pushed through the beaded curtain to the back of the shop, where I'd never been, and where a jumble of as-yet unsorted items (feather boas, a gold lorgnette, what looked like a real, no-kidding, mink coat) overflowed from cardboard boxes.

On the rear wall an old framed poster advised me curtly to BE HERE NOW. But still no Miss Halligan . . . until from behind the boxes came a low moan.

Squeezing past them, I found a sort of nest: a narrow mattress with blankets, an alarm clock, and a tiny TV. A romance novel lay on the plastic milk crate serving as a night table; this was where she slept, I saw, now that her own bed was no longer available.

And it was where she lay now; a burst of fury washed over me as I knelt. "Miss Halligan? What happened? Are you all right?"

A spot of blood stained her clipped white hair, and the lump on her forehead was swelling rapidly, turning an ugly purple.

Her eyes fluttered open. "Oh . . ."

"Was he here? Miss Halligan, where's the guy who's staying in your house? Do you know? And who is he, anyway?"

If I knew who he was, it might help me to find him, and get Ellie and Mika out of his clutches when I did. "Miss Halligan?"

And Marla as well; I couldn't imagine his intentions toward her were good, even if she'd gone with him willingly. This was all coming apart, whatever it was, and for a while she'd been a co-conspirator.

But now she was a witness against him. "Look, just tell me who he is and I'll get the police to go after him," I said.

But this didn't get the reaction I expected. "Who? Clark?" she said fearfully, struggling up. "Oh, please don't do that! He's my son. Please don't hurt him. He didn't do anything. He couldn't . . . He wouldn't be out in the daytime like this and be seen by anyone. He's got—"

Her mouth snapped shut, but I already understood: her son.

It explained why she let him live in her house, and why he wanted to. Because he knew she would no more betray him than I would my own.

"Warrants out on him, huh?" I said, and she nodded sadly.

Our tiny, remote town must've looked to him like a place he could hunker down in, I supposed, with a mother whose devotion he could depend on. He must've been the one who'd gotten Marla into whatever scheme she was involved in, too.

Miss Halligan shook her head mournfully. "Poor Clark, he's always had bad luck. First all the eye problems he had as a child and now—"

Yeah, poor Clark. "Was it him? Was he here? Did he hurt you?"

"No!" Miss Halligan climbed to her feet, tried vainly to put herself to rights.

"No, I'd just talked to him on the phone. He was at my house, when I heard someone out front in the shop."

I didn't believe her. "Who, then?" I followed her to the tiny bathroom, where she splashed water onto her face.

"Who, Miss Halligan?" Outside, the storm clamored wildly and the rain slammed down. "If it wasn't your son, Clark?"

Miss Halligan turned, her clipped white hair blood-streaked and her heavy black eyeliner running like dark teardrops down her cheeks.

"I saw a hand come up with something in it. Something heavy." She winced again, remembering. "I ducked, so it didn't hit square on. A glancing blow, but enough, I guess."

Her fingers went to her head again and came away red. "They must've been looking for something," she said about the front of the store's disarray.

Just as they had been at her house, in her little office, and at Marla's. But I didn't have time to tell her about that.

"After that, I don't remember anything, really, until you woke me up back there," Miss Halligan finished.

Outside, another couple of sirens wailed distantly. *Whatever*

Bob Arnold was racing to, it was big. But as I thought this, my cell phone *cheeped* at me and it was him.

"Yeah," he said through a background of wind noise and phone static, loud and electrical-sounding, "I'm jammed up out here, but I thought you ought to know."

The phone cut out briefly, then back in again. Bob went on: "State cops called. They've had pressure from the district attorney. They wanted to know if I thought Ellie'd be around tomorrow. Or if—"

The high whine of a tow truck winch interrupted him. I waited anxiously. "Or if she might hightail it," Bob finished.

Which meant they intended to take my friend into custody in the morning, and never mind that it was a holiday, unless instead they came and got her tonight despite the storm.

". . . told 'em she'd be here," Bob's voice came tinnily through my phone, "but I figured you'd want a heads-up."

"Yes," I shouted back; he was fading out. "Thanks, I . . ."

His voice came intermittently: ". . . accident . . . high tide now for . . . stuck here on the mainland side of the causeway until . . ."

The call dropped. But I'd heard enough. "Listen, will you be okay?" I asked Miss Halligan, and she smiled tiredly in reply.

"I'm a tough old bird, I'll be fine. Please don't call the police. And please . . ."

I turned from the door. Her eyes were tragic.

"If anything happens, try not to let them hurt him."

Back at the house I grabbed Sam out of the sunroom, leaving Roscoe chatting amiably with my dad. Once we were in the car, I told him what had happened: about Miss Halligan's son being the guy who'd followed us, and that Mika and Ellie were missing, and so was Marla Sykes, and that probably the guy had them all.

"Marla was in on it with him but now I'll bet he's turned against her. He can't get off the island until the causeway's clear, but then he'll run. So we don't have much time – "

Sam cut me off. "Ma, what in the world are you thinking?" He hauled out his cell phone and began punching numbers into it. "We've got to call the cops."

Right, only we couldn't. "Sam, look at this storm. You know that by the time anyone gets all the way out here . . ."

In Bob's absence it would be either the county sheriff or a state patrol officer, and in this kind of weather it could take a couple of hours or more for any of them to arrive.

Assuming, I mean, that they weren't all tied up with whatever was occupying Bob right this minute; a bad traffic accident in the storm, it had sounded like.

"And I'm sorry, but we've got to find them a lot faster than that," I said.

Sam grimaced, accepting this. On Water Street the incoming tide sent waves exploding upward like geysers between the pier's planks.

"Look," I said, "the one thing I know is that Marla Sykes was laundering money through her chocolate business."

She'd admitted that much. "But maybe Muldoon found out about it. If he did, knowing him, he probably threatened her."

"So to keep him quiet she got rid of him, and because she knew a lot about the Chocolate Moose, she was able to do it in a way that directed suspicion at Ellie?" Sam theorized.

"Right. She might even have been in the shop when George was doing the floor, so she'd have known about the trapdoor."

Wind buffeted the car. "Although," I added, still doubtful, "I'm not sure of that."

Sam scowled. "But then how'd she get hurt, herself? Or Miss Halligan, either? And why take Ellie and Mika?"

"I don't know." I gripped the steering wheel. I didn't know what the photos of Miss Halligan had to do with it, either. But maybe this was all a lot simpler than I'd thought. Sam pulled his phone out again.

"This is crazy, I've got to call someone."

"Fine, go ahead if you think it'll do any good. But I'm telling you, nobody can get here until the accident's cleared and the tide goes out, so the traffic can use the causeway again."

I pulled over on Washington Street and dug out my own phone, intending to call Wade. If I could get hold of him, he could come with us while we hunted for Ellie and Mika.

But no bars showed on the device. "Phones are out."

Probably the wind had damaged a cell tower. Even way out here it didn't happen often. But it did sometimes, mostly in the middle of bad storms, and now it had.

Sam sagged in the passenger seat. "You know where you're going now, though, right? I mean you have *some* idea of where—"

"Yeah, Sam, I'm not just driving around for the fun of it."

Saying this, I turned onto a narrow lane running down toward the bay, then turned again between granite boulders serving as driveway markers. Because there was one person still left that I hadn't really pressed about all this: the grieving widow.

And her house, perched at the edge of a cliff overlooking the bay, was plenty isolated enough for what I'd begun suspecting: the nearest-and-dearest theory of identifying murder suspects might have some usefulness here, after all.

MULDOON, said the sign at the end of the driveway. I followed it between beach-rose hedges to a low, glass-and-steel structure built into the side of a steep granite ledge.

"Ma," said Sam, "this is a dead end. They're not here. Mika and Ellie, I mean."

Then, squinting around, he added, "The place is pretty snazzy, though, huh?"

"No kidding." We got out and ran for the portico angled over the slate-tiled front terrace. "The Muldoons had it built here."

I pounded on the massive pine-slab front door. Until now I'd thought subtlety was our best strategy; for one thing, our snooping seemed always to be triggering someone's chasing and/or shooting behaviors.

But subtlety hadn't worked, and if the alternative included me at my pushiest, so be it. Ellie and Mika were in danger, and so was Marla, I now believed.

And they might be here. I hammered again and finally the sound of footsteps pattered from somewhere inside. Then the door opened and Sarabelle Muldoon stood there in a satin dressing gown and slippers.

With her pale hair pulled back and her face in disarray, she'd obviously been weeping. "What do you want?" she demanded harshly.

Good question, and I didn't know the answer for sure. But by now I was convinced that her husband's death had some-thing—maybe everything—to do with Marla's hidden money and Miss Halligan's criminal son.

So it was truth-telling time, or as much of it as would get us into the slate-tiled foyer, anyway.

"Ellie didn't kill him. I'm trying to find out who did," I said.

There was no muscle car parked in the driveway and nowhere to hide one, I'd noticed. Sarabelle's eyes gave away nothing, but she stepped aside. We followed her into a large, dim-lit sitting room so devoid of any personality, it was like a doctor's waiting area: beige rugs, nubby tan upholstery.

The only color in the place was in an elaborate wall hanging over the modern white-brick fireplace. It featured yarns in fantas-tic hues, with beads and feathers worked into the weaving. . . . My eyes fairly danced over the thing, as they were meant to do.

"Pretty, isn't it? I made that," she said wistfully. "A long time ago."

"'Pretty' isn't the word for it. It's beautiful."

More like tragic, actually. It showed me who she'd been, and perhaps still was behind all the determinedly applied makeup and jewelry she usually wore. Seeing it, you had to wonder what else she'd given up or lost, and under what kind of pres-sure.

But that wasn't what I was here for. "Sarabelle, I need to ask you a few things—"

Sam cut in. "Ellie White and my wife are missing from the Chocolate Moose. So's Marla Sykes. We need to know if you have any ideas about where they are, or who might've taken them."

"Or if they're here now," I might have added. But my probing gaze got that point across; Sarabelle's own dark eyes narrowed.

"I know nothing about them." Rain sheeted down the big plate glass windows at the far end of the room, where an elaborate exercise area included a gym-quality stationary bicycle, a weight machine, and a mat with a collection of free weights alongside it.

Sarabelle stood looking at the fancy apparatus for a moment, seeming not to have heard Sam. Then: "I'm sorry about the trouble Matt caused you. My husband just wasn't a very nice man—"

"Sarabelle, please," I interrupted. "First of all, you were the one behind the trouble he caused us. You wanted Ellie and me gone from the Moose so you could move in and have a bakery of your own. Why, you even looked at the shop space before we did."

Her brittle laugh rang out in the chilly room. "Is that what he told you? Oh, that's rich. He would blame it all on me."

She faced us, her dressing gown wrapped messily around her body, the satin slippers on her feet scuffed and worn.

"Matt wanted that shop space, not me. He took me down there and pushed the whole bakery idea on me because I *didn't* want to. But I never even went inside the place until the Moose opened."

She took a breath, shifting a strand of glittery white stones resting on her collarbone; even in her distress it seemed she just couldn't do without jewelry.

"As for what he did to you . . . like I say, he enjoyed making trouble for people. I mean, please," she added, "do I look to you like someone who wants to work in a bakery?"

She had a point.

"Right," I said, "but never mind that. I need to know if—"

She shook her blond head tiredly. "No. I already told you and the police, too, I don't know a single thing about Matt's murder, or about Ellie or whoever was with her being gone, or who took them."

It was all Sam needed to hear; he edged toward the door. I'd been hoping for a hint of that lemon cologne in the air, but there wasn't one.

So probably this was a wild-goose chase, as Sam had thought. But I wasn't done yet. "Sarabelle, please. I know I haven't been friendly." I nearly choked on the words. "But I'd appreciate your help. I need to know where Ellie and Sam's wife, Mika, are right now."

Stepping forward, she kept on moving me back toward the foyer, while the wind whistled crazily outside. Her lean, toned form wielded some surprisingly forceful body language.

"I told you I don't know anything. Except that your friend killed him and you want her to get away with it," she pronounced, edging Sam and me out onto the front terrace.

"Okay, then, just tell me this," I tried as she began closing the door. "Do you by any chance think Matt might've been seeing Miss Halligan? I mean . . . romantically?"

"What?" The door came open once more; her earrings sparkled like the falling raindrops behind us.

"Oh, dear," she said. "I'm afraid you've got Matt all wrong."

"Ma," Sam called impatiently from behind me. "Ma, come on." He climbed into the car and slammed the door.

Sarabelle looked pityingly at me as a new downpour rattled on the portico overhead.

"My husband was a hound, all right? Always sniffing around. Just not here at home in Eastport, where someone might catch him at it."

His trips for "meetings" at the health department in Augusta sprang to mind; she saw me thinking it and I realized suddenly that I'd misjudged her, that I'd been selling her short all along.

"Right," she said, comprehension in her eyes. "You don't know anything about me, do you? But since you're so curious . . ." Her look hardened. "Matt liked them young. That's what I put up with all the time I was married to him. Miss Halligan's a doll, all right, but she's out of the running by several generations," she said, and with that, she did close the door on me finally.

Out in the car Sam had the engine running and the defroster blower on, so I could see to back out. Unfortunately, I had no idea what to do or where to go now.

"The only way I can see any of this working," I told Sam, "is that Clark Carmody convinced Marla Sykes to do more than just launder the money he was getting illegally, somehow."

Because a one-third share argued for more than bookkeeping duties. And where had the other third gone, anyway?

Yet another question I didn't have the answer to. "And then what? He turned against her?" Sam asked.

"Yeah, that's what I think. He's probably got all three of them stashed somewhere by now. And if he killed Muldoon, he's surely desperate to get off the island, either with them or . . ."

Or without them, because he's already killed them, too, I finished silently; I couldn't say it to Sam. He knew, though, I could tell from his face.

Around us a few last stragglers of the tourist variety crept out of town with their headlights on and their windshield wipers slapping. But others had already turned around, their cars coming back in a steady stream.

"Anyway, whatever was going on, Muldoon found out about it," I theorized, "and made trouble about it, as he always did. So he had to die, and then Ellie and I started poking around."

A blown-down branch smacked the windshield and flew away; a flag sailed like a kite. "He probably thought I'd be at the Moose with Ellie just now," I said, "instead of Mika."

A makeshift sign on Washington Street said the causeway was still out; it was why all those cars were coming back.

"Sam, I'm so sorry. I just don't know what else to do."

Visiting Sarabelle had been especially useless. She hadn't cared much for her husband, but that cut both ways, didn't it?

Because I got the strong feeling she hadn't cared much about his infidelities, either, or at least not enough to kill him over them.

Sometimes the nearest really aren't the dearest. Sometimes, as with Sarabelle Muldoon, they just don't give a damn anymore. Sam sighed heavily as we pulled up in front of the Moose. Then he trotted through the drenching rain to peer into the shop.

"Nobody," he reported when he returned to the car, and when we checked Marla's Eastport house again and then Miss Halligan's, they were deserted also.

I thought briefly about the cheesecakes still waiting to be completed, but decided to forget them. After all, why bother? The auction, Ellie's catering business, probably even the chances of our continuing in the Chocolate Moose at all . . .

None of it means anything if something bad has happened to Ellie or Mika, I realized miserably.

"It's not your fault or Ellie's, either," Sam said. "It's whoever took her and Mika that I want to get hold of, and damn it, I'm going to."

Which was my feeling about it as well. I just didn't see how as I started back up storm-lashed Water Street, where wind-frayed Fourth of July banners hung like sodden laundry under the streetlamps glowing sullenly in the cloud-darkened daytime gloom.

But as we made our slow way up Key Street under power lines whining and whipping in the wind, Sam sat up straight, suddenly.

"Hey. I just thought of something. Ellie still has a boat, doesn't she?"

He'd been living right here at home back when she first got it, even helped with the launch the previous summer.

"Yes," I said. "But how would a stranger like Miss Halligan's son know that?"

My old house rose up ahead, lights glowing in the windows and a curl of smoke streaming sideways off the brick chimney-top.

Sam punched a bunch of numbers into his cell phone, which for a wonder was operating again, at least temporarily.

"Bella? Are Ellie and Mika there? Or Marla?" he said into it.

He shook his head at me, listening. Then: "Okay. And you have not heard from them. And Wade's not home yet, either?"

He was still working, probably; the boat basin when we passed it downtown had looked wilder than ever.

Sam hung up, then turned to me, looking thoughtful. "A boat," he said as if there had been no interruption, "that you could get off the island on. So . . . does Marla know about it?"

Like I said: *That's my boy.*

I stomped the gas pedal hard.

Debris littered the road to the boat dock: tree limbs, trash cans that had blown out of people's yards, some boat cushions and a big blue tarp, complete with the lines somebody had tried using to tie it down, all flew and tumbled as if possessed.

"Gnarly," Sam observed as we passed the low wooden Youth Center building. A hand-lettered cardboard sign in the window said BINGO TONITE, but from the way the building's shingles flapped in the gale, I thought the games would probably have to be postponed.

Then the lights inside the building—it was being readied to provide emergency shelter, I realized—went out. And stayed out.

"Try your phone," I said, and Sam obeyed.

"Nuttin', honey," he reported, so not only had the power gone out, but now apparently the phones had failed again, too.

The good news, though, was that no one would take a boat

out in this mess; not unless Davy Jones's locker looked viable as an escape route to them . . . or so I hoped.

At last we reached the dock, where the floating sections and the boats tied up to them seemed to fly up into the air in a slow, rippling motion each time a massive wave rolled in.

"I'm going down there," Sam said.

Wind shook the car. Out past the boats visibility was almost nil.

"I'm coming, too," I told him, spotting the Bayliner among the other vessels bouncing and lurching. Before he could object, I was out of the car and staggering toward the metal gangway right behind him.

Probably there was no one here. The dock, what little I could see of it through an atmosphere that was now mostly water, looked properly deserted, and there were no other cars around, either.

All of this seemed normal, given the weather conditions. But what did not seem normal, suddenly, was the sky brightening all at once and the wind dropping abruptly. There were no more of those intermittent storm bands coming in; this was the real deal now.

Sam pointed south toward where a break in the roiling clouds sent freakish-looking shafts of sunlight slanting onto the waves. "It's the eye," he said cryptically, but then I got it.

The eye of the storm. The thing was so powerful now that it was actually forming hurricane features. An odd sound came from somewhere, barely audible over the waves' crash.

Also a faint light gleamed in the Bayliner's cabin. Sam saw it, too. "Come on," he mouthed, charging forward.

Ahead lay the metal gangway, wet and slippery, slanting down to the water. At least, it wasn't low tide, so it wasn't vertical this time.

But high tide meant the water here was deep, cold, and likely fatal if you fell in when it was this wild. I gripped the railing with one hand, Sam held my other arm, and we proceeded down the ramp side by side like some fragile old couple, tottering and weaving.

At the bottom the dock's planks heaved wildly, trying to hurl us off. But we persisted, scampering to the Bayliner and gripping the boat's side rail to keep our balance.

"I don't understand," came a voice from inside the cabin. It was Ellie's. "How do you expect to get away with it?"

Then a new voice, recognizable also: "What do we care how the plan's supposed to work? This is ridiculous. Let me go right now!"

Sam grinned in spite of himself; it was Mika, sounding every bit like the no-bullshit woman I'd always hoped he'd marry.

But the grin didn't last. "You don't have to know my plans," another voice said.

My heart sank. It was Marla sounding as if she'd recovered very nicely from her head injury.

"Just rest assured I'm not going to let a bunch of dimwits like you screw them up."

There was the sound of metal snapping against metal. "So you two just sit there while I get this tub to where we're going. And be aware, if you stick your heads up out of the hatch," she added, "that I will shoot them right off your bodies."

So at some point she'd apparently gotten the handgun out of the lockbox I'd seen in her warehouse space. Wade probably still had his weapon, too.

And so did I. But it wasn't time to use it, yet, and now another idea struck me: that GPS tracker that Ellie's husband, George, had put into the Bayliner.

I hadn't turned it off. I didn't even know how to open the small black plastic box that held it, in the Bayliner's emergency gear compartment. That meant it was still there; now, once Marla set off in the boat for whatever her destination was, all we had to do was survive long enough for Wade to realize we were out on the boat, and start tracking the device's signal.

Without warning the hatch door flew open. But by now Sam

and I were over the rail onto the Bayliner's deck and then scrambling out to the heaving bow, where we dropped to our bellies out of sight between the rail and the cabin.

"They're okay," I mouthed at Sam, wanting to be encouraging.

"So far," he said silently back, not looking happy, and for a moment I saw his father in him: angry, stubborn. Meaning to get his way. But he'd forgotten that I had the gun and before I could stop him, he leapt up, rocketing off the bow to launch himself at Marla.

Spotting him with an ugly curse, she shot him in the foot, which of course launched *me* up. "Sam!"

I pulled out my weapon as he fell to the deck, a puddle of blood and rainwater sloshing around him. Marla cursed again, recognizing me.

"You guys just don't know when to quit, do you? Okay, gimme that." She gestured at my gun while keeping her own aimed at my son. "I mean it. Give it here, right now. Or I'll kill him."

Biting my lip, I obeyed. When I had and she'd tossed the weapon overboard, she crossed to the controls and dropped the engine into operating position.

"Darn," Sam managed through gritted teeth.

"Oh, shut up," said Marla, starting the engine. She pulled on a life jacket. "Be glad it's not your knee."

She gripped her own weapon, an ugly little metal pistol, in a way I found deeply unnerving; partly because she looked so comfortable with it, but mostly because now she was pointing it at me.

"Yeah," she said, seeing me putting two and two together: the gun, her comfort. "There's a lot you don't know about me."

"Oh, you think?" The woman had hurt herself so badly that she had nearly needed brain surgery, and even injured her own dog; of course, I hadn't suspected her.

Not until Roscoe told me she'd been the one who'd paid him to be a lookout. "The two of you," I said. "You and . . . Clark, is that right? Making it seem like he was after you . . . oh, that was clever."

I scoured my mind for some tactic that would keep her from shoving us both down in that hatch; the puddle Sam lay in was now as dark as wine with his blood.

"Who is he to you, anyway?" I took a step nearer to my son, his face now gray with pain. "The guy in the muscle car, I mean, who you're in on all this with?"

Sam groaned, and if she hadn't had that gun in her hands, she would already have been in the water.

Drowning, ideally. But she did have it, as well as a large canvas satchel, which she'd stowed in one of the boat's open gear compartments.

"He's my brother, all right?" she snapped angrily, squinting out to where the patch of sunlight moving over the bay was nearly upon us.

Oh, man. I hadn't even thought of *that* possibility. "But if that's true," I began, meanwhile scanning around desperately for anything I could use as a tourniquet.

"Right, it means your sweet little pal Miss Halligan is our mother," Marla snarled. "For all the good it's ever done us," she added bitterly.

She threw two more life jackets at me. "Get 'em on."

So at least she didn't plan on dumping us overboard. But Sam didn't need a jacket—he needed medical attention.

And he needed it *now.* "Marla, please. Leave Sam here on the dock. We can radio for help for him once we're away from here."

Since that was what she'd said she intended, to take the boat somewhere. She jerked the gun sharply at me again.

"Forget it. And the life jackets, too, on second thought. Just get below, both of you. I don't want to see any of you again till we get where we're going."

"*Which would be where?*" I wanted badly to ask, but she

aimed the little gun purposefully once more, this time at Sam's head.

So I hurriedly helped him up and toward the cabin hatchway. "Okay, just tell me one thing, then. Why'd you kill Matt Muldoon?"

Her face changed. "What? Why did I . . . Oh, hell, you don't know anything, do you?"

The boat bucked and yanked on its lines in the towering waves. "Get down there," she repeated, hauling the hatch door open and slamming it once we'd obeyed.

In the cabin I squinted around, letting my eyes adjust to the dimness of the small enclosure. Mika and Ellie, tied in the straps from spare life jackets, stared up at me with fear in their eyes. And sprawled beside them was my son, Sam.

Who if I wasn't mistaken was now very actively in the process of bleeding to death.

Thirteen

"Okay, lie flat. I'm cutting your shoe off." Sam's wife, Mika, crouched over him while I aimed the flashlight down at him.

With the box cutter from the vessel's toolbox, I'd made quick work of the life jacket's straps; by now Marla was too busy handling the boat to check on us.

Mika used the sharp tool on Sam's sneaker. The blood-soaked shoe fell away, and then his sock. Dark red blood bubbled from the round purple wound in his foot.

"Huh," said Mika unflappably.

She'd turned out to be not only a nurse, but also a surgical nurse-practitioner. "What's that, a needle?" she asked when I pulled the gleaming implement from the toolbox. Huge and curved, it was intended for mending the boat's seat cushions.

"Gimme that, will you? And how about some of that nice nylon thread fraying out of that pillow's seam, too," she said.

Then, "Sorry this sucks," she told Sam when she'd threaded the needle with the stuff.

She'd already probed the wound and found no bullet still in there to complicate matters. Now the rough seas we'd been bouncing through calmed briefly just enough so she was able to put the first stitch in.

Sam grimaced. "Oh yeah, it definitely sucks," he managed.

She put the needle in again; I'd have given him what was left of the rum from the galley, but of course I couldn't. Then after a few more stitches it was done, the bleeding mostly stopped and the wound itself dressed with the bandages from the first-aid kit.

Sam sat up, the color already returning to his face. "Yo," he said, fist-bumping his wife. I'd have done that, too, if I hadn't been so busy ransacking the rest of the boat's emergency supplies.

"You know how to pick 'em," I told Sam approvingly instead, and he beamed happily through his pain. But not for long:

"Hey, where are we?" I said as sunlight streamed through the portholes suddenly.

Ellie edged over to me, her face tight with anxiety. "We're in the storm's eye, I guess. But we're headed for the rocks again. Where we anchored the other night," she added to me.

Only this time nobody was watching the depth finder, to keep us off them. Not that it would've helped much; from the sound of the engine and the way we were slamming the waves, *thud-thud-thud,* the throttle was full out.

At that speed, the sharp underwater granite ledges we were approaching would take out the Bayliner's bottom like an ax blade through sawdust, before the depth finder even had time to notice them.

And before the GPS tracker's signal could bring help. But we'd notice, all right.

"Shit," said Ellie, which was very unlike her. And she wasn't talking about our speed. No, she was talking about . . .

"Damn," I agreed, peering past her to where she'd dug between two of the cabin's cushions to expose one of the bilge compartment hatches.

Sloshing sounds came from it, not a good sign. I took Ellie's flashlight from her and dragged the hatch cover off completely.

A salty smell rose up, the smell of seawater. Nice *fresh* seawater. "Oh, dear," I said weakly.

See, all boats leak. It's why they have bilge compartments at all, to collect what's always hoped will be only a minor amount of seepage. But now way more water was coming in from somewhere than the bilge pump could handle.

"The gunshot." It had gone right through Sam's foot. I looked around at the others. "Marla shot a hole in the boat, I'll bet."

"You mean we're sinking?" Mika demanded.

"Not yet," said Ellie, which I personally thought was a less-than-reassuring reply, but since I couldn't come up with anything better, I kept my mouth shut.

"But if we take on much more water, the boat's handling will deteriorate, and at this speed, especially in any rougher seas than this, we'll be in trouble for sure," she said.

As far as I was concerned, we were already in trouble. Then we did hit rougher water, much rougher. And as she'd predicted, each time the boat's bow hit a wave, it shimmied hard before settling again.

"Or the bullet could've fractured the fiberglass, like in a star pattern," Ellie said. "If it's bad enough, that'd mean the hull could fail."

By "fail" she meant "disintegrate." *Oh, terrific.*

"So let me get this straight," said Mika. "She's going to kill us . . . Why, again?" Sam's new wife still looked scared, but now she was starting to look pissed off, too.

"Marla killed somebody we knew and framed Ellie for it. Or her ex-con brother did the killing part, we're not sure," I said.

"And we were just about to figure that out, plus some other things, so she grabbed me, meaning to shut me up by killing me as well," Ellie told Mika. "She'd have gotten Jake, too, as soon as she showed up at the Moose. Only you were there instead."

Mika nodded slowly. "And now? I mean, how's she ever going to explain all of us being gone?"

"I don't know," I replied. "But I'm guessing she doesn't plan to explain anything. That big satchel she's got probably has money in it."

Probably she was the one who'd removed it from the cellar in her Eastport house, once her brother told her we'd been down there.

"She could just split with it. And meet her brother somewhere far away from here. We still don't know where he is," Ellie said.

She peered down into the bilge again—just as, without warning, the boat heeled over sharply. The engine lugged sullenly, a low gargling sound, and we all froze until the vessel righted itself.

But the fun wasn't over. Soon the water was liquid hell again; a gust slammed us, putting us into a sideways dip-and-shudder that I disliked very intensely.

The engine throttled down. Sam moved aside so the rest of us could see out as a row of islands slid by, their scant vegetation bent flat by the wind.

"We could maybe jump over onto one of those islands?" Mika suggested. "If we could get up on deck somehow?"

And overwhelm Marla with our superior numbers, I gathered she meant; I liked her thinking. Too bad Marla had the firepower.

Swiftly I explained this: "She's got a gun, see, and we . . ."

"Don't," I'd have finished, but I didn't say it because Ellie's eyes had just lit up, staring at the hinged metal box that hung above the galley sink.

CAUTION! the box read, and then some finer print I'd never bothered working my way through. Luckily, though, Ellie had.

"Okay. If I'm right about where we are . . . ," she began.

Which of course she was. Based on her fog-navigating feats of the other night, I thought she must have a GPS sensor built right into her brain.

Which reminded me again suddenly: "Ellie."

". . . then I think she must mean to dump us on Cemetery Island and just let the tide come in and . . . What?"

"Ellie. Ellie, listen to me. There's a tracking module in the emergency bin. I found it. I meant to tell you about it, but . . ."

They were all looking at me. I swallowed hard.

". . . but somehow I never got the chance," I said. "Anyway, I'm afraid George must have been . . ."

"*Keeping tabs on you,*" I was mustering up the nerve to finish. But then I'd tell her the good part: Sooner or later someone would come for us, because Wade knew about it. As soon as he realized the Bayliner was gone, he would start monitoring it.

But before I could say anything at all, Ellie laughed.

Not amused laughter. More like sad. "Oh, Jake, I knew about the tracker. George and I talked about it, okay? But it was disconnected. Or partly, anyway. It needs to be told where to send its data so it can work, and we undid that part of it."

What Ellie had just said made perfect sense to me. Of course they would end up discussing it; any idea of George hiding things from Ellie, or vice versa, was ridiculous, obviously.

Or it was obvious to me now, at any rate. "Oh," I said, feeling as if all the air had been let out of me.

So nobody was tracking us. Nobody would save us. The engine noise fell to an idle.

Another idea struck me. "Phones?"

But they were all dead, too, not a single bar on any of them. Which was no surprise; once a tower went down for good, it could take days to get it operating again.

Ellie took the flashlight and checked the bilge compartment once more, looking unhappy with what she saw. "The pump's still not keeping up." This was another way of saying that yes, we were indeed sinking, just very slowly.

The boat's hull brushed heavily against a half-rotted wooden piling that slid past us, black and dripping, so near I could've reached out through the porthole and grabbed it.

But I didn't because I'd tried that once before with another old piling, on one of my earlier trips with Ellie, and it'd nearly taken my shoulder off.

The hatch door opened and Marla peered down. She still had the gun. "Okay, all of you, up and out."

She waved us onto the deck under a sky still pelting rain. Sam hopped on one foot, leaning heavily on Mika and me. We were in a tiny cove with rock cliffs thrusting up on three sides, and a narrow inlet leading in from the open water on the fourth.

"Where are we?" Mika murmured. To our right the black stumps of additional old pier supports broke the water's churning surface; to our left stretched a thin strip of beach.

Marla jerked the gun at us, urging us toward the rail. When I realized what she meant to do, I couldn't believe it. "Marla, come on. You're really going to leave us here?"

No reply. The tide was still on its way in, creeping steadily a little farther across the rock-strewn sand with each foamy wave; when it reached its height, that little beach was history.

And so were we. Lightning flashed and thunder rumbled overhead as we all hauled ourselves over the rail. I dropped to the sand and fell heavily, but I managed to get myself back up again, while Sam eased over and let himself be lowered slowly and painfully by Mika and Ellie.

Then with a long boat hook, Mika pushed the boat off from the dock piling again and motored away, not sparing us a word or glance. The Bayliner moved, sluggish as an old barge, out into the heavy chop. Then, wallowing uncertainly, it nosed toward the cove's mouth and around it and was gone.

Mika crouched where Sam lay. The dressings she'd taped around his foot were soaked with red.

"There's still bleeding deep inside there. He needs a real OR and a trauma surgeon," she said, looking up worriedly.

Miserably we dragged him farther back from the water's edge, then huddled with him in the lee of the cliffs, out of the wind while the storm let loose on top of us.

No one spoke, but it was obvious to all of us what Marla had done. Maybe not directly, with a gun or a knife . . . or with a pastry needle, either.

But we were still being murdered.

"The tide'll be all the way in soon." Ellie looked scared, and she wasn't the only one.

"But . . . I don't know," she went on. "Maybe if we could find some dry brush or something, we could manage to start a signal fire? Sooner or later someone would see the smoke, I think," she finished, sounding discouraged.

There wasn't any brush. Also it was windy and pouring rain. Even if we could start a fire, which we couldn't, it wouldn't stay lit. And nobody would see it if it did.

But I didn't say any of that. I didn't have the heart to, especially after Mika spoke up. "The way Sam seems now, I'm honestly not sure he'll last that long," she said. And at the look I gave her: "Well, I'm sorry, but his pulse is thready and he's not fully alert," she retorted. "What do you want me to do, lie?"

I opened my mouth angrily, then shut it again; she was right. "Sorry. It's just really hard to hear." And when she'd accepted my apology:

"So, any other ideas?" I asked Ellie.

She shook her head. "The only way off this beach is up," she said, waving at the steep rock face looming over the sand.

"But even if we could climb one of these cliffs, *which we*

can't," she emphasized, "a million Eastport kids have come over here over the years and tried, and nobody's done it yet. . . ."

She took a breath. "Even if we could, there's nothing to burn there, either. Just bare rocks, and not only that, but in case you haven't noticed, it's drizzling a little."

So she knew it, too, that we were grasping at nonexistent straws. Meanwhile, each wind-driven wave rolled a few inches higher up the beach. Soon the tide would be splashing at the foot of the cliffs and then crashing there; judging by the dark line on the granite, the high-tide depth here was about fifteen feet.

Drowning depth, in other words. "I'm not talking about signaling, I'm talking about not dying," I told Ellie, measuring the cliffs with my eyes.

It looked steep and slick. But . . . "How high did the kids get, anyway? Halfway? Or even farther?"

That got her attention. "Huh, you're right. We wouldn't have to get all the way up," she conceded.

She glanced back at the ruined dock, with its rotting planks and the ancient lines dangling from it. "And I guess if the three of us could manage to push Sam up ahead of us somehow—"

"Ellie, *how high*?" Because if agile young high-school kids couldn't make it on a dare as far as we needed to go to save our lives, then we needed another plan.

"High enough," she called back, already heading for the dock with its loose planks and ropes. Mika and I followed, hurrying to yank planks off rusted nails, gather up as much usable line as we could, and haul it all over to where Sam still lay.

"Lash the planks to him the long way," said Mika. In addition to the many other wonderful qualities I was beginning to notice in my new daughter-in-law—courage, determination, even the ability to clean and suture gunshot wounds, a talent I always find attractive in a person—it turned out that for her job she'd taken a wilderness-medicine class recently.

"Wrap the rope over and under the slats, like weaving," she shouted over the wind. So we did that, too, and it took quite a while, but when we were done, we had Sam trussed tightly to three of the dock planks, laid side by side the long way under him.

By then the foam-capped waves nearly covered the beach. The tide around here didn't creep in; it was more like a gallop. Soon those green waves would be washing us off our feet.

"Don't try to carry him by the planks, though," Mika advised. "They're not strong enough. They're just to keep him straight."

Right, that made sense. So Ellie and I each took one of Sam's shoulders and Mika took his feet, and we shuttled him to the cliff base, where Ellie clambered up onto a jagged outcropping.

"Okay, get him vertical. Then you two push from below, and I'll pull. We'll start by hauling ourselves up as far as we can."

The wind snatched her words, but we got the idea. Half-blinded by cold raindrops smacking into our faces, Mika and I seized Sam's board-splinted legs.

"One, two . . . ," she shouted into the gale. The waves rolled nearer, their chilly edges now puddling around my feet.

Ellie screamed something at us, I couldn't hear what. But it didn't matter:

". . . *three!*" Mika and I straightened together, heaving Sam's body upward on his makeshift stretcher . . .

. . . which crumbled immediately into rotten black pieces that fell from their woven rope fastenings to swirl away in the tide.

"Oh." Mika was nearly weeping, trying not to show it. We held Sam up out of the surf, but I didn't know how long we could do it.

Forever, as far as I was concerned. But the water, already up to my knees and rising fast, would have its own ideas about that; it was so cold that I couldn't even feel my feet.

And that was that. We were going to drown, here, and there

was nothing more I could do about it. A burst of fear filled me, mixed with an awful rush of grief. *Good-bye . . .*

Ellie screamed again, and I thought it was in frustration, an emotion I surely shared. But then I heard what she was screaming:

"Boat!"

I turned in disbelief, barely able to make out a shape through the sheeting rain. Surely, it was my imagination, conjuring up our rescue, even though there was no hope of it remaining.

But when I looked again, I realized: someone was coming in a boat, a real boat with an engine, running lights, and a hull that didn't have holes shot into it.

"Sam," I whispered. "Sam, look."

Into the inlet's rocky mouth the approaching vessel motored slowly until it nudged what remained of the dock's rotted pilings.

And now . . .

I let out a breath I hadn't known I was holding.

Now it was here.

"But I don't understand. How did you know where we were?"

The boat was the Zodiac, a massive inflatable vessel out of Eastport's Coast Guard station, and on it were my husband, Wade Sorenson, plus four Coasties, whose piloting of the ungainly-looking craft through the storm had looked like fun.

For them, anyway. *Thump. Thump. Thump.* The thing didn't cut through the waves; it more like belly flopped across them.

Still, it was better than being under them. And the Coasties knew their stuff; within a few minutes of their arrival, they'd had us up and aboard the Zodiac, and headed for home.

Now Wade looked at me a little shyly, as if unsure how I might react. "So, do you remember the tracking module that George put on Ellie's boat?"

"Yes, but it wasn't set up to . . . Oh." The truth dawned as a few feet away the Coasties worked on Sam, using a first-aid kit that made the Bayliner's look like a toy.

Sam's eyes were open, he was responding, and he even accepted a hot drink; relief flooded me as Wade went on:

"Last night when I went to the dock to check on the Bayliner, tighten the lines and so on, I remembered that little gadget."

"Uh-huh." I let him continue, though now I thought I knew what must be coming.

"So I took a look at it, and when I did, I found out it wasn't wired up." Just as Ellie had said.

"And considering what was going on around here," he went on, "I figured you'd get that tracker operating yourself, if you knew it wasn't and you had time."

Correct. If I'd thought of it, and could figure out how, I probably would have; it would've been prudent. Like Wade.

"So I did it," he finished. He spread his hands in half apology, still watching warily for my reaction. "I figured what the hell, it might come in handy. I wasn't going to keep it secret, though. I'd have told you as soon as I got a chance," he added.

"The way I would've told you about our fog delay," I said, "and about nearly being hit by your freighter when we were out on our boat trip to Lubec," I said.

"Yep. So when you didn't show up at home, I got the satellite signal onto a screen down at the Coast Guard station, and here we are."

He looked at me again. "You'd have done the same. Set up the GPS. If our situations were reversed, I mean."

I let a big breath out. "Yeah. Yeah, I would've. So . . . where's Marla? Has the Coast Guard already picked her up, too?"

Because we were out on the water now, and the visibility here wasn't terrible anymore; I could see land.

But I didn't see the Bayliner, only gray waves surging and subsiding. I glanced back around the Zodiac's deck.

Mika sat by Sam, her hair in a thick towel and a Coast Guard blanket wrapped around her. Ellie looked up from where she sat on a bench, with her arms wrapped around her knees.

"She sank, didn't she?" I said, staring back out again at the cold, empty water, where the Bayliner should be. "I knew it. That bilge pump just couldn't keep up with so much leaking."

Wade nodded gravely. "We saw her go down on our way out here, actually, or we'd have gotten to you sooner. Got right to the spot where she was foundering. The bow went under and we were all ready with a life ring."

He sighed heavily. "But the water's pretty cold and choppy, and . . . anyway, it happened fast, and Marla never came up. I think that's the search-and-rescue helicopter I hear now, in fact."

A moment later I heard it, too, then saw the big orange-and-white aircraft circling, because, of course, they would keep looking for Marla until no hope remained for her.

"Her brother's in custody," Wade said. "Bob Arnold grabbed him up, trying to get off the island by driving around a road-block on the causeway."

Ellie got up, making her way unsteadily to the inflatable's rail. By now we'd reached the inside of Eastport's boat basin, where an ambulance waited on the dock for us, its cherry beacon haloed in rain and fog.

But something kept bothering me, something I just couldn't put my finger on as the Zodiac's plump rubber side bumped the dock rail. The EMTs off-loaded Sam; then over his protests they fireman-carried him up the steep metal gangway to the ambulance.

Mika went, too, and the rest of us followed; Bob Arnold met us at the top, looking apoplectic.

"Now wait just a damned minute," he said when Ellie tried to brush by him.

She turned. "Bob," she said calmly, but she wasn't. "Bob, I love you. I really do. But in the last couple of days, I've been stalked, chased, menaced, and kidnapped. Jake's been shot at, and Sam's *actually* been shot. Meanwhile . . ."

She sucked in a breath. *"Meanwhile,* all suspicion has remained squarely on *me,* and the people who have been doing all the chasing and shooting and menacing have been scampering around the island scot-free."

When Ellie gets mad, she actually uses words like "scot-free." Also I hadn't known eyes the color of violets could blaze like that.

"But now we *know* who, at least, one of the culprits is, on account of she nearly *drowned* us out there. And she *sank my boat,* damn it."

Oh, but she was hot. "So listen, Bob," she said. "You're my friend, and you have been for a long time. But right now I'm going back to the Chocolate Moose and don't you dare try stopping me unless you're arresting me for something, 'cause I have *other fish to fry.*"

Whereupon she actually did turn on her heel, stalking away up the breakwater toward Water Street and the Moose.

"Me too," I said into the silence that followed.

The big family dinner I'd planned would have to be postponed, I decided. Instead we'd ask Bella to bring us dry clothes; that way we could get those last few cheesecakes finished.

Which I was now even more determined to do. So I left Wade bringing Bob Arnold up to speed and dealing with the Coast Guard's incident report paperwork.

After they rescue you off a deserted island, after all, you can't just walk away as if nothing at all had happened; facts must be gathered and reports written. But they all knew us, and knew we weren't going far, and they were hungry for cheesecake, too.

I hurried to catch up with Ellie, who'd already gotten a big

head start. In the dying storm Water Street was sodden and deserted. A red-white-and-blue banner hung in shreds from a
lamppost; a flag lay across a puddle.

Inside the Moose all the lights were on. "Ellie?" I called.

She'd been here, if only briefly; the coffeemaker was burbling and the CD player oozed that damned syrupy Celtic harp
music, so sweet I could feel my blood sugar skyrocketing.

Somehow I didn't mind it so much anymore, though. Gazing around, I felt a familiar contentment come over me, a sense
of purpose mingled with the delightful smell of chocolate.
Home . . .

A soft thud hit the wall from over on Miss Halligan's side.
Then a voice cried out weakly: "No!"

I ran right over there, of course, but when I got inside the
Rose's front door, I stopped, gazing at all the many sequined
and embroidered and pearl-beaded dresses, sweaters, and
shawls arranged on the racks, hangers, and shelves.

Miss Halligan was a genius at using space; she needed to be,
with what little of it she had. Even in this tiny storefront area,
every item for sale was clearly visible, and there wasn't an imi-
tation jewel on any of them, I realized suddenly.

No cubic zirconia, no moissanite, no rhinestones.

"Where is it?" a harsh voice demanded from the tiny back
room, where the shop's elegant owner had been living recently.

"It's not in the Moose, I've checked every inch, and your
shop's the only other place I went after I—"

After she killed him. It was Sarabelle's voice, and now I did
remember what had been bothering me: that rhinestone Ellie
picked up.

The one Sarabelle had been scanning the floor for, probably,
the other evening in the Moose. Now she appeared in the doorway to the Second Hand Rose's back room.

Only it wasn't a rhinestone she'd found, I realized too late.

And what do you know? Sarabelle *didn't* have a gun in her hand.

She had a knife in it. "Hello," I said quietly. "Looking for something?"

She had her other arm clamped tightly around the front of Miss Halligan's neck.

"Hello, yourself," she snapped impatiently.

Miss Halligan's dark eyes gazed helplessly at me, the knife glittered wickedly, and where was Ellie, anyway?

"Where's my diamond?" Sarabelle demanded. "I've looked for it everywhere, one of you must have it."

"It must've fallen out while you were killing your husband," I said, unable to repress my sarcasm.

Hey, I'd had a bad day, all right? Including the hard mental kick that I gave myself now for my stupidity. I'd been sure that Sarabelle didn't care enough about her cheating husband to kill him, and even if she did, she didn't know about the trapdoor in our kitchen.

But she hadn't needed to know. When push came to shove, Miss Halligan had known enough for both of them.

Biting her lip, the proprietor of the Rose looked away from me. "She promised to get rid of Clark for me," she said dully, "to get him out of my house."

A sob escaped her. "I had to do something about him, I just *had* to. I couldn't live like this anymore. So . . . I told Sarabelle about him."

"So the two of you planned it together?" I asked. "You helped Sarabelle kill Matt Muldoon, in return for her evicting your son from your house, somehow?"

"Oh, don't be silly," snapped Sarabelle, "we couldn't have planned it the way it happened. We'd talked about it, how to get rid of Matt's body and maybe even pin it on someone else."

She eyed Miss Halligan contemptuously. "And how in return I'd get rid of her son for her, since she didn't have the nerve to."

"Make him go away, though, that's all. Not hurt him," Miss Halligan protested.

"Yeah, right." Sarabelle rolled her eyes. Clearly, her plan had been more permanent than that. She'd known, too, that before the lock set was replaced, the Moose's door had been so loose, it could be unlocked by digging at it with the tip of a knife blade.

Like the one on the knife she was holding right now.

"It wasn't so bad when only Marla was here," Miss Halligan said. "She'd want money from me now and then, or to push me around just because she could. But mostly she wanted nothing to do with me."

The sad, self-justifying words fairly poured out of her, as if she thought she could excuse all this somehow.

"I don't know why she decided to come here from Connecticut when she got fired from her job, except that I guess when she did need money, it was easier to get it out of me in person," she said.

"I see," I managed, half-choked with fury. But I had to keep them talking. Sooner or later someone would show up and get me out of this. . . . Wouldn't they?

"And then your son, Clark, got out of jail and came here, too?" I asked. "He must've decided that what worked for Marla might work for him as well?"

She nodded; Sarabelle just rolled her eyes long-sufferingly. The widow Muldoon was waiting for something, I realized, and then with a chill I knew what it must be.

"He barged in, took my house over, and the two of them teamed up together," said Miss Halligan. "Marla and Clark . . . she's just like him, selfish and bad. Only not so obvious about it, is all."

I imagined what it must take for a mother to say that about her kids. *Clark especially is a piece of work,* I thought. Marla's sudden retirement from teaching took on a new look for me, too. What had she done, not only to be fired, but afterward to want to leave the area entirely?

Meanwhile, Miss Halligan didn't know yet that Marla was dead. But I hardly thought now was a good time to tell her or Sarabelle; and when she spoke again, she confirmed my decision.

"You have such high hopes for them," Miss Halligan murmured. "You want everything for them when they're small. Don't you?"

I couldn't reply to this, on account of the lump suddenly in my throat. But Sarabelle could.

"Hush up, you old witch. To listen to you whining, a person would think you weren't hip-deep in all this yourself."

Miss Halligan went silent, which I thought was a fine idea on account of the knife.

"So just out of curiosity," I asked, hoping to distract Sarabelle further from her captive's vulnerable throat . . .

. . . and before it occurred to her that Miss Halligan could testify against her, too.

Oh, this is a fine mess we've gotten into, and where the hell is Ellie, anyway?

"What did Matt have to do with any of this?" I finished.

Because part of it was now clear to me: Marla Sykes and her ne'er-do-well brother had been in together on something lucrative and illegal, I still didn't know what.

But it was, like, gobs-of-money lucrative. What Muldoon's murder had to do with it, though, wasn't obvious at all, so I asked about it, still playing for time.

"That fool," said Sarabelle, with a grimace of disgust. "The whole thing was stupid. It all started when Marla saw him at some dive bar in Lubec."

"And I was with her," Miss Halligan put in earnestly; she did not, apparently, have the sense to shut up.

"I'd driven over to meet Marla that evening, she'd demanded

it," she went on. "Like I said, she liked to push me around, and that night she decided it would be fun to pretend we were pals."

She sighed, remembering. "Which might not have been so bad, but right away Marla got tipsy on those Irish coffees she likes so much, and started fooling around with her phone."

"Taking pictures. Including one of you and Matt," I said.

She took a shuddery breath. "Yes. And she teased him with it, telling him she'd show it to Sarabelle. I don't really think she would have, she was just . . . well, mean, actually."

Yeah, I'd noticed. "But she didn't know Matt very well, did she?" said Sarabelle tightly.

Still no Ellie, but by now I was starting to be glad that my friend hadn't shown up, because I was beginning to be sure that's who Sarabelle Muldoon was waiting for.

One fell swoop, in other words. And then she would . . . what, try to run, the way Clark Carmody had? Probably, but if she did, it wouldn't matter to me because I'd be dead.

"The very next day Matt started looking for something to use against *her*," Sarabelle said. "He took it personally, her having the nerve to threaten him even as a joke, and you know when he got started on something, he was a madman about it."

Yeah, I'd noticed. "Although," she added, "breaking into her house was a little over-the-top, even for Matt. The one here in Eastport, where she was keeping the money before depositing it."

She was relaxing a little; being able to talk about this must have been a relief. I measured the distance between us, calculated how long it would take me to cover it in a single bound. But Miss Halligan's throat would certainly be slit before I got there.

"So he found the money she'd hidden?" I asked, and Sarabelle nodded.

"There are limits on how much you can deposit at one time

and not trigger the bank's interest as to where you got it," she confirmed. "So she often had quite a lot of cash on hand."

"But when he found it, he didn't take it," I said. "Instead he must've watched her and her brother until he found out where it came from?"

I was just guessing, but Sarabelle nodded again. "Diamonds," she answered my unasked query. "In the cocoa paste she imports."

Of course, it would be something like that: small, valuable, easy to carry around. You could even put it into costume jewelry, replacing the rhinestones and cubic zirconia with real precious stones, and nobody would suspect you were wearing a fortune.

Sarabelle's masses of rings and bracelets glittered wickedly, reflecting the light of the shop's front window.

"But what Matt didn't know was that you were a partner in the operation as well," I hazarded, still trying to keep her talking. "Your job was to take the stones to the city and bring back cash?"

She already had contacts in New York's gemstone industry, I recalled, from her previous life in Manhattan public relations.

She nodded smugly. "It was easy. And if I ever wanted to get together enough money to finally leave him, I couldn't have Matt spoiling it."

Her face hardened. "Anyway, it's all over now. And I guess your pal Ellie's not coming to save you," she added meanly, "so when I'm done with you two"—she meant Miss Halligan and me—"I'll deal with that clan of yours," she finished to me alone, "then get out of here for good."

"You even *try* going anywhere near my family—" I began hotly, but she cut me off.

"Because who knows what you might've told them? Your husband, especially. Only this time Clark won't be around to help me."

So he'd been the one who'd sabotaged Wade's truck. Sara-belle went on: "A fire, I think," she mused dreamily, then met my gaze.

"Late at night. It'll be a shame. But all these old Eastport buildings really are terrible firetraps, you know."

And that, finally, was when I understood: Marla Sykes and her brother were mercenary, to be sure. Smuggling gemstones was the moral equivalent of selling the enslaved children who mined them; they don't call them "blood diamonds" for noth-ing, after all.

But this woman was scary. She'd killed her husband because he was a miserable son of a bitch and to keep him from fouling up her profitable scheme. And now . . . now she was *enjoying* this.

She gestured for me to approach her; a tiny upward jab of the knife at her captive's throat gave weight to her words.

"Please," whispered Miss Halligan, tears sliding down her powdery cheeks.

"Okay, okay," I gave in, stepping forward.

"*Oh, please,*" Sarabelle mocked cruelly, her voice thick with venom.

Which was when from behind her a big black cast-iron skil-let rose suddenly, then clonked down onto her head with a loud *bong!* She dropped as if shot.

"Wow," said Ellie, looking down at the sprawled form, then peering around the rest of the shop. "Anyone else need bonking?"

I crouched beside Miss Halligan, whose throat didn't seem too badly wounded; the bleeding had already stopped.

"Thanks *so* much," she croaked hoarsely.

She wouldn't be thanking me when I'd called the cops on her, but whatever. "How'd you get back there, anyway?" I asked Ellie.

"Heard you through the wall from next door. And you remember that our shop's trapdoor leads to the cellar, don't you?"

Oh, for Pete's sake, of course. "You went down ours, and up here by . . ."

She smiled beatifically. "Each shop has cellar access. Has to, right? So tenants can get to their fuse boxes and so on. That meant there had to be a trapdoor in this shop's floor, too."

I glanced at Miss Halligan, who suddenly looked much guiltier than before. No wonder she'd wanted the Moose's unreliable front door to be noticed, the morning after Muldoon's murder.

"You jimmied that door and left it open, and made sure there were scratches in the frame, too. To muddy the waters, so everyone would think it was how the killer got in."

It hadn't been important, as it turned out. But it could've been. Miss Halligan looked away as Ellie dusted her hands together in satisfaction.

"Well, we can figure out the rest of the gory details later. And the phones are back on, so I've already called Bob Arnold and he says he'll be here shortly."

She glanced around the Second Hand Rose, whose vintage charm seemed already to be fading without Miss Halligan's stylish verve energizing it.

"And once he is," Ellie added exhaustedly, "I'll finish those last dratted cheesecakes, then sit down before I fall down."

Just then Mika stuck her head in the door, took in the scene, and pronounced, "I'll get help," without missing a beat.

Which was when I knew for sure, finally, that Sam had been right to marry her, and when Mika returned—not only with Bob Arnold in tow, but also with fresh news of Sam's well-being (after a quick blood transfusion he was in surgery, but doing well, and likely to be home by tomorrow or the next day) she said she knew how to frost cakes. *Elaborately,* I mean, the way those remaining cheesecakes really *needed* decorating.

"Please?" she asked winningly. "Let me help? You really owe it to me, you know," she added. "Both of you."

After the wild ride we'd taken her on, she meant, and I liked her sense of humor, too.

"Oh, all right," I agreed, whereupon the frightening events of the previous few hours all caught up with me very suddenly and my knees went out from under me.

"Do that," I babbled happily from where I sat, feeling as if my body had turned to liquid. "Hey, do your thing, Mika. You go, girl. Knock yourself out."

In the shop's big front window it appeared that the storm had blown through at last and the sky had begun clearing, tatters of clouds streaming north toward Canada and the Atlantic. The tourists who'd remained in town gazed wonderingly at the washed blue sky and azure waves.

Ellie put a cup of hot tea into my hands, and not too much later Bob Arnold formally took Miss Halligan and Sarabelle into custody, and later still Wade showed up and took me home.

All the while, I kept trying to remember what it was that I still had to do, but to no avail. Not until later that evening in the sunroom, propped up on pillows in a chair next to my father's daybed, where we were eating our suppers together, did I realize this was it. This familiar old room, my old house, Wade and Bella and my dad, and now Sam and Mika and the beginnings of their family, too . . .

My dad ate with appetite while the dogs, Maxie and Fang, snored on their mat by the fire. Roscoe sat with us, showered and shaved and looking pleased with himself, while upstairs a pair of still-stranded tourists—their car had been the one washed off the causeway, it turned out—enjoyed the novelty of a two-hundred-year-old bedroom.

Later, of course, they'd be enjoying the novelty of two-hundred-year-old plumbing, which was a different matter entirely. But that would be later; tucked into the chair with me now was a pillow embroidered by Bella in some of her scarce leisure moments.

Count Your Blessings, it read. The terse instruction reminded me of the poster in the Second Hand Rose: BE HERE NOW.

And as I sipped my champagne and looked happily forward to Eastport's Grand Fourth of July Chocolate Cherry Cheesecake Auction, I knew the poster's message was right. *Be here now. . . .*

The pillow's too. *Count your blessings. . . .*

So I was, and I did.

Fourteen

The Fourth of July dawned breezy and cool in the remote island village of Eastport, Maine, the sky a clear, rain-washed blue and the sun's returning warmth a welcome arrival after the big storm.

"Last one," said Ellie as she slid a magnificently chocolate-frosted and cherry-glazed confection onto a wheeled metal cart.

We were arranging them in the Coast Guard station's big high-ceilinged garage, crowded with hoist chains, grease guns, power tools, and all the many other items of special equipment needed to keep small-to-medium-sized boats and trailers in tip-top shape.

Also its concrete apron was full of cheesecakes: twenty-eight of them to be precise, each glistening with Bing cherries simmered in their juices, generously piped with chocolate ganache, and drizzled across the top with a dark, sinfully semisweet version of Bella Diamond's extra-special homemade chocolate syrup.

"Do you think they'll like them?" Ellie asked anxiously, her look taking in the camera crews here for the event: two from the Bangor TV stations and one all the way from Portland.

"You could ransom an entire shipload of pirates with those cheesecakes," I told her just as Wade strode in.

Handsome in his blue denim shirt, weathered work boots, and jeans, he showed no sign of having been up all night, even though he'd sat by Sam's hospital bed until dawn. Now Sam was en route home, the tourists who'd been staying with us had gone, and our house was back to normal.

Almost. Wade slung his arm around me. "Hey." More prospective bidders kept arriving, eager for a look at the cakes.

"Hey, yourself." Up on Water Street, city workers were hard at work rehanging banners, flags, and buntings; on the breakwater wooden crates full of fireworks were being removed very delicately from a box truck with scary-looking EXPLOSIVES! icons stenciled on the back and sides.

"What's going on?" I asked. Ellie and I had been baking since four in the morning. The Moose would be open today, so we'd made chocolate chip cookies, fudge-nut pinwheels, and chocolate cupcakes with the rest of those Bing cherries mixed into the batter; Ellie hated waste.

"State guys're here," Wade said. "They're taking Sarabelle to the jail in Machias. Bob Arnold just unloaded on me about it."

She'd sat overnight in the lockup where Roscoe had been billeted, fuming and sputtering but refusing to call an attorney or anyone else, Wade said. Locked in, of course; Bob had policed festivals before and had already prepared the place with male and female deputies, to keep watch and to keep everyone safe.

"Miss Halligan's still in the hospital being checked over, but she'll probably get a state-cop visit real soon, now. Sarabelle's pretty good at shifting blame, you know?" Wade added.

Meanwhile, Roscoe had found a room to rent, and a job sorting bottles at Sprague's Redemption, the local recycling center. So he and his dog, Fang—by now it really was his animal, Bob having learned that its previous owner had abandoned it—were gone there, while Maxie the German shepherd had of course found a home with us.

"What about Clark Carmody?" I asked.

Wade eyed the cheesecakes. "Oh, he's in a cell, too. Waiting for some federal guys, they want to talk to him about a whole long laundry list of his recent bad deeds. Including his latest racket, diamond smuggling."

Besides hiding them in cocoa paste, they'd been bringing them into Halifax, Nova Scotia, on cruise ships, and then spiriting them over here to the U.S. side of the border by small boat, Sarabelle had said.

From what I'd heard, she was talking a lot. She was hoping for leniency, maybe, or simply dazed by the bop on the head Ellie had given her; if it was the former, I doubted it would work.

But that was not my problem anymore. A pink-cheeked, blue-uniformed Coastie in shiny black boots strode up to me, all spit-and-polished to within an inch of his life.

"Here's the check for the fireworks," he said.

"Thanks." I glanced at the slip of paper he'd handed me. But then: "Wait. This is too much money. *Way* too . . ."

The check amount had an extra zero on it.

"No, ma'am." The Coastie looked resolute. "Captain said that whatever's extra, you should put toward the cost of the fireworks for next year."

He thought a moment. "But if you wanted to send over some of your Toll House cookies in return," he added, "nobody would mind."

Then with his boot heels clicking sharply together, he favored me with just about the snappiest salute I'd ever seen and went back to his duties.

Wade grinned. "Looks like you've got some fans. They were impressed by the way you guys nearly had Sam pushed up that cliff. And since you and Ellie seem to have everything well in hand now, too, I'm going to go help rerig a guy's sailboat."

So he did, and then Ellie hurried up. "We're starting!" she exclaimed, looking pretty in a pink cotton shirtwaist and clean white apron. "Oh, I'm so *excited.*"

Me too, and the next hour was a blur; first the already-won cakes' top bidders were announced and then the remaining ones were auctioned. The bids fairly flew in; a homemade cheesecake, freshly swathed in gourmet chocolate and cherries, was a desirable item as it turned out.

Finally: "Sold!" cried the auctioneer for the last time, and it was over. The cake winners carried off their prizes to general applause.

Which was when Bob Arnold stomped up to me. "Now let me get this straight," he demanded.

"About what?" Ellie asked sweetly. Not being suspected of Matt Muldoon's murder had improved her mood tremendously, and so had the half-dozen interviews she'd done today about the Chocolate Moose: four with newspaper writers from all over New England and two on camera.

Bob held up two fingers. "First Marla threatened to blackmail Muldoon so he did it back to her. But what *he* found out, that Marla and her brother were in a smuggling scheme together—"

"Threatened Sarabelle," I finished for him, "who was in on the scheme, too. And she despised Matt, anyway, so—"

"So she killed him and framed me for it," Ellie added. "And in the process lost one of the diamonds she'd taken for herself."

"So those long, dangly earrings of hers . . . ," Bob began.

"Worth big bucks," I agreed. I'd had to get the rhinestone-that-wasn't back from Ellie, of course. "Also I found out about the shop lights being off that morning, and then going back on."

The fuses, it turned out, weren't fuses at all. Instead they were circuit breakers; just big switches, in other words, that you could flip up and down to turn the power on and off.

And as it happened, Morris Whitcomb had been working in

our cellar at the behest of the landlord, after he replaced our door's lock set. He'd flipped the wrong switch without realizing it, then had gone for coffee. So the power in our kitchen had been out for . . .

"About ten minutes," I finished to Bob. "Just long enough, and coincidentally enough, for me to think it must've been deliberate."

But there was one thing I didn't quite get: the timing of it all. "How'd Sarabelle know Matt would be in the Chocolate Moose? I mean that he'd be there alone, so she could kill him?"

"Hell, never mind that," Bob retorted. "How'd Sarabelle get in on the scheme Marla and Clark had going in the first place? That's what I want to know. And when you get done answering that, how'd a mutt like Clark Carmody ever get anywhere near a diamond-smuggling operation?"

To which I had a one-word answer: "Jail."

Bob raised an eyebrow skeptically; I went on, having gotten a good deal of this from Miss Halligan when we visited her in the hospital the evening before.

I hadn't meant to go. But when Ellie stopped by and mentioned that the vintage-clothing maven might like company, I knew that what she really meant was *let's talk to her while we've still got the chance,* and jumped at it.

"A New Jersey jail, to be precise," I went on now to Bob. "While he was in it, Clark met a guy who knew another guy who knew a shady gem merchant in Manhattan. When Clark got released, he went to the city and found this gem merchant, and hijinks ensued."

"Yeah?" Bob's eyes narrowed. "Fine, but what about Sarabelle? Don't tell me she and Marla met in the slammer, too."

I had to laugh. "No. They met when Marla was visiting her brother, and Sarabelle was visiting Matt. He was in for stalking and harassing the owner of a health food store, also in Jersey."

The only coincidence was in both of them ending up here.

But it wouldn't have been the only such recrossing of paths ever to happen in Eastport, Maine; I know a woman who bought an old house while she was vacationing here, only to learn, over a year later, that her own great-great-grandfather had built the place.

Anyway: "Sarabelle didn't know Matt would be there the night of the murder. But when he showed up in the Moose while she was next door with Miss Halligan—who, by the way, still won't admit they were planning a murder attempt at all—Sarabelle seized the moment."

Bob nodded. "Okay, so they saw Muldoon going into the Moose."

My turn: "Yes. Then Sarabelle went down to the cellar from Miss Halligan's shop, and up into our kitchen."

Bob: "Grabbed the pastry needle, stabbed him. But then she saw Ellie, here, coming back in through the Moose's front door?"

I agreed; he went on. "So Sarabelle hauled him down onto the cellar steps and pulled the trapdoor down over them both. And once Ellie was gone again . . ."

"Right," I said. "Sarabelle Muldoon hauled her dead husband up out of the stairway and . . . and don't ask me why about this part, all right? But she propped him up there, braced his feet so he'd stay—his own weight kept his middle flat on the table—and stuck his head in the chocolate. I don't know, maybe for a joke?"

Some joke. Or to sweeten him up, finally. Likely, we'd never know, but all of Sarabelle's exercise equipment had come in handy, at least. She'd had to be in good shape to pull all that fast, heavy lifting off successfully.

Ellie's look darkened. "You know what? I'll bet he didn't come back to yell at me again at all. He meant to sabotage our cheesecakes somehow, that's what I think."

Suddenly I recalled the empty salt container I'd found on the shop floor that morning. In the melted chocolate, probably . . . but I could tell Ellie about it later. I thought, too, about mentioning that Marla had tried casting suspicion on her own mother as soon as it started looking as if Ellie and I might cause difficulties. That's what telling us about the photographs of Muldoon and Miss Halligan had been in service of, I felt sure.

But that thought was too sad, so I didn't mention it, either.

"So if they're her kids, how come Marla and Clark have different last names from Miss Halligan? And from each other, too, come to think of it?" Bob asked.

"We asked her about that," I replied. "And it's simple: she was married when they were born, but went back to her maiden name after she got divorced. Marla was briefly married, too, but when *she* got divorced, she *didn't* take her old name back."

Bob frowned. "And Clark never changed his name at all," he concluded correctly. Then:

"Oh, one other thing," he said, pulling a familiar garment from a bag he'd been gripping. "Miss Halligan wants you to have this."

He held it out. It was the shimmery gray wool shawl from her shop window, the one I'd coveted.

My eyes prickled with sudden tears. "Oh. She . . . You're sure?"

He nodded firmly, pressing the thing into my hands. It was as wonderfully warm and soft as I'd thought it would be.

"Bob, please tell her . . ." I didn't know what to tell her. She'd been so grateful for company at the hospital, not realizing we were there to get information from her while we still could.

And of course we hadn't enlightened her. Lying there in that bed, she'd looked sad and defeated, and I'd disliked her two horrid children very intensely.

And Sarabelle Muldoon, too, of course. Now I understood

why Miss Halligan had felt so venomous about the murder victim's wife; the vintage-clothing seller had gone along with it all, and even helped when push came to shove.

But as far as I was concerned, Miss Halligan hadn't had much of a chance against the scheming husband-killer, or against her own two criminal kids, either; not really.

Gathering up the shawl in my two hands, I pressed my face into it, breathing in its faint lemon fragrance.

"Yeah," Bob said, understanding me perfectly. "Pretty sad all the way around, isn't it?"

I agreed, and it was the last time any of us talked about any of it for a while because the Fourth of July events were all back on schedule for the day.

These included, but were not limited to, the codfish relay race, the downhill bed races, the pie-eating contest, the musical entertainment, the greasy-pole contest, and of course the parade full of politicians glad-handing. There were also horse-and-wagon combos, baton-twirling marchers, bagpipes and flute-tooters, ball-gowned teen beauty-pageant winners, a steel band on a flatbed truck, a busload of fiftieth-anniversary high-school reunion attendees, and every single horn-and/or-siren-equipped emergency vehicle in downeast Maine.

So by that evening, when the sun had set and the fireworks were imminent, we were all tired, sunburned, and half-deaf from the firecrackers and cherry bombs going off all over the island.

But we were happy, crowded together on a blanket in the bed of Wade's pickup truck parked at the end of the fish pier. We'd even hoisted my dad up there and he looked extremely pleased with himself, surveying it all from the throne we'd built for him out of a lawn recliner and pillows.

"Oh!" breathed Mika softly when the first sparkling explosion burst across the night sky with a concussive boom.

Beside her, Sam smiled, not saying anything; he didn't have to. Earlier I'd suggested that we might get her estranged parents here for a visit soon, and she'd looked hopeful.

So we were content, and the fireworks crowd was huge, filling the whole downtown; even the health inspector who'd been in the Moose the day before was in the audience, eating fried dough and drinking what looked like a local craft beer out of a bottle.

He'd been in town, I learned later, to say all the complaints against us had been dropped. Matt Muldoon, as it turned out, had been a well-known gadfly at the health department, and no one who worked in any of its offices had ever believed a word he'd said.

Now I leaned against Wade as a boatload of the kids from the special-education class puttered by, their excited cries drifting faintly across the water at us.

"Hi," Wade said comfortably as another bright flower spread its glittering petals overhead. "How's your ankle?"

"Hi, yourself." The ankle was better; somewhere in all the activity lately, in fact, I'd forgotten all about it.

Resting my head on his shoulder, I spied Millie Marquardt and Lester Vanacore from the *Tides*. Morris Whitcomb grinned and waved; Ellie and George were around here somewhere, too, with their daughter, Lee, since as George said, "What good was any more money if you couldn't be with the only people you wanted to spend it on?"

So he'd picked his daughter up on his way home, and here they were. "Ooh," said the crowd as another bright bomb went off. Around us in the darkness the air smelled like cotton candy, fried dough, blooming onions, boat fuel, spilled beer, salt water, and backyard barbecues, all mingled with the sweet reek of burning gunpowder.

And of chocolate; to celebrate our success, Ellie was giving away cupcakes. There'd been a *lot* of those leftover cherries.

A toddler seated nearby with his family bit into one of the cupcakes. His grin widened around it as a red chrysanthemum with fiery white petal-tips burst overhead with a loud crackle.

Chocolate spread messily on the kid's face. "Yum!" he said.

Which was my feeling, too, suddenly.

About all of it.

Delicious.

CHOCOLATE CHERRY CHEESECAKE

Baking a cheesecake is a big project, but much easier if you do it in steps.

First, the crust: use a rolling pin to crush about 3 dozen chocolate wafers between two sheets of wax paper, reducing the wafers to fine crumbs. (You need about 2 cups of crumbs.) Melt 6 tablespoons of butter, add the melted butter to the crumbs in a bowl, and mix until all the crumbs are evenly moistened. Use your fingers to press the crumbs evenly into the bottom and about 1½ inches up the sides of a buttered 9" x 3" springform pan. Bake at 325 degrees for 10 minutes, remove the crust from the oven, and set it aside.

Now turn the oven up to 375 degrees and put a shallow pan of water on the bottom shelf. This preheats and humidifies the oven so the cake doesn't dry out when it's baking.

Next, make the filling: you'll need 32 ounces of cream cheese, 1 cup of sugar, 1 teaspoon of vanilla, 1 teaspoon of grated lemon zest, 4 eggs, and a cup of sour cream.

Use a wooden spoon to cream together the cheese, sugar, and lemon zest. Beat in the vanilla, the eggs one at a time, and the sour cream. Pour the batter into the already-made crust in the springform pan and bake for about 1¼ hours at 375 degrees. (Leave the pan of water in the oven during baking.)

Chill the baked cake overnight. Then slip a thin knife blade very carefully between the crust and the pan's side just to loosen it. Finally open the pan's latch and remove the side.

For the chocolate top: Put 4 ounces of chopped bittersweet chocolate in a bowl. Heat ½ cup of cream with a tablespoon of sugar to a simmer, stirring until the sugar dissolves. Pour the hot cream over the chocolate in the bowl, stir to dissolve the chocolate, let the mixture cool until it's the thickness you want, and pour/spread it over the top of the cake, allowing some to run down the sides.

For the cherries: 1 cup of frozen cherries, 1 tablespoon of sugar, ¾ tablespoon of cornstarch, ½ teaspoon of vanilla, ½ teaspoon of lemon juice, and ⅛ (or so) of a cup of water. Mix the cornstarch with the sugar, add the cherries and stir, add the water and vanilla, and heat the mixture to a boil, stirring constantly. Then quickly turn the heat down to simmer, cook until thickened (this happens fast!), and taste it. Add a little more lemon juice or sugar if you wish.

Group some of the cherries at the center of the cake top and distribute the rest evenly. Drizzle cherry syrup artistically.

Finally shave bittersweet chocolate curls off a chunk of the stuff and sprinkle/arrange them generously on the cake. Take a moment to congratulate yourself on your achievement, and then—

Enjoy!

FEB 03 2018